AF084820

ROBERT WEBBER
THE WHITE ROSE

THE Carlton CHRONICLES 1

Copyright © 2020 Robert Webber

The moral right of the author has been asserted.

Apart from any fair dealing for the purposes of research or private study, or criticism or review, as permitted under the Copyright, Designs and Patents Act 1988, this publication may only be reproduced, stored or transmitted, in any form or by any means, with the prior permission in writing of the publishers, or in the case of reprographic reproduction in accordance with the terms of licences issued by the Copyright Licensing Agency. Enquiries concerning reproduction outside those terms should be sent to the publishers.

Matador
9 Priory Business Park,
Wistow Road, Kibworth Beauchamp,
Leicestershire. LE8 0RX
Tel: 0116 279 2299
Email: books@troubador.co.uk
Web: www.troubador.co.uk/matador
Twitter: @matadorbooks

ISBN 978 1 80046 117 8

British Library Cataloguing in Publication Data.
A catalogue record for this book is available from the British Library.

Printed and bound in the UK by TJ Books Limited, Padstow, Cornwall
Typeset in 12pt Adobe Jenson Pro by Troubador Publishing Ltd, Leicester, UK

Matador is an imprint of Troubador Publishing Ltd

To my son, also born in Finland,
Nicolai

Prologue

Alex Carlsson was undeniably a complicated person. In his mere twenty-three years, he had already had four different names, which to somebody unaware of his peculiar circumstances would undoubtedly have been highly questionable. Suspicious his antecedents may have been, but each had been borne out of the peculiarity of circumstance and entirely justifiable in their own right. The most recent incarnation had been the construct of the backroom gnomes at the Secret Intelligence Service of Britain, who adjudged it to be sufficiently close enough to the name by which Alex was more generally known, yet adequately different so as not to be remarkably similar. Even the name by which he was more usually customarily identified, Alex Nicholas Carlton, was a derivation of his birth name, Aleksander Nikolayevich Karlov and he was, since the death of his father, a *vladetel'nyy graf*, or proprietary count at the imperial court of Russia. The son of a much-decorated nobleman who had given his life in a bid to save the imperial family from slaughter at Yekaterinburg in 1917; a man much loved by his mother, the Dowager Countess, but a man whom Alex had never met – and yet a man whose high standards of honour and propriety Alex strived to live up to.

Alex was debonair in a youthful sort of way. Although only twenty-two, his boyish charm and devil-may-care attitude had already marked him out to be something of a celebrity in the clandestine world of intelligence, which some may argue was a less-than-advantageous trait, considering the covert nature of such work. It had been during his training that he had exposed a fellow trainee as an enemy agent and rather than awaiting justice through a court of law, had shot him in the act of self-defence. If Alex was concerned about having dealt so finally with an adversary, it did not show in his demeanour; such matters were to be expected in a time of war.

It had only been a few short weeks since Alex had wed the rebellious but beautiful daughter of an overbearing war hero, Theodora, who was almost universally known as Teddy, in the most whirlwind of all marriages. She, wholly unaware of the adventure on which Alex was about to embark, believed him safely established in a bleak and remote area of Scotland, undertaking tedious but necessarily secret work for the Royal Navy. This deception sat worryingly on Alex's shoulders, but he acknowledged that ignorance was bliss, and he entirely preferred that his wife should not fret, as he knew she would have should the truth be known. Distress, Alex understood, was not beneficial for their unborn child. Of course, he knew the risks that he was undertaking, but Alex was keen to help his adoptive country in its time of need and anything that one could do to frustrate the intentions of Soviet Russia, he felt duty-bound to attempt.

The Bolsheviks had murdered the last tsar of his motherland, along with the tsarina and the imperial family; defenceless children callously butchered by machine-gun bullets was beyond the pale. Quite apart from that, they had killed his father, the man whom his mother had worshipped intensely and the man whom he knew he would have loved, also.

Since Stalin's Minister of Foreign Affairs, Vyacheslav Mikhailovich Molotov, had signed a non-aggression pact with his German counterpart, Joachim von Ribbentrop, it was clear that Stalin's intentions towards its former Grand Duchy of Finland were hostile. Indeed, it seemed as though half the Russian army and much of its air force were camped on Finland's eastern border, awaiting the word to advance and retake the land lost in 1917. Finland's loyalty both then and currently lay with the "Whites", the supporters of the Russian monarchy. When the country fought for its independence, their commander was Gustav Mannerheim, a former general in the Russian Imperial Army and a close confidant of the murdered tsar.

Alex's role for British intelligence was that of gathering information from Finland so that those more senior than he could strategise Finland's role in the war that had enveloped Europe. His arrival in Gothenburg was in anticipation of and preparatory to his departure for Helsinki in a few weeks. Alex fully expected to be briefed further about the precise nature of the role that he was to play, possibly even by his old school friend and recent best man, Simon Potts, who had secured a comfortable intelligence role with the British Legation in Stockholm.

On balance, although this was a simple fact-finding mission, where danger was considered only a remote possibility, Alex acknowledged that his role was fundamental and it was one into which he was eager to get stuck. There had already been far too many delays in getting him to Sweden; some, admittedly, of his own making, others the fault of circumstance, but he knew that much depended on his success and that was not a burden that Alex wore lightly.

I

It is a fact that Gothenburg, Sweden's second city, with its leafy boulevards and Dutch-style canals, steeped in history and culture, is considered a most attractive place to visit. Even so, one would have been hard-pressed to have applied such an adjective on the morning of the first day of November in 1939, when the skies had opened, and a deluge greeted those brave enough to venture outside.

It is also a fact that ships entering harbour and berthing, even at the best of times, are noisy beasts and the commotion associated with docking in the early hours is likely to waken all those who are not blessed with the deepest sleep – and Alex was a person who did not sleep deeply. Consequently, just as the clock in the first-class passengers' dining room chimed, 4.30am, the *S/S Suecia* docked with such a commotion that Alex roused from his sleep, and as he stirred himself to begin the day, he looked through his cabin window and was one of the first to acknowledge that November had started awfully.

Alex lay in his bunk, unable to get back to sleep as thoughts tumbled around his head in a confused manner until his inability to sort them into any resemblance of order prompted him to put uncertainty aside and go for breakfast. He was, quite naturally, anxious; on the one hand, excited by the adventures that lay ahead, but on the other, the awful weather meant that he was in no great hurry to leave the ship. Had this been a ferry, he may well have remained snugly on board and returned with the vessel to England and his wife, but the land that he had left was not destined to be his next port of call.

It had taken a full four hours since awakening before he mustered sufficient resolve to begin the day, and on entering the dining room, he was quite pleasantly surprised to find that few of his fellow passengers were joining him for breakfast. A couple of repatriated diplomatic wives on the ship acknowledged his presence with a smile or nod of the head, but Alex was relieved to discover that most of the passengers had already disembarked.

Choosing a table where he could surreptitiously watch who was entering the dining room, Alex called a steward to him and ordered, 'Skinka, äggröra, bröd, fil och kaffe' – ham, scrambled eggs, bread, sour milk and coffee – a typical Swedish breakfast. Alex picked up an old copy of a local newspaper from the next table and read what was happening in the world, according to the Swedish regional press. His breakfast, when it came, bore only a passing resemblance to what he had ordered – a slice of ham, some crispbread and a pot of coffee.

'Ursäkta!' – Waiter! – Alex called, but the steward had already left, and he reluctantly breakfasted on the food, even the coffee was disgusting. Alex had yet to acquire the taste of coffee first thing in the morning and far preferred tea, but in his life as a Swedish newspaper reporter, his personal preferences were laid aside as he adapted to more traditional Swedish customs.

Breakfast, in Alex's opinion, was never to be regarded as a convivial meal and he was glad that none of the ship's passengers sought to engage him in conversation, and as soon as he had finished, he returned to his cabin to finish packing his suitcase before his planned disembarkation at about 10.00am. He had not unpacked fully, so repacking was straightforward and took much less time than Alex had allocated, so he lay on the bed and took the photo of his young wife and smiled at it, clasping it close to his breast and wishing that it was she, in person, that he was holding. When they would meet again, or even if, was in the lap of the gods, but he fervently hoped that luck would be on his side and that the delay would not be too long before he was able to return and resume married life with his beautiful Teddy.

Alex rang for the steward and arranged for his luggage to be taken from the ship, and a short while later, after thoroughly checking his cabin to ensure that he had left nothing behind, he disembarked, carrying with him only his typewriter case. Opening his umbrella and proceeding carefully down the gangplank, Alex set foot on Swedish soil for the first time in his life.

*

Thus it was that, along with the few remaining passengers, the dock authorities shepherded Alex towards the *tullhuset* or customs house where a bored immigration officer stamped his passport after perfunctorily assessing him before waving him through to collect his luggage. Alex found a porter and for a few *kroner* persuaded him to carry his baggage out of the building and to find a taxi. It was not a difficult task, for having heard that there was a ship in port, most of the cabs of Gothenburg had descended on the dock area in the hope of picking up a fare, although Alex's driver was most unhappy to discover that his destination was the central railway station, only a few hundred metres away.

The imposing terminus of Copenhagen's central railway station stands proud and in the early part of the century was the last memorable building that many Swedes emigrating to America saw of their homeland. To Alex, it was the first remarkable sight of Sweden, and with the help of a station porter, he unloaded the taxi, paid the driver off and entered the station hall to buy a ticket for Stockholm. Alex purchased a first-class ticket and checked the departures board where he learned that the next train to the capital would depart in just under an hour, so finding the first-class waiting room, he settled in a comfortable armchair and ordered coffee and a traditional *butterkaka* cake. When the announcement came that his train was to depart from platform five, Alex collected his belongings and made his way to the departure gate, where he surrendered his ticket for clipping before joining his fellow travellers in seeking their carriages. For

Alex, it was a long walk, as the first-class carriages were at the front of the train, so he walked the length of the platform with his trusty porter following, dragging a trolley which contained Alex's luggage. Eventually, after walking a goodly distance, Alex joined the train and located his compartment to settle down with the latest copy of *Svenska Posten*, the Swedish newspaper that nominally was his employer.

In the efficient manner of most things Swedish, the train began its journey towards the nation's capital precisely on time, and Alex was grateful that the remaining seats in his compartment remained vacant. However, it was not long before his solitude was disturbed by the compartment door opening and of all people, his old friend Simon Potts entered.

'Är den här platsen upptagen, snälla?' – Is this seat taken, please? – asked Simon, and without awaiting a response, he entered the compartment and closed the door before pulling down the blinds and slipping the lock into place. Alex and Simon shook hands before Alex pulled his friend towards him and gripped him in a manly hug.

Releasing each other, the friends quickly caught up on all that had happened to each other since they had last met, and Simon handed over the address and keys of Alex's apartment in Stockholm. The four-hour train journey flew by in no time, and as the train was pulling into Stockholm's Central Station, Simon took his leave and told Alex that it was unlikely that they would meet directly again but to expect a contact shortly after settling in Stockholm. Simon gave Alex specific recognition codes for when he was contacted and instructed him to memorise them.

Stockholm Station was far busier than that of Gothenburg and much more substantial, but with the aid of yet another porter to assist with his luggage, he was quickly at the taxi rank securing transport to take him to the address that Simon had given him.

"Home", Alex discovered, was a chic apartment in Jungfrugatan in the Östermalm district of the capital, not far from the Hedvig Eleonora Church. While it was not a large apartment, the traditional Swedish furniture was tasteful, and although the kitchen was rudimentary, it was sufficient for Alex's needs. Alex unpacked his clothes and then went in search of a grocery store where he could purchase the essentials of life.

Much of the next week was spent orienting himself in Stockholm. Although Alex had read much about the city that was spread across fourteen islands, it was only by exploring that he was able to get to know the real feel of the town. He was walking around soaking up the atmosphere, shopping in stores like Nordiska Kompaniet or NK as it is universally known, or the Tempo store on Östermalmstorg. Even though winter was beckoning, Alex enjoyed walking in the Djurgården park or visiting the fabulous circular public library. He also went to the opera where he enjoyed one of the final performances of Verdi's *La Traviata* at the Swedish Opera house featuring the Swedish Caruso, Jussi Björling before the building was closed and turned into a dance hall.

During this time, Alex also spent long periods typing articles, including one about his time in England and his forced "repatriation" at the commencement of hostilities, which were collected regularly by a young sub-editor of *Svenska Posten* – a few even made it to publication. Alex only visited the newspaper once and was embarrassed when the editor-in-chief, Per Aslund, met him and told him in no uncertain terms that they would collect his work and that he should not revisit the newspaper's offices. It was evident to Alex that he was about as welcome as Banquo's ghost at the paper and Alex wondered why they had been so willing to give him the cover that was needed if he created such an embarrassment.

Towards the end of the second week, Alex received a short note in the mail informing him that his lost property had been found at the Grand Hotel and had been handed in at reception ready for him to collect at his convenience. Although perplexed, as Alex had not visited the Grand Hotel, Alex understood that he was to retrieve the "lost property"; it also implied that any surveillance that he had been under had found nothing untoward and that his cover was intact. Nevertheless, when Alex went to the hotel, he secreted his trusty FN pistol in the waistband of his trousers in the small of his back – just in case!

Alex arrived at the hotel just after 2.00pm and the receptionist handed over a small envelope. He thanked the girl and placed the letter in his inside pocket before going to the bar, where he ordered a beer, of which he drank about half before going to the guests' toilet, where he locked himself into a cubicle. After he was confident that nobody else was using the facilities, he carefully took the envelope out and slit it open. Inside, Alex found a single piece of paper that told him the location and time of the meeting the following afternoon. Alex was to wait outside the Skandia Cinema for the matinee performance at 2.30pm and to ensure that nobody followed him to the meeting.

*

Next morning, Alex woke early and carefully prepared himself for the day ahead. He shaved with care using the razor from the set that Teddy had bought him in London and applied a little eau de Cologne. The weather was turning colder, and Alex dressed in warm trousers and a pullover that had been one of his purchases from the NK department store earlier. He selected a stout pair of shoes and pulling on a drab anorak to hide the fact that the waistband of his trousers was again holding his pistol, Alex set out just before 11.00am and began an extremely circuitous route to the cinema. He dived into department stores and left by different exits, had an unhurried coffee and cake in a nearby cafe, doubled back and walked through parks, regularly but carefully checking that he was alone.

Alex arrived at the Skandia shortly before the appointed time and waited in the foyer for barely two minutes before a petite, young, blonde and strikingly attractive girl came to him. She put her arms around his neck and kissed him before slipping her arm through his and guiding him towards the booth. 'Buy a box so that we can be together,' she said.

Alex did as was suggested, and the couple made their way into the cinema and found their box. The girl slipped the latch on the door so that they would not be disturbed and it was clear looking across the auditorium that many other courting couples also bought boxes at this cinema for clandestine meetings. Alex decided that the girl had chosen the venue and film well. The movie was a light comedy called *Ombyte förnöjer*, or "Variety is the Spice of Life", starring Tutta Rolf and Elsa Burnett that had been released earlier in the year and was now doing the second round of showings, so the cinema was barely half full.

'Please listen,' the girl said in Swedish shortly after the movie started, 'my name is Sigrid Lind, and you have the agreeable fortune of being my boyfriend! You should feel honoured!' She smiled at Alex, who had recognised that the name was the same as that written on the back of the photograph in his wallet, that of Teddy, his wife. 'After we leave here, you can take me to a cafe and then we will go back to my apartment. I have some information for you that I will give you when we are alone. Before I forget, I am worried that you have not asked me to identify myself as you should have. Would you like me to identify myself?'

'Er, yes,' replied Alex. 'Sorry, I was rather taken by surprise. It is not every day that a beautiful woman unexpectedly kisses me.'

'I shall take that as a compliment,' Sigrid responded with a mischievous grin. 'Very well. "The sun is very bright today."'

Alex recognised the phrase as being the one that Simon had told him on the train, although as it was quite dull and overcast outside, he thought that the service might have chosen more appropriate codes. 'But there is a definite chill in the air,' he responded.

'Good,' said Sigrid. 'Of course, I knew who you were from your photograph, but you did not know me, and that is why we have recognition phrases. You need to remember that for your safety.'

They sat through the movie, which Alex thought quite amusing, and they laughed together frequently. When the film had finished, Alex and Sigrid left and skipped through the streets, laughing, and having fun as do boyfriends and girlfriends throughout the world. They went to a local coffee house where Alex bought coffee and cake, and they chatted conversationally about this and that, but never once about their lives or the mission that Alex was undertaking. Alex noticed that Sigrid was always aware and watchful of her surroundings, and he wondered whether he should be more alert, rather than enjoying being in the company of a beautiful woman.

Afterwards, Sigrid led Alex to a nondescript apartment block about a kilometre and a half from the cinema, where Sigrid let them both in and together they climbed the three flights of stairs to her apartment.

It was a charming apartment, not as well-appointed as the one given to Alex and undoubtedly that of a girl, as there was nothing masculine about the place at all.

'Come,' she said and led Alex to the lounge area, and they sat together on the settee.

'I work at *Svenska Posten* as well, although in a secretarial role, and I am to help you get your messages to London. When you send your articles, including the coded messages, I will send them on to my contact at the British Legation,' Alex wondered whether she meant Simon but decided not to ask, 'and they will send them onwards. You may ask why I do this, and I would say to you that my mother is English, and she works as a teacher in Stockholm. My father is an engineer, but my parents separated when I was twelve, and I have not had much to do with him since they divorced.

'As I have said, and as a precaution, you must encode your messages to me as this will protect us both. You should include the coded message in the reports that you write for the paper. The use of cypher is one of your best weapons against being discovered.' Alex recalled from his training at the Grange that good book cyphers are almost impossible to break and rely on both the coder and decoder having access to a unique text that becomes the codebook. The most important aspect is the codebook. If the book is commonplace and readily available, for instance, the Bible, then it is likely that a reasonable code breaker could quite easily crack the cypher, but if the book is obscure or better still a series of books, then the odds of breaking the code are infinitesimal.

'I think that the books that we shall use are good. I say "books" because we have a trilogy of books by the Swedish author Moa Martinson that are both contemporary and sufficiently popular as not to be remarkable. The first book, *Mor gifter sig*, "Mother Gets Married", was published in 1936; the second, *Kyrkbröllop*, "Church Wedding", in 1938; and then the last book *Kungens rosor*, "The King's Roses", has only just arrived in the bookshops.'

Alex did not know the author, but Sigrid handed him the trilogy. 'I suggest you read her books,' she recommended. 'Some say that Martinson is quite radical, but her writing is both insightful and sufficiently obscure as to be useful to us. I think she's exceptional!

'Next, we have to work out a methodology to formulate how the codes will be included in your messages. Firstly, you need to write your despatch backwards, and secondly, we need to find a key. I suggest that we use the time that you add in your message. If you time your message in the morning and use an odd hour, then I know to use *Mor gifter sig*; if you use an even hour, I shall remember to use *Kyrkbröllop*; and if you time your message in the afternoon, I shall understand to use *Kungens roser*.'

'How will I know what time it is sent?' Alex asked.

'You do not,' Sigrid said with a smile, 'but I said the time *you* include on your report, not the time it was transmitted. Most correspondents will date and time their reports so that we know when they were written as well as how efficient is the wire service.'

'Yes, of course.' Alex felt just a little foolish.

'That accounts for the books I shall use to find your message. Next, I need to know the pattern. I suggest we compile your report using letters rather than words and only the first six chapters of each book. The tens-of-minutes informs me which chapter you have chosen and the minutes tell me the sequence of letters. I recommend that you write in four-letter bursts and do not separate words.

'So, if you send me a report timed at 10.45am, I shall know to use *Kyrkbröllop*, chapter 4, beginning with the fifth letter. If that letter is an "F", for instance, I shall know that "F" equals the number one in our code and as "A" is the first letter of the alphabet, "F" will be "A". Logically then, "G" will represent the second letter of the alphabet, "B", and "H", the third, "C", and so on. I presume you have been taught how to use book codes in your training?' Alex nodded.

'Good. You should spend some time familiarising yourself with this cypher before you leave.'

They talked about the logistics of transmitting reports, and wherever possible and practical, the preferred method was over the wire services, but alternatives were available if that method became difficult.

'You will be leaving Stockholm shortly, although I am unsure when,' Sigrid continued, 'but certainly within the next two weeks. You will likely be travelling by ship from Stockholm to Åbo.' Was there a nod to colonialism by Sigrid's use of the Swedish name for the former capital of Finland, the city of Turku? Alex wondered, but he quickly concluded that it would be entirely reasonable for a Swedish speaker to use the Swedish name, and he made a mental note that he would have to do likewise.

'While you remain in Stockholm, you and I must often meet, so that everybody understands that we are a couple.'

Alex was concerned. 'You do understand that I am a married man?' he asked Sigrid.

'No, you are not,' Sigrid said sternly. 'Alex Carlsson is *not* married. It does not matter what you have left behind, here you are a bachelor, and you must act like one so that you do not appear unusual.'

It was the first time that Alex had encountered and appreciated the gulf that existed between his two lives, and he realised what Commander Jeffers had meant when he counselled Alex that the reason why the service considered marriage a complication for agents was that sometimes they must do things that would stretch adherence to the marital vows.

The time was nearly 8.00pm, and Sigrid decided that she was hungry. 'Come, now you can buy me dinner!' she said.

'Where?' Alex asked.

'I know a nice place that is…' she hunted for the right word '…discreet.' Sigrid grabbed her coat and threw Alex's to him before heading for the front door.

Restaurant Riche on Birger Jarlsgatan was one of those quintessentially Swedish restaurants where the food is simple, but at the same time wholesome, and for Kr3.50 for a three-course meal, it was exceptional value for money, so much so that Alex splashed out on a bottle of reasonable wine to wash down the food. Afterwards, Alex walked Sigrid home, and they parted with a slightly too passionate kiss for Alex's liking, but understanding that he was expected to reciprocate, he ignored his thoughts of Teddy and tried to respond in kind.

'*God natt*, älskling.' Sigrid bade him farewell, adding the mischievous "darling", and she let herself into the apartment, leaving Alex to go in search of a taxi.

*

Alex did not see Sigrid again until Saturday when she arrived at his apartment to deliver his tickets for the boat to Finland. He was leaving on the morning tide on Tuesday 28th November, and after a stop in the Åland Islands that form the archipelago between Sweden and Finland, he would arrive at Åbo/Turku late in the evening two days later. Sigrid explained to him that he was to stay at the Hotel Torni, in Helsinki, which she said was the residence of choice for many of the foreign journalists.

They spent the weekend together enjoying each other's company, Alex surrendering his bed to Sigrid and sleeping on the sofa, but in a worryingly candid moment, regretted that he was so generous – she was, after all, a beautiful young woman. When on Monday morning, Sigrid left to go to work, she gave Alex a message that had apparently come from Simon Potts, 'I must tell you a message,' she said, "*Your teddy bear has moved to Gloucestershire*" – as with many foreigners, she had difficulty with the pronunciation of English shires, calling it *glow-ces-ter-shire* – "*with Uncle Walter and is fine but missing you.*" I think it is a code and you know what it means?'

Those fifteen words took Alex back to his other life and fighting his emotions. he merely responded, 'Thank you.'

Sigrid then surprised him with her insight. 'It is good that you have someone to fight for. She is a fortunate girl.' She reached up and kissed him warmly, although not passionately as before, smiled and ran for a bus to take her to work.

*

Alex spent the rest of his time in Stockholm writing articles and trying to keep abreast of the changing situation in Finland in preparation for his departure, and the day when he was due to leave arrived far too quickly. He only saw Sigrid once more before he left when she came on Tuesday evening and cooked him an excellent supper before they spent the night together, although not as before, and then she went with him to the harbour, as one would expect of a loving girlfriend, to wave him off as he left for Finland. Alex was thoroughly ashamed of his weakness.

II

The *S/S Heimdall* was one of the vast numbers of tramp steamers that carry goods and passengers between ports, without a set schedule and usually purely on a charter basis. She had been built in 1915 for Sweden's Rederi line and had spent most of the past twenty-four years navigating the waters of the Baltic, but occasionally sailing through the Kattegat to the Atlantic coasts of Norway and Denmark. Although well maintained, after so many years of service, the ship was starting to show signs of her age – the once-gleaming white hull was streaked with rust and showed evidence of many careless encounters with docksides.

The ship's single stack was already belching black smoke as the engine room prepared for an early departure when Alex made his way up the gangplank and was greeted by an impatient sailor, clearly keen to set sail. The cabin allocated to Alex was reasonably proportioned, having room for his bunk and a chest of drawers, but little else. The passengers' salon and bathroom were down the corridor, and the whole passenger area looked as though, on the occasions when there had been none, it served as an additional hold for goods in transit.

Nevertheless, despite their intolerance of travellers who got in the way of leaving the harbour, the crew appeared efficient, and they navigated the ship through the picturesque channel from Stockholm and the archipelago to Mariehamn before turning towards their final destination of Finland's old capital.

The vessel arrived in Åbo/Turku just ahead of the predicted time on the last day of November 1939, and even though it was only early afternoon, it was already settling in for one of those dark and cheerless November nights. Alex remembered those nights from his childhood, walking home from the school in Loviisa in the depressing darkness of night that always descended early in November and December until the snow fell and brightened everything.

After thanking the crew and disembarking, Alex found an old Renault taxi to take him the relatively short distance from the port to the railway station. The driver only wanted to talk about was the news that the Russians had bombed Helsinki Airport earlier that morning. It seemed that Alex had arrived at the time when the Soviet-Finnish diplomatic crisis that was at the heart of his assignment had ended, and now Finland was at war with Soviet Russia. At the station, Alex managed to secure a first-class seat on the Helsinki express departing at 3.40pm, and he joined the mayhem assembled in the station. Hundreds of mild-mannered and peaceable citizens stunned that the Russians had attacked their country. Of course, it should not have come as too great a surprise as the world's press had been full of the expectation of war in the country for months, but hope is often vastly different to reality, and this is what Alex was experiencing. Just looking at the faces of the other travellers, he saw a mix of wonder and fear; something he had never come across previously but which he had seen on the newsreels in London of countries that had been invaded by the Nazis. It was so much more terrifying in real life.

Alex still retained the naïve view that Helsinki would be one of the safest places to be in Finland as he had been assured by Commander Jeffers and all the combined available intelligence that civilian centres in Finland would never be an objective of Stalin. If the invasion would come then the focus would be purely on military targets.

Despite leaving Åbo/Turku on time, the train did not arrive at its destination with the same punctuality since it was halted at the junction in Karjaa and held for nearly an hour with no explanation. When the train continued, it travelled much slower, almost feeling its way forward into the unknown, and when the train drew into Helsinki main terminus shortly before 10.00pm, it seemed to release the sigh of the exhausted athlete who had completed a gruelling marathon.

Collecting his luggage, Alex searched in vain for a porter on the platform at which they had arrived, but eventually found a two-wheeled trolley onto which he heaved his cases before following the other passengers into the crowd gathered in Saarinen's magnificent station hall. At the line of booking offices, queues of would-be passengers waited patiently for their turn – women dressed warmly in skiing trousers and jackets or luxurious fur coats and men in dark overcoats with hats, carrying business attaché cases. But it was the children that Alex could not understand being there – surely the children had already been evacuated from the capital weeks earlier? So, where had these come from, these youngsters of all ages, intently gripping the hands of their mothers and fathers, most with a look of bewildered fear on their faces? There were soldiers in the drab grey uniform of the Finnish army with their rifles hoisted over their shoulders, marching towards the platform where a train to Viipuri stood waiting. They did not whistle or sing as British soldiers did as they headed to war, but marched in silence with grim determination carved on their faces.

Alex found the luggage office and deposited his cases, receiving a ticket as his receipt before venturing outside to the square in front of the station, which was as black as pitch because all of the street lights were unlit. As Alex stepped out of the station, the wail of an air-raid siren sounded, and dark, shadowy beings emerged from the blackness of the night like wraiths, scurrying hither and thither trying to find sanctuary from the bombers – it was almost surreal. As his eyes adjusted to the dark, Alex saw that many of those moving through the blackness were soldiers, probably reservists being mobilised to protect the capital city. One cannoned into him, and he glanced at the face of a young soldier, who was scouring the dark skies looking for the bombers that the air-raid warning heralded. The boy muttered '*Anteeksi*' – Sorry – and resumed his search for the aggressor.

Alex held the boy's shoulder and asked, 'Hotel Torni?' and the boy flapped his hand towards a road heading right from the station. Alex followed the boy's vague directions and soon ended up on Helsinki's main thoroughfare, Heikinkatu, where he again asked for directions from someone else who was scuttling like a frightened rabbit to some unknown destination. The single word *Tuolla!* was his reply – Over there – accompanied by frantic pointing across the road.

Alex eventually found the hotel on Yrjönkatu and entered. He stepped through a heavy blackout curtain from abject confusion and turmoil into a calm orderliness where life continued in unflustered composure. He announced his arrival.

'Alex Carlsson. I believe I have a reservation,' he stated in Swedish to the elderly concierge who was on duty behind the reception desk.

'*Ja, naturligtvis, Herr Carlsson,*' the old man immediately responded in the same language. '*Har du något bagage?*' – Do you have luggage?

Alex told him that he had been unable to find a porter at the station, and perhaps the hotel could send someone to collect his trunk and bags? Filling in the hotel register and giving his address as the *Svenska Posten* offices in Stockholm, Alex was rewarded with a key and a clicking of fingers, summoning a bellboy to guide him to his room. Alex could not help wondering how long the youth would enjoy his comfortable position at the Hotel Torni before being called up to the military, and even whether he would survive to return to his job.

Taking the lift to the second floor, the bellboy opened a door for Alex to enter his room. Alex was pleasantly surprised by his accommodation. It was large and occupied a prime corner position, so out of one of his windows, he overlooked Kalevankatu and from the other, Yrjönkatu. The room was mainly furnished with comfortable art-deco furnishings and had a large double bed, a sofa and two chairs and a writing desk. There was even an adjacent bathroom with a large bath, lavatory, and washbasin, all standing on a black and white chequered tiled floor. The room, compared with many hotels where he had stayed and even places in which most people lived, was both modernist and palatial.

The bellboy coughed discreetly. 'We recommend, sir, at the moment, that the curtains are left drawn,' he ventured in Swedish. 'It will help contain the glass shards if we get bombed. If the sirens sound, provision has been made for guests in the cellar of the hotel. You will be guided from reception, but please do not use the lift if there is a raid happening.'

'Of course,' responded Alex and dug in his pocket for some loose change, which he gave to the bellboy, who nodded in gratitude.

After washing himself, Alex ventured downstairs to find a bar and see who else was resident at the hotel. It was too late to eat but, in any case, Alex was not hungry, so he settled at the bar where he ordered a beer and surveyed his fellow residents. It did not take long before he heard the English language, spoken with a thick Irish accent, and he observed a ginger-haired bull of a man playing cards with three others at the back of the lounge. Although it appeared as though they were not playing for money, it was clear that the luck of the Irish had deserted the son of Éirinn.

Alex wandered over to the table and introduced himself in accented English. 'Hello, my name is Alex Carlsson, and I have just come from England. I did not expect to hear English spoken in Helsinki so readily. I thought all the British had left?'

The Irishman looked up at Alex and seemed to weigh up whether to bother introducing himself, but in the end, offered a massive paw and said, 'Well, that would be because I am Irish, not British!' He looked with some amusement at Alex. 'Michael McMahon, universally known as "Mick", late of County Clare and now working for the *Clarion* newspaper in Dublin. Pleased to meet you, Mr Carlsson.'

'Alex, please,' responded Alex. 'It seems as though we are in the same game… I work for *Svenska Posten* and have been sent here to cover the troubles in Finland.'

'That is not surprising. This little backwater of the Baltic hardly rated the need for a resident stringer, but now mighty Russia is showing an unhealthy interest in the country, all of the world's press have descended on the capital! And it appears that this is the place where they put all the journalists,' McMahon said. 'There's about twenty of us here.

'This fellow is Jan de Smet from Belgium, who speaks passable English and who is far too lucky at cards.' De Smet smiled and nodded in recognition. 'This chap is called Olaf Pedersen, and he's from Norway – awful card player, but he can drink us all under the table.' The Norwegian raised his arm in friendly recognition. 'That is Charles-Louis de Bourbon who speaks not a word of English, but who reckons that he is distantly related to the French royal family, if you can believe a word he says.

'She, over there,' he indicated a forty-something attractive blonde woman sitting at the bar with a dark-haired woman of a similar age, 'is Margot Maddison of the *Chicago Tribune*, and her friend is Leona Guichard of *Le Nationaliste* in Canada. When I say *friend*,' he explained *sotto voce*, 'I mean the word in the biblical sense – they go everywhere together, and *la lionesse* is a very jealous woman! There are others, but they are not here at the moment.'

Alex joined the journalists at their table, but no sooner had he sat down than the air-raid siren began its mournful clarion call and half the patrons of the bar, including his new acquaintances, leapt from their seats and rushed outside. As he was hurrying to the door, McMahon called to Alex over his shoulder, 'Come on, slowcoach, or you'll be missing all the fun!'

Alex rose and hurriedly followed them outside, and it was clear from the searchlights that the bombers were concentrating on the docks area. Alex followed the other journalists along Kalevankatu towards the docks, until they veered left and went down a side street towards one of the most significant fires. The police stopped the journalists as they approached the Technical High School on Bulevardi, which was burning furiously, filling the air with acrid smoke. Alex looked around him, and it was evident that most of the windows in the vicinity had been blown out by the sheer force of the explosion. Somebody had laid flowers on some rubble outside one of the apartment blocks; a friend, a relative, perhaps a close family member mourning the loss of loved ones. Alex was horrified. He had not previously been so close to the after-effects of a bombing raid, and it was a fearful scene. The fire service was busily trying to extinguish the main blaze at the school, while in the debris of two adjoined apartment houses, the clearance squads were digging for bodies. Alex was mesmerised by the dreadfulness of what he was witnessing; he was rooted to the spot until a fireman pushed him unceremoniously out of the way as he unrolled another hosepipe to help quench the flames.

Alex pensively walked back down Bulevardi towards the centre, gathering his thoughts and trying to make sense of the enormity of what he had witnessed. He watched shopkeepers already starting to board up the fronts of their premises with timber, as additional protection against looting. But Finns were not like that, they stood together in a crisis, they would never steal from another man's misfortune. The nucleus of a story was starting to form in Alex's mind – the Soviet bombing of Helsinki, a city crowded with civilians, would have a far-reaching impact on the world. War was a terrible thing, and although the world had become used to hearing of carnage unleashed by Nazi Germany in their quest for European domination, those were German bombs, not Russian, and this would now change the whole perception of this war.

As he walked back to his hotel, Alex strolled through a park where he came across a young boy aged about ten years old, who was sitting on the ground and stroking a dead dog. 'Is that your dog?' he asked in a kindly manner and in Finnish.

'*Ei, se on siskoni koira,*' – No, it is my sister's dog, – the boy replied.

'*Missä siskosi on?*' – Where is your sister? – Alex asked. The boy looked over his shoulder at what used to be an apartment block but was now a pile of rubble.

'*Entä äitisi ja isäsi?*' – What about your mother and father? – The boy continued to look at the house with tears flowing down his dirty face. '*Siellä,*' – There, – he replied.

Alex silently held out his hand, and the boy tentatively reached up and took it, and without a word they started walking away from the devastation that had been the boy's life and family, leaving the once much-loved family pet where it lay.

Approaching one of the busier roads, Alex saw an ambulance parked against the kerb with two nurses sitting on the step inside the open rear doors, sharing a cigarette and a flask of coffee. Alex and the young boy walked towards the ambulance, and Alex explained that he had found the boy in the park near the ruins of his home and described that it was probable that the boy's family had perished in the air raid. The older of the nurses, probably a mother herself, looked at the boy and smiled before taking his hand from Alex and helping him into the ambulance.

Just before the nurse closed the door, Alex asked the boy, 'What is your name?'

'Juha,' the boy replied, almost in a whisper.

Alex delved into his pocket and pulled out a handful of Finnish *markka*, which he handed to the boy. '*Jumala olla kanssasi, Juha,*' – God be with you, Juha, – was all he said as the door closed.

*

That night, Alex reflected on the obviously inaccurate press reports that he had read in Britain about the evacuation of Helsinki's children on the orders of the government. He quizzed the other journalists in the bar at the hotel and learned that in October, when the threat was high, about a third of the city's population had left, even though it seemed that the Finnish emissary Juho Kusti Paasikivi had been doing well in the negotiations in Moscow. Someone mentioned that the even British Legation had moved most of the diplomats and diplomatic families to Sweden, which had surprised the Finns, who had believed in British resolution in adversity. An old *Punch* cartoon had been reproduced in a Finnish newspaper of the British enjoying "tiffin" even as marauding hordes were attacking the Governor's residence in some far-flung Indian outpost in the days of the Raj, with the caption *Missä Englanti rohkeus nyt?* – 'Where is English courage now?'

But in the weeks that followed, when the danger seemed to have calmed, and the threat of war had abated, the majority of those who had left drifted back – even the diplomats.

Stalin's demands for a protective belt around Leningrad, which would involve Finland giving up much of Karelia and the Hanko peninsula, were the subject of intense negotiations by the Finnish emissary, Paasikivi, which were somewhat hampered by the restrictions placed on him by the Foreign Minister, Juho Eljas Erkko, forbidding regional settlements. In the false belief that Paasikivi was doing well, on the previous Monday, the schools in Helsinki had reopened against the advice of General Mannerheim, who still believed the situation was grave. His fears had been justified most horrifically.

*

The next day brought bright sunshine, and Alex was up early walking through the streets of Helsinki that had been miraculously cleared of much of the evidence of destruction of the previous day; the traffic was flowing freely, and shops were open for business. Again, the sirens wailed and about ten minutes later out of the clear blue sky came the roar of the bombers. People ran for cover, but Alex stood firm. The planes were plainly visible, and the bright sunlight reflecting from their fuselages gave them an almost surreal appearance. As Alex watched, he saw tiny black flecks fall from the aeroplanes, and the whole city shook as the bombs exploded. Smoke and dust filled the air, and many people believed that the Russian bombers were dropping poisonous gas. The targets again appeared to be the docks and the area behind the Parliament building, where was located the city's main bus terminus.

Alex, together with the fire engines and ambulances, rushed to the area, and with them came the newsreel cameras of the Finnish Film Company whose footage of the bombing of the civilian population would be sent around the world to show the aftermath of this carnage. Later that day, the Finnish government announced that sixty-one people had perished and over a hundred and twenty were seriously injured. Alex telegraphed his account of the bombing to the offices of *Svenska Posten*, and for the first time in his fledgeling career as a journalist, his article made the front page. But it was only after reading an article in the *Helsingin Sanomat* newspaper that described the harrowing death of a twelve-year-old girl whose badly crushed legs had led to her death on the operating table, that Alex realised his journalism was amateurish by comparison.

In the bar of the Hotel Torni, the journalists tried to analyse the motives behind the air raids. Were they aimed at breaking civilian morale? Nobody seemed to know, but Mick McMahon suggested that all the bombs had fallen near legitimate military targets; some near the docks, some near the railway station, some near the airport, some near the parliament building, other bombs fell near the post office. He argued that this was pretty close to precision bombing and that there was no evidence of the Russians specifically targeting the civilian population. *Tell that to Juha*, thought Alex.

The Belgian, Jan de Smet, ventured that once the accounts of the bombing of Helsinki's civilian population, whether accidental or intended, were broadcast in other countries, it would have an immense effect on world opinion, and in Finland, it would make any peace negotiations almost impossible. Those in Finland who had proposed peaceful relations with Soviet Russia would have an uphill struggle to convince other Finns now.

McMahon confided in Alex that he had picked up a rumour that the full legislative assembly of Finland had been called that evening at the Säätytalo or House of Estates in Snellmaninkatu just north of the great Lutheran church, and if they hurried, they might just steal a march on the other journalists. It was a relatively short walk, but they arrived to find the doors locked, with a police officer turning cars away and redirecting them to a trades union hall somewhere in north Helsinki, which was supposed to be a secret meeting place.

'Some secret,' said Mick, 'if all you have to do is ask the policeman to where the meeting has been relocated!'

The two journalists flagged down a taxi and only just made it to the meeting before the doors were secured. Just after 7.30pm, the prime minister, Aimo Cajander, rose and after a short statement where he lamented the war that had come despite his government's best efforts, he asked for a vote of confidence. Every single hand in the hall was raised in support, and the prime minister then announced that the entire cabinet would resign so that the president could form a new government. The prime minister left the stage to telephone President Kyösti Kallio and soon returned to say that the president had notified him that Risto Ryti, director of the Bank of Finland, would be asked to form a new government.

'Well, I'll be buggered!' announced McMahon, somewhat disrespectfully as they both acknowledged the slight to the former prime minister.

'What do you know about Ryti?' asked Alex.

'Not much,' replied Mick. 'I know that he is considered to be a sound economist and that he did quite a good job at the Bank of Finland. As a member of the National Progressive Party, I think he is thought a moderate, even perhaps a little liberal, but I suspect that he will become a stronger prime minister than Cajander.'

As the delegates were leaving, McMahon noticed somebody that he knew and buttonholed him before the envoy could dodge out of the way. 'Kai,' he called and got the attention of the deputy, 'what does all that mean?'

'It means that we have a better chance of peace now that Ryti's in charge!' was all the delegate responded before pushing past and leaving.

III

When Alex's family left war-torn London for the peace and tranquillity of Gloucestershire, the move went much more smoothly than Teddy expected. Walter Compton, Alex's Uncle Walter, not being a person who would physically get involved in the removal himself, had engaged the services of a specialist removals company. They arrived at Onslow Gardens and Bedford Square almost simultaneously before taking charge, with military precision, of the entire operation of transporting all of the goods and chattels that were going to Ashton Court.

Alex's mother, the dowager countess, went ahead with Uncle Walter in his Rolls-Royce, while Teddy drove their housekeeper, Klara, in the Alvis. The journey took little enough time, even though military traffic heading westward out of London was unusually heavy. Teddy was becoming increasingly familiar with the roads to Gloucestershire. It was one of those beautiful late autumn days where the sun shone brightly, reflecting on the copper-toned leaves on the trees, but where the air was crisp and refreshing. As she approached Stow-on-the-Wold, Teddy saw the tower of St Edward's church standing proud and welcoming to the quaint Cotswold town. Her mind drifted back to the last time she and Alex had been there, only a few weeks earlier, and now she was back without him. Even though Klara was with her, she felt lonely, and she wondered how Alex was faring in Scotland.

Turning right off the Fosse Way onto Sheep Street, she continued along the Oxford Road until she saw the turn-off for Lower Oddington. It was a good job that she remembered the turn, as the signpost to the village had disappeared in the government's attempt to confuse any passing German parachutists or fifth columnists that happened to be in the area. As she swung through the gates of Ashton Court and past the imperious cedar tree, she immediately appreciated the changes that had occurred to the house in the past few weeks. Klara made a noise that caused Teddy to look towards her, and she smiled as she saw the gaze of wonderment on the housekeeper's face, 'This is home,' she said, but Klara was too awestruck to respond.

Uncle Walter's Rolls-Royce was already standing outside the front door of Ashton Court, and as Teddy drew up behind, the man himself, together with Alex's mother, came out to greet them with a warm embrace. 'Did you have a good journey?' the dowager countess asked Teddy.

'Surprisingly, yes,' she replied, 'a bit of traffic congestion around Burford, but nothing too bad.' Teddy smoothed her dress over the bump that was her unborn child.

Uncle Walter fussed around and wrapped his arm about her shoulders and guided Teddy towards the house. As she passed the Rolls-Royce, she noticed that the nearside wing mirror had disappeared and that there was a scratch down the passenger's side. 'Did you have an accident?' she asked Alex's mother.

'I found what I thought was a shortcut through the village of Icombe,' Uncle Walter stated flatly and with thinly disguised annoyance, 'and should have remembered that winding country roads have blasted tractors on them. Scraped the car on the hedge and a fence post avoiding one – bloody hedges are like barbed wire.' Teddy felt a little guilty as she suppressed a giggle at Uncle Walter's annoyance.

Entering the house, Teddy was again amazed at the transformation that had overtaken the building. No longer was there a sense of forlorn abandonment; there was furniture in place, new wallpaper and fresh paint on the walls, pictures hanging and rugs and carpets on the floor. 'My goodness,' she exclaimed, 'somebody has been busy.'

'It's still not finished,' said Uncle Walter, 'but with the builders have dealt with the essentials. The local furniture dealers have been most accommodating.' Did Teddy sense a feeling that Uncle Walter thought a bit of profiteering by the local tradesmen had occurred, at his expense? Uncle Walter looked at Klara. 'The upper rooms are still untouched, so we have allocated you a room on the first floor. It's a bit spartan, I'm afraid, but I am sure you will make it homely. We'll see if we cannot find a more permanent place for you shortly,' he said. Teddy understood that social division would remain until Alex's mother intervened.

'The old housekeeper's rooms are much larger, my dear,' she said, 'and you have the benefit of a sitting room and your own bathroom. I am sure that when they have been redecorated and furnished, you will find them far more comfortable. Perhaps you will help choose the furnishings to your taste?'

Klara smiled and thanked them both for their kindness. Uncle Walter suggested, 'The rest of the London furniture is arriving tomorrow morning, and we have not yet set up accounts with the local traders. The house is a little inhospitable at the moment as there is no food in the place, so why don't you girls go and get washed and whatever, and we'll all go into Stow for dinner?'

The King's Arms was just as Teddy remembered it and Alfred, the genial landlord, welcomed them as if they were long-lost relations. Uncle Walter was his usual ebullient self and before long was laughing and joking with some of the locals whom he had apparently met on previous visits. When called through for dinner, Teddy was surprised to find a jug of ale on the table. She could never remember Uncle Walter drinking anything except champagne and vodka, but it seemed that the order of the day was "when in Rome, do as the Romans do!"

Dinner was a huge success – a pot-roasted chicken followed by a delicious apple crumble, all washed down by the local ale, which was surprisingly good. Klara enthusiastically joined in the conversation, and it soon became clear that the "upstairs-downstairs" tradition of master and servant was not something that she regarded with any importance. Teddy was pleased; having married into the aristocracy, the protocols of service was not a part of her upbringing, and she was starting to form a bond with Klara that bordered on friendship.

*

It was seven o'clock in the morning when a loud knocking on the front door awoke the household. The London furniture had arrived. Alex's mother and Teddy dressed and came downstairs, to the delicious smell of bacon cooking. The family found Uncle Walter had already taken charge of the furniture removals and was instructing the foreman where precisely each packing case was to go. When he had finished directing operations, and not finding anybody in the dining room, he followed his nose and tracked down the source of the cooking bacon, discovering Alex's mother and Teddy already seated at the kitchen table while Klara was ladling bacon and fried eggs onto plates for them.

'Where on earth did this come from?' Uncle Walter asked.

'You said last evening that there was no food in the house,' said Klara simply, 'and so when we finished dinner last evening, I asked the landlord of the public house whether he could spare some eggs and a few rashers of bacon for breakfast. He also gave me some milk and a packet of tea.'

'Good God!' exclaimed Uncle Walter, rubbing his hands together in anticipation of his breakfast. 'You are truly a most resourceful girl. I think we shall all get along famously!'

Life over the next few weeks was busy, but not nearly as hectic as it ever was in London. The pace of living in the country was much slower, but surprisingly things were achieved far more efficiently. Alex's mother and Teddy spent the time working with the local craftsmen who had been engaged to restore the house to its former glory while providing modern-day creature comforts. They both enjoyed discussing plans for the gardens with a local landscaper and Klara was invited to plan a kitchen garden in the area where the previous one had long since become overgrown. For her own part, Klara negotiated with the local tradesmen and farmers firmly but fairly, and soon the larder and pantry in the kitchen were abundant. Indeed, so sharp were her negotiating skills that soon everybody felt sympathy for the local merchants trying to eke out a living while bartering with Klara's determination to get the best possible price.

The biggest compliment came from Uncle Walter who, after a particularly frustrating day in London, returned to Gloucestershire and as was his habit when he had had a bad day, he sat down to settle the household accounts. He joined Alex's mother and Teddy in the drawing-room afterwards and pronounced, 'If that girl ever decides to leave her post as a housekeeper, I shall instantly employ her as my head buyer. She has an excellent eye for quality and a sharp tongue for driving the price down!'

*

Over the weeks ahead, Teddy found it increasingly difficult fitting into her wardrobe of clothes, and despite Klara's best efforts with a needle and thread, Teddy's clothing could only be adjusted by so much. New clothes were needed, and at the same time, the nursery required decorating in preparation for the arrival of Alex and Teddy's baby. Neither Stow-on-the-Wold nor Moreton-in-the-Marsh had shops that would fulfil their every need, and even Banbury might not suit, so a day's excursion to Cheltenham with Alex's mother was deemed appropriate.

The train to Cheltenham from Stow-on-the-Wold was hardly an express. The line was a local branch line, and the trains stopped at every station along the route, all five of them. The four carriages and the locomotive were not in their first flush of youth, and even the one first-class carriage was so grubby that the dowager countess felt the need to cover her seat with a cloth before sitting down.

'They call this God's Wonderful Railway,' grumbled Teddy, remembering the popular nickname for the Great Western Railway, but try as she might on that branch line between Stow-on-the-Wold and Cheltenham, she could find nothing "wonderful" and even mentally removed a few letters thereby shortening it to a more apt adjective – "woeful".

The shopping trip, however, was a huge success. There was an entire department in Cavendish House dedicated to the expectant mother and Teddy was able to buy a whole wardrobe of clothes from a single store.

Perhaps they were not sufficiently fashionable for London, but for the shires, they were good quality and thoroughly practical. The shop was less successful at supplying nursery furnishings as there was nothing that she particularly liked. On the discreet recommendation of the helpful assistant in the furniture department, Teddy and the dowager countess left the store, crossed the Promenade and without difficulty found the quaint little side street where they found the recommended small family-owned furniture store that specialised in hand-crafted and bespoke nursery furniture. Teddy explained what she wanted, and the proprietor was able to make precise and surprisingly affordable suggestions that met her requirements exactly. Teddy was happy that she was able to purchase everything that she needed and for a slight additional charge even arranged for delivery to Ashton Court.

Teddy and Alex's mother had afternoon tea at the Queen's Hotel before returning to the station to catch the train back to Stow; it had been a very productive day, and Teddy had enjoyed the company of Alex's mother, although even Teddy admitted that the excursion had been somewhat tiring.

That evening, Teddy retired to bed early as the day's exertions were taking their toll, and she was feeling physically drained. As she climbed the stairs to her bedroom, she felt a twinge in her stomach, and having undressed and washed, Teddy lay on the bed in one of her new, larger nightgowns. The pains continued, and after about half an hour, she rang the bell for help. Klara answered her call and seeing the pain that Teddy was suffering, immediately telephoned for the doctor.

The doctor who came out was the complete opposite of Doctor McClintock, the straight-talking and somewhat dour Scottish doctor who had been Teddy's general practitioner when she lived in London. Dr Baxter was smooth and charming with an air of quiet authority and was evidently highly competent at his profession. Having examined Teddy thoroughly, he announced that she needed to slow down and take things more calmly. Otherwise, the doctor cautioned severely, she could harm both her own health and that of the baby. Apart from that, everything was fine, but he would prescribe a tonic to help boost Teddy's strength.

As the doctor was leaving, Uncle Walter thanked him and asked if there was anything that the family could do to help.

'Just make sure Mrs Carlton rests and does not worry unduly,' the doctor said. 'Is her husband at home?' the doctor asked as an afterthought.

'No, he's in the navy,' Uncle Walter replied briefly.

'Yes,' the doctor responded, 'that is often the case nowadays. Everything should be fine. Mrs Carlton just needs to rest.'

'Thank you, Doctor,' Alex's mother said as she joined the conversation.

'I shall render my account at the end of the month if that is acceptable?' said the doctor as he departed.

'Of course, thank you,' said Uncle Walter.

Despite the doctor's advice, Teddy was determined that nobody would mollycoddle her, although she did agree to slow down. Uncle Walter decided that Klara should learn how to drive so that if Teddy needed to go somewhere, she could be chauffeured rather than drive herself. When Klara heard of the plans, she protested nervously, stating that she could never possibly manage to learn how to drive a motorcar as it appeared so immensely complicated, but after much cajoling from Uncle Walter and the gentle reassurance of the dowager countess, in the end, she agreed to "have a go".

The medicine that Dr Baxter had prescribed was predictably disgusting, and Teddy was reluctant to take it the three times a day as instructed unless she had a cup of sweet tea to take away the revolting aftertaste, but after a few short days, it began to work its magic and Teddy started to feel much better. She had never been one to sit idly, and it was as much as the combined efforts of Alex's mother, and Klara could do to keep her from doing too much. Teddy hated the inactivity but soon adapted to life at a slower pace.

*

Meanwhile, in London, the division of military intelligence in London to which Alex ultimately reported, MI2, was also changing. Colonel Swann was promoted to brigadier and transferred to the Directorate of Military Intelligence under Major-General Frederick Beaumont-Nesbitt, and he was replaced by a Lieutenant-Colonel Rhys Llewelyn from MI3, the division that was responsible for European military intelligence. Unlike Swann, Lt-Col Llewelyn was not a Russian specialist, but he quickly came to understand the area of operation, and soon even Commander Jeffers appreciated the value of his new superior officer. Llewelyn was a quietly spoken Welshman who was staunchly religious, a confirmed teetotaller, who did not use or care for swearwords, but whose mind was razor-sharp. Whereas Swann had an exemplary military background and comprehensive knowledge of the area of operation, Llewelyn was a strategist – he saw through the "wood" and quickly identified the "trees"!

It was in the very early days of December that Llewelyn called on Commander Jeffers to review his department's operation, and the commander quickly gained the impression that Llewelyn was only concerned with one area.

'This chappie that you have in Helsinki,' he began.

'You mean Lieutenant Carlton?' Jeffers was keen that personalities should be acknowledged.

'Yes,' continued Llewelyn, 'tell me more about him.'

The commander took Lieutenant-Colonel Llewelyn through Alex's history with the service, culminating with a glowing endorsement. 'He has only been on the ground for a few days, and yet the intelligence on the nature of Russian bombing of Helsinki has been both thorough and insightful. May I ask why you are so interested?'

'Not just yet,' the lieutenant-colonel continued, 'but suffice it to say that there are those who are particularly interested in that theatre of war. Do you think that Carlton might be persuaded to be a little more…' he sought the right word, 'shall we say, proactive?'

Commander Jeffers resented being kept in the dark about his agents. Previously, Colonel Swann would discuss matters with departmental heads so that he could gain a full picture, but this new chap seemed to want to play his cards closer to his chest. It was clear that it was going to be a very different relationship with Lt-Col Llewelyn.

'Lieutenant Carlton is a remarkable young man who has a clear sense of duty and an extraordinary ability to understand situations and act appropriately. I am sure that if faced with a situation that requires "proactivity", he would act accordingly.' As the words fell from the commander's lips, he realised that they sounded pompous. Not that he cared particularly, he still had to get the measure of Llewelyn, but first impressions were not favourable!

They continued to fence for the next half-hour, Llewelyn offering up feints that Jeffers parried, but there was seldom a *riposte*, and not once did Llewelyn achieve a *prise de fer*. After much deflecting and countering, Llewelyn smiled and acknowledged Jeffers's skill by expanding a little.

'Please do not think that I am evasive, Roland,' the use of his Christian name somewhat took Jeffers aback, 'but there are concerns about Finland that some would like to address.'

Commander Jeffers sat back in his chair and silently invited Lt-Col Llewelyn to continue.

'Since Germany and the Soviets signed that outrageous non-aggression pact, just about the whole of the Baltic Sea is now controlled by the Nazis or the Soviets, except for the eastern seaboard of Sweden. That presents a logistical problem for the navy in that once German naval units get into the Baltic, they can hole up anywhere, and we would have little knowledge of where they might be hiding. The only control we have on ships is when they enter or leave the Baltic, but to monitor that effectively would tie up half the home fleet.

'There are some that believe assisting Finland to stay independent of the Soviets and therefore of Nazi Germany, would be of strategic value. I am inclined to agree.

'Besides, Churchill has drawn a comparison between our plight and that of Finland. He has likened our two countries to a pair of "Davids" facing the might of a brace of "Goliaths" and is pressing for military aid to be sent to Finland to help in her defence against Stalin.

'Having good intelligence from the war zone is crucial as it enables us to send the right type of assistance to best aid their efforts. Do you think your chappie would suit? He is, I gather, rather new to the game and a reservist?'

'I should think that Lieutenant Carlton would be very well suited to the task. He truly is a most resourceful and capable officer.'

'I gather he got himself into a spot of bother at one of the training units,' commented Lt-Col Llewelyn.

'Not so much "bother" – an unfortunate situation developed and he handled himself well. Moreover, he received a commendation from the subsequent inquiry,' responded Jeffers.

'Yes, I had read as much,' Llewelyn responded, 'and isn't he married to George Palmer's daughter?'

'He is,' Jeffers replied neutrally.

'I suppose he must be *exceptionally* gifted if he can handle Brigadier Palmer; he's not a man that I would readily cross. All right, Roland, let us see if anything comes of this initiative, but it might be sensible if he was prepared to move swiftly if we get the green light. Can you get a message to him on the QT?'

'I should think so, Rhys,' Jeffers responded, well, if Llewelyn was going to play the first-name game, Jeffers was not going to be left out, particularly as, at least on paper, he held seniority.

When Llewelyn had left, Jeffers asked his secretary, Miss Willoughby, to find 3/O Daphne Devine, his capable young assistant, and ask her to drop by at her earliest convenience.

'Hello, sir,' Daphne Devine announced herself a mere five minutes later as she let herself into the commander's office. 'You wanted to see me?'

'Yes, Daphne, come along in and sit yourself down.' She did as she was asked and crossed her legs in anticipation. 'We need to get a message to Lieutenant Carlton. Is there a way of communicating with him that will not arouse suspicion?'

'I should think so, sir,' she responded. 'I gather that Lieutenant Potts has made those arrangements.'

Simon Potts, as the Assistant Cultural Attaché at the British Legation in Stockholm, was responsible for handling agents in Sweden and other

Baltic countries, including Finland, and had been put in place primarily to manage the activities of his old school friend.

'Let me think about what we need to send,' the commander said pensively. 'We do not want to alarm the poor chap, but it may be that we need more of him than we originally thought.'

It was three days later that Lt-Col Llewelyn dropped by Commander Jeffers's office again. Without knocking, he opened the door and stuck his head inside. 'Roland? That Finnish thing, we're on. Would you set things up, please? I'll get my assistant to let you have the full details, but like most things they want it done yesterday!'

IV

After two days of bombing, the Saturday was remarkably calm. The German ship *Donau* had docked at Helsinki Harbour, having sailed from Danzig with instructions to evacuate the German colony in Finland, together with the Soviet diplomatic mission. It was due to sail for Tallinn on Sunday afternoon and about 3.30pm, Alex was struck by the eerie silence that had spread across the city. A rumour was circulating that after the Russian diplomats had left, a massive force of bombers would come and flatten the capital. The *Donau* was due to sail at four o'clock on Sunday 3rd December, and a large number of citizens that remained in Helsinki came to the harbour to witness its departure.

The *Donau's* sailing was delayed by the actions of Finnish customs officers who carefully went through every single piece of luggage that was brought on board by the Germans and even, despite strenuous objections from the Soviet Minister V. K. Dereviansky, every single bag carried on board by the Russian Legation. In fact, the ship did not get away that Sunday at all, but the expectation that the city would be safe did not lead to a peaceful night, as just after midnight there was a gas bomb alert. Finns feared a gas attack more than anything, as the country was not in any way prepared to handle such an assault with only a few officials having gas masks and none available for the defensive military or the general population. Newspapers had published instructions for do-it-yourself protection against poison gas with one even suggesting that people should urinate on a handkerchief and hold it to their faces to protect against gas attack.

Quite where the gas attack rumours had started nobody seemed to know, but the general opinion was that it was disinformation or propaganda spread by Soviet spies in the city to frighten Finns. If that was indeed the aim, it failed, as the Finns' resolve hardened.

Although the land invasion of Finland coincided with the bombing of Helsinki, the journalists did not receive notification until that Sunday evening when a junior official from the Finnish foreign office called them all to a conference room at the Hotel Kämp.

The official called the meeting to order and, in a deadpan voice, he read, '*Bulletin. Soviet troops began the invasion of Finland at dawn last Thursday, crossing the frontier in several places. Security detachments of Finnish troops fought them. Soon the fighting was in progress on all roads leading from Russia to Finland. The security detachments retreated according to the plan and between six and nine tanks were destroyed. The initial Russian attacks on the first day of war were in Lipola in Karelia and Suojärvi, north of Ladoga. At the same time, Soviet bombers attacked Aiipuri, Turku, Lahti, Kotka and the capital Helsinki, killing and wounding civilians as well as troops. That is all.*' Without waiting to take questions, the official left the room, and the journalists were left to speculate amongst themselves.

McMahon winked at Alex and indicated with a sharp movement of his head that they should leave. As they were departing the hotel, Mick said to Alex, 'I think we need to find out what that spokesman did not tell us.' Expecting Alex to follow him, Mick cut across the park that bisected the north and south Esplanade and headed towards the area of the city known as Gardesstaden or Kaartinkaupunki, where he entered a bar.

As they were taking the coats off, Mick spoke quietly to Alex. 'You can speak Finnish better than I, so when we find my contact, you can ask the questions.' Alex was a little upset at being brought along as the interpreter, but he also realised that if he were to get the same information as McMahon, he would have to put his pride in his pocket.

Mick spotted who he was looking for and clapped a man on the shoulder, greeting him in Finnish. 'Jarno, let me buy you a drink and introduce my friend Alex.'

He turned to Alex and said, 'Jarno here is a very senior clerical officer in the Ministry of Defence at Ohrana House.' With a great deal of deference to Jarno's position, he added, 'And what Jarno does not know is not worth knowing.'

Turning back to the man, who was preening himself and enjoying the accolades being heaped on him by the journalist, Mick asked, through Alex, 'So what actually happened with this invasion?'

'Whenever I see you, all you do is ask questions.' Mick shrugged and smiled at the Finn, who continued, 'It was just before 7.00am that we started to get reports of Russian tanks crossing the border near Lieksa,' Jarno explained, 'and it soon became apparent that the Soviets were advancing on all six of the roads between Russia and the Karelian Isthmus.

'We knew this is where they were likely to come from, so we had evacuated all the civilians from this area. We had mined the territory well, so when the Russian tanks and infantry crossed the border, they were blown up. Also, our troops had booby-trapped several buildings and shops, so when the Soviets went looting, they were blown up more.

'Our troops were well hidden in the forest, and they made sure that the Russians did not have an easy task invading our country. Thirty-two Finnish soldiers died on Thursday, but over 250 of the enemy also perished. Our soldiers did well.'

The next morning, after spending much of the night encoding specific details of the Soviet invasion into his report to *Svenska Posten*, Alex wired the article to Stockholm from Helsinki's war-battered main post office. As he was leaving, a Finnish soldier approached him and asked, '*Anteeksi, onko sinulla valoa?*' – Excuse me, do you have a light? – Although Alex did not smoke himself, he often picked up complimentary matches from bars and restaurants, so he delved into his pocket and found a box, which he passed to the soldier.

'*Kiitos*,' – Thank you, – responded the soldier, and as he handed back the matches, Alex noticed the soldier slipping a small folded slip of paper into the box.

'*Ole hyvä*,' – You're welcome, – responded Alex, replacing the matchbox in his pocket before turning to go back to the hotel. He had not walked far when the sirens began to moan their awful clarion of death and destruction, causing Alex to change direction and head towards a public shelter. Looking up into the dull grey sky, he watched nine bombers flying at about 2,000 feet.

Somebody near him called, '*Heillä on yksi!*' – They've got one! When Alex looked up, he saw one of the bombers falling out of formation, trailing black smoke from an engine. Abandoning his intention to seek shelter, Alex followed the path of the stricken aeroplane as it fell from the sky. It took him about half an hour to reach the wreckage in a small park in one of the western suburbs of the city. The crashed plane was on fire, but Alex saw that it was a twin-engined medium-sized bomber. The dull green tailplane with a faded red Soviet star had become detached from the main wreckage, and a bloodied tangled mess clad in a khaki-coloured tunic that was the remains of a crew member lay nearby. Quite a crowd had gathered, and unlike the rousing cheers when the shells had hit the aircraft, the atmosphere at the crash site was sombre. Perhaps seeing a corpse of a young Russian airman resonated with those onlookers as they reflected on their own family members who had been called up, or maybe it was just respect for a fallen warrior, Alex did not know, but the poignancy of that moment struck him.

Was this airman eager to fight for the Communist cause to build a better world? Was he after adventure and a better job? It mattered not; his life had ended that grey morning as he flew to deliver devastation to the people of the Finnish capital. It would only matter now to his grieving family and friends. Alex reflected on the strength and power of organised military campaigns and how little individual feedings counted. He watched as the onlookers picked up pieces of the aeroplane as mementoes before the police arrived with an ambulance. A van came with them also, carrying a film crew, and Alex watched as the body of the airman was heaved unceremoniously onto a stretcher several times so that the film crew got the "right" shot before the ambulance drove it away, and then he watched as the crowd dispersed as the police secured the area.

As Alex was walking away, he listened to the conversations around him; stories like those of a sixteen-year-old boy who had shot the aeroplane down from the roof of his apartment house, with his father's hunting rifle. Incredible as the story was, the people wanted a hero, but this was one of seven bombers that were brought down by Finnish anti-aircraft guns that day.

Back at his hotel and paying attention to the reports traded amongst the journalists, Alex heard tales of the Soviet bombers deliberately strafing civilians as they flew over the city, and two or three of his compatriots claimed to have either witnessed this as fact, others to have interviewed civilians who confirmed it. It was not something that Alex had seen for himself. The Frenchman, de Bourbon, claimed that one of the bombers had been brought down by an ex-world champion marksman, who had been serving with a machine-gun unit stationed atop the Olympic Tower at the city's stadium. The amiable Belgian, de Smet, claimed that he was at the same crash as Alex and that the police had announced that Estonian coins had been found in the pocket of one of the flyers, raising the prospect that the aircrew was not even Russian. Rumours and gossip were rife.

Just as Alex was about to go to his room, McMahon entered the bar and announced that Stalin had declared the creation of the Finnish Democratic Republic in a small town called Terijoki just inside the Finnish border of the Karelian Isthmus and had appointed Otto Ville Kuusinen as its leader. Stalin denounced the official Finnish government as a "clique of Whites and Bankers"! Alex would have much to write about in his report to *Svenska Posten*.

It was as he was lying on his bed, reflecting on the day's events, that Alex remembered the note in his matchbox. The message was simple, '*Helsingin Suurkirkko, 14.30, keskiviiko 6.12, rukoilla.*' – Helsinki Great Church, 14.30 Wednesday 6th December, to pray. An odd but fitting choice of date Alex thought; not only was it Saint Nicholas' Day tomorrow, but also Finnish Independence Day.

*

After waking and choosing to breakfast in his room, Alex spent the morning trying to sift fact from fiction from the various snippets of information and intelligence that he had gathered. The newspaper that morning was not only full of stories about the bombing, but there was an announcement that Prime Minister Risto Ryti had finalised his cabinet. Members were from every political party except for the Isänmaallinen Kansanliike (IKL) party, which was the ultra-nationalist and often considered the Fascist party, and the banned Suomen Kommunistinen Puolue (SKP), the Communist party.

Speculation that the delay in the composition of the new cabinet had been because Field-Marshal Mannerheim was against it, describing it as a "committee of bankers and businessmen", was promoted by various newspapers. Everybody knew that there was little love lost between the elder statesman of Finland and the new prime minister.

Alex concluded that the Soviets had blundered twice in recent days. Firstly, the bombing of Helsinki had shocked the whole Finnish nation to the core and now, that had led to the imposition of a government of national unity in the country. The prime minister had carefully selected his cabinet, as the country was no longer conducting a war on a military footing. It was fighting for its very existence, fighting for the system that was the foundation of its whole society.

Communicating this belief strengthened the morale of the Finnish working class, which accounted for about 60% of the Finnish population and who provided the bulk of the Finnish military. Since 1922, when the Act on the Acquisition of Land for Settlement Purposes, or *Lex Kallio*, was introduced, the majority of Finnish peasants had become individual landowners. They were no longer fighting over some diplomatic obscurity; they were battling to keep their farms. Alex reflected on the similarity with the Boer War, which indeed demonstrated what embattled farmers could do when defending their way of life. Furthermore, the upper echelons of Finnish society, the so-called "owning" class, understood that this was not just war between nations where compromise might be possible; it was a class war.

Secondly, it mattered not how "socialist" was the individual viewpoint. Finns resented the Soviet invasion and further begrudged the imposition of a quasi-Soviet government under Kuusinen. Communism by conquest clearly would not work.

Consequently, Alex surmised, those two initial actions would solidify the Finnish people behind Mannerheim and Ryti. So strong were the feelings against Otto Kuusinen that Alex noticed that the name over a renowned drapery store that shared the same name as the communist appointee, had the initial "K" hacked from the shop's sign by protesters, and throughout the time that he spent in Finland, the owners never replaced it.

Alex left the hotel just after midday so that he could follow his training and ensure that he was "clean" before arriving at his rendezvous. While walking through the streets of the capital, he quickly understood that the psychological shock of the air raids had partially achieved their aim – they had terrified the people of Helsinki. Alex recalled reading something that Leon Trotsky had written many years ago: *Individual terror is inadmissible precisely because it belittles the role of the masses in their own consciousness, reconciles them to their own powerlessness, and turns their eyes and hopes toward a great avenger and liberator who someday will come and accomplish his mission.* Nobody would ever believe Stalin was a Trotskyite, but as Alex walked through the streets of Helsinki, he pondered the sense in the author's words and wondered who that "great avenger and liberator" might be.

As he climbed the steps to the Great Church, the sirens began their mournful wail yet again. Although not overly religious, his immediate thought was that he would be safe inside – God would protect him there, especially in a church dedicated to St Nicholas on his patronal day; he was right, it was another false alarm. The time was just after 2.00pm, and Alex took a seat and waited, watching those others who were in the church that day. After about forty minutes, he sensed somebody moving into the pew behind him, who then leaned forward and muttered prayerfully, but somewhat ludicrously, 'The sun is very bright today.' It was not; again, it was grey and overcast.

Alex replied far more accurately, 'But there is a definite chill in the air.'

'Thank you,' muttered the voice from behind in heavily accented English. 'Please do not turn around. I have placed a package under my seat, and in a few moments, I shall leave. When I have gone, collect the package and return to your hotel. Included are your instructions. Please do not discuss them with anybody. Good luck.'

Alex waited as his mysterious contact departed, and in those quiet few moments, he reflected on the paradox of life. The beauty, peace and tranquillity inside Helsinki's great church amazed Alex and belied the fact that outside the cathedral's doors was the evidence of death and destruction wreaked on the city. Even though religion had never featured much in Alex's life until he had met Teddy, in that quiet moment his thoughts harked back to his days at Lassiter's where he learned that an omnipotent God treated all humankind as his children. Alex wondered how a loving Father could allow his children to kill each other. How could a caring Father discriminate between his children and decide which should live and which should die? How did that blessing go – the one they always used at school? "The peace of God that passes all understanding". It was the contradiction that made religion nonsense to him. But the quiet serenity of that place was inviting, it wrapped him in a protective cloak against the horrors of war.

Having waited longer than was necessary, Alex rose and took a step backwards before genuflecting and crossing himself three times in a most un-Lutheran manner, while he quickly recovered the package and secreted it inside his anorak. Would God worry about the irreverence of his actions? When the time came on that final day of judgement, when, if those who believed were right, Alex would repent of his sins, he would know the answer – but now such concerns were pushed to the back of his mind, as recovering the package was paramount.

Hurrying back to the hotel and in his room, Alex carefully locked the door behind him and placed the package on his bed. He sat in the armchair watching it, almost as if he expected the large envelope to burst into song. It was half an hour later when Alex plucked up the courage to open the package and examine the contents. He was surprised to see that the packet contained yet another envelope that again bore no name but was sealed heavily with red wax. Using his penknife, Alex carefully slit the envelope open, deciphered the message and read the coded instructions that it contained.

Alex was to form a relationship with an influential member of the Finnish Ministry of Foreign Affairs and to use his best endeavours to plant seeds promoting the notion that the United Kingdom was willing and prepared to offer military and humanitarian assistance to the Republic of Finland. Also, the British Ambassador to Finland, Thomas Snow, would be making representations to the president and government of the republic simultaneously. He was to spread the concept at each opportunity and be prepared to render such assistance as may be necessary to protect Finland's independence and victory in their conflict against the Soviet aggressor.

Alex burned the instructions and envelopes in the sink, washing the ashes down the plughole before sitting down again and contemplating his orders. Since signing the non-aggression pact with Hitler, Soviet Russia had unquestionably allied itself to Nazi Germany. The British government was understandably concerned that should the armies of the Third Reich be bolstered by the sheer vastness of Soviet military, then the odds would be overwhelmingly against Britain, France and all of the states that had not been invaded by the Nazis, ever succeeding in their struggle. Alex also understood the enormity of his task. He had been in the country for less than a week, and those contacts that he had managed to establish were tenuous and directly linked to Mick McMahon. Dare he trust his fellow journalist with the knowledge that he had recently gained? Did Alex know McMahon sufficiently for that trust to have been established? He decided not and concluded that any links and contacts that he found would have to be discreet. It was time that he bulldozed his way into the intelligence-gathering circle of the press corps and started to develop his own network of contacts.

Although Alex did not know it at the time, that day was when Soviet forces crossed the border at the village of Metsäpirtti on the shore of Lake Ladoga in the Karelian Isthmus, but Finnish troops brought in to protect the frontier repelled the attack. The Finnish daily newspaper, *Ilkka*, proudly announced the minor victory, some days later, with their headline, *Ryssät yrittävät turhaan Taipaleenjoella! Kiivat hyökkäykset torjuttu, Paljon tankkeja tuhottu, useita antautunut. Suomussalmella on 'lopputilitys' käynnissä Tolvajärvellä vihollinen jataka pankenemistaan.* – Russkies tried in vain at River Taipale! Vicious attacks repulsed, many tanks wrecked, many prisoners taken. At Suomussalmi, the enemy received their final coup de grace starting from Lake Tolvajärvi as the attackers continued to flee.

*

Over the next few days, the Finnish government evacuated two-thirds of the people from Helsinki; at least two hundred thousand were sent away. Considering the amount of damage inflicted on Helsinki's transport system, this feat was astonishing, not least because there was only one railway line available and the roads were slippery with ice and snow. The authorities commandeered buses, taxis and cars and shuttled people through fixed assembly points inside the city to predetermined locations on the five main roads leading out of the capital, at least 35 miles distant. Drivers filled their vehicles and motored at full speed to the drop-off location before turning around and returning for more loads. At the drop-off stations, the Women's Auxiliary Corps, known as Lottas, ran coffee stalls and "rest centres" in churches and schools that were warm and heated. From these initial distribution centres, citizens were transported further out of the city by a similar network of buses, cars and taxis, and so it went on like a massive spider's web. Outside the main industrial centres, Finland was principally agricultural, and farmers were glad of extra hands to help on the land, as most of the young men had been called up for military service.

In the first week of the war, the face of the city changed. Many of the hotels closed, shops were boarded up and padlocked, churches shut for the duration, orchestras disappeared from restaurants and just about all entertainment ceased – women and men even dressed alike, typically in ski trousers and boots. There was no need to encourage people to leave the city, the Soviet bombing had done enough to start the exodus, and the discipline of the Finns completed it. In those parts of Helsinki where attacks were most likely, large areas prohibited all civilians who did not have a special permit. Luckily, journalists could obtain passes with the correct authority to access most parts without question. Those workers whose jobs were critical to the war effort were not permitted to leave, and several of those who had already fled were ordered to return.

Alex decided that the easiest and quickest way of trying to establish contact with the Finnish Foreign Ministry was to try and get an introduction through McMahon's informant, Jarno, and so the next day Alex headed towards the Gardesstaden district to find the bar where they had previously met. He discovered the owner loading crates of alcohol onto the back of a truck that appeared to be half full of personal goods and chattels.

'What is happening?' Alex asked in Finnish.

'I'm getting out,' the owner said. 'I am off to my sister's in Hämeenlinna.'

'I am trying to contact Jarno who I met the other evening,' he told him.

'Jarno is an easy man to find,' the bar owner laughed. 'Go to any bar in Helsinki and sooner or later Jarno will walk through the door!'

'I had hoped to find him a bit quicker than that!' Alex persisted.

The bar owner stopped loading the truck and looked at Alex as if he were deciding whether to trust Alex's intentions, not wishing to bring trouble for one of his former customers. In the end, he shrugged his shoulders, tore a scrap of paper from one of the packages on the truck and using a thick stub of a pencil, wrote down an address.

'This is where he is staying,' he said, handing the slip of paper to Alex before turning back to the task in hand.

'Thank you,' said Alex and almost as an afterthought, 'good luck!' The bar owner acknowledged Alex's good wishes with a nod of the head before loading the truck with another crate of vodka.

'Here,' he said, offering Alex a bottle of good Russian vodka, 'you might as well have this. Jarno likes it, but there's not much call for Russian vodka at the moment.'

Alex took the bottle and thanked him again before heading off to look for the address that had been written by the bar owner. The apartment house shown on the paper was in Merikatu, overlooking the sea in the

Ullanlinna district of Helsinki. Being so close to the sea, the area had proved an easy target, and the apartment block three away from the one written on the paper was a smouldering shell of a building. The door of Jarno's apartment house was pockmarked with shrapnel damage and hanging uselessly on its hinges, so Alex let himself in and climbed the stairs to the second floor, where Jarno lived.

He knocked on the door of the apartment and heard a female voice responding, '*Mitä?*' – What?

Alex replied, '*Onko Jarno siellä?*' – Is Jarno there?

The door opened, and a young woman who appeared much more youthful than Alex had expected answered. 'He is out at the moment,' she said in Finnish, 'but he will not be long. Please come in.'

How trusting are these Finns, thought Alex as he entered the apartment, thanking the woman as he entered the hallway. '*Kiitos.*'

'I am Katja, Jarno's wife,' she introduced herself. 'Please come in and wait.'

'Thank you,' Alex responded. 'My name is Alex Carlsson, and I met Jarno the other evening.'

'You met him in the bar, I suppose.' There was a distinct sense of disapproval in Jarno's wife's voice.

'Yes,' responded Alex, 'I did meet him in a bar. A mutual friend introduced us, but I do not like to drink in bars too much myself, and I was only there because my friend took me.'

She warmed to this sentiment. 'I think Jarno spends too much of his time and money in bars. You would like coffee?'

'Yes, very much, thank you,' Alex conceded.

Katja left him and went to the kitchen to make coffee, and Alex looked around the comfortably furnished apartment. He knew that Ullanlinna was a select area in which to live and property overlooking the sea was usually much sought-after, but he wondered whether the views over the Merisatama harbour would make it dangerous, especially as it also faced the defence fortress of Suomenlinna. Katja returned with Alex's coffee just as Jarno returned.

Alex stood as Jarno entered the sitting room and greeted him.

'I know you. You're Mick McMahon's friend Alex, I think. What are you doing at my home?' he asked.

'I had hoped to meet you at the bar where we met the other evening,' Alex explained, 'but the owner was closing up and moving to Hämeenlinna to be with his sister. He gave me this for you, though.' Alex handed the bottle of vodka to Jarno.

'So, I do not think you have come here to tell me something that I already know. What do you want?'

'I want to talk to you,' Alex replied, 'but not in your home. Is there somewhere we could walk and talk, as I have heard something that I think may be of interest to your Ministry?'

'We can walk through the park to the sea if you wish,' suggested Jarno, 'and if you again tell me something that I already know, you can buy me a drink at another bar. If you tell me something that I do not already know, I might even buy you one!' Jarno smiled.

Opening the door to the hallway, Jarno called to his wife. 'Katja? I am going for a walk with Alex; I do not think it should take long.'

'That is good,' replied his wife. 'Dinner is cooking. Is your friend eating with us?'

Alex replied, 'No, thank you very much. I have another appointment, but it has been very nice meeting you and I hope that we shall meet again.'

'Of course,' she responded. 'I hope so too. Jarno does not bring many of his friends home.'

The two men left the apartment and walked down the stairs to the ground floor, and Jarno held the front door open for Alex. 'I must talk to the *talonmies* – caretaker – about this, anybody can walk in nowadays!'

They walked across the road and through the park to the sea wall. Barbed wire had already been added to the barrier to make it difficult for any would-be invader, and as they turned to walk alongside the water, Jarno asked Alex, 'So what is this information that you have heard?'

Alex replied, 'I expect that I am wasting your time and that you already know what I heard,' Jarno looked as if he had just won a free drink, 'but a contact has told me that the British have told your Foreign Ministry that they are willing to assist Finland in its hour of need. My contact says that this has come from the highest authority in Britain and I just wondered whether you had heard this rumour and whether it was true.'

Jarno looked at Alex suspiciously. 'You work for a Swedish newspaper. How would you have heard these rumours?'

'Yes, I work for a Swedish newspaper,' replied Alex, 'but before they sent me to Finland, I was working in London, and I still have friends there. To be a good journalist, you must have friends everywhere, and you must listen to what these friends tell you so that you can be a better journalist than the next man. If the story is true, I think it could help Finland, but if it is not true, it would be wrong of me to write about it because that could harm Finland.'

'I wondered whether you had heard this from Mick McMahon,' Jarno enquired.

'No,' responded Alex, 'I promise you that I have not heard this from Mick and I have not discussed it with him as he is one of the next men that this journalist would like to beat!'

'Good,' said Jarno, 'because I do not trust the Irish Mr McMahon very much. It seems to me that he is a man who does not let the truth stand in the way of a good story.'

'Tell me,' persisted Alex, 'is there any truth in this story?'

'I have not heard anything,' Jarno responded, 'but if the British are talking to the Foreign Ministry, that would not be unusual. They are like a clam. They keep what they know behind their teeth! If the British were talking to the Foreign Ministry, the Defence Ministry would be the last to know!'

'If there was some truth in this story,' mused Alex, 'do you think that the Finnish government would accept help from Britain?'

'Of course.' Jarno seemed confident. 'We are a small country, and we are facing a mighty foe. I think we would accept help from anybody. But I am surprised that Britain can spare any armed forces from the expeditionary force that they have sent to help defend France and the low countries against Germany. Why would they want to help Finland? We are not strategically important in the war that they are waging.'

'This worried me also,' said Alex, 'but my friend who told me this is normally very reliable. How do you think Britain could help?'

'Well, that's easy to answer,' Jarno replied. 'We have heard that the British Royal Air Force spends its time playing cricket on their airfields, as they have nothing to do. Send a few squadrons of Spitfires to Finland so that we can stop this bombing! Now, I think I promised you a drink.'

Jarno turned back across the park and before long they were warming themselves in front of a log fire in a bar.

V

It took Alex most of that night to compose his article for *Svenska Posten* and to encode and incorporate his report for London. He had planted the British government's idea in the fertile imagination of Jarno, and although he was not attached to the Finnish Foreign Ministry, Alex felt that it was probably more beneficial for the Defence Ministry to be aware of the offer that was on the table. If, as instructed, he had cultivated a lead in the Foreign Ministry, judging by what Jarno had intimated, they would probably have suppressed his information. However, the Defence Ministry, whose task was mobilising and maximising Finland's limited defence resources, would benefit much more from the knowledge that they did not stand alone and that help could be made available. It was a gamble going against his precise instructions, but Alex thought it worth the risk.

Breakfast at the hotel that morning was worse than ever. The choice of food was even less than it had been over the past week. No eggs were available, neither was ham, and Alex had to content himself with a slice of black bread and some tasteless cheese. Even the coffee tasted different, almost stale, as though it was from previously used grounds. After breakfast, Alex took the article that he had written the previous night to the central post office so that they could wire it to Sweden. Ominously, the clerk said rather pessimistically that he would try to send the article later that morning, but communications were difficult that day. Alex asked him to do his best, and the clerk gave Alex a look that said that he always did his best!

Alex was walking down Heikinkatu past the great Stockmann department store when McMahon appeared by his side.

'Hello, Alex,' opened Mick. 'I did not see you last evening.'

'Oh! Hello. No, I went out for a walk around the city and to see if I could make sense of this war that we seem to be caught up in,' responded Alex.

'And do you understand it?' asked Mick.

'Not at all! I think it is totally beyond comprehension!'

'Is that not the case with all war?' Mick questioned reflectively.

'I rather think it is,' replied Alex equally profoundly. 'Come, let us go and find some decent coffee. That muck at breakfast was undrinkable.'

They turned right off Heikinkatu and onto Bulevardi, finding a cafe that had some bread rolls and cakes displayed in the window. The warm fug of freshly brewed coffee enveloped them, but when they asked to buy one of the cakes, the waitress apologised and explained that they were only for display purposes. She could offer a Karelian pie, known in Finland as *Karjalanpiirakka* and maybe even some *munavoi* (egg butter), but still, that came from powdered eggs, she apologised. Alex and Mick accepted gratefully.

'Do you fancy a trip to the country?' Mick asked a little cautiously.

'What do you mean?' enquired Alex.

'I am getting sick and tired of only receiving sanitised information from the Ministry of Defence,' Mick explained. 'Even what I get from Jarno is censored. The military attachés at the legations are not being allowed anywhere near the fighting and have to accept what the government tells them. All the communiqués seem to disclose are lists of names, most of which are difficult to spell and impossible to find on a map. There are no troops back from the front who could tell us what it is really like, so I think it's about time I went and saw them myself!

'I have a contact in the army, and he has offered to get me to the frontline so that I can see the war up close and I'm sure that he would not mind if you came along also.'

'Why?' asked Alex. 'Surely, we are both competing for the same stories?'

'Bah!' replied Mick. 'We need to help each other. Your paper is in Sweden and mine is in Ireland, so we are not really competitors. Indeed, apart from neutrality, there is little similarity between our two countries – yours is a monarchy, mine a republic, *et cetera*. If we help each other, we both get good stories. Besides, I like you!'

'Of course,' Alex responded. 'I agree that it makes sense…' he left his response hanging.

'Naturally,' continued the Irishman, 'and I hope that if you had a lead, you would share it with me?'

'Naturally,' lied Alex. 'So what about this trip to the frontline?'

*

It was on Monday 11th December that Alex and Mick McMahon found themselves atop a small hillock, sheltering under a bivouac and watching through binoculars as, amidst the pine trees, a small group of men in white snow capes, with their rifles slung on their backs, moved swiftly over the landscape on skis. They watched as the men turned off the path and behind a small clump of trees where they crouched down and came to readiness. A dozen or so rifle shots echoed through the stillness like whipcracks, and then there was quiet, an intense almost deafening silence of the forest.

The mound from which Alex and Mick were observing was roughly halfway between the villages of Raate and Suomussalmi in the Kainuu region of Finland, about 650km northeast of Helsinki in what is known as the "waist" of Finland. Together with Mick's contact, a major wearing the insignia of the II Armeijakunta (2nd Army Corps), they had been flown north in a recently converted former Aero OY Junkers JU52 passenger plane, whose seats had been ripped out for cargo transport and replaced by ramshackle wooden benches either side of the fuselage. The aeroplane had landed on a hastily constructed temporary airstrip built on the frozen lake at Taivalalanen just outside Suomussalmi, and a helpful lieutenant had reluctantly surrendered his all-terrain vehicle. The Tempo G1200 was a

German forerunner of the Jeep, but hardly as versatile. They were about 30 miles inside Finland where Finnish troops were facing a Russian column that was attempting to cut across the country at its narrowest point.

Although it was only early afternoon, the evening was drawing in, and darkness seemed to settle on the forest like a shroud, even though snow covered the pine trees. As it darkened, what perspective there was, vanished. Trees, road and sky blended into a vacuous backdrop, and the trunks and branches were like scant pencil sketches on the background. Alex was almost captivated as dusk fell. His mind was abruptly brought back to reality as they watched a line of men emerge from the forest and trudge wearily towards them. The soldiers kept carefully to the shadows of the trees as they curved between the pines – some were on skis, others rode on sledges drawn by their comrades. All the soldiers wore white capes with hoods as camouflage. Alex thought they looked almost comical as he watched them trek towards where they had secreted themselves, but as they got closer, he saw the faces of the soldiers beneath the white cowls of the hoods, and there was nothing comic about them. Their faces with dark, exhausted eyes and unkempt beards with that resigned look of men who are on their way from war, the reality of what they had experienced etched deep in their faces, yet somehow thankful that they had survived.

The major, who was acting as their guide and whose name was Ville Koskinen, explained that these men were on their way back from what was believed to be the frontline, some 500 metres ahead. The Soviet had attacked that morning and had only been beaten back about an hour previously. When darkness came, everybody expected the Russians to try again. Alex asked whether it would be possible to go to the actual frontline.

'Frontline?' the major laughed. 'If anybody knew precisely where the frontline was, I would take you, but for all I know, we may be in Soviet territory right now. If the Russians have circled behind us, we may have to fight our way out. Nobody knows where the frontline is. It could be right here, or a kilometre ahead, or maybe a kilometre behind us. Anywhere where the patrols are. We are fighting a war without frontlines.

'Come on', the major decided, 'it will be pitch dark soon. We should start heading back.'

As they returned to the vehicle, the major explained that the Russian divisions were trying to find the weakest points in the Finnish defences, but such was the mobility of the Finnish frontier troops that they attacked the Russians every time they thought they had broken through the lines. The Finns drove the Russians back, and if the Finns thought that there was a weakness in the Russian front, they pushed forward. It was guerrilla warfare at its finest. In the forests and lakeland around Suomussalmi, the opposing sides had waged a battle for eleven days, and Major Koskinen told the two reporters that the troops that they were watching were returning to camp for the first time since the start of the war.

Further back and on the other side of the road, glimmers of orange flame from fires of pine logs were just visible through the trees. These were the fresh troops of the 27th Infantry Regiment waiting to move up, and the major turned the steering wheel into the woods towards the flickering lights. As Alex and Mick arrived at the camp, they wondered how many of these soldiers would survive the next battle, as the majority were obviously reservists. Their leather pull-on boots that came to just below the knee were all new, and they all had the turned-up toecap which was used to catch under the thong of skis. The soldiers carried the least equipment that they could get away with, and most of it was also new – an M28 rifle still smelling of the grease in which the manufacturer had encased it, a bayonet, a haversack of harsh new canvas. Each man had a *puukko* (knife) hanging from his belt, and a water bottle. None were wearing standard-issue steel helmets but were wearing grey fur caps with ear flaps that could be let down, each with a small blue and white army rosette on the front. Even though it was minus 10°C, none of the soldiers wore their ear flaps lowered – they wanted to hear the slightest sound. Very occasionally, Alex saw a soldier wearing the old khaki uniform from a time before the 1920s, under their cape. These men were veterans of some earlier campaign, recalled to fight for their country again, and he knew that the new and untested troops would look to these veterans for inspiration when the fighting began.

Sledges were piled high with ammunition and other military equipment and covered with a white canvas camouflage, ready to be dragged to wherever the fighting was taking place. The major suddenly stopped and held up a hand. Alex and Mick thought that he had heard something, but he raised his nose and sniffed. 'Come,' he said, 'it is supper time.'

They found the field kitchen supervised by two huge cooks. Army cooks throughout the world were large, Alex thought, and as the three men approached, they lifted the lid from a massive cauldron that contained a thick pea soup.

Major Koskinen commented, 'Good, *hernekeitto!*' They each received a metal bowl filled with the soup, a piece of the hard Finnish bread and a mug of milk. No cutlery, though, and they copied the men around them as they used the hard bread as makeshift spoons before it became soggy enough to eat; then they drank the glutinous soup straight from the bowl. As they ate, the major explained that pea soup was traditionally served on Thursdays but had become a staple of the Finnish soldiers' diet and was now likely to be served upon any day.

They had almost finished eating when a captain approached and saluted, inviting the major to join him in his command tent. All three got up and followed the captain to a bell tent, and inside, under the flickering light of a dimmed hurricane lamp, Alex saw a table spread with a detailed map of the district, which had several pins marking the position of the captain's troops. As they talked, they heard the faint chatter of a machine gun. The captain looked dog-tired, and Alex asked whether it had been hard, thus far.

'I think I have had about eight hours' sleep since the beginning of the war,' he replied. 'We are battling the Soviet 163rd Division, which has over fifteen thousand men, and they have at the minimum fifty field guns, and God only knows how many more mortars. Some of our reconnaissance parties have reported seeing tanks, but they haven't used them yet.'

'How many men do you have?' asked Alex.

'That,' replied the captain, 'I cannot tell you. I started with about a thousand, though God alone knows how many I have left. Maybe three or four hundred. Then there are the new lads from the 27th, but most have not long since grown out of nappies. I cannot send them into battle until they are better prepared. Altogether, maybe about a thousand if I'm optimistic. Last night, the Soviets put down a barrage on our forward positions, and we thought that they would follow that with an attack, but they did not. We sent reconnaissance forward to bring back any wounded, but there were none, and the bodies had their clothes stripped from them. It was clear that some of our men had been wounded, but they were shot dead before being stripped.'

The captain noticed the shocked look on Alex's face. 'The Russians only evacuate their walking wounded and shoot those that are more seriously injured. It might sound callous, but it is kinder than leaving a wounded colleague to freeze to death suffering terribly.'

'Why do they strip the dead?' Alex asked.

'Perhaps it is because the Finnish uniform is much better quality than those issued to Russians, I don't know. From what we have seen being worn by prisoners, they have not been kitted out properly for these temperatures; one prisoner we captured was wearing three uniforms – his own and two from dead comrades, just to try and keep warm.'

The field telephone jangled into life, and the captain picked up the receiver, listened for a minute and then barked a couple of orders. 'I think it might be better if you were to leave now, sir,' he addressed Major Koskinen. 'They are on the move again, and we might not be able to guarantee your safety if you remain.'

As they left the captain's tent, Alex thanked him and wished him good luck.

'Thank you, and please pray for us,' the captain said. 'Write kindly about us, and God willing, one day, I might even be able to read your story.'

'I will do that, I promise you,' Alex replied before leaving the tent.

As they returned to their G1200, they passed a troop of soldiers who slipped the toes of their boots under the thong on their skis and launched themselves down the track towards the sound of gunfire that had just commenced. Alex was amazed at the speed at which they travelled. Slaloming between the trees, they were quickly out of sight.

Climbing aboard the vehicle, Major Koskinen gunned the engine into life, and they headed off in the opposite direction. Although they were following the road, the snow and ice made driving difficult, and the headlight adaptors together with the low wattage bulbs that had been fitted further hampered progress. Not that the G1200's headlights were of much use anyway being located on the side of the bodywork just in front of the passenger cabin, the bulbous mudguard obscured much of the illumination from the lights, but the blackout precautions made them of even less use. Consequently, the major was driving cautiously and trying to prevent damage to the vehicle.

They had travelled about 6 kilometres when a Finnish patrol of five or six men, all on skis, stopped them. One man, presumably the officer, stepped into the road and raised his hand indicating that the vehicle should stop, and Major Koskinen slowed down.

Leaning out, the major called, *'Mikä hätänä?'* – What's wrong?

'Venäläiset ovat edessä!' came the reply – The Russians are ahead.

'Kuinka kauas?' the major asked – How far?

Alex was sitting behind Major Koskinen, and next to McMahon, so what he heard of the conversation was limited. He scanned the forest on the left-hand side of the road, and that was when he saw the slightest of movements if that was what it was, or maybe it was something out of place or even merely a perception of danger. He turned to look to the right and saw one of the soldiers start to raise his rifle.

Mick McMahon was the first to be hit, in his shoulder so that he fell sideways, and Major Koskinen was next as he was drawing his sidearm. Alex's instinct took over. As he rolled out of the vehicle, he pulled his FN pistol and coming to a firing position, he first shot the officer and then changing target slightly, shot the soldier who had fired at Mick McMahon. Ducking back down behind the vehicle, Alex span round and took aim at one of the other soldiers who was struggling to chamber a round in his rifle. As the soldier started to raise his gun, Alex shot him twice – the perfect double-tap. A gun barked from behind him and Alex span round, bringing his pistol up and seeing another soldier aiming at him. Alex pulled the trigger twice, and the soldier fell, hit by both bullets.

Realising his pistol was empty, he dropped it and picked up the major's weapon that had fallen out of the vehicle. Alex was pleased to see that it, too, was an FN, but the bulkier 1922 variant. Slipping off the safety catch and pulling the slide back to chamber the first round, Alex rolled around the front of the vehicle looking for another target, but the final soldier had disappeared and everywhere was eerily quiet.

Still using the vehicle as cover, Alex recovered his pistol and heaved Major Koskinen into the passenger seat. He was gratified to hear the major moan in agony, at least he was not dead. Alex pulled himself into the driver's seat and started the G1200, ramming the gearbox into gear, he let up the clutch a little too vigorously and launched the vehicle down the road. Adrenaline was still pumping, and Alex was not the most experienced driver, so his driving was far too fast and much too reckless.

They bounced, slithered and slid down the road for about another 12km before Alex noticed glimmering fires in the forest on the left. He found a track leading into the woods, and praying that they were not driving into a Soviet camp, he steered through the trees until he came to the encampment.

'Lääkäri!' – Doctor! – he yelled as he swerved to a halt, and again called the same.

Two soldiers ran up, and Alex yelled at them, 'I have two wounded, get a doctor!' and seeing the men were rooted to the spot, he bellowed, 'quickly!'

One of the soldiers ran back into the camp and quickly returned with an officer and two medics carrying a stretcher. Alex pulled himself out of the vehicle and addressed the officer. 'My name is Alex Carlsson, and I am a journalist with *Svenska Posten*. I was visiting the frontline with a colleague and Major Ville Koskinen of the 2nd Army Corps, who is wounded and in the front of this vehicle. My wounded colleague is in the rear. We were ambushed by a Soviet patrol about 10km down the road as we were returning to Suomussalmi.' Alex handed Major Koskinen's sidearm to the understandably dumbfounded officer.

'Come,' he said, 'I will take you to my captain. These men will look after the wounded.' The officer turned and headed back into the camp, expecting Alex to follow.

Dodging between the trees, they eventually came to a clearing, and the officer instructed Alex to wait while he reported to his captain. Finally, he returned with another older man.

'My name is Captain Urho Huhtala, and the lieutenant tells me that you met a Soviet patrol about 10 kilometres down the road. Tell me precisely what happened.'

Alex explained all that had occurred, and after he had finished, the captain stroked his stubble thoughtfully and asked, 'Are you sure they were wearing Finnish uniforms?'

'Yes, one of the attackers was wearing a fur hat with the Finnish blue and white badge on the front, and I recognised this type of hat as being the same as those worn by the soldiers with whom we had just eaten supper.'

'We suspected this to be the reason why dead Finnish soldiers had their uniforms removed. Come, join us, my men will be rising soon, and we must see about getting you back to civilisation.'

Captain Huhtala ordered coffee and then instructed his radio operator to send a message back to headquarters.

*

There is no dawn that far north in Finland during December. Indeed, the day is almost non-existent. In the "land of the midnight sun", the counter during winter is almost perpetual darkness. Dawn was marked by soldiers starting to go about their routines, and one woke Alex, who had fallen asleep in the captain's office in a chair. He had not even drunk his coffee, which was now cold. As he stood up and stretched, the captain returned.

'Ah, you have woken up, then?' the captain observed.

'Yes,' replied Alex, 'what time is it?'

'Seven-thirty,' the captain responded, 'and we are getting ready to move out. I am leaving you here with your friend and Major Koskinen and our medics. Headquarters are sending transport to get you out of here.'

'Thank you,' replied Alex. 'How are Major Koskinen and my colleague?'

'They are sleeping, but they will be all right,' the captain said. 'It is a good job that Russians are such terrible shots; both only have flesh wounds.' Alex smiled as he pondered the thought that both Koskinen and Mick McMahon owed their lives to the fact that not all Russians were awful shots!

The captain shouted at somebody to bring more coffee and then held out his hand to Alex. 'You did well to look after your friends. If you had not… well…' He left the rest of the sentence hanging – the captain saluted Alex and left the tent.

It was mid-morning before the truck arrived to take Alex, Mick McMahon and Major Koskinen back to headquarters, by which time both Mick and the major were awake.

VI

It was a couple of days before Alex returned to Helsinki. He was transferred by road to the hospital at Oulu, where he was methodically checked over by highly competent medical staff before being moved to a military base where Alex was questioned time, and again by different people from different sections, all of whom seemed most interested in why he had been suspicious of the patrol that had stopped them. They asked where Alex had acquired the pistol that he had used, and each time Alex was consistent with his answers – he became suspicious when he saw a member of the patrol bringing his rifle to readiness, and he had bought the pistol in Sweden a couple of years ago for his own protection.

On the fourth day since their visit to the front had begun, Friday 15th December, a Colonel Makkinen came and told him he was being taken back to Helsinki on the next available transport. He also broke the news that Mick McMahon had died the previous night; apparently, his wound had become infected, and he had been taken to the intensive care unit where, despite the best attention of the medical staff at the military hospital, he had suffered a fatal heart attack. Alex was shocked, and his immediate thought was that the Hotel Torni would be a drearier place without the geniality of Mick McMahon, but the good news was that Major Koskinen was being sent back on the same plane. The colonel thanked Alex for saving the life of a Finnish officer and shook his hand before saluting him and leaving.

The plane that was taking them back to Helsinki was a de Havilland Dragon Rapide, an aeroplane that Alex was familiar with from England. It could seat only a very few passengers, but the cabin was considerably more comfortable than the JU52 that had brought them north.

Major Ville Koskinen was waiting by the aeroplane as Alex arrived, and Alex saw that the major had his arm in a sling and he looked haggard.

'Alex,' he began in greeting, 'I hear you saved my life. Thank you. But I am very sorry to hear that your friend did not make it. I did not know him well, but he seemed a nice man.'

'I'm sorry,' Alex was surprised. 'I thought that you knew him quite well?'

'No,' the major said, 'I was on leave in Helsinki and was ordered to take you both and give you a tour of the front before returning to my unit. Now, I think my men must survive a little longer without me.'

The pilot leaned out of the cabin and said to the major, 'Shall we go, sir? We shall have to refuel at the military airfield near Jyväskylä on the way, and I especially want to get back today!'

'Have you got a date?' Major Koskinen asked, to which the pilot gave a knowing grin.

Both Alex and Major Koskinen laughed before clambering aboard the ageing bi-plane and strapping themselves into their seats. The pilot turned into the wind, and before long they were airborne and heading southwards. The brief stop at Jyväskylä was unremarkable, and Alex did not even catch a glimpse of the town, as the aerodrome was so far out in the country. They touched down at Malmi Aerodrome in Helsinki during the early evening, an evening where darkness had already enveloped the city. As they landed, Alex could just about make out the numerous bomb craters where the Soviet bombers had targeted the airfield, and he was amazed that it was still operational. The pilot taxied to the magnificent circular terminal building and no sooner had the pilot applied the aeroplane's brakes than the door was opened and the passengers assisted out of the cabin.

A smart lieutenant in the full dress uniform of an aide-de-camp greeted Alex and Major Koskinen and snapped to attention and saluted with such force that Alex winced in surprise. He addressed the major. 'Sir. Will you and Mr Carlsson please follow me?'

Major Koskinen and Alex both followed the lieutenant into the building and were surprised by the size of the reception committee that awaited them. A full major-general stepped forward, and Major Ville Koskinen was embarrassed. He could not salute his superior officer because of his injury, but the smiling major-general defused the situation by extending his left hand to the major and shaking his hand. He turned to Alex and shook his hand also, but Alex became uncomfortable when flashbulbs started to pop all around him, and journalists began pressing them both for details – it appeared that the news of their exploits had preceded them, and even though he tried to keep his head down and away from the cameras, he was only partially successful.

The major-general escorted Alex and Major Koskinen to a waiting staff car and whisked them back towards the city. They dropped Alex first at the Hotel Torni, and the major-general again thanked Alex for saving the major. Alex picked up his bag and entered the hotel to a rousing round of applause from his fellow journalists. All Alex wanted was to go to his room and sleep, but the other journalists had other ideas, and the celebrations began with a solemn toast to the memory of their recently deceased colleague, Michael McMahon. After that, the party became more of a wake.

It was during the party that Alex learned of one of the more ridiculous stories of the war. The day before Alex and Mick McMahon had left Helsinki on their adventure, Sunday 10th December, a whole battalion of Soviet troops attacked a Finnish supply depot near Tolvajärvi Lake to the east of Joensuu and the Finns quickly abandoned their positions, running into the forest to save their lives. The attack happened at the time when the Finnish troops were preparing to have dinner. Sausage soup was on the menu, and the cooks had prepared enormous cauldrons of the stuff. The Russians, having driven the Finnish soldiers off, promptly devoured the entire meal, for everybody knew that not only were the Soviet soldiers poorly led, they were also poorly fed!

The commander of the supply depot, a Colonel Pajari, gathered his men to him and counter-attacked, surprising the Russians as they were ravenously devouring the Finnish soup. Rumour has it that the entire battalion of Russian troops perished as they ate, and over one hundred dead Russian bodies were found in the field kitchen the next day. This short battle was already becoming known as "*Makkarasota*" or the Sausage War!

Alex left the party as soon as he was able and went to his room. He lay on the bed and started to mentally write the article that he would submit to *Svenska Posten* the next day, while at the same time formulating the report that he would have to encode into the piece, for London. He hoped that news of his exploits would not find its way to his superiors in MI2, but in the days of telegraphic communication, he soon realised that this was a forlorn hope. What would Simon Potts, the commander, his colleagues at MI2 and superiors make of his exploits? And God forbid that Teddy would see his photograph emblazoned across the British newspapers!

*

He set his alarm for seven the next morning, but even so, Alex woke early, and he made his way downstairs for breakfast, hoping to avoid meeting any of the other reporters. He had judged it right; nobody was awake yet and judging by the state of the hotel bar, the party had gone on to the early hours of the morning – only some would be awake before midday. The coffee was even worse than he remembered it to be, and breakfast was becoming even more paltry than previously; food shortages were starting to bite.

He wrote his article, which included a lengthy coded message for London, outlining all that he had seen over the past week, although he played down his actions considerably, merely describing it as a "fire-fight" in which most of the Russians did not survive. Satisfied with his efforts, he went to the post office to wire it through to Stockholm. As he walked through the streets, Alex felt as though he was under observation, and at the post office, the clerk was far more helpful than he had ever been previously, or was it Alex's imagination?

While Alex was returning to the Hotel Torni, a sailor hurrying to catch a tram bumped into him and apologised, but not before Alex felt the sailor's hand deposit something in his pocket. Another note. Back at the hotel, he read the message in his room: *Helsingin päärautatieasema, 18.00, tänään, odota kunnes yhteyttä* – Helsinki central railway station, 1800hrs today, wait for contact.

Alex spent much of that Saturday afternoon in the considerable public air-raid shelter on the north side of Heikinkatu. The sirens had howled their mournful tune of impending doom at about 2.30pm that day, and Alex had followed the crowd as they descended into the granite bedrock on which the city is built. Whenever possible, he had taken to using public shelters rather than the cellar at the hotel, as it gave him a unique insight into the morale of Helsinki's citizens. He had found that Finnish people were usually phlegmatic and unflustered when faced with adversity, but there were hints of mood changes that one could only notice when close to groups of Finns.

That day, waiting underground for the "all-clear" to sound, Alex again picked up the hardening of the collective resolve of the people. The initial shock of the bombing had increasingly given way to a strengthening of attitudes against Russia. When Alex left the shelter that afternoon, he was confident that if a division of the Red Army were to march down Heikinkatu that day, every single person in that shelter would give their life to prevent the capture of another metre of Finnish soil. He had not experienced the same resolve in the early days of the war in Britain, and he was impressed by the determination of the Finnish nation at that time.

The "all-clear" sounded just after five o'clock, and Alex spent the remaining time until his appointment ensuring that he was not under surveillance. He did not feel exposed, but his training demanded that he be sure.

Alex arrived at Helsinki's central railway station slightly ahead of schedule, and in the manner of most arriving at transport hubs, he surveyed the departure and arrivals boards as if trying to find his particular train. He turned into the magnificent hall of the station cafe and ordered a coffee with *pulla* (cake) before taking a seat, observing all those who were entering and leaving. Just after half-past six, a hand touched his shoulder, and a voice asked, in Swedish, 'May I join you?'

Alex automatically responded, '*Naturligtvis*' – Of course.

He looked up as Simon Potts, his old school friend and colleague, settled in the seat opposite. He was about to greet his old friend when Simon almost indiscernibly shook his head. Finns will seldom initiate a conversation, but Swedes are less reserved, so Simon asked, 'Excuse me, but I have just arrived from Sweden. Is there a good hotel in Helsinki?'

Playing the game, Alex responded, 'Most of the hotels have closed down because of the war, but a few are still open.'

'Aha,' replied Simon, 'has it been awful?'

'Yes,' Alex simply said and finishing his cake and coffee, he stood up to leave and looking at Simon, said, 'excuse me, I have to leave.'

'Of course,' responded Simon, and Alex left.

Alex loitered outside the station waiting for Simon to emerge, and when he did, Alex followed at a safe distance, always keeping his friend in sight while scanning for unwanted surveillance. Simon had crossed over from the railway station and was heading up a road towards the Esplanade, and Alex watched as Simon entered the Hotel Kämp before following his friend. Simon was registering, so Alex went into the bar and ordered a beer. He was immediately recognised by a Swiss journalist who came over and joined him at the bar.

'Alex, my friend,' the journalist said, slapping Alex on the back as he settled on the adjacent bar stool, 'has the Hotel Torni run out of beer?'

'Hello, David,' Alex replied. 'Not at all. I just fancied a change. Can I buy you a beer?'

'Ja, of course,' the Swiss replied with a smile. 'I never refuse free beer!'

Alex and the Swiss journalist were chatting when Alex became aware of Simon ordering aquavit next to him. Alex moved his barstool ever so slightly and glanced down at the bar on which Simon had placed his room key, and noted the number, 416, before resuming his conversation with the other journalist. He ignored Simon, who drank his drink and picked up his key before leaving the bar.

About twenty minutes later, after accepting a reciprocal beer from the Swiss, Alex made his excuses and left the bar. He went to the toilet and wasted another ten minutes locked in a cubicle before emerging and making sure that the Swiss correspondent was not about. He caught the lift to the fourth floor, found room 416 and knocked lightly on the door.

Simon opened the door, and as Alex entered, they embraced each other.

'Pottsie, you old sod,' Alex greeted his old friend in English. 'What the hell are you doing in Helsinki?'

'I've been sent to keep an eye on you,' answered Simon. 'It seems that you cannot keep a low profile anywhere you go, and somebody, somewhere, had the inexplicable notion that I might be able to keep you under control. God only knows why they should think that!'

Simon and Alex spent the next three hours reminiscing and bringing each other up to date with what was happening in their separate lives. Simon complained that he had been due to go on leave in January and had planned to marry his long-term girlfriend, Cordelia, but London had cancelled his leave indefinitely when they ordered him to Finland.

'Not surprisingly,' Simon said, 'Cordelia is most upset.'

'I hope not with me?' Alex asked.

'No, of course, she doesn't know about you,' Simon explained, 'but when we do get married, I doubt the commander will get an invitation!'

Alex empathised with his friend but cheered up immeasurably when Simon told him that Teddy was safe in Gloucestershire and had already joined the church choir at St Edward's, Stow-on-the-Wold. By all accounts, Alex's family were doing well, including Uncle Walter, who was on the shortlist for an essential role in the newly formed Ministry of Supply.

Simon explained that he was now attached to the British Legation in Helsinki to add weight to Britain's offer of aid and assistance to Finland. His role was an extension of his cultural attaché role in Stockholm, although as he succinctly put it, 'Frankly, I cannot see how a tour by the London Symphony Orchestra could remotely benefit the war effort of Finland, even if we could muster enough musicians to form an orchestra!'

It was apparent that Simon was there for other reasons, and one of those was to make sure that his old school friend focussed on intelligence-gathering rather than traipsing around the country and taking on the Red Army single-handedly. Not that Simon needed to worry; the wings of the press corps had been substantially clipped since Alex and Mick McMahon's adventure to Suomussalmi, ostensibly because they could not guarantee their safety and did not want to suffer the embarrassment of losing any other foreign journalists.

*

The next evening, Sunday 17th December, Alex tracked down Jarno, who greeted him like a long-lost brother and with considerably more deference than previously. He answered Alex's questions honestly, and Alex learned how the Finnish interpreted the Russian tactics of war. He understood that the Russians had intended to split Finland swiftly in two and had deployed two divisions to the north to seize the road junction at the village of Suomussalmi. It was apparent that the Russians planned to protect their right flank and allow them to advance safely towards the paper and pulp town of Kajaani, which was the primary military objective in that sector, as it shielded the approach to the Limingo Plain and the road towards Oulu, on the Gulf of Bothnia. It was also on the main railway line running across country westwards.

At the same time and to the south, another full Soviet division had targeted Lieksa on Lake Pielinen to capture the north-south railway there before driving north to link up with the other troops at Nurmes to strengthen the attack on Kajaani.

Ironically, the Soviets were helped in this offensive by the Russian-built Finnish railway system that had been constructed during tsarist times with the same broad gauge as the Russian railway network; of course, at that time, it formed part of the Imperial Russian Transport System. The Russian designers of the Finnish railway system had demanded that the railways were all constructed on the Russian side of the lakes because they wanted the water to lie between the railway and any enemy coming from the west. Now that Finland's enemy was coming from the east, the Finns had some difficulty defending the railway system. Alex learned that any railway line that did not lie on the Russian side of the lakes was a line built after 1918.

Jarno explained, 'The Russians had one significant advantage, they concentrated their forces right on the border, and when the war started, they came flying across with all their might – tanks, troops, armoured cars and artillery, but we have had nearly three weeks' of fighting, and our troops have held their ground. Yes, we have had losses, many; but nowhere near the number that we have inflicted on the Russians. We have used small groups to attack Russian troops, and this has confused them. Our army dashed around using skis, and that has baffled them also.

'There is no doubt that the Russians are good soldiers. It is just that these troops are unused to fighting the type of warfare that they are experiencing.'

Alex's report that he submitted the next day was to be his last before Christmas, but when what he learned from Jarno was received in London, the Christmas festivities were put on hold.

VII

Alex met General Kurt Wallenius two days before Christmas when he arrived in Helsinki to bask in the publicity of the Finnish success at the recent Battle of Kemi River.

Before the press conference, Alex read up on the man and quickly decided that he was not much awed with his track record. His association with the hard right-wing Lapuan movement was well known, and this group had been active in the kidnapping of the moderate former president of the republic, Kaarlo Ståhlberg and his wife. Moreover, Wallenius had been part of the leadership of the Mäntsälä Rebellion in February 1932.

So, it was an unenthusiastic Alex that left the hotel with the Belgian journalist, Jan de Smet, and as they made their way to the barracks where Wallenius was to give the press conference, he asked conversationally, 'So, what of this Wallenius fellow?'

'By all accounts,' the Belgian replied, 'a pig of a man, but an outstanding soldier. Many have called him the "Winston Churchill" of Finland but without the charm or diplomacy! He's utterly ruthless and probably one of the very few men who could save Finland – he hates communists with a passion!'

At the press conference, to which practically the entire foreign press corps had been invited, Alex thought Wallenius was an implausible figure. The general entered the room with all the panache of a Hollywood film star, smoking a pipe which he lay down on a side table on the dais from which he was to talk.

His opening gambit was to ask in faltering English, 'Please, are journalists present from Britain?' A few hands were raised, including that of Simon Potts, who was sitting some distance from Alex and with a cadre of British and American journalists. He continued, with the help of an interpreter, 'In July 1918, I fought against British troops, or I should say, Finnish Bolsheviks that were commanded by British Officers. They were led by Major-General Charles Maynard, who was a thoroughly decent man but was leading a ragamuffin hoard of communist bandits. I think, by the time it was over, we could declare a draw!' The general guffawed with laughter at his private joke.

'I have never learned the English language because, in that war, we had the alliance of Germany. Earlier, I had the honour of serving with the *Royal Prussian 27th Jäeger Battalion*, so the only foreign language I speak is German.'

Wallenius certainly knew that Britain and Germany were at war and the British press took his comments as a slight against Britain. Indeed, after the British newspapers reported his comments, it almost derailed the aid package that Churchill was trying to put together to help the Finns, and rumours were rife afterwards that General Mannerheim was so annoyed at Wallenius's insensitivity that he sharply reprimanded the man.

The general was not unusually tall, but he was well-built, and he did exude a massive presence. Alex gained the impression that even if you could not see Wallenius in a room, you would definitely be aware of his being there. Despite his ego, there was a sense of informality about the press conference, and Alex recalled reading that Wallenius had, for a time, been a war correspondent, so in dealing with the world's press, he was on familiar ground.

The briefing was in Finnish, but reasonable copies of the general's account were made available in a variety of languages on roughly printed sheets. The session was one of the most thorough that Alex had attended, and Wallenius was undoubtedly enjoying publicising what he patently saw was his success.

He began, 'The Russians captured the remains of Salla village on 10th December. Half a division of Soviet troops, with many tanks and much artillery, went straight on towards Kemijärvi by the southernmost and most direct route, while the other half of the division advanced along the north road towards the Kemi River and the village of Pelkossenniemi, intending to attack Kemijärvi from the north. They did not meet much resistance, as the main force of the Finnish army had been withdrawn to regroup, but our gallant army fought them on both roads with the limited resources at their disposal.

'On the southern route, Finnish troops dug in at Joutsijärvi near a small frozen lake across which the road ran. It was a good position, and they fortified their defences well; the frozen lake gave an excellent field of fire, and behind them, between Joutsijärvi and Kemijärvi, they created five wide defence strips of land by felling trees and covering the areas with barbed wire, even laying mines. Even a small body of troops could defend the southern route well, and for some time, but things were different in the north.

'The only defensible position on the northern route was the broad and frozen Kemi River. Of course, troops who were well dug in at the village of Pelkosenniemi could defend against a direct crossing, but if they were outflanked by forces crossing either further up or downstream, their defence would be unsustainable. Our concern was that if the Soviet troops crossed the Kemi River, they would have a straight road to Kemijärvi.

'It was clear to me that our weak spot was in the north and this is where our defence must lie, so I ordered all but two companies to leave the southern section to reinforce the northern lines. Our intelligence had shown that we were facing an entire Russian regiment of tanks, heavy artillery and at least six thousand men. We urgently requested reinforcements and were sent a battalion of reservists, most of whom had not seen battle previously. I ordered our troops to defend Pelkosenniemi to the last man and to stop the Soviet advance at all costs, but by the time the reinforcements had arrived, the Russian advance forces had already crossed the Kemi River, so we had to beat them back.

'The gallant Colonel Villamo, at his command post in Pelkosenniemi, gathered all of the intelligence that our scouts were bringing. The Soviets' supply column had made camp about 2 miles from the river and a force, which we estimated to be a battalion, was marching up as reinforcements. We had to decide. We did not have enough troops to hold both the Kemijärvi road and the road to the Arctic highway. We made the decision to defend Kemijärvi, and I sent a patrol to monitor the Arctic highway route, just in case I was wrong.' The general again smiled at the prospect that anything he did could ever be construed as "wrong".

One of the Finnish journalists called out, 'How many men did you send to monitor the highway, sir?'

It was evident that Wallenius did not appreciate being interrupted, but he answered, 'Three,' and then continued. 'Yes, it was a gamble! If the Russians had attacked the Arctic highway route, they would have outflanked us, but we relied on the Soviets following their plan of attack rigorously, and on balance, from their viewpoint, Kemijärvi was a better strategic victory.

'It was mid-afternoon when I received the news that the Russians were moving towards Kemijärvi and that our gamble had succeeded. We set our defences, but we also sent a force of men to cross the Kemi River north of the Russian army and attack their supply column. I have always thought it a good strategy to attack the enemy from the rear while defending the main assault. Our troops defended Kemijärvi heroically, and when the Russians received the information that their supply column was also under attack, they realised how precarious was their situation, as they had no idea of the strength of our forces that they were facing.

'The battle lasted until midday on the twentieth of December before the Russians retreated across the Kemi River – they had been defeated. The retreating army had abandoned most of their equipment and left their wounded behind as they scurried back along the road to Savukoski, with Finnish troops chasing them and continually harrying them. It was a great victory against a force of so many.'

'How many Finnish soldiers died?' a journalist asked.

'Far too many. A lot,' Wallenius replied. 'In war, there are casualties, but we must only focus on victories.' Was there a tinge of remorse in his voice, Alex wondered, or was it pathos for dramatic effect?

Alex asked, 'Alex Carlsson, *Svenska Posten*, would it have made any difference if you had more troops at your disposal?'

'Mr Carlsson, I have heard tell of your courage in Suomussalmi.' He smiled at Alex. 'Of course, it is often argued that the more troops a commander has, the easier his task. I think that if I had had more soldiers, then I would have employed a different strategy. But the plan that we used worked. Let me give you an analogy that I unashamedly borrow from Tolstoy's *War and Peace*. In the game of chess, each player can consider each move that they make, and they are not limited for time, but there is also another difference – a knight is always stronger than a pawn, and two pawns are stronger than one.

'In war, a battalion is on occasion stronger than a division and sometimes weaker than a company. The strength of bodies of troops can never be known to anyone. A small force that is well commanded can easily defeat a more significant force that is poorly led, and we knew that Russian commanders do not think, they follow orders. This is their great weakness. Our troops fought tenaciously in defence of our country, and that was the difference. The passion that burned in each of our soldiers' hearts saw this battle won.

'You must come and see us again on the battlefront,' Wallenius concluded with a smile.

*

Over what remained of the weekend, Alex tried to gain independent verification of General Wallenius's claims. Much of it seemed too good to be true. How could a small and mostly untrained army so comprehensively defeat the might of the Soviet Union? Only on Christmas Day, after he was given access to the Tilkan Military Hospital in the Pikku Huopalahti district of Helsinki so that he could talk to survivors of what was becoming known as the Battle of Kemi River, did he realise the full extent of the victory. The building was truly spectacular; built in the so-called "Functionalist" architecture of the pre-war era it was distinctive by the huge semi-circular balconies around the main stairwell. The wards were light, airy and highly efficient, and it was evident that the Finnish authorities really cared for their injured warriors.

Alex and two other journalists obtained free access to all patients who were not in the most critical care wards, and they found several who had survived the battle at Kemijärvi. One soldier, whose name was Martti and whose leg had been amputated at a field hospital before he was evacuated to Helsinki after sepsis had set in, described the battle graphically.

'I was part of the relief column,' he recalled, 'as we marched towards Kemijärvi, we came upon the first corpses. They looked like bundles of rags. I turned one over. He was a Finnish boy, yes, not much more than a boy, dressed in a brand new uniform – somebody's son whose life had ebbed away in that godforsaken place after being shot in the chest. He was no more a soldier than I was. God knows how long he had lain there, but his body was frozen stiff. Before that, it had been an adventure. Now we understood what sort of hell we were entering.

'The sun, such as it was, shone like red fire behind the hills in the distance. We marched down the last hill into Kemijärvi, and a sentry halted us and checked our orders. At the side of the road, there were five Soviet tanks and some heavy machine guns, along with piles of Russian rifles that were being guarded by another sentry. Our officer, who was little more than a boy himself, joked that the Soviets had dropped the guns and run away when they saw the Finnish army at Pelkosenniemi, but I doubted this was true. For an officer, the boy was a good man and liked by his troops.

'It was incredible that even amid that carnage, farmers were still herding their animals into barns to give them shelter and food. In Kemijärvi, the shops were all boarded up, but we saw young girls hurrying to buy whatever provisions were available. They watched us with awe, and we whistled at them, making lewd comments – they ran away, giggling. We halted outside the troop canteen, and we were told to go and get something to eat and drink. The mess was being run by the Lottas, and the one who served me was a real beauty – I still think about her!

'Having eaten, I went outside, and I stood by the side of the lake. There were boats tied up but solidly fixed in place by the ice around their hulls. I remember wondering why their ropes still tied them when the ice held them so solidly. Outside the town's hotel, where the officers were staying, there was a thermometer that said 31° below zero. God, it was cold! But, I tell you, if it were not for the soldiers, that town would have been beautiful.

'Suddenly, the air was split by a horrible screeching from the observation post, and everybody started to run. One soldier shouted at me to hurry up and take cover because the bombers were coming, and I ran also. I saw them in the sky: little specks that emptied their cargoes of destruction over that beautiful place. A sergeant in the shelter near me said that this time, we were safe because they were trying to hit our positions at Joutsijärvi. We felt the explosions, and then the all-clear sounded. I went back to the canteen and had coffee.

'Our officer gathered his men, and we set off down the road out of town. That is where they ambushed us. The gunfire came out of the pine forest, and our officer fell. Luckily, the sergeant knew what to do, and we took as much cover as we were able and started to return fire. Ten of us were ordered to try and get into the woods and attack the enemy from the rear. We were successful, and as we crept through the forest, we saw the Soviets shooting at our comrades. Suddenly a soldier in a dirty brown uniform stood up in front of me, and we looked at each other. While his comrades were firing at our soldiers, this boy was having a crap,' Martti joked. 'The boy looked so young and scared, but he was the enemy and was reaching for his rifle. He had just started to shout a warning when I shot him, and that innocent young face disintegrated in a pot-mess of blood and bone. It was the first and the last time that I killed a man.

'They had discovered us, and I was in shock, so when they came at us, I was rooted to the spot like a statue, and that is when a soldier bayoneted me in the leg, I think because he was running at me and tripped. I would be dead if that Russian hadn't stumbled!

'I was lucky because my comrades took to me to a field hospital, which was more like a butcher's shop. The smell was terrible – not just blood, guts and death, but fear. The surgeon took this away,' he indicated his leg, 'and patched me up as best he was able, and I was put on a stretcher and taken back to Rovaniemi, but after a while, I started to sweat even though I was cold. The hospital at Rovaniemi was full up, and we remained on our trucks. We were moved on and moved on again, everywhere was full. Eventually, they loaded my stretcher onto an aeroplane, and I ended up here.'

The soldier displayed that pragmatism that Alex knew was the Finnish way and was not surprised that the soldier's main concern did not lie with whether he would live or whether he could ever work again, but whether he would never play ice hockey again.

Alex spoke to several other survivors while he was at the hospital that day and heard similar stories of courage and determination. He heard more about the horrors of war, including a story from one soldier who had arrived at a farm only to find the farmer and his family butchered. But of all the stories that he had heard, it was the soldier's, Martti's, which he used to write his account for *Svenska Posten*, little realising that it would be networked around the world.

Alex encoded his report for London into the story and spoke of the lack of modern equipment that the Finns needed to be more effective in their efforts against Russian might but to carry out a more complete analysis he argued that he again needed to get closer to the action, to see for himself.

Constantly badgering the military administration, ostensibly for a flying visit to the front before crossing the border and returning to Stockholm to see his editor, eventually paid off and Alex found himself on a transport plane heading northwards, on Wednesday 27th December. A brief stopover at the military airfield at Tikkakoski allowed Alex to ask the pilot of the transport plane what would make a real difference to the war. He got the reply: 'The sad and much-lamented death of Uncle Josef!'

When the aeroplane landed at Rovaniemi, Alex found that General Wallenius had laid on an impressive staff car to drive him the 90 kilometres east to Kemijärvi. As they pushed further eastwards, the wide-open spaces narrowed to a single track through the pine forest, and it was there that Alex saw the first twisted corpses, either strewn in the ditches or even on the road itself. It was a grisly trail that they followed to the hillside above the Kemi River. As they ventured over the river ice, they passed the truck, abandoned where the Russians had left it. Alongside the truck lay the bodies of several men dressed in the drab Russian uniform.

About a kilometre and a half along the road they came to the destruction that had been the central column, and they pulled over to allow a large truck to pass, loaded with the corpses of still more Finnish soldiers; even after nearly three weeks, the Finns were still collecting their dead comrades. It was a matter of honour that the remains of fallen Finnish soldiers were gathered up and sent home to their families for burial. At the head of the column, they passed a Russian truck with the corpse of the driver still in the driver's seat. His skull shattered by a bullet and laying half in and half out of the lorry was an officer, his body riddled with bullets. The cold had frozen the corpses in the positions in which they had fallen and given them the appearance of waxworks. Indeed, the entire road looked like a diorama from Madame Tussaud's.

Alex counted the trucks in that column – there were forty and two tanks as well. The lorries were old with hinged sides, and they appeared poorly maintained. Alex wondered how they had made it that far. Somewhat strangely amongst the debris of the column, Alex saw household items and even children's clothes, and he had no idea why they would be on a Russian truck heading towards the battle. His driver provided the answer: 'They loot anything that is not nailed down, and even things that are nailed down but easily prised up, they also take.'

The memory of the carnage on the road to Kemijärvi would stay with Alex for the rest of his life. Most of the Finnish corpses that he saw, frozen after death like meat at an abattoir, were not soldiers; they were boys, many hardly out of their teens, and in a country of such low population, he wondered how the nation would survive. Even the remains of Russians looked young, and many were Oriental in appearance, probably drawn from the southern states of that vast empire. Would their families even know the fate of their loved ones?

Alex reached Kemijärvi when it had already turned dark, and the car was flagged down by a sentry on the outskirts of the town. Alex's mind naturally went back to the last occasion he had been flagged down on a remote Finnish road, and his hand went instinctively to his FN pistol – he was not going to be caught out again. He need not have worried, and both Alex and his driver produced their papers and asked where General Wallenius was based.

'He has flown back to Rovaniemi,' was the reply. 'He left a message that you were to return there also.' The driver turned the car around and headed back the way they had come, muttering darkly about what he thought of officers in general and in particular Wallenius. Alex rather agreed!

VIII

It seemed to Alex that there was no escape from the howling of air-raid sirens even in Rovaniemi, and when it woke him, a glance at his watch told him that it was eleven o'clock, although he had no idea whether that was in the morning or the night. The blackout in his hotel was a simple affair and fixed permanently in place as it comprised thick brown paper that had been painted black and stuck on the window. He pulled the window open, and as a gust of arctic air rushed to warm itself in the comfort of his bedroom, Alex saw that it was daytime on 28th December before he rammed the window closed.

The hotel in which General Wallenius's staff had billeted him was right next to the main bridge on the road to Kemijärvi and as such, in Alex's opinion, was a bloody dangerous place to be during an air raid. If the Russians wanted to stop military aid reaching Kemijärvi, then bridges on the main road and especially in the region's capital were inevitably going to be prime military targets.

Dressing in the warmest clothes that he could immediately find, Alex left the hotel and with grim determination headed towards the shelter that was right in front of his hotel. It was all very ordered; the air-raid warden held the door open for people to enter while at the same time scanning the skies for any sign of the bombers. Most people sheltering that day were women – nurses, hotel waitresses, Lottas, shop girls, farmhands, all chattering incessantly. Alex squeezed into a space between a man and a woman, hoping that he was not coming between husband and wife. Muttering '*Anteeksi*,' – Excuse me, – he made himself comfortable on the rough wooden benches.

The man asked, in Swedish, 'You are Alex Carlsson, aren't you?'

Alex agreed that he was, to which the man continued, 'Felix Nyström, *Svenska Dagbladet*, pleased to make your acquaintance.' The man offered his gloved hand.

To have been recognised by Felix Nyström, especially as he had wrapped himself warmly against the biting arctic wind, was unbelievable. Nyström was Swedish journalistic royalty, having won several awards for his articles, and his stories were a regular on the front page of Sweden's premier daily newspaper.

'And I yours,' Alex replied. 'Do you come here often?' he asked with a smile.

'Too often,' responded Felix. 'I heard about your exploits on the eastern front,' he continued. 'It must have been quite exciting?'

'I'm not sure "exciting" is how I would describe it. It was definitely terrifying,' Alex answered, 'bloody terrifying!'

'I heard about your article, also,' Felix said non-committally.

'I hope you heard good things.' Alex was hopeful.

'I'm not sure "good things" is how I would describe it,' the Swede parodied Alex's response, 'but I was damned jealous of it! It was an excellent story.'

Alex's inner temperature substantially warmed as they heard the drone of the approaching aeroplanes. They passed by overhead, apparently intent on another target further afield, and after a short time, the all-clear sounded. 'Join me for a drink?' Felix asked Alex.

As they left the shelter, Alex saw a group of soldiers abandon the two machine-gun posts that were on the roof of the hotel and return to whatever it was they were doing before the siren sounded. The sky was pale above the forest with the glow that was both the sunrise and the sunset in January. As he walked to the hotel bar with Felix Nyström, he wondered thoughtfully what it would be like in summer, when the sun did not set. He imagined the complete antithesis of what he was experiencing that day.

'I guess you have travelled often to the Arctic Circle?' Felix asked as he returned to the table with a tray of drinks.

'Not really,' replied Alex, 'my father was in the Corps Diplomatique, and I spent much of my life in other countries.'

Felix Nyström reminisced about the pleasant holidays that he had shared with his family in northern Sweden and Finland. 'It is like two different countries, so verdant and green in summer and so clean and pure in winter. It is like God practised on the rest of the world and then when He had achieved perfection, He topped off the earth with the Arctic Circle!'

'I can imagine,' Alex said.

'So, you have not been in Finland long?' Felix fished.

'No,' Alex was entirely open. 'I was in London before. It almost seems that in whichever country I arrive, a war breaks out!'

Felix smiled. 'Yes, I was in London about four years ago. It was such a vibrant city. I suppose it has changed now?'

'I agree that much of the vitality has gone, probably with the men as they have been called up into the military, but you can still find some life if you know where to look.'

'I hear that you are here at the invitation of the great and glorious General Wallenius?' Felix continued his fishing trip.

'I am,' responded Alex, 'it was very generous of the general.' Alex did not know in which political direction Felix Nyström leant, so he erred on the side of caution.

'Oh, yes,' Felix continued, 'he's a very generous host. He billets us in a key military objective and then is the most difficult man in the region to pin down for an interview. I have been here since the battle and am still waiting. Still, there are worse places to be, I suppose. The booze is cheaper than in Helsinki and the food in the restaurants more plentiful if you like reindeer.'

'I only arrived yesterday and have not yet found anywhere other than the hotel,' muttered Alex.

'Well,' said Felix, 'you must let me buy you dinner tonight. I know a nice little place where the food is excellent and, besides, I am getting on famously with one of the waitresses. You know, they get paid a pittance, only about 500 Finnish markka a month!'

Alex thought that a well-known Swedish journalist could have had the pick of the local girls if their pay was so low. His brain had already worked it out to about two pounds and ten shillings, and yet still, they smiled warmly.

'Yes,' Alex accepted gratefully, 'I would like that.'

'Then I shall meet you in the bar at about seven o'clock.' Felix knocked back his drink, clapped Alex on the shoulder and went to his room.

'Would you like another drink?' asked the pretty blonde waitress.

'No, thank you.' Alex got up and drained the remains of his drink and remembering what Felix Nyström had said, he left an over-generous tip for the girl.

*

Despite being the largest town that far north in Finland and notwithstanding the Finnish government pumping many hundreds of thousands of Finnish markka into the place in an attempt to develop it for the pre-war tourist trade, it still had an old-fashioned charm. Even though the government had built modern hotels, like the Pohjanhovi where Alex was staying, and a new co-operative store, the construction of most buildings were still wooden, and many had stood for over a hundred years. It was the town where the reindeer herders, farmers and lumberjacks came to spend their money, and in many ways, it reminded Alex of places that he had heard about in America, where the gold prospectors would go for relaxation. In both the summer and winter, many Finns and Swedes had brought tourism to the town; in the summer, for the beautiful and wild tundra and crystal clear waters in the lakes, and in the winter for sport.

Alex's hotel stuck out like a sore thumb, with its grey concrete walls and the vast expanse of glass, in this traditional town, but it provided all the creature comforts that modern living demanded. The porter even proudly announced that the hotel elevator was the most northerly lift in the world!

Rovaniemi was only about 10 kilometres south of the Arctic Circle, and this alone was enough to ensure wealth from tourism. It was to a tourist restaurant that Felix Nyström took Alex later that evening, and it is where, for the first time in his life, Alex ate bear meat. He decided it tasted like venison, but the texture was much coarser. Felix said that the bear's diet determined the flavour of the meat, and even animals that came from only 10 kilometres distant would often have an entirely different taste.

Alex asked, 'How do they keep meat fresh here? I cannot imagine hunters going out to shoot bear when there's a war on.'

'It's simple,' replied Felix, 'we are living in the world's natural deep freeze. The animals are hunted and placed in outhouses to freeze. Very often, you will find homes with two or three reindeer stacked in the outhouses for the family to eat throughout the year.'

The meal was delicious even though all through dinner Felix and the young, pretty, dark-haired waitress were flirting outrageously. Alex was introduced to the local beer, which he initially thought was utterly disgusting, but his taste mellowed with the quantity that he consumed. After the meal, the waitress brought two small glasses of what she described as *lakkalikööri*, which was entirely the opposite of the rough beer; absolutely delicious, if a little sweet for Alex's taste. As they were leaving the restaurant, Felix suggested that they ought to take a sauna together sometime, indicating a low bathhouse. Taking a sauna was a Finnish tradition that Alex had tried to avoid. The prospect of sitting in a steamy room with a group of sweaty naked men, who took turns to beat each other with birch twigs before either jumping in an ice-cold lake, or rolling around in the snow, did not appeal, but he made noncommittal noises to indicate that he might be willing sometime in the future.

*

The following day, Friday 29th December, Alex was up early and waiting at General Wallenius's headquarters hoping for an audience with the man, but again he was disappointed. It seemed that the general was long on promises and short on deeds as far as foreign journalists were concerned, even those who had "impressed" him. While walking back to the Pohjanhovi hotel, he studied the industry of the town and realised that everything was focussed on the war effort. There were people waxing skis for the soldiers, little old ladies sitting outside their homes, knitting warm hats, or gloves, and making leggings out of the skins of reindeer. The Lottas were industriously packing first-aid packages of bandages and ointments into little boxes marked with a red cross that each soldier would receive, others were working in the soldiers' canteen, or busily recycling uniforms taken from those who no longer needed them. Those men who had been too old to be called up for active service were filling the essential roles of those that had gone to war: operating the fire appliances, or repairing bomb damage, or teaching what few children remained in the town. Everybody was busy ensuring the maximum war effort, except Alex and, as he discovered when entering the hotel lobby, Felix Nyström.

'Greetings,' hailed Felix, seeing Alex entering the hotel. 'I bet the glorious commander of the north was again too busy to see anybody?' Alex nodded. 'I've stopped going to his headquarters now; if he wants me, he knows where I am!'

'My trouble is,' said Alex, 'I feel so redundant. Everybody here is working so diligently, and all I am doing is waiting to get a few minutes with the general. I just feel as though I should be doing much more.'

'Bah!' exclaimed Felix, 'it's not our war, so why concern yourself? I tell you what, though,' Felix had Alex's attention, 'if Wallenius will not talk to us, why don't we go and find somewhere more interesting and get our own stories?'

'How?' Alex thought the notion was a little far-fetched as all transport movements were being restricted for military use only.

'The father of my girlfriend, Jaana, the waitress from the restaurant,' Felix began, 'has an old car that the military did not seize – and it is full of petrol. She said I could buy it for a few markkas if I wished. We might need to appropriate a few more cans of petrol, but it beats sitting here scratching our arses.'

'Fair enough,' agreed Alex. 'If Wallenius has not seen us by tomorrow, let us go and see what we can find. I still have the pass that he signed, so that should get us past any checkpoints,' he suggested.

The rest of the day was taken up planning for the adventure. Felix managed to obtain some more petrol, although he continually moaned about what it had cost, and he also came up with some food for the journey. After dinner at the family restaurant, Felix was ceremoniously given the keys by Jaana's father, and she took them out to a ramshackle garage behind the restaurant. Inside was an old Volvo taxicab, whose once-gleaming paintwork was pitted and flat from years of neglect. Alex's heart sank; what was this wreck? But when Felix jumped into the cab, and Alex swung the starting handle, it fired up the first time.

'It's good, yes?' Jaana asked.

'It will do well,' Felix responded, and he gave Jaana a kiss that suggested that their relationship was far from platonic. Felix said to Alex, 'Come on, let's get it loaded up ready for the early morning.' They took the old car back to the hotel and parked it around the back and away from prying eyes.

IX

With some reluctance, Teddy had been slowing down since the doctor warned her about being too active, but getting more involved in the church at Stow-on-the-Wold had been her saviour against boredom. The rector had welcomed her with open arms, and she had quickly found herself singing in the choir and becoming immersed in many other aspects of church life. Alex's mother grew more and more concerned that Teddy was doing too much and would have far preferred her to have stayed in bed during her pregnancy until the baby was born, but stopping Teddy from being an active young woman was a feat that she acknowledged was impossible. The dowager countess did, however, assign Klara to watch over her daughter-in-law and report back if there was a doubt that Teddy was overdoing things.

Klara was probably the least reliable person to keep watch on Teddy. To begin with, she morally resented being asked to spy on her employer, and secondly, she enjoyed a good relationship with Teddy that she did not wish to spoil. Reluctantly, Klara did agree to accompany Teddy whenever she went into Stow-on-the-Wold, which meant that they both became more involved with the church. Like Teddy, she had been brought up in the Roman Catholic faith, and although she was as "lapsed" as Teddy, having not been to confession since her marriage to the staunchly "Chapel" Rhodri, she held a closer affinity with the Roman church. Nonetheless,

Klara enjoyed their trips to Stow-on-the-Wold, and when the rector learned of her proficiency as a pianist, he persuaded her to play in the church, whenever she felt the urge. Soon, she had progressed on to the organ, and while she found the foot pedals challenging, it was clear that she was enjoying herself and was not going to let it beat her. Whenever Teddy sang in the choir, invariably Klara was press-ganged into playing the organ, and even old Mrs Matthews, who had stepped in when the last regular organist had been called up, was willing to surrender the accompanist's role to somebody with such a light touch on the keys.

The Advent season, in the run-up to Christmas, and the festive season itself, is always one of the busiest for the church. Carol services and other activities leading to the celebration of the birth of the Christ child was one of the most exciting times of a church's calendar, but Teddy's willingness to be part of the festivities was often frustrated by the icy weather that had descended on Gloucestershire in the two weeks before Christmas. Perversely, this pleased Alex's mother, but it exasperated Teddy, who was noticeably getting more frustrated by her enforced confinement. Conceding that her plan to use Klara to restrict Teddy's enthusiasm was an abject failure, Alex's mother had eventually enlisted Uncle Walter's assistance. He, rather than approach the problem head-on, worked on the rector and others to ensure that they did not overload Teddy.

It was two days before Christmas Day that the telegram boy carefully rode his bicycle up the drive of Ashton Court bearing a message for Klara that Lance Corporal Rhodri Williams of the 1st Battalion the Welsh Guards had been killed while serving with the British Expeditionary Force on the Franco-Belgian border. Klara was devastated, but Teddy was magnificent in her support. The death of Klara's husband brought a dark veil of sadness over the approaching festivities, and even though no one else had met Klara's husband, cheerlessness ruled the house.

Uncle Walter kept away from the melancholia and chose to spend much of his time in London. He was the first to admit that he lacked natural empathy, and his manner was a little too brusque to be indulgent of mourning. After the initial shock of that impassive and formal communication, it took a week before a letter arrived from Rhodri's commanding officer, saying how sad the entire regiment was to have lost such a magnificent baritone and respected comrade. He explained that Rhodri had not even lost his life in combat, but had died when a section of the fortifications in the segment of the line which his regiment was guarding had collapsed and buried both him and one of his comrades. Even though he had not fallen in combat, the army buried Rhodri Williams in France, with full military honours. Klara was both heartened that Rhodri had not suffered and his comrades missed a valued comrade-in-arms, but equally distraught that she could not exercise the widow's right of giving her husband a funeral. That small comfort quickly evaporated when Rhodri's mother refused to talk to her when she telephoned, and Klara was given the cold shoulder by her husband's entire family – even in death, his family resented their marriage.

Klara's response to the loss of her husband and her in-laws' attitude was to dress in sombre widow's weeds and throw herself into her work. She woke early and went to bed late, and for the entire time she was awake, she diligently applied herself to the various tasks at hand. Furniture was polished until it gleamed, carpets vacuumed to within an inch of becoming threadbare, pots and pans scrubbed until they glowed; and all the time, Teddy tried to coax Klara into slowing down – how those tables had turned. Ironically, it had the much-needed effect on Teddy as it forced her to take life at a slower pace, and even though Alex's mother was grateful that her daughter-in-law was reducing her workload, she fervently wished that it had not come at the expense of Klara's husband.

*

Life returned to a semblance of normality in January after Christmas. Over the festive season, the cold weather and snowy conditions had almost paralysed the county, and on the one occasion that Uncle Walter had managed to get back to Gloucestershire from London, he found himself stranded for four days. Uncle Walter's appointment to the Ministry of Supply had begun on the first day of the year, and he was uncharacteristically anxious when he was unable to get back to London.

It was not a promising start to his new role; even the telephone lines were down.

On the fourth day, and with a slight improvement in the weather, a determined Uncle Walter set off in the Rolls-Royce as soon as old Bert Foskett, the local farmer who had taken it on himself to clear the roads with his tractor, had done so. It took Uncle Walter all day to drive to London, and by the time he arrived at Bedford Square, it was as dark as pitch, and he was exhausted.

Arriving at the Ministry the next day, Uncle Walter was surprised that many, if not most, of his colleagues and employees, had also failed to make it into work during the bad weather, and that just about every function had ground to a halt. At the time he had been appointed to the position, the urgency of coordinating the supply of essential materials and refining the supply chain had been impressed on him as being crucial to the war effort. Never one to be accused of inactivity, Uncle Walter quickly mobilised those staff that had turned up with the determination of an engineer turning the starting handle on a large machine. Slowly and surely, he got the engine running – not, perhaps, at full speed, but at least the cogs were turning.

Eventually, when the newly appointed Minister of Supply, the Rt Hon. Leslie Burgin arrived back from his Luton constituency where he had been spending time with his family, he found Uncle Walter in his shirtsleeves at the Ministry, driving the team to ensure no disruption to the continuation of essential supplies. He knew they had selected the right man for the job.

*

Not that far away, in Broadway Buildings, the atmosphere was equally as fraught. Christmas was a distant memory and those that had managed to spend some time with family and friends were expected back on St Stephen's Day or "Boxing Day" as they call it in Britain. 3/O Daphne Devine was sitting at her desk on that 26th December and idly pondering the origins of "Boxing Day". She vaguely remembered that it had something to do with charity when churches opened the alms boxes and the money collected was distributed to the poor of the parish in memory of the first Christian martyr, St Stephen. She had argued the previous day with her nine-year-old niece that it had nothing to do with throwing away the boxes in which were wrapped the Christmas presents, and Daphne's mother had scolded her for her insensitivity at making the child cry.

Just before Christmas, Daphne's fiancé had been promoted to command the newly delivered *HMS Sea Trout*, an "S-class" submarine that had just been completed by the Birkenhead shipbuilder, Cammell Laird, and he had spent Christmas Day working the boat up on her final sea trial before commissioning. They had hoped to spend the holiday period talking about their wedding plans for later that year, but when her fiancé had been given his half-stripe and told of his new command, she knew that the old naval wives' tale that sailors were "married" to their ship first and their bride second, was right. Of course, Daphne was happy for him, but he had just returned from a lengthy trip to the Mediterranean, and she had hoped that he would have had some shore leave over the Christmas period.

When the telephone had rung on the afternoon of Christmas Day, and she was instructed to return to Broadway Buildings the next day, Daphne was half relieved. Family life at her parents' semi-detached house in Enfield, with her parents trying desperately to bring some pre-war cheer to the festivities, was an endurance for Daphne. Her elder sister spent the entire time dogmatically arguing that because Hermann Göring had not yet bombed London, her decision to bring her children home from the country was the right choice, and this alone spawned more quarrels than happiness that year. Yes, overall, Daphne was glad to be back working, but still, there was that niggling doubt that she could have tried harder to make her family's Christmas happier.

Commander Jeffers had breezed into the office just after ten o'clock, having spent most of the morning in consultation with Lt Col Llewelyn and the other section heads. The discussion had centred on trying to piece together the intelligence that had been gathered from both MI2 and MI3 and to try and predict when the "phoney war", as the popular press was dubbing it, would end. The consensus had been by March, although some had the temerity to suggest that Hitler was delaying any assault in the hope of reaching a negotiated peace with Britain. Privately, Jeffers suspected that any negotiated peace would require the subjugation of Britain to Germany and that was unacceptable in his eyes. He fervently hoped that sheer common sense would prevail over the appeasers.

The subject of Alex was not discussed at the meeting, and only a few of those outside the close confines of Jeffers's section knew much of his activities. Lt Col Llewelyn had the reputation of backing his subordinates to the hilt, and in Alex's case, not disclosing what had happened in Suomussalmi was the best stratagem for protecting the role that Alex was fulfilling.

'The purpose of the Secret Intelligence Service is that it gathers secret intelligence secretly and that intelligence is best kept secret by circulating it very much on a "need-to-know" basis,' he argued logically. 'With regards to most things that Lt Carlton gets up to, the fewer the number that knows, the better!' Commander Jeffers tended to agree.

'If he was not doing such an excellent job, it might be time to reconsider our options in that area,' Llewelyn continued, 'but I do not know the man apart from what I have heard and read. Roland, tell me more about the real Alex Carlton.'

Commander Jeffers sat back and considered his answer carefully. 'In many ways, some would argue that Alex Carlton is wholly unsuited to this type of work,' Jeffers began. 'He's not someone who flies in line with the geese. Colonel Swann called him a "maverick", and it is also true that he almost failed his training. But there is something about him, some...' he searched for the word, 'some inexplicable quality that seems to work.'

'I do not have an issue with mavericks,' the colonel interjected, 'and the problem with those that fly in line is that they are often the first to get their tail feathers shot off. What I want to understand is the man himself.'

Jeffers continued. 'You are aware of his family background, I presume?'

'What's in the file. Of course,' replied Llewelyn.

'Then you know that his ancestry is Russian?' Jeffers ventured, and the colonel nodded slightly. 'If you believe the rumour, his mother delivered him in Finland as she was escaping from the terrors that followed the Bolshevik uprising in 1917, and when they eventually made it to England, Walter Compton took them under his wing – the man who Alex still calls Uncle Walter.

'Walter Compton, or as he is less acceptably known, Count Vladimir Mikhailovich Komarov, is an old family friend who knew Alex's father when they were children. Komarov is or, more accurately, was active in the *Soyuz Russkih Monarkhistov*, the Russian Monarchist Union, and as Alex's father was a hereditary count in his own right, he was duty-bound to render assistance, but I suspect that because of their old family ties, he would have done so, anyway.

'He sent Alex to Lassiter's School, which is where he met Simon Potts, who recommended Alex to us. On leaving Lassiter's, Compton used his influence to get him a position with Inkerman's, in the City.'

The commander suddenly remembered. 'Did you also know that his father was a war hero who died trying to save the imperial family and that since the confirmation of his father's death, Alex has inherited his father's title?'

'No,' said Llewelyn thoughtfully, 'but there were few enough who were prepared to lift a finger to assist the Russian royal family during their hour of need, something that I believe will come back to haunt us, in the future. Why on earth, then, was he considered suitable for this mission?'

'Largely because he spoke Finnish, Swedish and Russian,' Jeffers replied.

'And there were no concerns that he might have been a little too close to the cause and may seek to settle old scores?'

'Not at all,' the commander responded. 'After his faltering start, Alex eventually came through the training with flying colours. He is a most level-headed young man who has an ingrained sense of duty to this country. I had my doubts when young Potts recommended him, but in all my dealings with him since, I have become more convinced that he was an inspired choice. Count Aleksander Nikolayevich Karlov is one of those rare beasts in our calling, a natural.'

'It is as I suspected, Roland,' Llewelyn confirmed, 'and that is why we must do all we can to protect him from those who would happily hang him out to dry at the first opportunity, just to even a score with this department and to harm him personally. The Baker Street Irregulars are unlikely to forget his exposing one of their cock-ups!'

'I hear that Simon Potts has been reassigned to the legation in Helsinki to assist with this aid package with which Winston is trying to tempt the Finns?' The commander changed tack, and although posing the enquiry like a question, it was actually a statement of fact.

'Yes,' replied Llewelyn, 'we thought he might add a "cultural" dimension to the negotiations, and besides, it will strengthen our numbers in Finland at a time when we need as much intelligence as possible from that particular area.'

'I agree,' approved Jeffers, 'and besides, Simon Potts and Alex Carlton could be a formidable team. Potts has one of the sharpest strategic minds that I know, and Carlton sees things that others miss. They will need to work closely but also maintain a distance. I cannot imagine any good reason why a Swedish journalist should have a source at the British Legation!'

'That's already resolved,' the lieutenant-colonel confided. 'Potts has also assumed the role of "press liaison" at the Legation, so he will hold press briefings for all the press corps based in Helsinki. Plus, there is also an English professor at the university who has indicated his willingness to be of assistance, if required. We thought that Lieutenant Potts might look after them both.'

X

Alex and Felix Nyström never did begin their road trip, as on the penultimate day of the year, there was suddenly a flurry of activity in Rovaniemi. Everything that was out of place was squared away, and soldiers who had not bothered shaving for days were queuing at the bathhouse for a sauna and shave. The last remaining hairdresser in the town saw her regular business triple as lines of officers and NCOs queued to have their hair cut, and the laundry was overwhelmed with officers and enlisted men trying to get their uniforms cleaned quickly. Felix provided the answer to this unprecedented level of activity when he spoke to the head porter at the hotel, who was wearing his pre-war concierge's uniform and medal ribbons from the Civil War – Mannerheim was coming. The man whom many regarded as the "Uncrowned King of Finland", Field-Marshal Carl Gustaf Mannerheim, who had been instrumental in Finland gaining its independence from Russia in 1918, was coming to Rovaniemi.

At first, neither Alex nor Felix could believe the rumour, and then Felix speculated, 'To my mind, either General Wallenius has achieved something significant to warrant this huge accolade, or he has screwed up massively, and Mannerheim is coming here to relieve him of his duties. Either way, to not be here when Mannerheim is here is likely to get any less-than-diligent newspaper man rightfully dismissed!'

None of either Alex's or Felix's contacts knew when the great man was arriving, or if they did, nobody was saying. Felix decided that the best plan was to watch the road to Salmijärvi, the lake that was doubling as the landing strip until completion of the new military aerodrome, and when the staff cars left, Alex and Felix would follow in the borrowed taxi. The plan worked well, and shortly after midday a few days later, a motorcade of staff cars with motorcycle escorts swept out of the town and headed out in a north-easterly direction. Alex and Felix tagged on to the back of the convoy and were almost successful in reaching the landing strip, but as they approached the lake, a guard stepped in front of them and brought them to a halt. Despite Alex showing his pass and much cajoling by both journalists, the soldier was not to be moved, and they were forced to observe the arrival of Mannerheim from a distance. Not that they could see much, as they were blindsided by the aeroplane's fuselage, and the first indication that the great man had landed was when the convoy came back through the gate and sped towards Rovaniemi. Alex and Felix leapt back into the old taxi and tried to keep up, but it was a hopeless task, and by the time they had crossed the river back into the town, the convoy had deposited its dignitaries at General Wallenius's headquarters. It was two very dejected journalists that returned to the Hotel Pohjanhovi to drown their sorrows in a vast quantity of alcohol.

Just before seven o'clock the following morning, while Alex was struggling to find a way of recuperating from the phenomenal hangover brought about by Felix and he drinking into the small hours and drowning their sorrows at not having been able to see more of yesterday's activities, he was woken by a discreet but persistent knocking at his hotel room door. Reluctantly opening it, if only to cease the persistent knocking, he discovered the duty porter bearing a message that a car had been sent from General Wallenius to collect Alex and bring him to the military headquarters. Alex quickly showered and shaved to try and make himself look vaguely respectable, before dressing warmly and reporting to the reception in less than ten minutes. As Alex walked from the hotel, the rear door of the staff car was opened for him, and when he settled into the back seat, the driver drove carefully towards the military base. On arrival, Alex was received by a lieutenant, who saluted and told him that the general was very busy that morning, but remembering his promise to give Alex an interview, Wallenius thought that they could share breakfast together. The lieutenant showed Alex into a room with a table laid for two and no sooner had he taken his coat off than General Wallenius entered the room and shook Alex's hand.

'So,' the general began, 'are they looking after you at the Pohjanhovi?' and without waiting for an answer, he continued, 'I am sorry that it has taken this long for us to meet, but I have been occupied trying to save Finland from the Soviet!'

'I quite understand,' Alex reassured him, 'but I understand that the tide has turned in Finland's favour.'

'That is quite true,' the general replied. 'Our soldiers are just mopping up the last few pockets of resistance, very successfully. But there will be other encounters before we get rid of the menace, so whereas we have won this battle, we must still win the war.'

'I have heard rumours that the British prime minister, Winston Churchill, has suggested that Britain is willing to assist Finland by providing military aid. Have you heard these rumours, also?' Alex thought he would plant an early seed in the mind of the general.

'In war, Mr Carlsson,' Wallenius responded carefully, 'there are many rumours; some of which may even be based in fact. History shows us that previously Britain was not that concerned with Finnish independence and our struggle was better supported by Germany. Now that Germany has allied itself with our enemy, we must also consider our former friend as our enemy, but does that mean that the enemy of our enemy must, therefore, be our friend?

'I can see no strategic advantage in Mr Churchill wishing to help Finland in its war against Soviet Russia, but if he wants to help, then that is something that our politicians must consider. As a military commander, I hope to have the right tools to fight the enemy, but whatever means I have at my disposal, I must use them to the best advantage. Of course, the more and better tools that I have to use, the better is my chance of securing a victory; but I wonder what Mr Churchill could spare to aid us and how much help they would be?

'Would British aeroplanes be able to fly in such cold weather as we have in Finland? Or would the fuel in British tanks not freeze? Would British soldiers be able to stand the extremes of cold that our soldiers have to endure? Or are they able to adapt to the type of war that we are fighting? Much as I appreciate the kind offer of help, I wonder whether the assistance offered might not become a hindrance. And then I come back to the central question of whether Mr Churchill could spare any military aid to assist us when he has sufficient troubles of his own with which he has to contend.

'So, to answer your question, yes, I have heard the rumours, but I cannot base my strategy on rumours of what may, or may not, come to be; I have to deal with the reality of what exists.'

What the general said made perfect sense, even to Alex, and he wondered how he might convey the message to his masters in London in a manner which would not offend.

Alex was quite surprised at how relaxed he was in Wallenius's company. They were chatting together as if they had known each other for many years, such was the ability of the general to feel at home in any company. In many ways, despite all the background information he had read on Wallenius, Alex was starting to warm towards the man – it was clear that he was a man of passion, and that his enthusiasm was focussed solely on defeating the Russian invaders of his country.

As Alex was pondering this new-found respect, the door opened, and a tall, imposing and upright soldier entered the room. The general rose and saluted, for which he received a nod of acknowledgement.

'Good morning, sir,' the general began. 'I apologise, but I was just breakfasting with Alex Carlsson of the Swedish newspaper *Svenska Posten*.'

Alex quickly realised that he was in the presence of Field-Marshal Mannerheim, who looked towards him with what could be best described as disdain. Alex felt distinctly uncomfortable as one of the most famous men in the country stared down his nose at him. He knew that Mannerheim rigorously avoided any contact with the foreign press as the field-marshal did not trust journalists and made it very clear that he would not entertain any interviews. Alex knew that it was almost impossible for reporters even to catch a glimpse of the man and unheard of that they would receive an audience, and yet here he was, sitting at the general's breakfast table, in the presence of Mannerheim himself.

'Mr Carlsson,' the field-marshal began courteously, 'I am so very pleased to have met you, but I am sure that you will appreciate that General Wallenius and I have much to discuss in the limited time that I have in Rovaniemi, so perhaps you would excuse us?'

By this time, Alex had risen to his feet. 'Of course, sir,' he responded respectfully and started to gather his hat, coat and gloves.

'Please forgive me,' the field-marshal suddenly said, 'but I have the feeling that we have met previously, but I cannot recall…'

'Sir, I have only been in Finland for a few short weeks, and I can assure you that I have not previously had the privilege of meeting you, but am very glad to have done so now,' Alex responded, 'although I shall not impose on your time further.'

He thanked the general for his hospitality and shook hands with both men and was about to leave when Field-Marshal Mannerheim said, 'Mr Carlsson, I have been very remiss. I recall now where I have heard your name – were you not the journalist who was involved in that incident at Suomussalmi?'

'Yes, I was,' Alex responded, 'but in all truth, it was blown up out of all proportion.'

'Nonsense,' the field-marshal stated, 'you are a civilian and a civilian from a neutral country. What you did was extremely courageous. Notwithstanding that a diplomatic incident may have ensued, your actions saved the life of a valuable commander, and for that, Finland is in your debt.' Mannerheim extended his hand again and shook Alex's, and as he did so, his face broke into a most genuine and welcoming smile.

It was on the way back to the hotel that Alex realised that the meeting with General Wallenius had been a deliberate ploy to introduce him to Mannerheim, for what reason Alex could only speculate. It seemed as though General Wallenius had a Machiavellian streak, and that was reason enough to be wary of how much he trusted the man, despite Alex's new-found respect.

*

Alex had hoped to surprise Felix while he was still at breakfast and to give him the news that he had met Mannerheim, but Felix was not in the restaurant. Alex ran up the stairs two at a time and knocked on Felix's door, before twisting the handle. The door opened and the sight that greeted him as he entered, of Jaana's young body straddling that of Felix and her riding him to an ecstatic climax, somewhat took Alex's breath away. Alex backed out of the room and quietly closed the door, hoping that his intrusion had gone unnoticed in the culmination of passion in which the two lovers were engaged.

Alex returned to the hotel lounge, and when, some half-hour later, Felix joined him, there was no sign of Jaana, nor any indication that they had even noticed his intrusion. Felix said that he had been concerned for Alex when, having asked the porter of his whereabouts after Alex had failed to come down for breakfast, the concierge said that Alex had been taken to the military base early in the morning. Alex thought, somewhat sardonically, that his concern had not prevented him from returning to bed and making love with Jaana.

'I was worried that you had been arrested, probably for being so disgustingly drunk last night, but it seems not. So, what happened?' Felix asked. 'Did the concierge misinform me and because of too much alcohol, last night, you were sleeping it off? Or did you get lucky with one of the Lottas?'

'Wallenius sent for me early, and we breakfasted together at the base,' Alex replied.

'So, you managed to get an audience with the general, then?' Felix inquired incredulously with more than a hint of envy in his voice.

'Yes,' responded Alex, before adding, 'Mannerheim was there also.'

'You met Mannerheim?' Felix was doubly astounded.

'I did,' Alex was enjoying mocking his colleague, 'and what a thoroughly nice fellow he is, too!'

*

Alex took time to reflect on what he knew about the Finnish field-marshal before he wrote his article for the newspaper, which was to incorporate General Wallenius's views on military aid. Who was this man who was either loved or abjectly hated, the man who was regarded as either *Pyöveli Mannerheim* (Mannerheim the Executioner), or as the saviour of an independent Finland?

Indeed, he was, without a doubt, the most fascinating figure in Finland at that time, and Alex tried to delve deeply to discover the character of the man. For some, who could never forgive the massacre of the workers in Finland in 1918, he was yet again condemning even more Finnish men to butchery in another war. Others saw him as a saviour who had stopped the spread of Bolshevism at the end of the previous war and was again standing up against the might of the Soviet.

It was clear that he was not a politician, having neither the guile nor aptitude for beating Kaarlo Ståhlberg in the presidential elections of 1919, but on the other hand, he was undoubtedly a very astute military commander.

Alex learned that Mannerheim was born in Askainen to Swedish parents who had settled in what was then the Grand Duchy of Finland and part of the Russian Empire; he had served with distinction in a cavalry regiment of the Imperial Russian army, rising to the rank of general at the age of thirty, the youngest in Russia. Because his allegiance was to the Whites, he was deeply anti-Bolshevik. A definite favourite of the imperial family, Mannerheim even had the privilege of escorting Tsar Nicholas II and the Princess Alix of Hesse and by Rhine, as she was, to the altar on their wedding day in November 1894, less than a month since Tsar Alexander III had died, and Nicholas had succeeded him. Even Mannerheim's own marriage to his estranged wife, Anastasia Arapova, had been arranged by the Dowager Empress Maria Feodorovna.

Many myths and legends surrounded the man, some of which must have been true and others based on folklore, but in Alex's mind, there was no doubt that ideologically they had much in common.

*

As January progressed, it became apparent that the fight had forsaken the north of the country and that the war had moved to the area around Lake Ladoga and the so-called *Mannerheim-linja* – Mannerheim Line – that stretched between Koivisto and Taipale, south of Viipuri. Nevertheless, the Soviet bombers still maintained their regular attacks on Kemi, Rovaniemi and Oulu as well as other military and civilian targets. Throughout January 1940, there were over six hundred different air raids on over two hundred different towns or villages and conservative figures estimated that over twenty thousand bombs had been dropped on the country in this period, and yet surprisingly less than four hundred civilians had lost their lives.

Alex discovered that the reason why there were so few casualties was threefold. Firstly, the Finns were extraordinarily disciplined and had an excellent air-raid precaution system, and the network of air-raid shelters was second to none. Of course, no air-raid shelter is protection against a direct hit, and several got obliterated by a bomb that occasionally hit the mark. The second reason was the architecture and town planning of Finnish centres – single-storey wooden houses spaced widely along broad streets often meant that even a direct hit would not cause the fire to spread. Most towns and villages were rural, and when the bombers came, the Finns evacuated and went to hide in the forest, and this was supported by a government directive that prevented shops from opening until after 3.00pm in the afternoon when dusk had descended, and the Russian bombers seldom came.

Ironically, the third reason was more to do with Russian strategy. Despite earlier misgivings, it was evident that the Russians were not deliberately targeting civilian centres, with a few exceptions, and were focussing their attacks on military objectives. The main railway junctions at Kemi, Tampere and Riihimäki were clear targets and raided repeatedly. Likewise, the bombers regularly targeted the industrial centres of Tampere and Lahti, but also places that had limited military significance were attacked – towns like the port of Vaasa were repeatedly bombed in January, even though it was already icebound.

The much-respected Finnish navy also received a fair amount of attention, even though their two cruisers, the *Väinämönen* and *Ilmarinen*, named after the heroes in the Finnish epic poem, the *Kalevala*, were icebound in Turku Harbour. They regularly used their anti-aircraft guns to ward off enemy bombers but did not take part in any naval encounters, as they were stuck in port. The rest of the Finnish navy comprised little more than some fast patrol boats, minesweepers and old gunboats dating from the early part of the century. Not that the Russian navy was much better equipped, and both Soviet Russia's and Finland's navies were little more than coastal defence forces. Compared to Germany's Kriegsmarine, they were both about twenty-five years behind the times.

The Finnish custom of looking after some of their military wounded in civilian hospitals was too well known and served to turn them into military targets. The Russians saw them as "fair game" in their bid to reduce the supply of troops to the Finnish army – it was almost as if the red cross painted on the roofs of these buildings merely acted as an aiming point for the Russian bombers. Of course, there was also some element of trying to demoralise the citizens of Finland by consistent bombing throughout January, but it was a measure of the Finnish *sisu* – determination – which is omnipresent in their national culture, that their resolve remained unbroken.

Mannerheim left the town with the same amount of haste as he had arrived; the motorcade swept out of town to Salmijärvi, and he was gone. The atmosphere in Rovaniemi changed instantly. No longer was there the air of expectation, and the whole place almost seemed to deflate after the great man had left. Not long after Mannerheim departed, General Wallenius also departed, heading north practically as far as you can go without getting your feet wet, to a battle that had been continuing for some time but had never attracted the headlines that the more significant actions achieved. The town of Petsamo nestled between the Russian and Norwegian borders at the northern extremity of the country.

Almost as though they were waiting for the dignitaries to depart before resuming the bombing, the Russian air force returned the very next day after General Wallenius had left. After weeks of false alarms, a level of laziness had set in at Rovaniemi, and when the air-raid sirens sounded, many people ignored them. Others casually sauntered to their air-raid shelters. Only a few joined Alex and Felix in taking the threat seriously.

On 10th January, just after breakfast, as workers were leaving their homes, Rovaniemi was hit by an attack from the Soviet air force. They targeted the hospital, the hotel, the military headquarters and the vital railway and road bridges. A wing of the hospital was severely damaged, and those killed were civilians, another bomb hit an air- raid shelter just outside the hospital, where nurses were sheltering. Many burned to death. No sooner had the raid come than it had gone – fifteen minutes of death and destruction. People came out to see the damage that had been caused by this flagrant attack on a civilian centre, and while they were lamenting the loss of loved ones or property, the second raid hit. Some might have argued that people should have awaited the sound of the all-clear before coming out of their shelters, but they didn't, and the second raid hit without warning. People fled across the river, hoping to find sanctuary on the opposite bank, but the Russian aeroplanes machine-gunned them as they were running.

These hit-and-run raids continued over the next two days, and eventually, the town council decided that the town would be evacuated before nine o'clock in the morning when citizens would cross the river to a makeshift camp that was being set up in the woods of Ounasvaara on the opposite bank. Merchants, restaurant owners, bankers, all loaded their wares onto sledges and skied across the river in the early hours, dragging their sleighs behind them, and they remained there until after three o'clock in the afternoon when they would return to discover what else in their town had been attacked and destroyed. Just a skeleton medical staff at the hospital were left to care for the severely injured and unmovable patients, and the duty fire and police officers. This mandatory evacuation ensured that these raids killed very few other civilians in Rovaniemi, but both Felix and Alex felt that they had outlived their usefulness in Lapland and decided it was time to return to the capital.

XI

In the late afternoon on Thursday, 18th January 1940, Alex and Felix managed to arrange travel warrants to return to Helsinki by train and Alex telephoned ahead to the Hotel Torni to secure a room for Felix. They departed from Rovaniemi the next morning on an overcrowded train and headed south, and as the train gradually pulled out of the station, Alex was surprised to see Jaana forcing her way through the crowds of people on the train and struggling with her suitcase, to find Felix.

'Hello,' Felix began, 'what are you doing here?' Although Felix pretended innocence when he saw the restaurateur's daughter, Alex had the distinct impression that this was prearranged, even though she played along with the act.

'My father thought that Rovaniemi was becoming too dangerous,' she said simply, 'so he is sending me south to live with his brother and his brother's wife in Järvenpää. He hopes I will be safer there.'

'See,' Felix turned to Alex with a smile, 'my one regret about leaving Rovaniemi is resolved – Jaana has come with us.' He turned to Jaana and said, 'Perhaps you will come and see us when we are in Helsinki, I would like that very much.'

Even though he was at least twice the age of Jaana, there was no doubt that Felix was smitten by the girl and more to the point – she was enjoying it! She simpered her willingness to see Felix in Helsinki, and Alex could not help feeling some sympathy for the girl, as he knew Felix was in his early forties and already married with two children back in Sweden – this, Alex thought, was going to end in tears.

Nevertheless, having Jaana as companionship for the journey to Helsinki was like having a breath of fresh air in the otherwise stuffy train compartment, especially as it turned out that she was a good conversationalist and quite well educated. After leaving school, Jaana had enrolled in a local college to learn secretarial skills and had graduated top of the class, and this was a skill that she hoped to put to good use in the capital, as she had not had the opportunity to use it at all in Rovaniemi, which frustrated her. Alex had thought that she was in her late teens and was a little surprised when he learned that she was twenty-three years old, the same age as was he, and he put her youthful complexion down to the clean air in Lapland and the relatively healthy diet of berries and other locally produced products.

It took nearly four hours for the train to venture south from the Arctic Circle to Oulu, and during this time, the conversation was lively. Alex sat one side of the compartment and Jaana snuggled up to Felix on the other. Whether this was intended romantically, Alex was unsure, but the heating on the train was scarcely working, and Alex could well understand that they were huddling together to keep warm. As the train pulled into Tervola station, Jaana slipped out to use the toilet, and this allowed Alex to enquire after Felix's intentions. He felt somewhat like a Dutch uncle, quizzing somebody with the reputation of Felix Nyström about a girl whom he hardly knew; for all Alex knew, they might have been much closer than he believed. Felix tried to brush it off as a matter of little consequence, and when Alex persisted, he felt that he was overstepping a line and encroaching into the precluded territory between friends.

'Look, Alex,' Felix attempted to bring the matter to a close, 'I have known Jaana for a couple of months now, and we get on well together. She likes me, and I most definitely like her. One thing this war has taught me is that you should seize your opportunities when they are presented! My wife did not want me to take this assignment and has not written to me in the six months that I have been in Finland – I do not know whether she is waiting for me or has found somebody else. It is quite likely as we were hardly ever strong with me travelling all over the world and she staying in Sweden. Women are fickle, they change their minds and men can waste a lot of their lives hoping for the impossible.'

Alex was shocked. He held his marriage to Teddy as sacred, and apart from the dalliance with Sigrid in Stockholm, it had never crossed his mind that either he or she would ever stray from the commitment that they had made to each other.

There was a three-and-a-half-hour wait in Oulu for the connecting train to Helsinki, which left at 4.30pm, so all three found the lounge and warmed themselves by the roaring log fire, hoping that the next train would have better heating! It did not, but it was much busier with soldiers going on leave, so the body warmth of other passengers helped, even though most smoked continuously, which Alex found uncomfortable. More uncomfortable for Felix, however, was the fact that he and Jaana were sitting on opposite seats, and none of the other passengers seemed willing to move to allow them to sit together.

After about an hour's travelling, one of the men took out a bottle of *Jaloviina*, the Finnish cut brandy, and handed it round to the other soldiers in the compartment. As their tongues loosened, it became clear that they regarded civilians who were of military age and not in uniform as cowards.

One growled at Alex, '*Sinä! Miksi olet siviili?*' – You! Why are you not in uniform?

Alex replied equably, in Swedish, 'Because I'm a Swedish journalist.'

Felix joined in the conversation, 'As am I.'

The soldier turned to Jaana. 'And you, what do you do for Finland, or are you a Swedish chicken, too?'

The atmosphere in the compartment was worsening, and Jaana was visibly afraid. Just about all of the soldiers she had met at her father's restaurant in Rovaniemi had been cheeky, some even playfully taking liberties, but none had the aggression of these soldiers.

Felix stepped in to help. 'She's with me.'

'What? Is she your daughter or your niece?' There was no doubt as to the inference implied by Jaana being Felix's niece.

'She is my girlfriend,' Felix replied simply, and received a roar of amazement from the soldier and a charming smile from Jaana.

The soldier said to Jaana, 'You don't want to go with old men, *kulta*, you need a young man!' and with that, he placed his arm around the terrified Jaana and started to reach for her breast.

Felix launched himself across the carriage and grabbed the soldier's wrist. In his other hand, he held a lethally sharp-looking puukko that had appeared from apparently nowhere. 'Now, just so that we are clear,' he snarled at the frightened soldier, 'if you continue disturbing my girlfriend, you will know the name of the man who has sliced you open like the pig that you are. My name is Felix Nyström of the *Svenska Dagbladet*, and my friend is Alex Carlsson of the *Svenska Posten*, and we are here to cover the war at the invitation of your government, to make sure that the world gets a true picture of what is happening in this godforsaken country. Do you understand?' The soldier squirmed with the pain inflicted by Felix on his wrist. 'Okay, now that we understand each other, you are going to get your shitting arse out of that seat, and we are going to change places so that I can sit with my girl and you can go fuck with your boyfriends.'

The venom with which Felix spoke these words shocked Alex. This was entirely another side of the journalist that Alex had not previously encountered, but it worked as Felix's grip on the soldier's wrist tightened, and he hauled him out of the seat next to Jaana before depositing him in the place that he had just vacated.

An older sergeant who was sitting by the door asked Alex, 'You! He said your name was Alex Carlsson?'

'Yes,' responded Alex cautiously.

'You were at Suomussalmi?' the captain continued.

'Yes.' Again Alex agreed despondently; did everybody know about Suomussalmi?

'I also,' the officer replied. 'Seppi,' the sergeant addressed the soldier, 'I have heard of him, he is a friend. Leave him alone, eh?'

The soldier resentfully accepted what the sergeant had decreed and sank into his seat, drinking his liquor and no longer offering it to his colleagues.

The sergeant rose and addressed Felix. 'I apologise for my friend's manner, we have just been given leave after many months of fighting. It is not an excuse, but it is a reason, and I am sorry if our actions have offended you and your young lady. Please accept our apologies.'

He extended his hand to Alex, who shook it and then to Felix, who did so also, although more grudgingly. The sergeant smiled at Jaana, who nervously smiled back. The rest of the journey continued without incident; Alex, Felix and Jaana were included in the conversation between the soldiers, but the offensive Seppi did not join in and eventually drifted off to sleep in an alcohol-induced stupor.

The soldiers left the train when it arrived in Tampere at about half-past eleven that night, leaving Alex, Felix and Jaana, the entire compartment to themselves and all three, settled down and slept. So tired were they that they were completely unaware that the train halted at Riihimäki for a couple of hours, as there was damage to the Helsinki line from an earlier bombing raid, and when eventually the train pulled into the capital, it was almost 3.30am.

'Well, it is going to be a few hours before you can catch a train to Järvenpää. What will you do until then?' Felix asked Jaana.

'It is not a problem,' she replied. 'The waiting room here is warm and cosy. I will wait here.'

'You can always come and stay at my hotel,' suggested Felix, adding hurriedly, 'I am sure they will have a spare room.'

'No, that's very kind, but it will be expensive, and I would not want to be an imposition on either of you,' Jaana stated.

'You would not ever be an imposition,' Felix said. 'Besides, we are residents, so they might even open the bar for us.'

Alex felt it was time to be chivalrous. 'If Jaana is happy to stay at the station, I will gladly wait with her until her train comes.'

'Please, I shall be all right.' Jaana tried to stamp her authority, but Felix was not to be swayed.

'No, Alex is right, if you are staying at the station, at least one of us must remain with you. It is all right, Alex, I shall wait with Jaana. You go on to the hotel, and I will see you later today.'

It was plainly not a battle that he was going to win, so Alex picked up his suitcase and typewriter and headed out of the station, having first shaken Felix by the hand and given Jaana an affectionate peck on the cheek.

'I will see you later, then,' Alex said as Felix and Jaana left. 'Good luck!'

*

At dinner that evening, Alex was not at all surprised to see Felix and Jaana enter together, and they came over and sat at his table.

'You decided against the station, then?' he asked with only a hint of sarcasm.

'Yes, they turned the heating off, and it got cold,' Felix explained, 'so Jaana took me up on my offer of a bed for what remained of the night,' and smiling at Jaana, he said, 'and for the rest of the day, we just could not find the motivation to get out of bed.'

Alex thought that Jaana looked radiant that evening as she tucked into the dismal offering of dinner, and after what he had seen in Rovaniemi, it did not take a genius to work out how she had worked up such an appetite. He concluded that he had tried to help and stop her heart from being broken, but some people were beyond help – all you could do was wait and try to patch them up when it all went wrong.

'What are your plans for tomorrow?' Felix asked Alex.

'Nothing particular,' Alex replied, 'I have some writing to finish, and I should get something sent to Stockholm or my editor will think I have gone on strike. Apart from that, I think I might try to find out what has been happening since I was away. What about you?'

'The same, I think,' Felix responded. 'I've promised to show Jaana the sights of Helsinki tonight, so tomorrow morning I shall see her off on the train to Järvenpää and then get back to work. Shall we meet in the bar later and compare notes?'

'Yes, a good idea,' replied Alex, 'but do not expect me to give you a hint about the "scoop" I shall be writing. I shall let you read it in the next issue of *Svenska Posten*!'

Alex was true to his word. He spent the morning of the next day beavering away, writing an extended article and several smaller feature articles for his newspaper. Seeing that the time was approaching lunch, he went in search of sustenance and found himself in the hotel bar where the only other occupant was the Canadian, whom he recalled Mick McMahon had referred to as "the lioness". Taking the seat next to her at the bar, Alex ordered aquavit and after murmuring *'Skål!'* to nobody in particular, swallowed the drink. As the liquor made its way down his gullet, Alex felt the warmth spread through his body, and as it landed at its destination, he experienced the usual sensation of a catfight occurring in his belly, with the animals trying to rip his stomach lining apart in a bid to escape. It was always like this with the first drink of the day, and he waited until the burning subsided before turning to his fellow journalist and introducing himself.

'Alex Carlsson of the *Svenska Posten*,' he said. 'I don't think that anybody has formally introduced us.'

'That's right,' Leona Guichard responded, 'I do not think anyone has.' Not that she bothered trying to rectify the situation and just sat staring at her drink.

'Pleased to meet you,' Alex tried again.

'I imagine you are,' Leona responded.

Even as he uttered the next sentence, Alex realised how crass it would sound. 'Do you come here often?'

'Jeez, I don't believe it,' Leona muttered under her breath. 'That has to be the worst pick-up line ever.'

'I'm not trying to pick you up, but you are drinking alone in the bar, and I just thought that I would be civilised. Still, if you find that disagreeable, then I apologise.'

'*Non, je suis désolée, je ne passe pas une bonne journée. S'il vous plaît, pardonnez-moi.* –No, I'm sorry, I am not having a great day. Please excuse me.

Alex dropped into his rusty French: 'No, it is not a concern. I just thought it would be nice to get to know each other…'

'Yeah, I guess,' she answered, without displaying much enthusiasm in doing so.

To many men, such an apparent disinterest would have been sufficient for them to have given up on the conversation, but not to Alex – this was now becoming a challenge, and he was determined to have a meaningful discussion.

'I hear you are Canadian,' Alex persisted. 'They say it is a beautiful country, although I have never been myself.'

'Some parts of Canada, possibly; but some other parts are so wild they defy description. Indeed, where I was born, Montréal is very beautiful.'

'So how come you ended up here?' Alex asked.

'You mean,' she said in an almost mocking manner, using another clichéd pick-up line, 'what's a nice girl like you doing in a town like this?'

'If you like,' Alex responded.

'I guess it's because I am such a pain in the ass to my editor that he sent me here to get me out of the way.'

Alex drained his drink and asked Leona whether she would like a refill.

'Sure, why not, but just because I let you buy me a drink does not mean that I will let you screw me,' the Canadian replied.

'Good, I'm glad about that,' Alex responded, 'you're not my type – far too old,' he said with more humour in his voice than hurt.

'You really are a cheeky young bastard.' If she was shocked, she hid it well. 'And before you ask, Margot Maddison is not my type either, although it seems that most of the hacks in this place reckon that we are together.'

'Really?' Alex appeared surprised. 'I had not heard that.'

'So, Mister Alex Carlsson, tell me about yourself,' she enquired.

'Not much to tell,' he replied, 'born just outside Stockholm, spent much of my childhood being brought up by my grandmother, and much of my youth travelling with my diplomat parents. Decided to become a journalist because my father had little good to say about journalists and I thought I could change his mind, but then inconveniently he died before I had a word published.

'My family got me the job at *Svenska Posten*, and they sent me to England to get me out of the way, and when Britain declared war on

Germany, the paper sent me here, and I suppose I will stay here until my editor finds me an equally dangerous assignment to undertake.'

'Do you enjoy it?' she asked.

'Well enough,' he said thoughtfully. 'My time in Finland has certainly been eventful!'

'So I hear,' she said with more than a hint of jealousy. 'That business in Suomussalmi, then you get an interview with Wallenius, which nobody else seems to be able to do, and he even introduces you to Mannerheim. You are quite the golden boy.'

'Believe me,' Alex was a little wounded, but even more surprised that news of his meeting Mannerheim was such everyday news, 'none of it was planned. It was just circumstances; I would not even declare it as my good fortune, as I would not have wished Mick McMahon to die…'

'Sure, if you say so,' she responded. 'Look, I've got a meeting. Nice to have met you, Mr Carlsson – and maybe, if I let you hang around, some of your good luck will rub off on me!'

With that, she left, leaving Alex alone at the bar wondering whether the other journalists at Hotel Torni felt the same.

XII

Following the tremendous successes in early January when the Finnish forces won the Battle of the Raate Road in which the vastly outnumbered Finnish 9th Division held out against and decimated the Russian 163rd Rifle Division, and the Battle of Suomussalmi when using the strategy known as *Motti* – siege tactics – the 44th Soviet Rifle Division was annihilated, and the Soviet advance stopped.

Alex learned the whole story having drunk several vodkas and beers over two nights with Jarno in one of the many bars that he habitually attended after work before going home to his long-suffering wife. Since the death of Mick McMahon, Jarno had become less reticent about what he discussed with Alex, or perhaps it was that he considered Alex as an ally after his exploits at the start of the Suomussalmi campaign.

'Colonel Hjalmar Siilasvuo knew only too well that if the two Russian divisions consolidated, then it would be game over,' Jarno explained to Alex. 'His tactics of splitting his force and driving a wedge between the two Russian divisions was a gamble that paid dividends. The 44th Rifle Division was a fast-moving mechanised unit sent to reinforce the 163rd at Suomussalmi, but it was hampered by the terrain, and although they had plenty of skis, few of their number could actually ski!

'Dividing his force to prevent the 44th from joining up with the 163rd was a considerable risk, but it enabled Siilasvuo to focus on beating the exhausted 163rd Rifles Division, before turning his full attention to the 44th. Although his troops were battle-weary, they rallied and successfully took on the reinforcements of the 44th Rifle Division, capturing a vast quantity of Russian equipment.' It was to go down as one of the most significant Finnish victories of the war.

From the Soviet perspective, however, the aftermath of those losses saw the Soviet Brigade commander, Alexei Ivanovich Vinogradov, and three other officers who had escaped in a tank, being executed in front of the remnants of the 44th Rifle Brigade on the direct orders of Stalin. Ironically, they were not killed for cowardice or for having lost the battle, but for leaving so much of their equipment behind when retreating, for the Finns to capture.

After these two defeats, the Russians needed to regroup, and for the rest of January, apart from the continuous bombing of cities and military targets, the war seemed to stall. Naturally, this also benefited the war-ravaged Finnish forces, and it enabled them to replenish stocks of ammunition, equipment and men.

That January was one of the coldest that Finland had experienced, with the temperature dropping to as low as minus 45 degrees centigrade. It was a time of taking stock and reflecting on how the war was progressing. The consensus seemed to be that Finland was holding its own against a much stronger military adversary, and Alex spent much of the time analysing the information that his sources had given. Could it be that plucky little Finland could actually conquer the might of the Soviet? The recent victories suggested that it might just be a possibility. Felix, meanwhile, spent much of his time shuttling between Järvenpää and Helsinki, strengthening his relationship with Jaana.

It was during one of the rare occasions that Alex and Felix found themselves together in the bar of the Hotel Torni, exchanging opinions and news over a relaxed game of chess, that Alex learned that Felix's wife had eventually contacted him. A letter had arrived telling Felix that his marriage was over and that his wife had found somebody who would be at home to help bring up his children, rather than gallivanting around the world in pursuit of news. She intended a divorce and hoped that Felix would not object. On the face of it, Felix seemed wholly unconcerned, and Alex learned that Jaana was becoming much more of a fixture in Felix's life.

'Out with the old and in with the new,' Felix quipped as he sacrificed a rook in a move that Alex had anticipated, and one that allowed him to move his white knight to achieve an inevitable checkmate in three. Realising the trap that he had been lulled into, Felix toppled his black king with a wry smile. 'It seems I have mixed fortunes tonight!'

*

As January melted into February, there was a definite sense of anticipation in the air, and Wednesday 4th February typified the new hope that was sweeping the country like a pandemic. The day was a typical midwinter's day in Helsinki; not too cold at only minus 7 degrees centigrade in the capital, but overcast and drab for the entire day. At least, thought Alex, the low cloud base would keep the bombers nicely hangered at their aerodromes across the Baltic, well away from Helsinki.

As he was leaving the hotel, the concierge called him back and handed him a neatly type-written letter inviting him to a press conference at the British Legation's offices on Etelä Esplanaadikatu on Friday at 12.00 noon, where they would get lunch before the meeting. Alex wondered what calamity necessitated such a highly unusual step to be taken by a foreign legation to summon a conference, without there being a hint of what was afoot amongst the foreign journalists – and there was nothing in the informal intelligence circles of the international newspaper correspondent's, known as the "rumour-mill". Even Charlie Wattis, the usually soused, but incredibly well-informed stringer for the *Daily Express*, professed to know nothing, which Alex genuinely believed because Charlie was not renowned for hiding his self-perceived superior knowledge if he thought he could use a snippet of information as currency for something more significant. Although he was usually "three sheets to the wind", Charlie Wattis had a nose for a story like a truffle hound has for fungi – if Charlie knew nothing, then there was nothing to know!

Alex eventually concluded that Churchill had probably persuaded the Cabinet to support Finland and the announcement would come at this meeting, perhaps with some functionary of the Finnish Ministry of Defence in attendance to offer their country's eternal thanks for the generosity of the British government.

He was wrong. Friday came, and Alex took his seat at the Legation's offices along with Felix Nyström and the others from the "Torni Drinkers' Club", as Charlie Wattis described those who were billeted by their newspapers in one of the city's more expensive hotels, while he had a small flat that he was paying for by himself. The lunch was excellent, and so was the drink, and just before the main event was due, Alex went to the toilet and shortly afterwards Simon Potts joined him. Simon waited until they were alone and then suggested coffee at Fazer's café, the next morning. Alex readily agreed before returning to the reception.

At precisely 2.00pm, the new Envoy Extraordinary and Minister Plenipotentiary of the United Kingdom, His Excellency George Vereker, stepped up on the dais accompanied by Field-Marshal Mannerheim. After an appallingly dreary speech, the Minister announced that it was his very pleasurable duty to officially bestow upon Field-Marshal Carl Gustav Emil Mannerheim, the honorary rank of Knight Grand Cross of the Order of the British Empire, which had been conferred by King George VI two years previously. The field-marshal gave a sufficiently short response of gratitude, translated from Swedish into English by a staff officer, shook hands with Vereker, and after a suitable time shaking hands and taking compliments, while studiously ignoring all journalists, he departed. It was over, rather an anti-climax, Alex thought, but he was glad to have arranged a coffee with Simon the next day.

Just as Alex was about to leave, the staff officer who had so ably translated the field-marshal's thanks, approached him and asked whether Alex would be available to dine with Mannerheim that evening at the barracks, before the field-marshal returned to the war. Alex was both stunned and astounded to have received the invitation but readily agreed, even when pressed to keep the meeting confidential from his colleagues.

'Can you find your own way to the barracks?' the captain asked, and Alex indicated that he could. 'When you get there, tell the sentry that you have a meeting with me, Captain Toivonen, and I will ensure that the guards know you are visiting.'

Alex took his time preparing for his dinner with Mannerheim. He bathed, but ensured that he did not use any perfumery, he shaved ensuring that there was not a vestige of stubble remaining, Alex selected a conservative lounge suit and accompanied it with a plain tie, and shone his shoes until he could almost use them as a mirror. Deciding against walking, Alex took a taxi to the army base, and when he announced his arrival, he was shown through the gate to wait at the guardhouse. Within a few moments, a lieutenant arrived and escorted Alex to Mannerheim's quarters. The first thing that struck Alex was how modest was the accommodation of Finland's most senior military man, almost spartan, and when the field-marshal arrived, Alex noted that he was still formally dressed in his uniform. Did this man ever relax?

'Forgive my tardiness,' Mannerheim greeted Alex, 'it is entirely unforgivable.' Alex acknowledged the apology. 'Would you care for a drink? I shall have a small glass of water, but may permit myself a glass of wine with dinner.'

Did Alex detect a hint of uneasiness from the field-marshal? Surely not!

'A glass of water would suit me also, sir, very well,' Alex agreed, although privately he would have welcomed something a little stronger.

Mannerheim poured two glasses and offering one to Alex suggested, 'Shall we sit? Dinner should not be long.'

They sat in the two armchairs and engaged in stilted small talk until dinner was ready, and they went through to the dining room, which was equally as modestly furnished.

'You will excuse the meal, I am sure,' the field-marshal began, 'but I always insist on eating the same food as my men. If I expect it to be good enough to sustain them as they take up this fight, then it must also be good enough for me.'

The logic was as impeccable as the food was almost inedible, but the field-marshal ate his meal with appreciation and Alex did so also, even though Finnish sausages were not to his taste, and the last time he had eaten *näkkileipä* (crispbread) was when he had been in Suomussalmi, and he had enjoyed field rations of soup with the troops.

'Tell me of your parents,' the field-marshal requested over coffee, and Alex gave him the rehearsed version of his background. Mannerheim appeared interested, and he continued, 'I understand that you were working in England before your newspaper sent you to Finland?'

'That's correct, sir,' Alex responded.

'I have much admired the British,' the field-marshal stated, 'good warriors. Alas, I have not had the privilege of visiting the country, but I believe it is delightful.' Alex agreed that it was. 'Perhaps, one day when I am less busy, I might have the opportunity of visiting and thanking King George personally for the medal and Mr Churchill for the aeroplanes he has sent. I think the Bristol Blenheims will prove useful for us to bomb our enemy.'

It was the first time that Alex had heard of the approval of Churchill's plans.

'Of course, we know and respect these aeroplanes as we have had several since 1936, but another twenty-four will expand our air force greatly. Mr Churchill has also said that we can make the aeroplanes ourselves at the state aeroplane factory at Tampere. Did you know we have an affectionate name for the Blenheim? We call it *Pelti-Heikki* or "Tin-Henry". He has also promised some Hawker Hurricanes and some other aeroplanes, as well. We are most grateful for his efforts; it is most generous considering the situation that Britain is facing.'

Alex wondered where this conversation was going, but just as quickly as it came, the field-marshal changed the subject again and asked Alex whether he was enjoying Finland.

'I am, yes, sir,' Alex responded. 'I am sure that the country would be even more beautiful if it were not at war, but wherever I have been, I have been very impressed.'

'Have you visited Finland before?' Mannerheim asked.

'No, sir,' Alex lied to keep with his legend. 'I believe we holidayed once on the Åland Islands, but I was a child then, and I do not remember it at all.'

'They are truly scenic,' reminisced the field-marshal.

Thus the conversation continued until it was time for Alex to leave and the field-marshal to retire for the night, which he always attempted early so that he could be awake before reveille the next morning. Alex thanked the field-marshal for his hospitality and assured him that their meeting and conversation would remain private. He hoped that building trust with one of the most influential members of Finland's ruling elite would pay dividends later, particularly as the field-marshal did not trust journalists in the slightest.

It had been a strange meeting, almost strained. Alex had the impression that the field-marshal was distinctly uncomfortable on the one hand but reaching out into unfamiliar territory with the other. It had not been an easy encounter, and he was surprised at how tired he felt afterwards.

When Alex returned to the hotel, there was a gaggle of journalists all gathered at the bar exchanging stories of increasing magnitude with each other. Alex felt that his news would have trumped the lot, but true to his promise, when asked where he had been, he merely said, 'Following up a lead that turned out to be a blind alley!'

Felix Nyström assessed Alex's smart appearance and did not altogether believe Alex's tale of time wasted. He tried to press his friend a little when they were alone, but still, Alex maintained that he had been led on a fool's errand and that he had nothing significant to share.

'What about you?' Alex asked Felix.

'Bah! Nothing!' came the reply. 'I was supposed to meet with Jaana this evening, but she has a cold or something and left a message that she could not make our rendezvous, so I'm kicking my heels around the bar hoping to pick up a snippet from which I can expand something resembling a story.'

'Do you want me to beat you at chess again?' Alex ventured.

Felix smiled. 'You can try,' he said.

Alex bought his friend a drink, and they settled down in the corner of the bar to play one of the least exciting games that Alex had played – it was clear that Felix's mind was elsewhere. The first two games ended in a stalemate and in the third Alex achieved checkmate in ten moves.

Felix stretched and said, 'My mind is not on the game tonight. I'm going to bed,' and with that, he stood up and left the bar with hardly an acknowledgement to Alex as he left. Alex understood that something was profoundly troubling his friend.

*

The next morning, Alex arrived at Café Fazer on Kluuvikatu ahead of time and was reading of Mannerheim's award in the *Sanomat* newspaper when Simon came and sat opposite him.

Alex, in greeting, cheerily imitated Lennox's greeting from Shakespeare's Scottish play: 'Good morrow, noble sir!'

'And "good morrow" to yourself,' responded Simon. 'What ails thee?'

'Boredom and the need of sustenance,' Alex responded. 'Boredom because since I have been back in Helsinki, it seems to be nothing but continuous air raids and little other action. It appears as though our war is becoming mundane, and I feel the urge to go and find something worthwhile that I can write about. Perhaps this journalism is beginning to get to me. Sustenance, because although I am in a good hotel, the food is dire, the coffee undrinkable and the company tedious. Even the illustrious Felix Nyström is becoming tiresome – all he wants to do is fall helplessly in lust after a chit of a girl who is young enough to be his daughter!

'The hardships of this place is depressing. Half the shops have closed, the cinema only shows newsreels that heighten my urge to get out and do something more constructive, restaurants are on rations so what is available is poor and damned expensive. God knows I am hardly religious, but I am thinking of trying to find a church on Sunday so that there is a highlight to the week!'

Simon smiled at his friend's discourse and commented, 'At least you meet people with a grip on reality. I have to endure diplomats… and the endless round of functions, even in these constrained times, means that all I hear is the blatherings of those who have more opinion than sense. In honesty, I am of the certain belief that the three most important qualifications for a career in the *diplomatique* are the ability to ignore the blindingly obvious, the skill of obfuscation, and the capacity of a reservoir when it comes to alcohol!'

Having poured out their woes, each to the other, they smiled and then laughed at the other's predicament, before calling over a waitress and ordering coffee.

After it had arrived, Alex said to Simon, 'So, Churchill is doing something to help the Finns, then?'

'Sorry?' responded Simon innocently.

'I hear that Finland is getting Blenheims and Hurricanes and other planes, courtesy of Mr Churchill,' Alex said.

'Really? I've not heard anything.' Alex did not know whether to believe his friend's denials. 'But I would be interested in learning from where you heard that morsel of tittle-tattle.'

'I had dinner last evening with someone senior in the military,' Alex explained.

'Well, it's nonsense, of course,' said Simon. 'I do wish that these generals would learn the folly of spreading false rumours. I suppose it was Wallenius?'

'No, Mannerheim,' said Alex quietly.

'Shit!' said Simon, 'how did you… I mean, where did… sorry, with whom?' Simon was speechless.

'Mannerheim. I had dinner with Field-Marshal Mannerheim. You know, the chappie to whom your Minister attached the gong, yesterday. I know it sounds implausible, knowing his wariness of journalists and foreign ones in particular, but I had dinner at the military headquarters, with Field-Marshal Mannerheim. His aide-de-camp, Captain Toivonen, set it up at that reception, yesterday.'

'Bugger!' Simon was clearly in favour of profanity that morning. 'What he told you is supposed to be highly confidential. You're not going to write an article about it, are you? Not that it matters, it would not get published anyway. Bugger, bugger, bugger, the ink is not even dry on the agreement yet. God, if this gets out, there will be hell to pay!'

'Oh, for God's sake, Simon, calm down,' Alex urged his friend. 'Of course, I am not going to write the story. Mannerheim asked for my discretion, and I gave him my word that it would go no further. I only told you because I'm supposed to feed information back through you.'

'Yes, well, the deal was signed late last week, and I only learned of it yesterday. Winston was determined to do his bit and try and help Finland – I only hope that it does not all blow up in his face.'

'Is it likely to?' Alex asked.

'We hope not, but everybody realises that the successes that Finland has been enjoying on the battlefield are not sustainable. Finland has lost too many men of military age and is now considering expanding the ages whereby citizens can be called up for military service. If their losses continue with the same magnitude, I doubt whether Finland can survive until summer, so rumour has it that they are looking for a peaceful settlement. They have certainly bloodied the Soviet nose, but the sheer might of Russia's military is too great for Finland to defend against, in a protracted war. I understand that Prime Minister Ryti has already made initial representations to the Soviet, but whether anything comes of them remains to be seen. If they do agree on terms, will Finland remain neutral? That is the big question to which nobody seems to have a definitive answer.'

'Bloody hell!' Alex said. 'What have the last months all been about?'

'God only knows,' Simon responded stoically.

Simon and Alex finished their coffees and Simon gave Alex some brief instructions about what the department was keen to understand before they shook hands and Simon left. Alex sat and ordered another coffee and reflected on what he had learned. One thing was sure, Alex was not going to get the answers sitting and twiddling his thumbs in a cosy hotel room in downtown Helsinki.

XIII

It did not take long for news to reach Helsinki that the Finnish army was again under attack in the village of Summa, which was one of the main gateways to Viipuri on the Karelian Isthmus. Finland had won the first battle just before Christmas the previous year, and although there had been skirmishes in the ensuing six weeks, the Russians appeared to be reluctant to try their luck again lest they got their noses bloodied once more. So apart from the occasional shelling by Russian artillery, or bombing by their air force, January on that part of the Mannerheim Line was entirely peaceful. Finnish soldiers had plenty of rest, and some had even received home leave. Modernised weapons were issued to troops, and any that proved defective were quickly replaced so that by the end of January, the Finnish forces were both well-rested and well equipped.

Of course, the Soviet had not been resting on their laurels during this period either, and the Russian General Timoshenko had been strengthening his position while testing the defences of Finland. By the time February had arrived, both the Russian 7th and 13th Armies had been deployed in the area, supported by heavy and light tanks, artillery and a sizeable proportion of the Soviet air force. Facing them was the Finnish 3rd division, which was still under-strength despite having been swelled by new recruits.

Alex arrived in Viipuri on Thursday, 8th February having endured a ten-hour journey from Helsinki, originally by train to Rikkilä and then scrounging lifts in whatever transport was heading in the right direction, as the railway to Viipuri had been heavily shelled earlier that day and was impassable. The last ride he found had been in a truck full of newly trained soldiers with their uniforms still bearing the freshness of the first issue. Their spirits were high, and they laughed and joked about kicking the Soviet bear back to its lair in Leningrad. Alex doubted that the soldiers would find it that easy to achieve their ambition but did not dampen their morale. He joined in and laughed and joked with them, knowing that some, perhaps many, would not be making the return journey to their barracks, and if they did, some would have terrible injuries.

Even though it was on the frontline, Viipuri was still home to about six and a half thousand people. The hotel in the centre of the town, where most of the journalists were staying, tried its hardest to provide comfortable accommodation, and the waitresses at dinner were extraordinarily pretty, small compensation for the poor quality and limited choice of food on offer. Even though he was a guest at the hotel, Alex had to wait in a queue of prospective diners, most of whom were soldiers, and he soon became convinced that the waitresses provided a higher level of service than just waiting at table.

Having settled and eaten, Alex went for a walk, and it was not long before he came across workmen building anti-tank defences to protect the town against attack. As he was returning to his hotel, the air-raid siren sounded, and a squadron of Soviet bombers came, laden with bombs to bring death and devastation. Considering that this was a regular occurrence by all accounts, Viipuri had survived well – many of the wooden houses still stood undamaged, as did the church. Nobody seemed particularly concerned by the bombing, and unlike Helsinki, where people would take shelter as soon as the sirens sounded, here, people just continued with their lives, perhaps occasionally stopping to watch where the next bombs were falling.

Back at the hotel, he asked one of the other correspondents, 'Why does nobody take cover during air raids?'

The reply came, 'Because the Russian bomb aimers are bloody useless and their bombs are even worse! Most of the bombs miss their target and those that do get anywhere near, seldom explode. The people of the town have been living with this for many months – it is now part of their way of life.'

Alex went to bed and wondered what the next day would bring.

*

Getting to the front was more straightforward than Alex had imagined, although frowned upon by the authorities, just about every troop transport was willing to take a correspondent or two with the soldiers, hoping they would become famous in a story written by their journalist. He joined the clutch of other correspondents outside the hotel, and soon he was on his way in a truckload of fresh-faced and inexperienced troops. Their lieutenant was a Swedish-Finn by the name of Lundberg, who welcomed the opportunity of chatting with somebody in good Swedish as most of his men were Finns, with only limited conversational skills in his mother tongue.

Lieutenant Lundberg was quite a handsome young man with a shock of pitch-black hair and the bluest eyes that Alex thought he could remember. He spoke in a well-modulated and educated tone, and Alex soon discovered that before being called up to serve, he was training to become a lawyer at the university in Turku. Alex learned that the lieutenant had grown up in Kristinestad in Ostrobothnia, where the majority of the population were Swedish-speaking. He had an elder brother serving with the Finnish air force and a sister who was still at school. Although he looked much older, he was only twenty-four years old.

Alex asked the lieutenant about the rumour that General Wallenius was being tipped to take over command in Salla.

'Bah!' said the lieutenant, 'if that buffoon is ever made commander down here, then God help us! He is not such a good commander – he just got lucky up north, and most of his troops fear him. To Wallenius, soldiers are cannon-fodder. No more than tools to get the job done.

'Completely unlike General Laatikainen, who commands here. He genuinely cares for his men, and when they die, it truly affects the general. I think it must be because he was once a schoolmaster. He wants the best for everybody.'

'Yes,' Alex replied, 'I have heard good things about his skills as a commander. I hope I might meet him while I am down here.'

As they approached Summa, Lieutenant Lundberg was more alert. 'The Russians put up observation balloons, and their artillery will target anything that moves on our side of the lines, so we need to advance carefully and use the trees as cover,' he explained.

As if on cue, shells started whining overhead and crashing down either side of the track that they were driving along. 'Take cover!' Lieutenant Lundberg shouted at his men, and the truck emptied quickly as his men sought whatever cover was available. Alex found a large boulder and Lundberg slid in beside him. 'Shouldn't take long, they soon get bored,' he smiled. He was right, the barrage lasted less than five minutes, and their truck remained wholly unscathed.

'Come on, lads,' the lieutenant called, 'let's get out of here before Boris wakes up again.' They all clambered back onto the truck, and the driver drove away from the area as quickly as he was able.

'If they could get their gunners to shoot straight,' Lundberg smiled, 'we might even be in trouble one day!' The corporal driver laughed, and even Alex had difficulty keeping a grin off his face.

The driver stopped, and everybody got out of the truck and formed a loose column. 'This is as far as we can get with the truck,' Lundberg said. 'The camp is only one and a half kilometres from here, so we shall walk the rest of the way. Do you want to come with us, or go back with the driver?'

'I have come this far,' Alex said, 'I might as well travel the rest of the way.'

'Good man!' Lundberg said and called his men to order before marching them down the side of the track leading to the forward positions; Alex walked with the lieutenant.

Soon, they arrived at where the main force had gathered. To call it a "camp" would be stretching the truth as it was merely the place in the forest where the troops assembled. Lieutenant Lundberg told his major that he had brought a Swedish correspondent with him and the major was distinctly unhappy, judging by the gruff barking that emanated from his tent.

A bearded and dishevelled major, dressed in the remains of what had once been a uniform, emerged from a trench and bustled towards Alex. 'We cannot have any civilians here,' he started. 'It is far too dangerous, and I cannot take responsibility for your safety. I will organise transport back to Viipuri for you. Wait there, and hopefully, the good news of our victory will soon come to you!'

'Thank you, major,' Alex said calmly, 'but I think I would rather wait here and witness it for myself.' He thrust out his hand in greeting. 'Alex Carlsson, *Svenska Posten*.'

'You are Carlsson?' the major asked suspiciously. 'Who was at the Battle at Suomussalmi?' Alex inclined his head slightly. 'Then, sir, you are most welcome, providing that you do not get in the way of a bullet. If I were responsible for the fate of Alex Carlsson, then I think my career would be very short-lived!' The major grinned and explained to the perplexed lieutenant just who his passenger was.

Whereas Alex did not relish the fame that his exploits in the north had brought him, it certainly opened doors with soldiers who typically had little time for war correspondents.

Alex was astounded by the sheer confidence that the Finnish troops could repel a Soviet invasion in the area. The major, whose name was alliteratively Auno Ahonen, was particularly bullish. 'We beat them back in December; we can do the same now. The Finnish soldier will stand his ground and defend his country to the end.'

'Surely the troops you had in December,' Alex tested his resolve, 'were seasoned soldiers, whereas many of your troops today are fresh from training?'

'That is true,' Major Ahonen responded, 'but they have been trained well and understand modern warfare.'

'But do you not think that the sheer weight of two Soviet armies, which must be over a quarter of a million troops, will be overwhelming?' Alex persisted.

The major was starting to get tetchy. 'Our Third Division numbers nearly two hundred thousand men, and everybody knows the Finnish soldier is worth two of Uncle Joseph's. We shall win this battle decisively and with it the war!'

As a jingoistic battle cry, it was acceptable, but in reality, even Alex knew that the Russians had close to half a million troops and the Finns, about one hundred and fifty thousand. The Russians also had over three thousand tanks and artillery pieces and over one thousand aircraft. That said, often battles are not won by the sheer force of one side, but by commitment and belief, and the Finnish troops had that in spades! They were perhaps justified, as in just about every action of the war thus far, the Finns had won handsomely against all the odds.

The night was drawing in, and Major Ahonen invited Alex to stay overnight in his trench dugout, but before retiring, they both, along with Lieutenant Lundberg, drank several bottles of vodka together. It was as they opened the second bottle that Ahonen opened up. Before the War of Independence, Ahonen said he had studied psychology at the university and had hoped to follow his father's footsteps into a professorship at Helsinki University, but the war had brought a change of career. The military life suited him – it was disciplined and with a real sense of purpose. After the war, he had stayed on and had eventually gained promotion to captain – then this war happened, and he found himself a major. He was quite reticent, but as the vodka loosened his tongue, Alex appreciated a dark humour that was quite infectious. Alex had thought that the major was in his late forties or early fifties, and was quite surprised to learn that he had only just turned forty. 'Clean living, the love of a good woman and a bottle of vodka a day,' was his recipe for looking so handsome, he quipped. Alex almost believed him.

The next day, Friday 9th February, saw the Finnish troops woken by the usual dawn chorus of an artillery barrage from the Russians. It began just before six o'clock and continued for nearly two hours. In truth, Alex was scared witless! Although having been close to the frontline on several occasions in the past few months, he had not been in the thick of it and close enough to witness such comprehensive pounding. Lieutenant

Lundberg had fetched Alex just before the bombardment began and taken him to his dugout; he appeared not to be unduly worried, and Alex wondered how many of these barrages he had already endured.

'We shall consider ourselves extremely unlucky if one of their shells finds us,' he said to Alex as they were taking cover. 'They make a lot of noise but seldom hit anything! All the time you can hear them, they say you will not get hit – but you do not hear the one that has your name on it!'

'Let us all pray that today is not the day when they learn how to shoot straight!' Alex commented, sardonically.

'If that day is upon us, I doubt that prayers will help much,' the lieutenant grinned. 'When this is over, Major Ahonen said it would be better if you return to Viipuri, so I will get you onto a truck going back there. When you write your piece, be kind to us. It may be of comfort to our families.' It was the first time that Alex had witnessed any doubt that the Finnish forces would prevail.

'Of course,' was all that Alex could think of to say.

When the shelling had ended, and the lieutenant was sure that an attack was not following it, he and Alex scampered back to the track, where several lorries were having canvass camouflage covers removed, ready to load with any dead and wounded going back to Viipuri. It transpired that there were few because the Russian aiming had been particularly poor that day. As the soldiers removed the truck's camouflage, a brace of Polikarpov fighter planes swooped out of the sky and strafed the lorries – everybody dived for cover as they came back for a second bite at the cherry, but they completely missed all of the trucks and troops. When the planes had flown away, Lundberg propelled Alex towards one of the waiting Maavoimat trucks, waving farewell as he did so. Alex clambered into the cab and smiled at the driver, who looked at him without any expression at all.

The drive back was almost entirely without conversation, apart from the occasional *'Perkele!'* from the driver when he hit a bump in the road and the moans from the injured soldiers in the back of the truck. Alex used the time to reflect on his experience, and he found that he was much in awe of the sheer determination of the Finnish soldier. Many had been stationed at the front for several weeks and were not only filthy but had signs of disease – but still, they fought tenaciously. On the whole, Alex was quite gratified when the lorry pulled up outside the hotel. Even though he did not usually indulge, Alex spent much of the evening in the sauna trying to get the stench of warfare out of his pores, and he had only experienced one day at the front.

The next day, Alex and the other correspondents were woken at 5.30am by a harassed-looking hotel manager who told them that they were to be evacuated to Helsinki immediately and that the army was organising transport – they had half an hour to get ready. Bleary-eyed and cold, the journalists gathered outside the hotel in the darkness of that Saturday, and shortly two Volvo military buses, with peculiar stoves fitted to the rear to generate wood gas – because petroleum was in such short supply – arrived to collect the correspondents.

Apart from a slight smell from the conversion units, the buses were surprisingly comfortable and warm. It was not long before Alex, and several other passengers had fallen asleep. After a few hours, the buses arrived at Lappeenranta railway station, where a train was waiting to take Alex and the other correspondents back to Helsinki. When they disembarked from the bus, they could hear the shelling in the distance, and Alex wondered whether today would be the day that the Russians would attack. The journalists climbed aboard the train and were quickly on their way back to the capital – most were glad to be heading for the relative safety of Helsinki.

It is always challenging to try and ascertain the strength of a foe when you are living in the opposing territory, but Alex spent the day talking to various contacts to try and understand what exactly Finland was facing. It was common knowledge in Helsinki that the Soviet 7th Army, commanded by General Kirill Mereskov, had been strengthened by seasoned regular troops as opposed to the conscripted soldiers that had previously made up the army. There were strong rumours that Stalin had ordered the reorganisation of the 7th Army and had reinforced it with about one thousand light and heavy tanks. A 200mm rail-mounted gun was brought up specifically to bombard Viipuri from a position that was unreachable by any of the Finnish artillery.

Despite the optimism of just about everybody in the Finnish government or military that the Mannerheim Line was impregnable, the collective view of most military attachés was that if the Russians attacked quickly, they could achieve a breakthrough. If, however, they waited a few weeks until the March thaw set in, then the odds would swing dramatically in Finland's favour mainly because the area around Viipuri was marshland, and if it started to thaw, the attackers would find it impossible to fight their way through the swampy terrain. It was inconceivable that the Russians would not be aware of this fact, and the consensus was that the Soviet forces would begin their assault within the next seven days.

*

Rumours that the Russians had begun their attack in several places along the Mannerheim Line, but that the Finnish troops were containing them, hit Helsinki like a hammer blow on Sunday 11th February. Alex started to write a piece for *Svenska Posten* of his time at the front and included such facts as most Finns still having bolt-action rifles, while captured weaponry from the Russian side suggested that they had been re-equipped with semi-automatic rifles. Alex's encoded piece highlighted the futility of resistance, saying it would only be a matter of time before the Finnish opposition would crumple. Alex predicted that once there was a breach of the Mannerheim Line, Russian troops could be in Helsinki within seven days. He had just finished his report and was getting ready to go to the post office to send it to Stockholm when the air-raid sirens sounded. The weather had been too bad recently for the Soviet bombers to leave their Estonian bases, but clear skies meant that Helsinki was due another battering.

Remembering that government offices closed during a raid, Alex went down into the public shelter on Heikinkatu, where he met Felix Nyström and Jaana, holding hands and looking very much in love.

'Hello, you two,' Alex greeted them.

'Alex!' Felix exclaimed, jumping up and embracing him. 'You are back! When did you return? How was Viipuri?' The questions came thick and fast.

Alex sat with them and recanted his tale of life on the Mannerheim Line, and even though he was a seasoned and somewhat cynical journalist, Felix was spellbound. When Alex had finished, Felix whistled tunelessly through his teeth, as if in wonderment.

With time, it transpired that the Russian plan was only partially successful. The frontal assault on the Mannerheim Line was just one of the elements of a concerted attack that was calculated to eradicate Finnish opposition. The whole plan involved reinforcements for the besieged Soviet 18th Division between Syskyjärvi and Ruokojärvi, around the northern shores of Lake Ladoga, that would have allowed the Russians to seize the north-south railway between Viipuri and Kajaani, enabling them to swoop down behind the Finnish troops defending the Mannerheim Line, effectively cutting off their retreat. This part of the plan failed as the Finnish forces held back the Russian advance so that when the Mannerheim Line was breached, the Finnish troops were able to withdraw. Moreover, having checked the Russian progress in the north, the Finns counter-attacked, forcing the Russian forces to retreat. The Battle of Ladoga resulted in massive Russian losses and the cutting of some of their supply chains to the divisions in the north. However, had the Finns not committed so many troops to Lake Ladoga, it is possible that the Mannerheim Line would have held and Finland would not have been forced to negotiate peace.

XIV

The second Battle of Summa was to prove the turning point of the war. In all, from when it started on 1st February with consistent shelling of the Mannerheim Line, it took a further twelve days before a minor breach occurred near the village of Lähde some 10 kilometres to the east, which led to the collapse of the Finnish defences.

It came as a shock to Alex when he realised that he had visited the front only a few days before the Russian troops burst through, and it was not until Tuesday 13th February that Alex understood that he must have been one of the last correspondents to have been on the frontline. He thought about Major Ahonen and Lieutenant Lundberg and wondered what had become of them. The piece that he filed with *Svenska Posten* was a poignant tale of the great courage of the Finns fighting in that area.

The article was able to provide further detail of the Russian tactics. The shelling of the concrete fortifications along the Mannerheim Line was relentless to such an extent that many had been unearthed and were lying at dangerously acute angles to the ground, made it difficult for the soldiers within that had survived to bring any of their artillery to bear on the Soviet forces when they attacked. It told of Russian soldiers of the 49th, 100th and 103rd divisions who were able to cross No Man's Land with the aid of heavily armoured sledges drawn by the advancing tanks and how persistently they fought the Finnish troops – but still, the line held, and the Russians could not force a breakthrough. In many cases, the fighting was hand-to-hand using bayonets and puukkos as the Finnish ammunition became spent. Alex wrote of how the Finns fought valiantly, but the main breach eventually came near the village of Summa when, despite overwhelming odds, the Russian troops forced their way through a defensive line of Finnish reservists, causing the Finns to retreat. Once through, the Russians poured through the breach with every soldier and tank that they could muster.

Alex portrayed in the most graphic of detail everything that he had gained from talking with a captain whose commanders had ordered his reluctant evacuation with his wounded troops. He was not physically injured, but when Alex met him, his eyes stared manically, and he almost stuttered every second word. The captain's mind had gone completely, but he was still able to tell Alex of how the Finns had not given up easily and had hurled their crack regiment into the sector to try and seal the breach. Of how over the next two days, this elite cavalry regiment had fought heroically before being almost wiped out. Even despite the courageous efforts of the Finnish army, on 15th February, Mannerheim ordered a general retreat. Alex explained that the only area where the line held was at Taipale on the eastern end of the Mannerheim Line at Lake Ladoga, but the resistance there was to little avail as the breach at Summa meant that the troops, had they not withdrawn, would have become cut off and surrounded.

Many of his fellow correspondents wrote of the foolhardiness of Mannerheim in committing so many troops to certain death, defending a hopeless position; some even brought out the old soubriquet *"Pyöveli Mannerheim"* – Mannerheim the Executioner – that he had acquired in the War of Independence. But Alex's writings were always balanced and extremely fair to the courage of the Finns and their leaders. Alex understood that Mannerheim needed to buy time to allow the Finnish government to sue for peace. Had he not sacrificed so many soldiers, the Russians would have swarmed through and been in Helsinki in less than a week, forcing the capitulation of the proud nation.

The Russian advance was held up by the defending Finnish army and the Soviet marshal, Timoshenko, decided to create a pincer movement by attacking a narrow strip of land at the extreme western side of the isthmus, near the town of Äyräpää. It was here that Alex learned that Major Ville Koskinen had lost his life fighting a rearguard action as the Finnish troops tactically withdrew when faced with many thousands of Soviet troops.

Alex only saw Simon Potts once during this period, and that was to say farewell. Simon, along with other unessential members of the British Legation, was being shipped out. His role had been that of support to Churchill's offer of aid to a beleaguered country, but with Finland trying to reach a compromise with Stalin, the British prime minister certainly did not want any supplied British weaponry to fall into the hands of the enemy, so the British government had suspended the promised support. Consequently, Simon was going back to his old role in the embassy in Stockholm, but before he left, he arranged a meeting with Alex.

'Be careful, old friend,' Simon cautioned when they met at a bar on the Esplanade in Helsinki. 'If the Finns get the peace that they want, the best we can hope for is that they retain their neutrality in the region, but if Stalin pushes for more, then Finland could again become a puppet state of Soviet Russia. That could make staying here problematic, and we should have to consider pulling you out.'

'Dear Simon,' Alex responded, 'it has always been my intention to take good care of myself! Before I signed up for this lark, I made a pact with myself that history would not repeat itself, and that I was going to be very much part of my child's life. Besides, for you, this is a great opportunity. You must surely be due some leave, and that might just be enough incentive for you to eventually make an honest woman of Cordelia! I'm just sorry that I will not be available to be your best man. If you see them, give my love to Teddy and Mamma and tell them that I am thinking of them constantly.'

'I will,' promised Simon, although both realised it was a "piecrust" promise – one easily made and just as easily broken!

*

Major Ville Koskinen's corpse was brought out of the battlefield on a sledge dragged by one of his men, and his body was sent to his family in Hämeenlinna for burial. Alex attended the funeral at the starkly simple yet delightful Hämeenlinnan Kirkko – Hämeenlinna Church. The coffin, covered with the Finnish flag, was brought into church on the shoulders of six surviving soldiers from Major Koskinen's unit, and the service was minimal, but even so, it was moving. Alex was surprised that the major's father was a Lutheran priest, and he conducted the service with dignity, although his voice caught as he reminisced about his son, who had been full of life. Ville Koskinen's wife, Soili, and his two young sons, Valtteri and Henrik, were there and they almost, though not entirely, succeeded in not showing any emotion.

As the mourners left the church, the major's father asked who Alex was.

'My name is Alex Carlsson, and I met your son last year. I liked him very much,' was all that Alex could think of to say, but added, 'I am so very sorry for your loss.'

'I know your name,' Ville's father said, and then the floodgates burst as the man understood who Alex was, and he flung his arms around Alex in an entirely unexpected display of emotion. When he had recovered his composure, wiping away the tears, Ville's father said, 'I know that you saved my son last year. He told us all about it when he was recuperating. Please allow me to introduce you to my wife and his family.'

'Sir,' Alex said gently, 'I came as a mark of respect to your son, not to intrude on this sad time for his family.'

'Please,' Ville's father said, 'it would not be an intrusion, it would be a pleasure. My daughter-in-law is with child, and that is a gift that would not exist, had you not saved my son. We owe you so much, and so does Ville. Your courage gave us more time with him.'

He took Alex by the elbow and steered him towards the waiting family. Having introduced Alex, Ville's wife instinctively touched her abdomen and smiled at Alex before gently reaching up and kissing him tenderly on the cheek. She plainly said, '*Kiittos!* – Thank you.

Ville's family asked Alex to stay and eat with them, but he felt that he had already intruded sufficiently on their grief, and so kindly declined the offer. They formally exchanged contact details with promises to write, although Alex doubted that either would, and he made his way back to the train station to catch the next train back to Helsinki.

*

On his return to Helsinki, Alex learned from Felix Nyström that the army had evacuated one of the final bastions of Finnish resistance on the Karelian Isthmus, the impressive fort at Koivisto. The remaining troops had removed the great 280mm guns from the fort and had transported them over the pack ice on huge sledges, rather than let them fall into Russian hands. So heavy were these guns that the ice cracked, and it was only by sheer luck that the troops did not find themselves sailing down the Baltic on sheets of ice.

The ultimate strategic plan, Alex learned from Jarno, when Alex caught up with him for a drink, was for Finnish troops to hold the Russian forces for as long as possible. Staunching the advance would enable a new defence line to be built down the Vuoksi Valley towards Imatra and culminating at the Gulf of Viipuri near Juustila. It was a last-ditch attempt to halt the Russian troops and prevent a mass invasion of the country while the politicians negotiated peace. The more time that the Finns could buy through slowing the Russian advance, the more prolonged negotiations could continue, but nobody was under any illusion that in the event of the line breaking, the Russians would demand Finland's unconditional submission.

Jarno went on to explain, 'The problem is that our troops are tired, even those we are bringing in from other parts of the country. The Russians are fresh and very well- trained seasoned troops, not like those we faced previously. But we must hold out until the thaw. It is our only hope.'

Alex was most concerned that the foundations of Finnish military strategy depended on the weather changing and slowing down the Russian advance. When he encoded these facts in his regular column for *Svenska Posten*, he could well imagine the disbelief of his commanders back in London.

Eventually, the grapevine was proven correct, and Jarno confirmed that General Wallenius had been appointed to command the Finnish forces on the Karelian Isthmus. It seemed that there was a strong belief that as he had managed to snatch victory from the jaws of defeat in the north, Wallenius could achieve the same miracle on the isthmus.

*

Alex had been spot-on in his prediction about his superiors in London reading his report; they had done so with wholesale astonishment! Lieutenant Colonel Llewelyn burst into Commander Jeffers's office in Broadway Buildings and demanded to know whether Alex Carlton had taken leave of his senses.

'His latest report,' Llewelyn said, 'seems to suggest that the Finns are relying on divine intervention to save their country!'

'There is a precedent in that part of the world,' the commander said equably and, seeing the querulous look on Llewelyn's face, explained, '1812? Napoleon's defeat in Russia? After Moscow, it was the Russian winter that saved Tsar Alexander – maybe the Finnish spring can save Finland from the Russians?'

'Surely,' Llewelyn continued, 'this new defensive line is only to be a delaying tactic while the Finns regroup their army behind the central lakes? That would force the Russians into the open and give the Finns a chance of fighting the decisive battle on their terms?'

Commander Jeffers was sceptical, and taking a red Chinagraph pencil, he also grabbed a detailed map of Finland. 'So you are saying that if the Finns pulled back and defended a line from, say,' he drew on the map, 'Nurmes in the north to Joensuu in the south and perhaps Joensuu in the east to Varkaus in the west or even Jyväskylä, then that would be better?'

'Strategically, it would be far more defensible,' Llewelyn maintained.

'But it would mean the loss of the capital, Helsinki, and much of the industrial south of the country. Do you seriously think that the Finns would even consider this?' Jeffers was unconvinced.

'No, probably not,' Llewelyn responded resignedly, 'but tactically, it is most likely their best hope. The trouble with naming defensive positions after military commanders is that they get personal, almost as if the line-breaking spells the beginning of the end to hostilities! The breaching of the Hindenburg Line in September 1918 was the beginning of the end of the German defence. I know the war dragged on for a couple more months, but breaking the line was so psychologically defeating to Germany, they capitulated. That and the almost public arguments between von Hindenburg and Ludendorff.

'Mannerheim is sufficiently egotistical that I am sure he will want this new defensive line in the south to hold and protect the capital, but I doubt it will. He will see it almost like the second Mannerheim Line!'

'Some would agree,' Commander Jeffers ventured. 'It would be like us drawing a line from Norfolk to Bristol and falling back to defend Birmingham or Manchester!'

'Precisely!' the colonel said in an unguarded moment, and when the penny dropped, Commander Jeffers was shocked.

'You mean,' he sought clarification, 'if Germany invaded England, we could abandon London and the south and retreat to the north?'

'I'm not saying that it would happen, but in such cases, any option is on the table!'

'Good God!' exclaimed Jeffers. 'I suppose we would call it the "Churchill Line", or something equally as absurd!'

'Well,' Llewelyn continued, 'currently GHQ is proposing naming them after colours; green, blue, red, etc. But I am sure that if they thought that renaming them after an inspirational leader was beneficial, they would do so in a trice!'

'Interestingly, it seems Wallenius has been brought in to take over from Österman on the Isthmus,' Jeffers suggested. 'It is just possible that Mannerheim has no stomach for surrendering the south of the country. Wallenius does have a track record of success!'

'Yes,' Llewelyn agreed, 'let us hope that it pays off! In any event, young Carlton is going to be kept very busy trying to make sense of what the Finns are up to!'

'And not forgetting Ryti's peace negotiations. That might bring the whole matter to a close if Paasikivi can reach a compromise with the Soviets that does not involve unconditional surrender.'

'Get a message to Carlton,' Llewelyn instructed, 'and tell him to keep his ear to the ground and a weather eye on developments. We need to understand their intentions.'

Jeffers agreed, even though he winced at the mixed metaphor!

XV

Alex's instructions came in the form of a telegram from his editor at *Svenska Posten*, Per Aslund, praising his work and stating that he should *"use his best endeavours to continue providing readers with such insightful narratives of developments in Finland, especially of any peace negotiations."*

As February drew to an end, Alex was amazed at the continued optimism of the propaganda that was being generated by the Finnish government's press liaison department. Every briefing told of victories that Finnish troops were inflicting on the Russian forces, aircraft being destroyed on the ground by the Finnish air force, using the bombers that had arrived from Britain, the significant number of tanks that the Finns had wrecked, the vast quantity of Russian soldiers left dead on the battlefield after each resisted attack. None of the foreign correspondents believed a word of it and most had independent sources in various departments of the Finnish government who were telling them something closer to the truth. Alex's primary source, Jarno, had become increasingly more morose over the past few days, and Alex knew that things were not going well for the Finns.

Alex regularly met Jarno at a bar in Annankatu, only a few steps from his office at the Ministry of Defence in the Okhrana House at Korkeavuorenkatu, which some would have argued was a bit too close to where the man worked to be a secure meeting point. Caution, however, seemed to have been thrown to the wind in these dark days as Alex learned the increasing real plight of the Finnish forces. Chronic lack of ammunition, exhaustion of the Finnish troops, training being curtailed to a minimum to get fresh troops to the frontline. It all spelt desperation. He learned that the Russian forces were relentlessly keeping up the pressure on the centre and the left-hand side of the second Mannerheim Line and that although they were losing many hundreds of soldiers, fresh well-trained troops were being brought up to replace them. Wallenius had identified a threat coming over the pack ice in the Gulf of Viipuri and had strengthened coastal fortifications along a line from Uuras south-west of Viipuri to Virolahti to prevent an outflanking attack over the sea, where the ice was still as much as 3.5 metres thick and well able to withstand the weight of a light tank. The Finns also increased their fortifications on the islands of the archipelago.

At the same time, Russian troops were trying to breach the Finnish lines north of Lake Ladoga, and still, the Finns held the position. So the constant probing actions at various points along the entire second Mannerheim Line meant that the depleted Finnish forces were too thinly spread, and although the line was holding, Jarno warned that it was unlikely to resist for much longer. If only the much-promised Anglo-French relief force arrived, the Finns would be able to hold out for longer.

Alex knew this was a forlorn hope. Sweden and Norway were still maintaining strict neutrality and refusing to allow the force to cross their lands, even though it was mobilised and was eagerly awaiting deployment from their Scottish training grounds. The relief even had an operational name allocated to it: *Operation Avon Head*. The best that Sweden was allowing was that "volunteers", who were travelling independently and not part of an organised unit, could cross their territory, and by the end of the war, over five hundred of these "volunteers" had done so.

Felix, in the meantime, seemed to have been almost conspicuous by his absence. When Alex eventually tracked down his friend in the bar of the Hotel Kämp, he asked what ailed the Swede.

'It was as I thought,' he began morosely, 'I have been served with divorce papers, and she says that she intends keeping our house for the kids. I imagine her new boyfriend will be moving into the house we had bought together. I suppose I asked for it, but it is still hard to swallow, and I really don't know what to do. Should I try to win her back? Do you think there is hope?'

To say that Alex's sympathy was in short supply would not be an understatement. 'You could always thank her and make an honest woman of Jaana,' he suggested. 'I thought you said your marriage was all washed up, anyway. Look at it as a new beginning.'

'Do you think so?' Felix asked with an air of desperation. 'Do you think Jaana would be interested in an old newspaper hack?'

'Only you can answer that question,' Alex told him, 'but from what I can see, she seems smitten with you. Whether that is the basis of a good relationship is anybody's guess, but rather than wallow in your self-pity, why not ask her if she wants something more permanent?'

'You are right!' Felix agreed. 'I will speak to her tomorrow. Now, old friend, let me buy you a drink.'

*

The next day was Thursday 6th March and rumours were starting to filter through to Helsinki that the Russians had attacked the coastal defences with such force that Wallenius's troops were having difficulty holding them at bay. In a daring move, the Russians had crossed vast distances of ice and attacked the very extremity of Wallenius's line at the coastal village of Virolahti. They had suffered huge losses, but it showed that Soviet tactics had changed and that more troops had to be deployed to strengthen the coastal defences. At the same time, the Russians had crossed to and attacked the islands of Suursaari and Haapasaari, both of which were defended well by the Finnish troops stationed on the islands, with substantial Russian casualties, but it had the desired effect of unnerving the Finnish general staff.

At an impromptu meeting with Jarno on Saturday, Alex was amazed when he was told, 'It seems as though Wallenius's luck has run out. The

Russians have secured positions on the islands in the Gulf of Viipuri and are shelling our coastal defences on the mainland. Russian bombers are constantly bombing our positions, and although the Finnish Air Force is attacking Russian positions, they are too strong.'

'What's to be done?' Alex asked.

'God only knows,' was the reply. 'If only the bloody Swedes and Norwegians had let the British and French through.' Then realising that Alex was working for a Swedish newspaper, added, 'I am sorry for being angry with your countrymen, and I know you have done much to support our cause, but I think Sweden and Norway have abandoned Finland to satiate the hunger of the Russian bear!'

Alex believed him. Sweden and Norway had acted in their own self-interest in the hope that neither would get dragged into a war with Russia, or, more worryingly, with Russia's ally, Germany.

General Wallenius had openly complained about the role of commander of the coastal defences, saying it was a "poisoned chalice" and guaranteed to fail, plus he had taken to drinking heavily, and this gave Mannerheim the excuse to relieve the general of his command and to replace him with General Lennart Oesch. Shortly afterwards, the general staff had dishonourably discharged General Wallenius from the army and rescinded his rank, removing his name from the army list to add to the snub. When Alex next saw Wallenius, he was holding court in the Writers' Room at the Hotel Kämp and telling anybody prepared to listen that Mannerheim had betrayed him by not supporting the coastal defences with enough troops and artillery – he was thoroughly drunk, and Alex felt a small measure of pity for the man whose failure had cost him dearly!

Two nights later, the heavy shore batteries on the defensive island of Suomenlinna opened up after the Russians landed aeroplanes on the ice outside Helsinki Harbour. This one act alone led to the mobilisation of reserve civil guard to protect the capital – troops that might otherwise have reinforced the Mannerheim Line. Helsinki was not the only place where such testing incursions occurred; Kotka also received unwelcome attention from the Soviet. The Russian plan, if that is what it was, was masterful, as it significantly reduced the troops available for frontline duty.

*

Peace negotiations began in earnest on 7th March 1940. A Swedish-registered aeroplane landed at Moscow's Khodynka Aerodrome carrying a Finnish delegation of the Prime Minister, Risto Ryti, accompanied by the Finnish special envoy, Juho Kusti Paasikivi, a close confidant of Field-Marshal Mannerheim, General Rudolf Walden, and an academic expert in Karelian history and former government minister, Professor Väinö Voionmaa.

The fact that Stalin was prepared to negotiate with the Finnish prime minister was a mark of acceptance that had begun earlier in the year when the Russian envoy in Sweden had indicated that the Soviets might entertain an approach from Ryti's administration to negotiate. Previously, the only government that Stalin recognised was that of the communist puppet, Otto Ville Kuusinen and the Finnish Democratic Republic.

It was soon apparent that Stalin was keen to rid himself of the Russo-Finnish war. This small and relatively insignificant country had laid waste to vast numbers of the Soviet military. It had become a massive embarrassment to the Soviet leader, and he had long given up on the original hope of establishing communism in Finland – now, it was all about borders and territory. Moreover, it had been clear right from the start that Finland did not want to prolong a war with Russia. Ever since Risto Ryti was appointed prime minister, he had been open about seeking peace with Moscow, but even the intervention of the United States of America and Sweden had not convinced Stalin. An open invitation to discuss terms, sent by radio broadcast during December 1939 from the Finnish Foreign Minister, Väinö Tanner, to Vyacheslav Molotov, his counterpart in Moscow, still failed to persuade Stalin to reach an accommodation.

In the early days of the war, Stalin had believed Finland was a minor inconvenience that could be crushed by the might of the Soviet military

– a quick military victory was feasible. World opinion nevertheless sided with Finland – after all, they had not sought the war and were merely defending their sovereign state against the mightier aggressor.

Even as negotiations for peace were occurring, Alex tuned into Russian radio to hear Molotov reiterating that the Soviet-Finnish talks had started on 12th October 1939. The reasonable request of the Soviet government, as repeatedly stated by letter, had been to ensure the security of Leningrad and to safeguard the strategic position of Soviet Russia in the Baltic and the Arctic without in any way impinging upon the sovereignty of Finland. But President Aimo Cajander had irrationally refused to discuss any compromise.

The Molotov report continued that even though Russia had modified its position and some of the requests made to the Finnish government, they refused to move an inch. It had all come to a head when on 26th November 1939, a confrontation occurred in which Finnish artillery fired on Russian troops, which (naturally) Russia had to take as an act of belligerence. The Finns rejected the rational pleas of the Russian government for the withdrawal of the Finnish forces to an agreed distance from the Soviet-Finnish border. Over the next few days, other clashes ensued until finally, on 28th November 1939, the Russian government was forced to go back on the 1932 Soviet-Finnish Non-Aggression Pact.

Consequently, and very reluctantly, at midnight on the 29th November 1939, in a radio broadcast to the Soviet peoples, Molotov had himself confirmed the breakdown of diplomatic relations with Finland, with hostilities breaking out between the two countries on 1st December 1939.

Even as late as February 1940, the Soviets had sought peace by asking the British government to act as intermediaries, and Ivan Maisky, the Soviet Envoy in London, was surprised when Chamberlain refused his appeals. The Russians had tried right until the last minute to secure peace by using their diplomatic mission in Sweden to entreat the Swedish government to intervene. Now the new Finnish prime minister, Risto Ryti, had come to Moscow to beg for peace from a generous and forgiving Soviet Russia.

It was masterful propaganda and clearly intended not just for the Russian masses, but also for those in Finland who, illegally, listened to Radio Moscow. It did, however, conveniently ignore the bombing of Helsinki on 30th November 1939, the day that Alex had arrived in the capital, and the Finnish request for a truce that Alex knew was delivered to the Russians on 5th March 1940 by the Swedish government, which was refused point-blank.

Alex and the other correspondents learned that the Finnish delegation had negotiated peace, in a hastily convened press conference held at the Finnish Ministry of Information on Tuesday, 12th March 1940 and that a ceasefire would exist from 11.00am the following day.

It was over.

XVI

The news of Finland's surrender reached London through the Foreign Office channels, and it was not long before there were loudly voiced opinions from all levels of government. One of the loudest was, predictably, that of the First Lord of the Admiralty, Winston Churchill, who was critical of just about everyone involved. He criticised Lord Halifax, the Foreign Secretary, who had advised the prime minister, Neville Chamberlain, against precipitous action that may have led Britain into a war with Russia. He was derisory of Per Albin Hansson, the Swedish prime minister and Johan Nygaardsvold, the Norwegian prime minister, for not having given the support to Finland that the Copenhagen communique of 19th September 1939 and subsequent Heads of State Conference in October 1939, promised. In fact, hardly anyone who had even the remotest of connections with the Finnish situation escaped his wrath – except, of course, his own association through the Secret Service.

Colonel Llewelyn hastily organised a meeting of his departmental heads to discuss the developments, and Commander Jeffers, accompanied by Daphne Devine wearing the additional stripe denoting her recent promotion to the rank of Second Officer, attended. The meeting wavered between recommending full support for the Finns in rebuilding their country in the aftermath of the war, to doing nothing and not risking any hostility from Soviet Russia. At one point, Jeffers became concerned that

Llewelyn was about to divulge the existence of an asset in Finland, but after a discreet cough and slight shake of the head, the colonel took the hint and steered the conversation to safer ground. The meeting eventually came to the conclusion that Military Intelligence should await further details and developments before committing to a recommended course of action. It was the traditional British compromise of kicking the ball into the long grass!

As the meeting broke up, Colonel Llewelyn asked Commander Jeffers to wait behind and when they were alone, asked why he had been reluctant to reveal Alex Carlton's role in Finland.

'Lieutenant Carlton's operation in Finland was never officially sanctioned. It was at the whim of the First Lord of the Admiralty, who has always felt that Finland could hold the key in the Baltic. To reveal his existence now might compromise his future value to the department. I can imagine that Churchill will want Carlton to remain *in situ*, feeding back information in the post-war period, so that he can continue lobbying for aid, but until the First Lord has been consulted and appraised of the situation, I felt it better to keep this operation under our hat. The First Lord has ordered a meeting as soon as Carlton's next report is at hand.'

'Why was I not appraised that Carlton's operation was clandestine?' Llewelyn asked tetchily.

'I was unaware that you did not know. I would have thought that Brigadier Swann had briefed you upon handover. It is one of the reasons why Carlton holds a naval rank, rather than in the army. The fact is that the First Lord places the highest store on good intelligence and I am aware that there are other operations that he has sanctioned that are, shall we say, under a cloak of ambiguity – but as far as I am aware, Carlton is the only one in MI2.'

'That bloody man is impossible!' Llewelyn cursed. 'He seems to run the Admiralty like his own personal fiefdom. He plays fast and loose with government funding and seems to regard authority and the natural order of things with disdain.'

'Yes,' agreed Jeffers, 'but he is awfully effective and frightfully well informed, and that gives him the edge when arguing for a particular course of action. And, let's face it, he is seldom wrong – that's what makes him so formidable.'

'As may be, but the fact remains that we have an operative working in a war zone that nobody has officially sanctioned and who does not seem to even exist outside the knowledge of a very few people.'

'Oh, he exists, all right,' Commander Jeffers explained. 'He is on the navy list and shows as being attached to Naval Intelligence. We are not going to make the same mistake as the Baker Street Irregulars made by running "ghosts". There is a slight muddying of the waters surrounding precisely what he does for Naval Intelligence, but the total success of any secret service is that it must remain secret to be effective.'

Changing tack, Llewelyn asked Daphne Devine, 'Did you know about this?'

'Yes, sir,' she replied, 'when I took over from Lieutenant Potts, he fully briefed me.'

'I see,' the colonel stated brusquely.

'The fact remains that until we know what is to happen with Lieutenant Carlton, his existence in his current role should remain obscure,' Jeffers emphasised.

'I suppose we have little choice,' Llewelyn commented, 'but I want to be fully briefed about his activities, preferably before Churchill knows.'

'Of course,' Commander Jeffers agreed, adding, 'and congratulations on your promotion.'

'What?' Llewelyn was surprised. 'I didn't think that was common knowledge yet. It certainly has not been published in the *Gazette*.'

'I know,' Jeffers responded with a smile, 'but that's what having a good intelligence network is all about, don't you agree? I suppose I shall have to start calling you "sir" now.'

'Yes, I suppose you will,' Llewelyn responded, 'and thank you.'

*

Alex's report on the peace negotiations arrived on Commander Jeffers's desk the following morning. Peace had forced Finland to surrender more land than they had lost in the war, which included nearly all of Finnish Karelia, including Viipuri, Käkisalmi, Sortavala and Suojärvi and the whole of Viipuri Bay with its islands. The Finns also ceded a part of the Salla area, the Finnish part of the Kalastajansaarento Peninsula in the Barents Sea, and in the Gulf of Finland the islands of Suursaari, Tytärsaari, Lavansaari, Peninsaari and Seiskari. Lastly, the lease of the Hanko Peninsula to Soviet Russia for use as a naval base for thirty years, against a paltry payment of eight million markkas per annum, was particularly hard for the Finns to accept; the Russians added the Enso industrial area to the ceded regions at a later date. Apart from land concessions, Finland also had to surrender more than seventy-five railway locomotives, two thousand railway carriages, and many cars, trucks and ships. It was a hard price to pay and considerably more than the Russians had demanded before the war.

Commander Jeffers had 2/O Daphne Devine type the report, and he made an immediate appointment to see the First Lord of the Admiralty, for later that same day. He instructed that a copy of the report be sent through internal mail to Colonel Llewelyn, as a matter of priority, openly acknowledging that the statement had been despatched to the colonel in advance of Jeffers's briefing of the First Lord, thereby complying with the spirit of Llewelyn's instructions, if not the letter.

To say that Commander Jeffers was looking forward to his meeting with the First Lord of the Admiralty would be a considerable overstatement. Breaking any bad news to Churchill needed a skill that Jeffers was unsure he had quite honed to perfection. When the commander handed Alex's report to Winston Churchill, a scowl deepened over the First Lord's brow; a grumbling emanated from the man's inner being that grew louder the more he read. In the end, a calmness settled on his demeanour, and he said quietly, 'Your boy, Carlton, has done well.'

'Yes, sir,' Jeffers responded.

'His reports have made for good reading, and he has made some useful contacts in Finland that may be beneficial to us in the future.'

'Yes, sir,' Jeffers repeated.

'But it has been to no avail,' Churchill glowered.

'Sir?' Jeffers asked for clarification.

'We had a golden opportunity to do some good in a country fighting the same odds that we are facing, and all the time, Chamberlain, at Halifax's behest, dragged his heels. Helping Finland to beat Stalin back would have sent a clear message to Hitler that Britain is a force to be reckoned with!'

'But surely it was the Swedes' and Norwegians' refusal to allow troops through their countries that stymied the plan?' Jeffers asked. 'Didn't Norway threaten to sink our ships if we tried to land a force for Finland?'

'Words, Jeffers, words,' explained Churchill. 'Sir Victor Mallett, our esteemed Envoy Extraordinary and Minister Plenipotentiary to the King of Sweden, was hampered by being required not to ask too loudly! The British government squeaked like a mouse – it did not roar like a lion!'

'I see,' Jeffers responded cautiously.

'Operation Avon Head would have given the Finns the time it took for the thaw to set in and then Stalin would have been stuck on the wrong side of a quagmire and on a group of islands, from where the Finnish navy could have polished them off. Chamberlain and Halifax between them have made a nonsense of any pledges that we have made to Sweden and Norway; they have turned our government into liars!'

The crescendo of rage had been seething under the surface of the First Lord, and it eventually burst in a roar of exasperation that quite took Commander Jeffers by surprise. Anybody who knew Churchill was aware of his mood swings and his petulance if he did not achieve what he wanted, and now Jeffers was experiencing the uncontrollable rage from which few survived. "Black Dog" is what senior naval officers called these rages, and this dog was as black as they come!

When tranquillity returned, Jeffers asked what the plans for Alex were and whether his assignment was over.

'Over?' Churchill asked, almost distantly. 'Carlton has to stay on the ground; we need him to build bridges. We need to convince the Finns that Britain has not deserted them, or God only knows, Germany will. They have lost the war. We must help them win the peace.'

'It might be useful, sir,' Jeffers ventured, 'if you explained your thinking to Colonel Llewelyn. He is starting to dig around and unearth a few skeletons, like the semi-official nature of Carlton's operation.'

'I will see what we can do,' Churchill said enigmatically, 'but if he rocks too many boats, we may have to consider his continued future in intelligence.'

The meeting concluded, and Jeffers returned to Broadway Buildings, wholly unsure whether he had released a malign genie from the bottle, or not.

*

The membership of the "Torni Drinkers' Club" had much depleted in the aftermath of the signing of the peace treaty. Alex remained, along with Felix Nyström and Leona Guichard of *Le Nationaliste* in Canada, but of the others, most had already left. The same was the case at the other central journalist hotel, the Kämp, where only a smattering of correspondents remained. One was Gunther Weiß of *Völkischer Beobachter*, the official newspaper of the Nazi party in Germany. Gunther was an amiable old-style newspaperman who had survived the transition from the old *Vossische Zeitung* when it was shut down in 1934. His liberal roots were tolerated by Goebbels's propaganda ministry because much of what he wrote was staunchly supportive of the greater Germany, but his liberalism had earned him banishment to a journalistic backwater in Helsinki – until the war came. Up until the signing of the peace accord, Weiß wrote strongly advocating that Germany should not abandon Finland, whom it had significantly helped during the War of Independence. Since the armistice, his writings strongly argued that Germany should help Finland rebuild its infrastructure and economy. He was a close confidant of Kurt Wallenius, and Alex had met Weiß on several occasions.

Alex quickly understood that Finland was soon to be the subject of a post-war race over who should play the most significant role in helping to rebuild the country; Germany, Sweden or Britain. Both Germany and Britain were ambivalent over any part that the Swedes undertook, but there was to be intense competition between each other.

The telegram to return to Stockholm for a briefing was waiting for Alex when he returned to the Hotel Torni shortly after a heavy afternoon of drinking and reminiscing, in the company of Wallenius and Weiß. More intriguing was a second telegram from the editor-in-chief of *Svenska Dagbladet*, inviting him to discuss a matter that could be "mutually advantageous". Alex had no idea what this matter could be, principally as *Svenska Dagbladet* was the newspaper for whom Felix wrote.

Alex tried to find Felix to ask him, but Felix seemed to have disappeared. Nobody had seen him for a couple of days, and Alex concluded that he must be with Jaana somewhere. A chance encounter with Charlie Wattis, the stringer for the *Daily Express*, intimated that Alex might try a dive of a bar in the Katajanokka district of Helsinki, not far from the prison. The area surprised Alex, as Katajanokka was not a district that either had frequented and was one of the least salubrious parts of the city. He found the bar without difficulty and also Felix at a table littered with empty glasses – he looked awful.

Alex shook his friend until he was almost conscious. 'Felix.' He shook him more until his friend was awake. 'Felix, what has happened?'

Some semblance of recognition eventually dawned on Felix. 'Oh, it's you,' he mumbled drunkenly. 'Alex, my so-called friend, just do me a favour and fuck off!'

'What do you mean, "fuck off"? And what do you mean, "so-called" friend?' demanded Alex. 'Come on, I'm getting you back to the hotel to get you sober.'

Alex tried to drag his friend from the seat, but as with most drunks, the deadweight proved too heavy, and Felix sprawled on the dirty floor of the bar. Alex took a fire bucket in which many customers had extinguished their cigarettes and threw the revolting water over Felix.

The elderly barman decided to intervene. 'Hey, what's happening here?' he demanded.

'My friend is a little unwell, and I need to get him home,' Alex said.

'Your friend is a little pissed,' the barman laughed, 'but you cannot come in here and throw water over the floor!'

Alex became annoyed. 'Why the fuck not? Even the disgusting water in your fire bucket is an improvement on your even more revolting floor! Now, either you help me get my friend out of this shithole, or I am coming over there to beat you fucking senseless for getting my friend pissed. Which is it to be?'

Weighing the odds, the barman decided to help Alex and hauled Felix up the stairs to the door, which he pushed open, and threw Felix into the gutter.

'Take your friend and bugger off! I don't want to see either of you again!' the barman scowled as Alex left the bar. The barman closed the door and locked it behind them.

It took a bribe almost the size of a king's ransom to persuade a very reluctant taxi driver to drive them both back to the Torni, and even there, the driver did not want to help Alex get his friend out of the cab. As Alex hauled Felix out of the car, the driver sped away, leaving them standing by the side of the hotel. The night porter, well used to assisting drunken newspaper correspondents back to their rooms, helped Alex in getting Felix to his bedroom and Alex gave the man a sizeable tip for his help – the porter beamed in gratitude.

As dawn broke over Helsinki, so Felix recovered consciousness and groaned loudly before throwing up over the bed. Alex pulled the soiled bedclothes from under him and threw them in the bath, before getting Felix a large glass of water. Felix drank it in one gulp and held the glass out for more, which Alex poured.

'What has happened?' Alex asked his friend gently.

'Everything has happened,' Felix moaned.

'Tell me,' Alex invited.

'Jaana has left me for a wounded cavalry captain who lost his arm fighting in the war. My wife is not interested in having me back, and my editor thinks I should write more like you! The *Dagbladet* has let me go!' Felix complained. That, thought Alex, explains the telegram from Felix's editor, they want to offer me Felix's job.

'Tell me about Jaana,' Alex asked.

'Doh! I should have expected that. She was so much younger than I. It seems her uncle did not much care for me, as I was two years older than him. He thought our relationship was "unwholesome", whatever that means.

'Anyway, he introduced Jaana to the son of a neighbour, a recently wounded cavalry captain who lost his left arm fighting at Lake Ladoga, and encouraged them. At least it was his left arm, so he can still play with himself.' Felix was obviously bitter towards the man who had replaced him in Jaana's life.

'So, I have been replaced by a fucking cripple!' Felix continued. 'Then I telephoned my wife, and she told me that she was happy with her new man. Finally, my editor fired me saying I should take lessons from you on how to write about war – it seems that more people are reading your stories than mine! My life is a fucking disaster!'

Alex refrained from suggesting that much of Felix's woes were down to his own actions, although he knew there was some element of truth in the thought. Instead, Alex cleaned his friend up as much as was possible and covered him with a fresh blanket from the wardrobe, and when he had fallen back to sleep, went back to his room to sleep.

Alex woke at just after nine o'clock in the morning and went for breakfast, where a sense of gloominess hung over the breakfasters. At about eight o'clock that morning, Felix Nyström had drawn a bath, shaved, dressed in his best suit, taken his trophy Russian Nagant pistol and blown his brains out.

The life that he considered had become such a disaster, was no more.

XVII

Alex arrived in Stockholm on Tuesday, 19th March 1940, onboard an Aerotransport Douglas DC-3 from Helsinki. He was met at the airport by Sigrid Lind, who threw her arms around him and kissed him passionately. Alex was acutely embarrassed. They spent the next days together doing most of the innocent things that boyfriends and girlfriends do when reunited after a period of absence.

Sigrid told Alex that he was a bit of a celebrity in Stockholm's newspaper society and a regular contributor of front-page news stories in *Svenska Posten*, and his by-line had now become *Alex Carlsson – Our Special Correspondent in Helsinki*. Per Aslund, the editor who had given Alex short shrift when they had met, now considered him to be one of the paper's greatest assets, as circulation had more than tripled since Alex began reporting from Finland – typically at the expense of the *Svenska Dagbladet*.

Although he had not once considered the financial aspect of his role as a newspaper correspondent, he was amazed to learn that his earnings had been substantial. His income from the newspaper comprised a low retainer topped up by a fee for every column inch of his reporting that they published, with a bonus for column inches on the front page. Realising that Sigrid had mostly rewritten his articles after extracting the encoded messages for London, he treated her to a meal at one of

Stockholm's more elegant restaurants and bought her a new fur coat, as her old one was looking decidedly threadbare. It was unclear how much of his earnings Alex would be allowed to keep, as officially his pay was still that of a naval lieutenant, so he figured that spending some of his assumed employer's money might just keep it out of the hands of the British treasury.

Alex's meeting on Wednesday morning was at ten o'clock, and he travelled into the *Svenska Posten*'s offices on Rålambsvägen arriving well ahead of schedule. Alex was given coffee and shown into a wood-panelled meeting room, and at ten o'clock precisely, the editor, Per Aslund, together with a suave-looking gentleman, entered.

'Alex,' Aslund began, 'first, I want to congratulate you and to thank you for your excellent reporting from Helsinki. If you ever give up your calling, I would happily employ you full-time.' He held out his hand, smiling and shook Alex's vigorously. How things had changed since their last meeting, Alex thought. 'This is Richard Liscomb from the British Embassy, and I am now going to leave you together.' With that, he left.

'Good morning,' drawled Liscomb. 'I am sure you would have preferred to meet with Simon Potts, but he had some leave owing and a rather pressing desire to get married, so I have been asked to brief you.'

Alex shook the diplomat's hand. 'Good morning.'

'Simon knows your situation better than I, but I have received detailed instructions from Commander Jeffers. In short, you are to return to Helsinki and try to persuade the Finns that Britain is their friend and His Majesty's Government wants to do all it can to help Finland restore its greatness, following the recent conflict.

'Of course, HMG profoundly regrets not being able to support Finland more actively during the war, but the intransigence of Sweden and Norway tied our hands by refusing to let our military aid cross their territories. We thought that Sweden would have been more compliant as they had allowed the aircraft that we sent to refuel en route, but they even threatened to impound troop transport aeroplanes and personnel, if we tried.

'But Sweden has given us assurances that they have no objection to our sending economic aid to Finland and will give us every assistance in transport. Commander Jeffers is keen to emphasise that the First Lord to the Admiralty urges that everything is done to dissuade Finland from turning to Germany for aid, as we consider Finland a strategic ally in the Baltic region.'

'I see,' said Alex, 'and has the First Lord any advice on how a mere correspondent might achieve such a mammoth task?'

'No,' replied Liscomb, 'but you appear to have been quite resourceful, thus far.'

'I shall do my best,' was all that Alex could think of in response. 'On another matter,' Alex continued, 'it would seem that *Svenska Dagbladet* is interested in making me an offer to work for them! Their correspondent, who was a good friend and trusted colleague of mine, was recently fired and committed suicide. As a result, now they seem to want me to fill his shoes. Out of respect for Felix's memory, I could not ever accept, and besides, I doubt they would be as accommodating as *Svenska Posten*, with my other life.'

'I doubt it also,' Liscomb responded. 'Besides, I suspect they would not have such resourceful employees as young Sigrid.'

'She may be resourceful, but I find it hard to reconcile spending time with her as "boyfriend and girlfriend" when I am a recently married man,' Alex stated.

'They tell me you are about to become a father.' Liscomb neatly sidestepped Alex's concerns.

'Yes, in May,' replied Alex. 'It would be nice to think I might be home by then.'

'Who knows?' Liscomb responded. 'But I have been told to let you know that your wife is doing well. I have some letters here from her. You should reply only to the latest one as the others have already had a response. If you care to pen a response now, I will ensure that it goes in the next bag – I have some paper and a pen of the type that you have previously used in response. Please do not seal the envelope as it has to pass through the censor.' He handed Alex several sheets of standard-issue writing paper and a fountain pen, together with a neatly tied bundle of Teddy's letters to Alex over the past few months, and a sheaf of transcripts of the replies.

*

Alex spent the next hour and a half reading of life in Gloucestershire and how Teddy was adapting to impending motherhood. His mother, the dowager countess, was in excellent health and doing much in the community, while Uncle Walter was spending more time in London ensuring that supplies reached their destination promptly. Klara had developed into an exceptional driver, and she now chauffeured Teddy around most of the time, as Teddy found it challenging to drive in her condition.

Uncle Walter had employed two gardeners to bring the gardens at Ashton Court back to their former glory, but it was almost impossible to get all the supplies they needed. In any case, before long, most of the garden would be turned over for agricultural use, and when they brought the big field into use later that year, Uncle Walter might even qualify for a girl from the Land Army. The family now had two additional maids, and Klara had adopted the role of housekeeper, although she still ran the kitchen. Teddy had only been to London once, with Uncle Walter, about a month ago, to see a specialist about her pregnancy, but there were no problems, and the house in Onslow Gardens was all right if looking a little forlorn at being shut up. Life in Gloucestershire was spectacularly ordinary, and Alex, for the first time, felt distinctly homesick.

His reply was mostly a tissue of lies, as he could not even begin to describe his life in Finland. Alex wrote how bored he was without Teddy (which was correct) and how he missed being with her (also accurate). Alex wrote how fed-up he was in Scotland, fully expecting the censor to eradicate that sentiment, and replied to several of Teddy's concerns and said how grateful she must be to have Klara with her and even joked how life would have been different had they chosen one of the other two candidates for the job. It took all of five sides of carefully considered prose to say nothing of any consequence, and eventually, he told Liscomb that he had finished. The embassy man neatly gathered together all the various documents into several piles and placed them carefully in his briefcase, before taking Teddy's letter and inserting it into a separate envelope and putting it into the inside pocket of his suit.

Liscomb rose and, with a genuinely warm gesture of comradeship, he shook Alex's hand and said, 'I cannot begin to imagine what you have had to endure in Finland, but God go with you and may your operation continue as successfully as it has been thus far. I shall pass your good wishes to Simon Potts and his bride when next I see him. Goodbye, Lieutenant Carlton.'

He left the room, and Sigrid Lind came to tell Alex that a flight had been arranged for the next day to take him back to Helsinki. That evening, she said, they should spend together, and he should leave work with her at six o'clock. After writing to Teddy, spending the evening with Sigrid was not high on Alex's list of priorities.

The evening with Sigrid was a muted affair, even though they dined at one of Stockholm's most elegant restaurants. During the meal, Sigrid pointed out a striking woman who had humorous eyes, but a hard mouth, in the company of a distinguished-looking gentleman and another larger lady.

'That is Alexandra Mikhailovna Kollontai, Minister of the Soviet delegation in Stockholm, and the couple with whom she is dining are Viktor zu Wied, the German Minister, and his wife. I wonder what they are discussing. You should pay particular attention to Madame Kollontai, as there are rumours that she may be appointed to the Soviet Embassy in Finland when it reopens.'

'Really?' Alex sounded surprised.

'Do not be fooled by her demeanour; although considered by some as a liberal, she is a hard-nosed communist. They say she has been in prison in the early days of Bolshevism and that the party executed her second husband last year. She is a dangerous woman, and it was largely her threats to the Swedish government that prevented the Swedes from granting safe passage to the British/French relief force.'

'Not somebody I should get to know, then?' Alex was intrigued.

'Oh, I don't know,' Sigrid said humorously. 'She is rumoured to have had a string of lovers.'

Alex replied sardonically, 'And why should that interest me when I have a beautiful girl like you as my girlfriend?'

That response totally confused Sigrid; was Alex being sincere, or was he playing with her? When she looked to Alex for some encouragement, he was inscrutable. She got her answer later that evening when they returned to Alex's apartment. He laid in bed next to her and put his arm around her protectively; he even kissed her goodnight, as a brother might kiss his sister, but intimacy was conspicuous by its absence.

*

The next morning, Sigrid rose and made Alex coffee, which she brought to him in bed. 'Your wife,' she said, 'is truly an extremely fortunate woman.'

'I know,' teased Alex and pulled Sigrid back to bed, 'and you are a lovely woman, who in a different, less confusing life, I know I might love very much. But circumstances are what they are, and there can be no future for us. My life is far too complex already without complicating it further. Maybe you should find somebody else?'

Sigrid looked at Alex and said, 'I am being paid to do a job, and we must both play by the rules to ensure a satisfactory conclusion. Besides, there is someone else.'

Alex looked at her and raised his eyebrows, inviting her to continue.

'I have a flatmate who shares my flat with me. She works for a small shipping company and is often away, but we are close.'

'I see,' said Alex non-committally.

'I have never been very interested in boys,' Sigrid explained. 'When I was at school, I met a boy who was a couple of years older than I, and he was very rough; he took my virginity, and I was in agony for days afterwards. I hated having sex with him. Then I met a girl, and sex was gentle and loving, so I have always preferred being with other girls. Later, when I met you, and we made love before you went to Finland, you were so gentle and kind, I doubted my choice. You were the first man who I had slept with since the boy at school, and it was a very different feeling, it was marvellous. So, your wife *is* very fortunate to have found you, and if she does not ever appreciate you, you can always come back to Sweden to me!'

'Oh, *käraste Sigrid.*' Alex held her gently in his arms, appreciating the confidence that she had just shared. 'I genuinely regret that you and I cannot be more to each other. You are a beautiful and lovely person, and although there is a shadow of remorse over what we did before, I am delighted that it was as significant for you as it was for me. There are many men like the boy from your school, but there are more who are not.

'You must find happiness in your life, but you must also appreciate that I cannot make you happy, much as the prospect is appealing. We could have an affair; it would be easy, but you will be the one who gets hurt when I go back to my other life. That would make me no better than the boy from your school who hurt you physically. You have come to mean so much more to me than someone who I could use and then discard.

'Who knows how long I shall live, but I shall always remember you with fondness and…' Alex faltered, 'yes, love. But that love must surpass our wanton desires. In doing what we do, we must not hurt each other by trying to be something that we can never become.'

Alex raised her head and saw the dampness of tears that had rolled down her beautiful face, and he kissed them away before gently kissing her lips.

'This life that has been thrust upon us is one that we have chosen; it comprises much darkness and evil, but occasionally there shines a sunbeam. You must see that if I become unfaithful to my other life, I would be a shallow cad and bounder, not worthy of you.'

'I do,' replied Sigrid quietly, 'but it does not make life any easier.'

'I know,' Alex responded.

They lay together, holding each other, with Alex gently stroking her blonde hair, for a good half-hour before Alex gently raised her head again, kissed her gently, and said, 'We should get ready for whatever the day might bring.'

*

Alex's flight departed from Bromma Airport at half-past four that afternoon, and Sigrid came to see him off. They kissed as he left and she stood to watch him go until he was out of sight, before wiping a tear from her eye and returning to work.

The flight back to Helsinki was both uncomfortable and uneventful. The three-engined Junkers aeroplane was not anywhere near as comfortable as the DC-3 that had brought him to Sweden, but it served its purpose and touched down more or less on time at Malmi Airport in Helsinki. During the flight, Alex pondered on the developments that had occurred during his time in Stockholm, particularly his redefined role in persuading the Finns that Britain was keen and willing to help.

The manager at the Hotelli Torni was delighted to see Alex return that evening. Several of the other correspondents had left that week, and the hotel now had more empty rooms than occupied ones. Alex gave him two one-kilogram packets of coffee that he had smuggled out of Sweden in his luggage and asked for some proper coffee in his room. The manager beamed with delight and promised that he would see to it personally, handing Alex a note from Leona Guichard telling Alex that Felix's funeral was to be held the following Monday, the 25th March, the day after Easter, at the Gamla Kyrkan, or Old Church, in Lönnrotinkatu. The manager said how sad all the hotel staff were that Felix had died, although the sincerity of his sentiments had to be questioned as Felix's room had been unavailable since he had killed himself, initially at the insistence of the police and latterly because it needed to be fully redecorated before another guest could use it. Alex was quite surprised that the service was being held in a church, knowing that many Christian creeds had strong views on suicide, and he had not considered Felix to have been in any way religious, but he decided that Felix was a close colleague and that he would attend the service.

He was glad that he did; the only mourners were fellow correspondents, and an elderly couple, who Alex presumed were Felix's parents. Felix's wife had not bothered to travel from Stockholm with his children, and even Jaana, Felix's erstwhile lover, chose not to attend. The funeral was being paid for by Felix's former employer, *Svenska Dagbladet*, but they had not sent a representative, and they had apparently not spent a lot on the coffin or burial. After the service, Alex and his colleagues expressed their condolences to Felix's parents, who tearfully thanked them all for coming. Later, the correspondents gathered in the bar at the Torni and got drunk, remembering the good times with Felix, and afterwards, they organised a collection to pay for a headstone, as otherwise, Felix's grave would have likely remained unmarked.

XVIII

It had been a couple of weeks since Alex had met with Jarno and he was quite surprised at the change in the man since they had last met. Jarno had always been a bit of a cynic, but now he seemed to have developed acute fatalism, and that worried Alex.

'I hope you have brought me some good news,' Jarno said to Alex when they met in the bar in Annankatu.

'I would have thought that peace would have brought a huge amount of relief to your Ministry?' Alex countered.

'Peace? Is that what you Swedes call it?' Jarno snorted. 'Finland capitulated to the might of the Soviet Union. It was as if the War of Independence had never happened. I come from a town called Sortavala in Karelia, and until recently, my parents lived there in the house we have owned for generations. After this "peace" they were given ten days to pack everything and leave when the town became part of Russia again. My mother and father are living with Katya and me in our small apartment until the government decides what to do with them. My father was a doctor in the sanatorium until he retired. He is a proud man who believed in an independent Finland; now nobody wants responsibility for the old people who are displaced.'

'So, what happens now?' Alex asked, 'Finland is rebuilding. Perhaps it will be stronger, now that there is peace?'

'It is possible,' Jarno said, 'but Finland will need a strong hand to guide its future, and the question is, does Ryti have a strong enough hand?'

'Surely having a prime minister who was courageous enough to negotiate an armistice with the Soviets, is strong enough? The alternative does not bear thinking about. At least Finland retains independence.'

'But he signed away so much of the country.' Jarno was unconvinced.

'So, now Finland must take what it has left and build itself into a great country once more,' Alex suggested. 'I want to help by writing and telling the world of the opportunities that exist in your country. I believe that Finland, with the right support, can even be better than it was before!'

'And from where will this help come? Sweden? Are we to become a vassal state of the old imperial power? Was this why they did not let Britain and France help us in the war? So that they could pick over the corpse of the country afterwards, like vultures? I am sorry, Alex, to feel so bitter about your country, but we feel that Sweden and Norway left us to our fate!' Jarno was clearly bitter.

'No, I understand the bad feeling towards Sweden. You know how much I strongly advocated their letting the aid through,' Alex protested.

'Yes, but it did not get us far, did it?' Jarno countered. 'Where else? Britain? I should think Britain has enough of its own problems to worry about Finland. Maybe Germany? Perhaps we could invite the Third Reich into our country and end up like Austria and Czechoslovakia? Where else is there? Possibly America? But why would Roosevelt be interested? No, Finland will have to do this by themselves!'

'Anyway,' Jarno continued, 'it seems as though the Ministry of Defence is less important now, and many of my colleagues are moving on to other jobs. Even I have been given a sideways promotion to the *Valtiovarainministeriö* – Finance Ministry – so as a war correspondent, I am not sure how much more I can help you.'

'Congratulations!' Alex toasted Jarno. 'I, too, got a promotion. I am now the special correspondent to Finland and have been asked to stay on and report on the rebuilding of your country, so maybe we can be of mutual assistance in the future?'

'It seems as though the ending of the war has brought us both good fortune,' Jarno said wryly as he threw back the remains of his vodka and prepared to leave. 'There is a good bar in Sofiankatu that I expect I shall use when I move offices, just around the corner from the Sunn House on Senate Square. Maybe I shall see you there sometime?'

'Maybe, you will.' Alex was deliberately non-committal, although he knew he would be seeking Jarno out very shortly.

*

The following evening, Alex caught up with one of the members of the delegation that went to Russia to negotiate peace, Professor Väinö Voionmaa, at a lecture he was giving at Helsinki University on the subject of "The Social History of Finland in the 18th Century". However, judging by the number of newspaper correspondents in the audience, it was unlikely that the published subject was going to receive much coverage.

Voionmaa was a rather bookish man; unfashionably dressed in a shabby tweed suit and round steel-rimmed glasses, he was every bit the archetypal image of a university professor, but Alex knew that he had an incredibly sharp mind. As soon as he started his discourse, one of the newspapermen asked a question about the peace negotiations. To give him his due, Professor Voionmaa tried to keep his lecture on track and only talk on the published subject, but it soon became apparent that it was a lost cause. All that anybody wanted to discuss was the peace negotiations with the Soviets.

The professor halted for a moment and polished his glasses on a handkerchief, gathering his thoughts before continuing. 'The Finnish delegation went to Moscow to negotiate terms, but the Soviets had already decided what they wanted and, in truth, there was only token negotiation. General Vasilevsky arrived with an old pre-independence map on which the Soviets had drawn a line in ink, and their proposed border passed through many villages. The chart they used was vastly out of date, and several of the places that their line went through were no longer villages, but medium-sized towns. The drafting of the final agreement occurred after we had acceded in principle to their demands, and I sat with Vasilevsky and Marshal Shaposhnikov to try and create a workable demarcation but, it has to be said, they were less compromising than were we.

'When the Finnish delegation complained about the extent of the land that we were expected to hand over to the Soviets, Shaposhnikov stated, "We demand just enough ground in which to bury our dead," which General Walden took to be a back-handed compliment of how well the Finns had fought.

'In the end, we had to cede about thirty-five thousand square kilometres of our territory to Soviet Russia, and we have had to evacuate over four hundred thousand citizens who wished to remain Finnish nationals.

'Persuading our Parliament that this was the best deal available, was no easy task. Several prominent ministers objected and voted against the plan, but there were few options. Rejection could have seen Finland at war with the Soviet again, and our military was too weak to sustain another conflict. So despite the protestations, the proposals were agreed in Parliament.

'It fell to Minister of State Paasikivi and me to travel to Moscow and submit our agreement to the Soviets on 20th March. We shall re-establish diplomatic ties with the Soviet Union, and many in government pray that future conflicts might preferably be resolved diplomatically rather than down the barrel of a gun.' The professor continued in this theme for about an hour, before summing up.

'This was not intended to be the subject of this evening's talk, but seeing few students and more correspondents in the audience, I should have realised that your collective interests lay elsewhere than in the Social History of Finland in the 18th Century.'

Professor Voionmaa opened the floor to questions, and after a couple that sought to apportion blame on the delegation that negotiated peace with Russia, the professor looked at Alex.

'Alex Carlsson, *Svenska Posten*,' Alex began, and did he notice a slight recognition of the name?'Thank you, Professor, for your clear explanation this evening, and I feel confident that most gathered here acknowledge that your delegation faced many challenges in negotiating peace.

'But now we must look to the future. Are you able to give any insight on how Finland will rebuild itself, now that there is peace? Has, perhaps, the Finnish government received any offers of help in rebuilding its economy and infrastructure?'

'I imagine they must have received many such offers,' the professor responded. 'When the animal lies mortally wounded, many come to where it fell, not all intending to see the beast recover. Many come for their own selfish reasons, hoping that should the animal not recover, that they may carve up its carcass and divide it amongst themselves for their own profit.' *Philosophical*, thought Alex.

'Your country, for example,' the professor continued, 'may well offer assistance to Finland to assuage its guilt in not having given aid when we were fighting for our very existence. Please do not think *I* am critical of Sweden. They acted as they did out of neutrality, but many might feel justifiably unsympathetic of their actions.

'No doubt there will be others claiming to act out of pure altruism.'

'Like whom, sir?' Alex persisted. 'Much of mainland Europe is engaged in their own battles. I worry that Finland might seem inconsequential in comparison to their own troubles and that a weakened Finland may fall prey to a voracious predator – and I do not exclude the country with whom you have recently been at war.'

'That is an interesting perspective, young man,' the professor continued, 'and one that is not without some merit.'

Alex recalled his school days when his masters had taught that double negatives were acceptable in mathematics, but not in language – when used verbally, they were invariably the solace of those who were uncomfortable with the conversation. Alex sat down.

A few questions later and another correspondent raised the issue of a closer alliance with Germany, which the professor dealt with non-committally, giving Alex the opportunity of asking a supplementary question.

'Accepting the existence of the Treaty of Non-Aggression between Germany and the Soviet Union, and imagining that Stalin is content with not poking the Nazi wasps' nest, should these two countries become more closely aligned, might not the acceptance of aid from Germany be tantamount to allowing the Russians into Finland through the backdoor?'

'Mr Carlsson,' the professor responded, 'it would seem that you have a better grasp of the paradoxes that confront our nation than many in our government.' He paused for a brief recognition of his wit and was rewarded with a giggle of laughter. 'This is a concern, and I am sure those in government will weigh the merits and shortcomings in each case.'

'One also has to accept that Britain was keen to help but was frustrated by my country and Norway; might Mr Chamberlain not be petitioned to assist Finland in restoring the country, as they were in defending it? Surely, neither Norway nor Sweden would object to such aid passing over their borders?'

'Perhaps that ought to be a question best asked of your government, Mr Carlsson?' the professor suggested.

'And it shall be one that I ask,' Alex replied. He had enjoyed the verbal skirmish with the professor and felt that he had acquitted himself well enough.

*

The report for London that Alex included in his next article confirmed that Alex had undoubtedly planted the seeds of British aid in the ears of influential members of the Finnish government and that he would continue monitoring the situation. As a report, it was bland and entirely unremarkable, but the story that surrounded the account received the literary attention of Sigrid and made the front page of the newspaper. In many ways, Alex enjoyed the recognition that accompanied his stories regularly appearing so prominently, but at the same time, he understood that in his business, attention was not always and, indeed, seldom was, advantageous.

At the embassy in Stockholm, Simon, who had recently returned to duty following his marriage to Cordelia, was summoned to meet with the Head of Station.

'Ah, yes, Potts,' the Head of Station greeted his subordinate, 'take a seat and tell me of this chappie Carlsson or Carlton, in Finland. He appears to be featuring rather too prominently on the front page of his newspaper, don't you think?'

'His reports to London are of the highest order and extremely valuable,' Simon countered in defence of Alex.

'That may well be the case, old son,' the Head of Station wanted to appear avuncular, 'but would you not agree that he is becoming just a little too visible?'

'We all do things differently,' Simon answered, 'and I have known Alex Carlton for many long years. He is a very shrewd operator, and I am sure that his visibility is a carefully considered ruse to gain the trust of those in the Finnish government. He is extremely well placed and seems to be doing rather well.'

'Let us hope he continues to do so,' Simon was told, and he made a mental note to get a message to Alex suggesting a lowering of his profile, although he doubted that his friend would take any notice.

*

As March drew to a close, Alex travelled with several other correspondents to the seaside town of Hanko on the peninsula, to see how preparations for the evacuation of its citizens was progressing. The leasing of Hanko to the Russians had been the prize of Stalin's war reparations. Russia had secured the mighty fortresses with their massive guns, which would provide a fearsome arc of firepower to protect Leningrad from invasion by sea. In peacetime, the town had a population of over twenty thousand, but fewer than 10% had remained during the war, so the evacuation was a relatively straightforward affair. Those that had abandoned the town were now teeming back to recover possessions before the Red Army took over the area, and this caused much congestion on the only serviceable road onto the peninsula.

Military lorries that were stacked high with ammunition and other military hardware barged their way through the civilians as they took whatever was moveable from the fortresses. Part of the lease agreement was that the fortifications and guns should be surrendered intact, but that did not include anything that was not nailed down – Finnish soldiers were keen that the Soviets got as little as possible.

Life in Helsinki was becoming mundane, and the correspondents were vying with each other to try and find a new twist on the redevelopment programme.

Alex found an incident that none of the others had latched onto through a contact that he had been nurturing in the German Embassy. Although Germany was at war with England, the embassy in Helsinki was far from a Nazi party enclave. The Ambassador was an old-school diplomat; Wipert von Blücher was not a strident party member, and many of the staffers at the mission held similar views. Alex had found himself in a bar with a second secretary at the embassy, and it was from this meeting that Alex learned that the Finns had captured over five thousand Russian prisoners of war during the conflict.

As part of the peace negotiations, Finland repatriated these prisoners to Soviet Russia. Almost as soon as they crossed the border, Soviet Secret Police (known fearfully as *Obyedinyonnoye Gosudarstvennoye Politicheskoye Upravleniye pri SNK SSSR* or OGPU) seized them and transferred the repatriated prisoners to secret prison camps of the Interior Ministry, the *Narodnyy Komissariat Vnutrennikh Del* (NKVD), in the wilds of Russia. The Secret Police interrogated every single prisoner and then executed them. Try as he might, Alex could find no independent corroboration of this story, but in his opinion, it was probably accurate. The Soviets did not condone failure, and the leadership considered that being taken a prisoner of war was a prime example of abject failure.

XIX

So it was that the war was over, and Finland had lost. The peace treaty that Finland had signed on 13th March appeared to rip the heart out of the proud nation, with so much of their precious country ceded to Russia, but Finns are a philosophical race, and whenever he spoke to civilians and old soldiers alike, Alex understood that the whole nation was determined to grow from this conflict.

In the period immediately following the cessation of hostilities, Alex spoke to a good cross-section of the population. From soldiers recently returned from the frontline to those who had provided essential services to the citizens that had remained in Helsinki, from those who were staunchly conservative to the stalwart socialists, men and women, young and old, he was determined to understand what came next. He was not surprised to learn that the Finnish resolve had not been shaken. Many of those who had been communists felt betrayed that the Soviet bombers had dropped propaganda leaflets urging Finland to seek peace at the same time as they were dropping bombs on the capital.

'The mastery of the peace agreement,' Alex learned from his discussions with a government spokesman, 'is that as a nation we are emasculated. The defensive Mannerheim Line is no more, and Russia will be able to build better defences at Viipuri, and with the port of Hanko in Russian hands, they effectively control the south coast. They have a functioning airbase from which they can launch an attack on the capital and Finland is even building them a new railway line to strengthen their grip on the north of the country.'

Alex walked around the city and was amazed to see how quickly the signs of war were being covered up and renovated. Slowly but surely, shops began to reopen, and as time progressed, more and more items were finding their way onto the shelves for the Finnish consumer to buy. Retailers had to import most of their stock, as manufacturing was only slowly being re-established, and factories were focussing their output on war reparations, but once this debt was clear, the country would have set the foundations for growth.

In his articles for *Svenska Posten* and his reports for London, Alex identified the areas of greatest need, and help was forthcoming from both directions, although logistically most came through Sweden. On one occasion, Alex walked towards the docks, retracing the steps that he had taken with the other correspondents on his first night in Finland. Alex walked through the park where he had found Juha cradling the corpse of his sister's dog, and he wondered what had happened to the young boy. He made a mental note to try and find out but acknowledged that unless the authorities could find a relative, Juha would likely grow up in a state orphanage.

The hotel, once desperate for the patronage of correspondents, now considered their discounted rates as short-changing the potential of higher profits brought by the businessmen who were slowly returning to the capital, and who were prepared to pay premium prices for the best accommodation. The hotel manager strongly hinted that Alex might like to move to another room and vacate the spacious and delightful accommodation that he was currently occupying. The manager looked determined, almost as if he was about to argue when Alex told him he was perfectly happy to remain in his current room, until Alex offered to make up any shortfall from his own pocket.

'That is most generous,' the manager responded, 'shall we say an extra hundred markka a week?' After a quick calculation in his mind, Alex realised that this was less than ten shillings per week.

'Yes,' Alex agreed, 'as long as the coffee improves in the morning!'

The manager smiled at his victory.

*

Simon's message arrived the next day in the form of Sigrid Lind, who turned up unexpectedly by air from Stockholm. The fact that Sigrid had not sent him any message and had come without warning both thrilled and worried Alex. Arriving back at the hotel the next afternoon, Alex found Sigrid dressed in her Sunday best sitting primly in the hotel lobby, with a small valise on the floor by her chair.

'Alex,' she called as he entered the hotel, causing him to spin round and almost lose his balance when he saw her sitting there.

'Sigrid! What on earth are you doing here?' Alex asked, somewhat ungallantly.

'Well, that was hardly the welcome that I expected!' Sigrid smiled. 'I had a few days' of vacation owing, so I decided to visit my boyfriend and see what he was up to in Helsinki.'

'No, er, yes.' Alex was clearly flustered. 'Well, it is absolutely wonderful to see you, you just took me by surprise.' Alex took her in his arms and gave her a warm hug.

Sigrid whispered, 'I have a message and some instructions, and our masters thought it better if I delivered them personally.'

Turning to the hotel manager, Alex asked, 'My girlfriend has arrived unexpectedly from Stockholm. Do you have a room for her?'

'I'm sorry, sir,' the manager responded, 'we have nothing available. Now the fighting has stopped, everybody seems to be coming to Helsinki. But this is not a problem, sir. We have some temporary beds, and we could install one in your room – if you think it is necessary.'

It was clear that the hotel manager thought that Alex must be mad to want another room or an additional bed for such an attractive young woman.

Alex looked to Sigrid, who smiled demurely and nodded imperceptibly. 'No, it is all right,' Alex told the manager. 'I am sure we can make do.'

'Yes, sir, I am sure you will.' The manager almost winked at Alex. 'There is, of course, an additional charge for double occupancy. Shall I add it to your account, sir?'

'Yes,' Alex replied tetchily, before picking up Sigrid's bag and allowing her to loop her arm through his as they went to the lifts and made their way to his room.

'This is very pleasant,' said Sigrid as he let them both in.

'It is,' agreed Alex, 'but the settee is bloody uncomfortable, and that is where I shall be sleeping. You can have the bed,' Alex made up his mind.

'Of course,' agreed Sigrid, although Alex thought that he detected a slight disappointment as she continued, 'I wouldn't have it any other way.'

Rather than trusting the dubious quality of the hotel's restaurant, that had still not regained its pre-war eminence for dining, Alex chose a small and cosy restaurant just off Fredrikinkatu to entertain Sigrid that evening. The food promised mediocrity, the service appeared distinctly average, but the alcohol was plentiful, and it had the definite advantage of not attracting any of the foreign correspondents who tended to frequent the trendier establishments.

'This is,' Sigrid sought the right word, 'intimate.'

'Yes, I saw it the other week and thought it looked interesting.' Alex did his best to sound debonair.

They chatted as old friends would talk over a surprisingly good meal of some sort of fish served with potatoes that more than satisfied their hunger. As they walked back through the park towards the hotel, Alex told Sigrid the story of his first night in Helsinki and how he met Juha, by the end of which Sigrid was sobbing, and Alex put his arm around her, drawing her to him.

'How awful,' Sigrid said.

'Yes, but I am sure there are many other Juhas in this town,' Alex responded philosophically.

'I wonder what happened to him,' Sigrid speculated.

'Who knows?' Alex attempted nonchalance, but it was clear that the fate of Juha still played upon his mind. Changing the subject, he asked Sigrid, 'Why are you here?'

'Oh, yes.' She clearly did not want to break the moment with thoughts of why she had been sent. 'There is a concern that you are becoming too noticeable and London suggests that you stop being so good at your job. I have been told to downgrade your articles so that they do not get printed so often on the front page. The service thinks you should be less conspicuous. Also, they are asking about what is happening outside the capital. How are the people in the country faring now that hostilities have ceased? How strong is the concern that Finland might still fall prey to Russia again?'

Alex was pensive as they walked back to the hotel arm in arm; he wondered what he had done wrong. He genuinely thought that he had been doing well, but now Sigrid was here telling him that Alex was too successful, in the wrong way!

Arriving back at the hotel, Alex was dismayed to see the group of his fellow correspondents gathered at the bar.

'Yo! Carlsson!' Leona Guichard called, 'Come join us!'

Alex rolled his eyes at Sigrid and called back, 'I'm tired. See you tomorrow.'

La Lionesse staggered over and insisted on buying Alex a drink, grabbing his arm and pulling him towards the bar. Then she saw Sigrid. 'Ho, ho, ho! What have we here, who is this beauty?'

Before Alex could respond, Sigrid spoke in faltering English that Alex knew to be an act, as Sigrid's English was almost perfect. 'Hello. My name is Sigrid Lind, and I am the girlfriend of Alex. How do you do?' She held out her hand to Leona.

'My,' said Leona in admiration, 'what a cutie. Now I know why you are not interested in this old warhorse if you are dating a beauty like this! Where are you from, Miss Lind?'

'Oh, please to call me Sigrid. I live in Stockholm,' Sigrid responded falteringly. 'I have just come from there today, and I am fatigued.' To Alex, she added, 'We go to bed now, please, *min raring?*'

That brought a roar of drunken laughter from Leona. 'Ja, you go to bed now, Alex,' she said, and Alex guided Sigrid towards the lifts.

'What a vixen!' Sigrid said as soon as the lift doors had closed.

'She's all right, really, and very good at her job, but she does take some getting used to.'

The lift came to a halt on the second floor, and Alex was quite disappointed when the doors opened and he was no longer in such close proximity to Sigrid. They let themselves into his room, and Alex almost regretted his virtue in not sharing a bed with Sigrid. Nevertheless, he set about trying to make the settee as comfortable as possible.

'Are you really going to sleep on that thing?' Sigrid asked.

'I am,' replied Alex. 'You and I have become too close, and that cannot be.'

'I know that elsewhere you are married,' Sigrid sighed, 'but we did agree that Alex Carlsson was not, so we must keep up appearances. Imagine what the maid would think if she let herself in and saw you sleeping on the couch. She might think we had quarrelled!'

As an argument, it was unconvincing, especially as the maid had not once since he had been at the hotel ever disturbed him. Alex went to Sigrid and gave her a tender kiss on the forehead. 'Then I shall put the "Do Not Disturb" sign on the door and the damned maid can deduce from that whatever she wants! Do you want to use the bathroom first?'

*

To start the next day, Alex and Sigrid breakfasted together and then went out to explore Helsinki. Alex took her to the Töölö district to see the magnificent Olympic Stadium that the Finns had hoped would host the 1940 games after Japan lost them, but as a result of the war in Europe and the Winter War, that was not going to happen, and the games had been abandoned. As a monument to functionalist architecture, the stadium was truly magnificent, even though it had suffered badly at the hands of the Soviet air force during the war.

They walked back along Töölönlahti, the lake that used to be part of the Gulf of Bothnia, and towards the central station. Spring was just starting to show in the trees and bushes along the pathway, and Alex wondered that even after the war, nature always delivered a new beginning. Alex showed Sigrid Helsinki's Lutheran cathedral, and from there they walked to the harbour, before turning up the Esplanade and heading back to the hotel. As they walked, they talked, and Alex learned more about Sigrid's life as she grew up in Stockholm. It is always dangerous when one agent knows too much about another, as capture would likely lead to torture, and very few were able to resist giving information for long under extreme pain. But Alex and Sigrid talked and grew to know each other better, even though Alex maintained his guard about what he divulged. There was no doubt that a strong friendship was maturing, and one that would have likely developed further had circumstances been different. Nevertheless, they were keen to enjoy each other's company while it lasted, especially as Sigrid was returning to Stockholm the next day.

That evening, Alex took Sigrid to one of the oldest restaurants in Helsinki. Although named Bellevue, French for "Beautiful View", the restaurant was, in fact, Russian and located in the Katajanokka district of Helsinki, in the shadow of the Orthodox Uspenski Cathedral. It was the first time that Sigrid had tasted Russian food, and although the restaurant was suffering the same rationing as the rest of the capital's eating places, the food was delicious. Sigrid was torn between whether she preferred the *blinis* or the *pelmeni*, and Alex confessed that he found both delicious. Alex introduced Sigrid to good Russian vodka, drunk ice-cold, and even though Sweden had a vodka tradition stretching back to the 15th century, this vodka was far superior. Sigrid announced that it was the best vodka she had ever tasted!

A taxi took the couple back to the Hotelli Torni, and Alex steered Sigrid away from the bar and towards the lifts. Sigrid was keen to make their last night memorable, but Alex was determined that he would not succumb to her feminine wiles. She collapsed onto the bed and dragged Alex down beside her. He held her close and gently stroked her hair until her breathing was rhythmic, and she was unmistakably asleep. 'Godnatt, min ängel,' he whispered and kissed her gently on her cheek before making himself as comfortable as possible on the settee.

*

The next morning, after breakfast, Alex escorted Sigrid to the aerodrome at Malmi so she could catch her flight back to Stockholm. As he watched her walk across the tarmac to the waiting aeroplane, he thought with a tinge of sadness that she was indeed a wonderful young woman who would make somebody an excellent wife, in the future. As she was about to board the aeroplane, she turned and searched for Alex, and when Sigrid found him in the small crowd that had gathered, she waved before taking her handkerchief and wiping her nose. Clearly, it was an emotional parting for them both.

Arriving back at the hotel from the aerodrome, the manager greeted him as if he was his long-lost brother and announced conspiratorially that a messenger had delivered an official letter for Mr Carlsson. Alex looked at the manager expectantly, but it was apparent that he was in no hurry to divulge more, so Alex asked for the letter. The manager reluctantly passed it over, and Alex was surprised to see an official-looking wax seal joining the flap of the envelope, and the crest of the president printed on the top left-hand corner. The manager looked more than a little disappointed when Alex put the unopened letter in his pocket without opening it.

'I'll read it later,' Alex said casually before taking his key and heading for his room. There was a palpable sense of unrequited expectancy from the manager as Alex left the reception.

XX

Alex had decided to travel east on the King's Road and see how the towns and villages that were closer to the frontline were faring in peacetime. He had momentarily thought to revisit Rovaniemi, but the memories of his time there with Felix were still too recent, and he really did not want to travel so far to understand what was happening elsewhere. A trip towards Viipuri should suffice, he concluded.

Early the next morning, as he was preparing for his trip eastwards, Alex remembered the letter that the manager had handed to him the previous evening and retrieved it from his jacket pocket. He carefully opened the envelope using his penknife and discovered an official-looking invitation, that read in a neat copperplate text:

THE PRESIDENT OF THE REPUBLIC OF FINLAND, KYÖSTI KALLIO, CORDIALLY REQUESTS THE PRESENCE OF MR ALEXANDER CARLSSON AT A RECEPTION TO BE HELD AT THE PRESIDENTIAL PALACE ON TUESDAY, 16TH APRIL 1940, COMMENCING AT 7.00PM. R.S.V.P

Alex was astounded. Why was he being invited to a presidential reception? This was undoubtedly the most formal of occasions, and Alex's evening suit was either in the wardrobe at Onslow Gardens or in a packing case in Gloucestershire. He had not even contemplated bringing such a suit with him to Helsinki. Nevertheless, this was a minor complication and one he could quickly resolve. The invitation would enable him to get closer to those whom he had to convince of Britain's continued interest in Finland – perhaps even the president himself.

Alex sat at the desk in his room, and taking a sheet of the Hotel Torni's notepaper, he wrote his acceptance note before sealing it in an envelope. He handed it to the hotel manager with the instruction that it should be delivered at their earliest convenience. Alex asked if there was an accommodating tailor in Helsinki who could arrange something suitable to wear.

'There are two,' the manager advised, 'both of whom are exceptional. Ekman's on Eerininkatu is the closest to the hotel, but Katz's on Roobertinkatu is possibly the better choice for quality. Of course,' the manager added by way of additional information, 'neither will be open today.' Alex thanked the manager and decided to try Ekman's first, on Monday, as it was just around the corner and he wanted to leave on the midday bus.

Ekman's was an unprepossessing store. A single suit stood on a tailor's dummy in the window, and there was a distinct atmosphere of shabbiness with the faded, peeling paintwork. Nevertheless, the tailor was most obliging, and Alex was impressed by the way that his measurements were swiftly taken down. The choice of cloth was limited, but Alex was happy to accept the recommendation of a bolt of pre-war wool cloth that was of particularly excellent quality. The tailor scheduled an appointment for Alex's only fitting for that Friday afternoon so that any final adjustments could be made to the suit before collection on Monday.

After being measured for his suit, Alex caught the midday bus and travelled the 50km to the medieval city of Porvoo. Although only 50km from Helsinki, the bus moved slowly, continually stopping for traffic coming in the opposite direction. The old King's Road was the main thoroughfare to the recently ceded city of Viipuri, and those rendered homeless by the peace treaty were still heading west, carrying their belongings on all manner of carts and trucks. The similarity of his mother's flight from St Petersburg back in August 1917, when she had travelled on a merchant's wagon escaping the Bolshevik uprising, carrying her unborn child inside her, was not lost on Alex. That look of desperation and misery on the faces of the modern-day refugees as they trudged westwards, brought home the realisation of the suffering that his noble-born mother had endured to save her own life and his.

The distance between Porvoo and Loviisa was only about 30km, and Alex decided to return to the small town where he had been born and where he had lived his early childhood with his mother, who had sacrificed much for the sake of her child. He wondered whether Lisbet and Edvard Nylund would still be at the farm where he grew up, and although he realised how dangerous it would be to allow his two lives to come together, the proximity was too much of a temptation for Alex not to go and see.

Eventually, when the bus pulled into the station in Porvoo, Alex was quite surprised to see that, at least on the surface, the city seemed to have escaped the ravages of war. The wooden houses of the area around the cathedral were still standing and were completely intact, as was the bridge that spanned Porvoonjoki. On the corner of Rantakatu and Lukiokatu, Alex found the *Folkademis Hus* – Folk Academy House – which was still operating as a field hospital, nursing soldiers injured in battle. To say that the matron welcomed Alex with open arms would be far from accurate; indeed, with so many of her nurses and Lotta assistants discharged at the end of hostilities, to have a nosy newspaper correspondent snooping around her domain was very low on her list of priorities.

'You can come back at 6.00pm,' the matron instructed, 'and I will see if I can find somebody prepared to talk to you. Until then, I'm busy!'

Alex looked at his watch. The time was just after 3.30pm, so he had two and a half hours to spare. In the town square, he found a café, and Alex settled himself in with a copy of the local newspaper and a coffee.

An elderly and suspicious lady who had entered the café after Alex asked, '*Vem är du?*' – Who are you? The question somewhat surprised Alex as Finns and Swedes are notoriously reticent in making the first move in conversation.

'My name is Alex Carlsson, and I am a newspaper correspondent with *Svenska Posten*,' Alex replied in Swedish.

'*Bah!*' the old woman replied and sat down with her drink and then ignored Alex for the rest of the time he was in the café.

Alex ordered another coffee, and the proprietor asked in Swedish, 'You say you work for the *Svenska Posten?*'

'Yes,' replied Alex, 'I'm their correspondent in Finland. Alex Carlsson.'

'Were you that correspondent at Suomussalmi?' the café owner asked.

'I was, yes,' Alex replied, trying to keep the indifference from his voice.

'So was my son, Gustav,' came the reply, 'stayed there, too.'

'*Mina kondoleanser för din förlust*' Alex said. – My condolences for your loss. Alex read between the lines of what the owner was saying and commiserated.

'*Tack*' –Thank you. The café owner continued: 'He was a good boy, bright at school and very good at hockey. He wanted to protect his mama and me, so he lied about his age and joined the army. Of course, they did not check. Otherwise, they would have known he was only fifteen, but a big boy for his age. They just wanted pawns to throw against the Soviet and to plug the lines. They brought him back in a box and despite the kind words of his commander telling us what a brave boy he was, it could not bring Gustav back to life. Broke his mother's heart, it did. Now there's just me.'

Alex settled down to talk to the owner. 'How did he die, do you know?'

'Not really,' the café owner continued. 'I gather it was during one of the attacks by the enemy when they were trying to break through the lines. Gustav was in the wrong place at the wrong time. It happens. That's war.'

Alex filed away the information, to be used in a future article, and thanked the café owner. When he offered to pay for his coffees, the proprietor waved his money away, but Alex insisted, pushing some markka notes into the man's hand. 'Buy some flowers for your son's grave,' he said, smiling sympathetically.

Still having time to spare, Alex walked through the streets, past the wooden houses to the cathedral, which he entered and sat down to reflect on his current life. He thought of Mick McMahon, of Ville Koskinen and of Felix Nyström; he thought of the fifteen-year-old son of the café owner and the thousands of other Gustavs who had perished in the war; the countless families who had lost fathers and sons and of the innocents like Juha whose lives had been turned upside down by the war. Was it worth it? Was it ever worth it?

Alex checked his watch and was shocked to discover it was six-thirty. He was late for his meeting with Matron at the *Folkademis Hus*, so he gathered himself together and hurried out of the church. Arriving at the hospital, he found the matron was in even less good humour than earlier.

'You are late,' she scolded, to which Alex smiled charmingly. 'Well, come on then.' Matron brusquely ushered him through the door and strode off down a corridor, evidently expecting Alex to follow.

They entered a ward that had ten beds neatly arranged around the walls and a central desk for the on-duty nurse. 'Nurse,' the matron gained the attention of a pretty young nurse, 'this is Mr Carlsson who is here to see Lieutenant Lundberg. He can have half an hour only, and make sure he does not tire the patient with his questions.'

Without further acknowledging Alex's presence, the matron turned on her heels and marched out of the ward. *Lundberg?* Alex thought. *Surely not?*

It was. The nurse showed Alex to a bed in the corner of the ward where a familiar face peered over the bedsheets at Alex as he approached. The shock of black hair had been joined by a scruffy black beard, giving the soldier an almost piratical appearance.

'Anton,' the nurse spoke to the patient, 'this is the correspondent who has come to see you. Matron says you can have half an hour together.' She smiled warmly at Alex and went back to her desk.

'So, we meet again,' the lieutenant said to Alex, 'how are you keeping?'

'Well enough,' Alex replied. 'It is good to see you again. Are you all right? Tell me what happened.'

'Yes, I'm fine now,' Lundberg responded. 'A few more holes in my body since last we met, but they tell me it is nothing serious. Unlike some.'

'What of Major Ahonen?' Alex asked.

'I do not know,' Lieutenant Lundberg replied. 'My section was one of the first that was hit. Nobody seems to know – or, at least, they are not telling me – what happened to the rest.'

'What happened?' Alex continued.

'We knew something had changed,' Lundberg reminisced. 'Their artillery was getting more accurate. Whereas before they were missing more than they were hitting, suddenly everything changed. It was almost as if different gunners were firing at us.

'You remember me telling you that you do not hear the shell that has your name on it? I now doubt its truth. In a barrage, all you can hear is a deafening cacophony of shell bursts. I cannot say whether the shell that did for my section was one that I heard or not but one minute we were in our dugouts praying that they would miss us, the next our prayers failed, and it was a pot-mess of blood and guts everywhere. I do not even know how many of my men survived, but I doubt many did.'

'Where did they get you?' Alex asked.

'In the shoulder and my side,' the lieutenant explained. 'My sergeant took the worst of it, and I just got hit by the shrapnel that didn't hit him. Good man, Sergeant Aho, good man – a family man too. He stopped most of the burst, which was lucky for me and bad luck for him.'

Alex could not understand whether Lieutenant Lundberg was sardonic or just stating a fact. 'How long will you be here?' he asked.

'Not long now. Apparently, I'm almost as good as new, so they will be sending me home soon. I gather the doctors will be invaliding me out of the army, so I suppose I shall be going back to my legal training. Back to my parents in Kristinestad, though quite what they will make of me now, God only knows. What about you?'

'Oh, I'm here for a while,' Alex said. 'My paper wants me to cover the rebuilding of Finland, and I am now known as their "special" correspondent in the country. I have to say, I am looking forward to seeing Finland without the war and getting to know the Finnish people when they do not fear for their lives.'

The young nurse interrupted and said that Alex's time was up, so he rose and shook hands with Lieutenant Lundberg, offering him the opportunity of a future meeting, should he come to Helsinki soon.

'I would enjoy that,' Lundberg said.

As Alex walked with the nurse towards the exit, he asked whether the lieutenant really was as well as he had told Alex.

'Oh, yes,' the nurse said brightly. 'Anton will make a full recovery physically. He will have a few scars, and he will probably suffer a few more aches and pains later in life, but he will be all right. He will need more help in forgetting the horrors that he has seen, he suffers from terrible nightmares.'

'I see,' said Alex as he shook the nurse's hand on leaving. 'Thank you very much for letting me chat to Anton and please thank Matron also for her kindness.'

The nurse smiled at Alex; somehow "kindness" was not a word that readily came to her mind when thinking of Matron. As an afterthought, Alex turned back to the nurse and asked, 'Do you know whether there is a hotel in the town that is open?'

'I am not sure,' the nurse replied. 'There is a hotel in Välikatu, but I am not sure whether they have any vacancies.'

'Where is Välikatu?' Alex asked.

'If you wait a few minutes, I will show you,' the nurse said. 'I have just finished my shift, and it is on my way home.'

'That would be very kind,' Alex said, and then introduced himself. 'Alex Carlsson from *Svenska Posten*.'

'Minna Koskela,' the nurse announced. 'Pleased to meet you, Mr Carlsson.'

The nurse disappeared and returned about five minutes later, dressed in a long coat and hat. She looked much smaller and more youthful than she had when in her nurse's uniform.

'Shall we go, Mr Carlsson?' the nurse asked.

'Please, call me Alex. Mr Carlsson sounds too much like my father,' Alex responded, and the nurse smiled.

As they walked, they talked, with Alex asking, 'So, Minna, do you come from Porvoo?'

'No, my family come from Espoo near Helsinki, but when I got married, we moved to Vantaa,' she replied.

'What does your husband do?' Alex asked.

'He ran a small hardware shop with his family. Jussi was a few years older than me,' Mina replied before continuing. 'He died in the first week of the war.'

'My condolences,' was all that Alex could think of to say.

'Thank you. We had not been married long,' Minna explained, 'but I still miss him. I was working as a nurse at our local hospital, but they sent me here after Jussi died.'

They had arrived at the hotel, and Alex turned to the nurse and said, 'Thank you for showing me the way.'

'Thank you for listening,' Minna replied, and Alex smiled.

The hotel had one room left, and Alex went upstairs. It was a simple room; a wooden bed with a chest of drawers and a small wardrobe. There was a handmade rug on the floor covering the bare floorboards that had been smoothed to almost a shine by many years of guests walking on them. Alex put his travelling bag on the chest of drawers and transferred the clothes into two of the drawers and secreted his trusty FN pistol amongst his clothes.

Dinner comprised a thick and nourishing fish soup served with fresh bread that had probably been baked in the hotel's kitchen. It was delectable and just what Alex needed before he settled down to write up the notes of his visit to the hospital, before retiring to bed and sleeping soundly until the morning.

XXI

The weather that greeted Alex as he pulled back the curtains was wet, and when he went down for breakfast, Alex momentarily considered whether he could be bothered to continue his journey to Loviisa, or whether he should stay in Porvoo and wait for the bus to Viipuri. It was only a fleeting doubt that was quickly suppressed by his memories of childhood – there seemed to be an inexplicable magnet drawing him back to where he grew up before he left for England.

Having eaten breakfast, he thanked the hotelier for a comfortable night, paid his bill and left to walk back to the bus station, where he planned to catch the local bus to Loviisa. He had not walked far when he heard his name called, and turning, he saw Minna Koskela hurrying down the road towards him wearing the same long coat and hat that she had worn the day previously.

'I thought it was you,' she said after they had greeted each other. 'Was the hotel comfortable?'

'Very,' said Alex. 'Did you have a good night, also?'

'I was a bit restless,' Minna confided. 'I do not often think of Jussi now, but when I do, I usually have a restless night.'

'I'm sorry,' Alex said, realising that their conversation of the day before must have triggered the memories of her husband.

'No, it is all right,' she reassured Alex. 'Have you heard the news?'

'No,' replied Alex. 'What news?'

'Germany has invaded Denmark and Norway,' Minna stated matter-of-factly.

'But Norway was neutral, and Denmark had a non-aggression pact with Germany.' Alex could not believe his ears.

'It seems not to matter to Mr Hitler. Germany invaded both yesterday, so the wireless said,' she stated. 'Anyway, where are you going next?'

'I'm heading east,' Alex replied, still reeling from the news of Norway's plight. 'My paper wants me to write about how the people in the regions are coping after the war, so I thought I would visit a few towns and villages towards what used to be the frontline.'

'It must be fascinating, visiting all these places,' Minna observed.

'I suppose so,' Alex replied, 'but you get used to it!' He smiled.

Alex and Minna parted company in the town centre so that she could go to the hospital and he the bus station. The local bus to Kotka that called at Loviisa was due to leave at 9.45am but was already at the station collecting passengers, even though there was still half an hour before departure. Alex paid the few markkas for his fare and settled down to wait. He glanced up as the driver started the engine and briefly glimpsed what he thought was a familiar long coat, waiting near the terminus. He thought nothing more about it, as he knew Minna Koskela had gone to work.

The bus pulled out of the station on time and began the journey eastwards. It drove slowly as there were still far too many people travelling in the opposite direction carrying their belongings with them. The journey that would typically take no more than forty-five minutes took over an hour, and Alex was glad when the bus pulled up by the railway station. He regretted that trains had still not been reinstated on the route following the war, as he was sure that train travel would have been far more comfortable.

It did not take Alex long to get his bearings in the town of his birth. The town church was immediately recognisable behind the station, and he remembered the Sunday mornings when he and his mother had accompanied Lisbet and Edvard to the church service. He recalled that he had not liked church very much, as the usual priest was very stern-looking and had a loud voice that scared him as a young boy. He remembered how he had often feigned a cold or cough on Sunday mornings so that his mother would keep him at home, but how miraculously the ailment had cured itself by the time that Lisbet and Edvard returned.

'*Bön är kraftfull medicin*,' Lisbet used to say. – Prayer is powerful medicine!

Alex retraced the steps that had somehow been retained in his memory, never once straying from the path until he came to the ruin of the farmhouse that had been his first home. The building had fallen into disrepair and was clearly no longer lived in. Feeling a slight pang of remorse and a definite sense of anti-climax, he made his way back into town. He passed by the school that he had attended and where his mother had taught; it had not changed much. Eventually, he saw the old bakery where his mother would occasionally buy him a cake as a treat, and coming out from the door was a middle-aged woman dressed in the uniform of a postwoman. Alex hurried across the road before she had time to mount her bicycle and pedal off.

'*Anteeksi*,' he called in Finnish. – Excuse me.

The postwoman stopped and looked at Alex. '*Mitä?*' she asked. – What?

'Hello, my name is Alex Carlsson, and I'm a distant relative of Lisbet Nylund,' Alex introduced himself, 'and I have just been to the farm. Do they not live there anymore?'

The postwoman looked at Alex suspiciously. 'You do not know that Lisbet lives in the hospital now?' she asked.

'No,' Alex explained, 'my family went to live in Sweden, and we lost touch after a few years. Is she still alive? And what about Edvard?'

'Oh, Edvard died many years ago.' Alex felt a distinct sadness. 'Lisbet ran the farm for as long as she was able, but it got too much for her. Her nephew from Porvoo came over to help them about six or seven years ago. They still live there, but Edvard would be spinning in his grave if he could see how they have let his farm go to ruin.

'Erik has gone off to war. I do not know what came of him, but Siri and her daughter Ines still live on the farm. Lisbet used to look after her until she became ill.'

'I'm surprised.' Alex was astonished. 'I have just been up there, and it looks long since deserted. Are you sure it is still inhabited?'

'I don't get to deliver to the farm too often,' the postwoman said, 'but last time I was there, I left the letters, and it looked as though Siri had got some help with the farm. There were workers in the fields.'

'Thank you for your help.' Alex smiled at the postwoman. 'I shall go and look more closely to see if there is still anybody there. Do you know which hospital Lisbet was taken to?'

'The main one in town,' the post lady replied, 'if she is still alive.'

Alex decided to walk back up to the farm to see whether Lisbet's niece and daughter were still living there. It was starting to get dark as he approached, and Alex noticed a light shining dimly from one of the windows. *Good*, he thought, *there is somebody there.*

Alex walked up to the farm and knocked on the door, expecting it to be opened by either Siri or her daughter. He was quite surprised when it was opened by a large man wearing dirty brown trousers and braces.

'Sorry,' Alex started, 'I was looking for—'

Alex did not complete the sentence, as he was struck from behind by something wielded with much force. When he awoke, it was dark, and he had no idea where he was, but he did know that his hands were tied together and attached to a rope affixed to a very solid beam.

Alex's eyes took time to adjust to the gloom, but he eventually identified that it was a barn or another sort of outbuilding. He could hear a noise coming from the corner and assumed that it was a rat whose home Alex had invaded.

'*Perkele!*' Alex cursed and realised that when the chips were down, he had started to swear in Finnish! He then made a conscious effort to curse again, but in English: 'Shit!' The rat responded by scurrying in the corner. He tried to make himself as comfortable as possible so that the thumping headache would go and he might wake up to discover it was all a bad dream.

It wasn't. When Alex woke again, he saw two men in the barn with a plate of bread and some water. One came over to him and kicked him, but something told Alex to remain quiet, so he rode the kick and did not make a sound. The other grabbed a pile of rags from the corner where Alex had heard the rat the previous night, and he dragged a girl of about sixteen to her feet.

'Here you are,' he said, though the girl did not respond. She probably did not understand what was being said, but Alex did – the man had spoken in Russian. What were they? Deserters?

The other man, the one who had kicked Alex, laughed and grabbed the girl, dragging her to the far side of the barn where Alex could see an old bed had been left. He threw her onto the threadbare mattress, and after undoing his clothes, he was on her, pumping away and ignoring her cries, while his colleague stood and laughed.

'You want food, you have to work for it,' he said as his friend finished what he was doing. The man who had just satisfied his needs with the girl dragged her back to the rags and threw her down before readjusting his clothing, and they both left, laughing. Alex remained silent, listening to the girl's whimpering in the corner.

After a while, Alex whispered in Finnish, 'Is your name Ines?' The girl stopped sobbing and went very quiet.

Alex tried again but in Swedish. 'Is your name Ines?'

'Ja,' she breathed back.

'My name is Alex,' he whispered. 'Try not to be afraid, but please answer my questions.'

'Ja,' the girl murmured again timidly.

'Who are these men?' he hissed back to her.

'I don't know; they came a few weeks ago.'

'Where is your mother?' Alex asked.

'They shot her and buried her out in the back yard,' Ines sobbed. 'They were going to shoot me too, but then they realised that I was a young girl.'

Alex fully understood the men's intentions when they had saved her from the same fate as her mother.

'I need to think about how we are going to get ourselves out of this mess.' Alex tried to sound positive, but with his hands tied tightly, he did not know how he would begin.

'It is not possible,' Ines said dejectedly. 'If we try to escape, they will kill us. I know they will.'

'Nothing is impossible.' Alex tried reassurance. 'You just need to find a way of making the impossible possible! How many of them are there?'

'Four,' Ines whispered.

'Shit!' Alex cursed. One or two was a possibility, but four was too many. He leant back, hoping to find the reassurance of his pistol in the small of his back, but it was not there. He heard footsteps outside, and another man entered the barn, coming over to where Alex was laying. He kicked him lightly.

'Come on, I know you are awake. Nobody sleeps this long even if Ivan has hit them with a shovel,' the man said in Russian.

Alex grunted.

'Tell me your name,' the man said.

'Sergei Mikhailovich Anokhin,' Alex replied. 'I'm a deserter.'

The man laughed and left the barn.

When they were alone, Ines said, 'I do not understand. You said your name was Alex, but I think you just told him your name was Sergei.'

'My name is Alex,' he said quietly, 'but if we are going to get out of this mess, we might have to tell a few untruths.' He smiled at her.

All four men returned together, and the one whom Alex had not yet seen asked, 'You say you are a deserter? Which division?'

Alex said the first that came into his head. '54th.'

'54th, eh?' the man asked. 'Who was your commander?'

'General Gusevski,' Alex responded.

'Where did you escape?'

'Kuhmo,' Alex replied. 'My section got hit by a patrol, and I played dead. When the Finns had gone, I got up and sneaked off.'

'Kuhmo? That's some distance! How did you get here?'

'Mostly I walked,' Alex said. 'I occasionally managed to get a lift or I jumped a goods train, but mainly I walked.'

'What happened to your uniform?'

'I got rid of it and stole clothes from washing lines,' Alex explained. 'Finns were not going to give a Russian a lift, so I needed to change my appearance.'

'You speak Finnish?' the man asked.

'No, but I do speak Swedish. My mother was Swedish.'

'Why did you come here?' the man questioned.

'I was going to Borgå,' Alex answered, using the Swedish name for Porvoo.

'Why?'

'If you want to hide a tree, you plant it in a forest,' Alex responded. 'I speak Swedish, but not Finnish, so hiding in a Swedish community is easier than in a Finnish- speaking one.'

'Why did you come to this farm?' the man persisted.

'I heard in the town that the people who lived here were Swedish Finns and that the man was in the army and his wife needed a man to help out, so I came to offer my services.'

'You won't be much good to her in the place where she has gone. I must talk to my friends to see if we believe you. If we do, we might let you join us. If not, we will kill you.'

The men left, and Alex relaxed on the straw.

'What did they say?' Ines asked.

'They were interrogating me,' Alex replied. 'Let us hope they believed my story.'

XXII

Alex spent a fretful night, worried that the story that he had spun his captors would not stand the test of scrutiny. The secret, he recalled, about lying is that the untruth must be believable to the person being lied to. He had no idea from which division these men had deserted, but he was gambling on them being from a unit that had fought in the south and that they might not know anything of the troops who fought in the northern sectors.

He eventually drifted off to sleep when the night was at its darkest. Ines was still sobbing amongst her rags, and Alex wondered what was to become of her if they managed to extricate themselves from captivity.

The dawn rose on Friday 12th April and the morning light leached through the badly warped planking of the barn walls. Alex called quietly to Ines to see if she was awake.

'Ja,' she responded.

'Good,' he whispered. 'Now, whatever might happen today, understand that I am going to try and find a way out for us. Do not do anything to annoy these people, and just act normally.'

'All right,' she murmured.

As if on cue, the door was hauled open, and all four of their captors stood in the barn looking at Alex.

'You!' The one who seemed to be in charge pointed at Alex. 'It seems that your story has convinced two of my friends. Maxim here remains to be convinced.' Alex recognised the man who had brought the bread and water for Ines the previous day.

Alex sat up and waited to see what was coming next.

'Where do you come from in Russia?' the leader asked.

'Leningrad,' Alex replied.

'Excellent,' the man said and continued, 'what is the name of the main street in Leningrad?'

Alex remembered having read about how the main street in St Petersburg had been changed from Nevskiy Prospekt to mark the October Revolution of 1917. 'Prospekt 25 Oktyabrya,' he replied.

'The Museum of the History of Religion and Atheism on Prospekt 25 Oktyabrya used to be what?' the man asked, and as Alex took his time in answering, a smile of satisfaction crept across the face of the one they called Maxim.

'Kazanskiy Kafedralniy Sobor,' – The Cathedral of Our Lady of Kazan, Alex ventured.

The man looked at the other called Maxim and asked if he was satisfied.

Maxim looked at Alex and asked, 'What is the name of the Leningrad ballet?'

'Kirov,' Alex replied, and the man looked crestfallen, almost as if he wished Alex had given the wrong answer. 'It used to be called the Mariinsky until the murder of Sergei Kirov when they renamed it in his honour.'

The leader looked at the man called Maxim, who shrugged and nodded, before turning back to Alex. 'Finally, where did you get this?' He pointed Alex's FN pistol at Alex's forehead.

'I took it from a dead Finnish officer,' Alex replied nervously. 'He had no further need for it, and I thought it might be useful.'

'Cut him free,' the leader ordered, and one of the others slit the bonds that bound his hands. 'He is Russian.' The leader turned to Alex, 'My name is Ilya Vladimirovich Glushenko, and I was a starshina in the

44th Rifle Division. This is Boris Sergeivich Kovalchuk, that is Andriy Stepanovich Zelenko, and Maxim is Maxim Mikhailovich Pavlyuk. All of us but Andriy were in the 44^{th,} and he was in the 163rd Rifle Division.

Alex now understood how easy it had been to convince these men that he was a deserter – they were all Ukrainian and had probably never been to Leningrad, as neither had Alex. Glushenko gripped Alex in a bear hug and said, 'You are welcome to join us, but I think I shall keep this for myself.' He held up Alex's FN pistol.

'Now, come and have some breakfast, unless you want to fuck the bitch first. We all do,' he laughed.

'No, breakfast would be great. Maybe later,' Alex said.

'Well, if you don't want her, I do,' Maxim said, and grabbing Ines by her hair, he dragged the young girl to the bed. The sound of Ines screaming as he went for breakfast was one of the most painful sounds that Alex had ever heard.

Over the weekend, wherever Alex went, one of the others went as well. It was almost as if they still did not trust him to be on his own. On Monday evening, they said he should take the girl her bowl of thin soup and use her while he was there, and Alex picked up the bowl and plate and went to the barn. As he put the soup down, he heard someone behind him, and he looked up to see Glushenko standing by the door.

'Go on,' he said, 'take her. Or do you only do it with boys?'

Realising this was a test, he looked apologetically at Ines, and as carefully as he could, he dragged her to the bed before whispering, 'I am not going to do anything, but make like I am hurting you. They seem to like that.'

As he threw her on the bed and climbed on top, Ines screamed in his ear to stop as he was hurting her. Alex smiled at her, and as he got up, he whispered, 'Soon. Be ready.'

*

Life progressed in this manner for the next few days. Whereas Glushenko had accepted him as a fellow deserter, Alex felt that the others did not fully trust him, so he did whatever was necessary to gain their trust. He fetched and carried, worked on the farm, cooked, cleaned; in fact, anything they asked of him, to bolster his standing in their group. There seemed to be some kind of casual rota as regards the use of Ines, where each had rights to use her on different days. Hardest for her was when it was Boris's day as he seemed insatiable and often used her more than once. He was also not worried about how he used her and often bragged about the various unnatural acts he had forced Ines to commit on him. Alex was included in this rota and was forced to be with Ines twice more during that first week, although on each occasion the act was simulated and Ines did her bit by making appropriate noises of suffering while he was with her.

Alex did not get an opportunity to strike until the Sunday of the following weekend. He was instructed to go with Maxim to take Ines food and wait while Maxim enjoyed her. He put the food down, and as Maxim grabbed Ines to drag her to the bed, Alex stepped behind him, and with a deft move, he extracted his puukko that had remained secreted in his boot and neatly slit Maxim's throat. There was no noise, but the look of sheer astonishment on Maxim's face was remarkable.

'Take him to the bed and make out you are doing it,' Alex instructed and then called Glushenko to the barn. 'Hey, look,' Alex said, laughing, 'the bitch is bleeding.'

As Glushenko stepped forward to see better, Alex gripped him under the chin and pulled his head back before swiftly and accurately pushing the puukko straight through Glushenko's heart. The man fell to the ground silently, and Alex ran his hands over the leader's body until he found the Russian's pistol tucked in his waistband.

Alex pulled Ines out from under Maxim's dead body, smiled at her and whispered, 'That evens the odds a little bit. Now, let me go and deal with the other two. Stay silent.'

Alex walked through the door into the farmhouse and saw Boris and Andriy playing cards at the dining table, sharing a bottle of vodka of which they had drunk most. Andriy looked up as Alex entered, and Alex shot him straight through the eye, the back of his head disintegrating as he fell backwards. Boris drunkenly tried to rise, and Alex shot him twice in quick succession, going over to make sure that both were dead. He dragged them together, and stripping the dirty tablecloth from the table, he covered their bodies before returning to the barn to fetch Ines.

Entering the barn, he checked Glushenko's body to make sure that the man was dead. He was, but there was still a strange gurgling from Maxim, so Alex shot him in the head at point-blank range, to make doubly sure that he was lifeless.

Taking Ines by the hand, he said, 'Come, we must get you cleaned up and then we will go into town to get help.'

*

The news of Alex's apparent disappearance set off a chain reaction that reached the highest level of government. When he failed to attend the presidential reception the previous Tuesday, a messenger was sent to the hotel to check if he was all right. The manager explained that he had not seen Alex for over a week and that the hotel had received a message from Ekman's the tailors when Alex had failed to attend for a fitting but had thought little about it as Mr Carlsson was a very busy man, and they assumed he had merely forgotten.

Svenska Posten was contacted and asked when they had last had a report from Alex Carlsson, and they said that it was not unusual for correspondents not to file anything if there was nothing to report. Despite sounding unconcerned, Sigrid was worried and secretly contacted the British Legation and notified Simon Potts that Alex was missing. Simon contacted Commander Jeffers in London, and he briefed Colonel Llewelyn. Colonel Llewelyn suggested that it might be time to repatriate Alex if and when they found him alive, and Jeffers found himself agreeing. The commander just hoped that Alex was all right. Llewelyn instructed Jeffers to keep the matter "under his hat" until they knew more, and although tempted to brief the First Lord of the Admiralty, Winston Churchill, he managed to tame the urge.

In Finland, the civilian police were asked to try and locate Alex, and at the same time, the security police also became involved. The joint investigation led the search as far as Porvoo, where Minna Koskela was interrogated, and she reported that she had last seen Alex catch the bus to Kotka. The investigation stalled when the driver could not say where Alex had alighted, but he thought it may have been when they reached Kotka. The hotels and bars of Kotka were searched, the hospital visited, but nobody had any recollection of ever having seen Alex. The report said that Alex had disappeared, but in a country where so many citizens were on the move, one more missing person did not raise too many concerns with the police.

*

Back at the farm, Alex had gently encouraged Ines to come into the house, and he prepared her a bath of warm, but not too hot, water. While she went to what had been her bedroom to see if she could find any of her clothes, Alex dragged the two dead bodies out of the house and took them to the barn, leaving Ines to bathe in private. In the barn, Alex searched the bodies and found that two of the deserters had kept their identity tags, so he took them and put them in his pocket. He also collected a variety of papers and other personal effects and wrapped them in a piece of oilcloth that he found in the barn, securing that package with twine.

After about forty minutes, Alex knocked on the door and asked Ines if she had finished, and she called him into the living room. She had cleaned herself thoroughly and dressed in what must have been her Sunday best. The transformation was remarkable; gone was the disgusting and smelly urchin that had lived in the barn as a prisoner and object of sexual gratification for her captors. She had been replaced by a wholesome and attractive young lady with a shy smile and pigtails, wearing a loose shift dress that had clearly been made by hand.

Alex smiled at her and said, 'Let me get rid of that filthy water,' and he struggled to drag the tin bath out into the farmyard, where he tipped it up and poured away the evidence of Ines's degradation.

When Alex returned to the house, she said, 'I had to scrub myself nearly raw to get the stench of those men from my body.'

'I know,' Alex said, 'but it is over now, and tomorrow we shall go to town and see if we can put things right. I am sure that there will be an investigation, so you must continue to be brave.'

'I will try,' Ines assured Alex.

Alex found a pan and made a sort of soup with whatever meagre rations the deserters had left. It comprised mainly vegetables that they had scavenged from the farm, and he served it with hard black bread that was stale. Nevertheless, Ines complimented Alex on his cooking skills and announced that it was one of the best meals that she had eaten.

After dinner, they sat in the farmhouse and chatted. Alex told Ines of his life as a newspaper correspondent and of all his adventures in Finland and London. She politely said that it all sounded exciting and that she thought she might like to visit London one day. Ines told Alex that her seventeenth birthday had been two months ago and she had been at school until the previous year when she had left to help with the farm. Because Ines had come to the school late and was Swedish-speaking, not Finnish-speaking, she had found it difficult to fit in with the other children and had not even been kissed by a boy, let alone had a proper boyfriend. She said she had hoped to train as a teacher, but when the war had come, and her papa had to go to war, her mother needed her to help run the farm.

At the mention of her mother, Ines's eyes welled up, and she started to cry. Alex put his arm around her protectively and said that before they left in the morning, they must make a cross and place it where the Russians had buried her mother. Ines nodded in gratitude.

It was evident that Ines was getting tired, so Alex picked her up and carried her to the bedroom, where he gently placed her on the bed. 'Go to sleep, your nightmare is over. I shall sleep in the living room and make sure nothing more harms you and tomorrow we will go into town.' Ines nodded and fell asleep, and Alex looked down at the frail young girl, wondering whether the mental scars would ever heal.

XXIII

The next morning, Alex was awake early. He went to the barn to check on the bodies and found them all where he had left them. Alex collected two pieces of planking and took a roll of twine down from a shelf. He searched the barn and eventually found an old tin of paint and a brush, then he returned to the farmhouse.

Ines was still asleep, but she soon woke when Alex started to make some coffee and to reheat the remains of the soup from the previous night. She wandered into the living room wearing a nightdress that she had seemingly changed into when she had woken during the night.

'*God Morgon*,' Alex greeted her in Swedish. 'Did you sleep well?'

'Not really,' Ines replied, 'but better than when I was in the barn.'

Alex smiled. 'Coffee? Soup?' Ines nodded, so he poured both for her.

'I was wondering,' Ines ventured, 'why did you come to the farm? Why would a newspaper correspondent come to this farm in particular?'

'I once knew Lisbet and Edvard Nylund who used to own the farm and just wanted to see if it had changed,' Alex replied.

'Uncle Edvard died, and Aunt Lisbet is in the hospital,' Ines told him.

'I know,' Alex said.

'Mama and I used to go and visit her sometimes, but she is not well,' Ines told him.

'That is a shame. I have fond memories of them,' Alex said. 'Perhaps we might visit her before I leave if you would like to?'

'I think I would,' Ines said.

Ines went to dress, and when she was ready, Alex made a rough cross from the planking he had taken from the barn, and Ines painted her mother's name on the wood before they went out behind the barn to a piece of freshly dug earth and Ines gently placed the cross in the ground.

They stood for a moment in silent prayer before Ines wiped away her tears and whispered, 'Goodbye, Mama. God bless you.'

Ines smiled awkwardly at Alex and said, 'Shall we go?' They both picked up their bags and started walking towards the town.

When they walked into the police station in the centre of the town, Alex asked to speak to whoever was in charge. The duty officer looked them both up and down, before nodding to a hard bench by the wall and instructing them to wait. After a few moments, he returned and asked what their names were.

'Ines…' Alex looked at her, and she added, 'Lindgren.'

'And Alex Carlsson.' Alex completed the introductions.

The duty officer went away, and there was suddenly a commotion in the back office that led to another policeman coming out of a side door and looking at them intently.

He said to Alex, 'You are Alex Carlsson?'

Alex nodded.

'Come with me,' the policeman instructed, and they both followed the officer into the back of the police station. They entered the area where prisoners were detained, and the officer opened a cell door.

'Please,' he invited Alex to enter, 'you are not under arrest, but we have been asked to hold you until somebody comes from Helsinki. We need to make sure you stay here. We will put your friend next door.'

'Before you close the door, why are we being held?' Alex asked.

'I do not know, but the chief received instructions last week to look for you and hold you. I just follow orders.'

Ines was looking frightened, so Alex said, 'We have to make a statement to the police, so will you please contact your superior urgently? Also, if I give you my word that I will not try to escape, please can the young lady stay with me? She has suffered a lot recently and is very frightened, which is what we want to say in our statements.'

The policeman looked at Alex, weighing up the situation. On the one hand, if Carlsson escaped, he would be in serious trouble, on the other hand, the message from Helsinki had said to "hold" Carlsson, not to "arrest" him, and they were in the cell area, which was completely secure. He looked at Ines, who was visibly shaken and close to tears.

'All right,' the policeman decided. 'I will not lock the cell door, and your friend can stay with you until the inspector arrives. He should not be too long, as he has already been summoned.'

Ines joined Alex in the cell, and the door was left open. After less than a quarter of an hour, the senior officer arrived and introduced himself as Komisario Erkki Laakso. The inspector invited Alex and Ines into his office and asked the reason for them wanting to make a statement.

Alex explained, 'This is Ines Lindgren, and she lives at the Nylund farm just outside town on the Gislom road.' The inspector nodded, acknowledging that he knew the place. 'A few weeks ago, the house was taken by four Russian deserters who killed Ines's mother and buried her on the farm. Ines was spared and held captive for their gratification.

'About ten days ago, I came to visit the Nylund's, who my family knew many years ago, and I was also attacked. Because I speak Russian, I managed to convince the deserters that I was also on the run from the Soviet army, and they let me join their group. I had no choice, and I am sure they would have killed me otherwise. At the first opportunity, yesterday, I killed the deserters and freed Miss Lindgren, and now we have come to report it to you.'

'How did you kill them?' the inspector asked.

'I used my puukko on two and the others I shot. They are all lying in the barn at the farm,' Alex explained.

'I will have your story checked out, and if it is true, I will take statements. Also, Miss Lindgren should see a doctor if what you say is true, and I will arrange that. Meanwhile, you will have to accept our hospitality as some people are coming from Helsinki to talk to you.'

'Do you know about what?' Alex asked.

'No,' the inspector replied. 'I am just a provincial policeman who is long overdue retirement. They don't talk to me about such things.'

The inspector left them in his office while he went to give orders to his men to go to the farmhouse straight away and report back what they found. Alex stretched his hand out to Ines and took hers, giving it a squeeze of reassurance.

'What is happening?' she asked.

'The inspector is checking our story. Don't worry; everything will be all right,' Alex assured her.

It did not take long. After less than half an hour, the inspector returned with the news that his men had discovered four bodies at the farm and a recent grave. He asked how Alex could be sure that they were Soviet deserters, and Alex took the identity discs and other items he had recovered from the bodies from his pocket and handed them to the policeman who put them into an envelope and sealed the flap.

'We need to get something taken down on paper, so can Miss Lindgren go with another officer and answers some questions, and I will take your statement?' Inspector Laakso asked. Alex looked at Ines, and she smiled and nodded. He squeezed her hand supportively and smiled back.

It took about an hour to answer all of the policeman's questions, by which time Alex felt drained. He hoped that Ines was being treated well by the officer who was taking her report. Shortly afterwards, the other officer returned and handed a sheaf of paper to his superior, who read the document through before pronouncing that everything seemed to tally and that both statements were in agreement. A kindly officer brought Ines back to the inspector's office, and she smiled nervously at Alex.

Alex asked, 'My main reason for coming to Loviisa was to see Lisbet Nylund, and I am sure that Ines would like to see her aunt, also. Is it possible that one of your men could come with us to the hospital? It will be a shame if I have to go back to Helsinki without paying my respects.'

The inspector thought for a moment. 'Two of my officers will accompany you. You appear to be a bit of a will-o'-the-wisp, Mr Carlsson, and I really do not want to have to explain that you vanished from our custody, by the time that the people from Helsinki arrive.'

Alex and Ines were taken to the hospital and shown into a ward by a nervous nurse; she was not used to having visitors escorted by the police.

'Mrs Nylund is not well,' the nurse explained. 'She may not recognise you. But please do not tire her out.' They were shown a bed in which an elderly woman lay staring at the ceiling.

'Lisbet? There's someone to see you,' the nurse spoke gently to the old woman. It was not as Alex remembered Lisbet Nylund from the days when he was a child. She had always appeared healthy and mentally sharp. The old woman lying on the bed was a husk of the former farmer's wife who had taken so many risks to protect Alex and his mother.

'Is that you, Edvard?' the woman asked.

Alex threw all caution to the wind and drew closer to the old woman before saying clearly, 'No, Aunt Lisbet, it's Alex.'

The old woman's eyes focussed on his face, and there appeared to be a spark of recognition. 'Tell Tatjana that she will have to make dinner tonight, I'm too tired.'

The fact that the old woman had used the name that Alex's mother had been known by when she lived in Finland showed Alex that Lisbet's reason had not altogether abandoned her.

'Is this your wife?' she asked Alex, looking at Ines.

'No, Aunt, it's your niece, Ines,' Alex explained.

'I'm sure you will live as happily together as did Edvard and me,' the woman said distantly.

The nurse touched Alex on the arm and said, 'I think Mrs Nylund needs to sleep now.' Alex nodded and gave the old lady a peck on the cheek, as did Ines, and they left.

*

When Alex and Ines arrived back at the police station, the inspector told them that the people from Helsinki would be coming shortly and that

Alex was to wait for their arrival. He had not had any instructions about Miss Lindgren, so she was free to leave if she wished.

Ines looked horrified at the prospect of returning to the farm without Alex, and she gripped his arm tightly. Alex said that Miss Lindgren was in shock and she would need help to recover from the trauma she had experienced. Perhaps it would be better if she waited with Alex. The policeman smiled a knowing smile, although he was probably quite far distant from the truth, with his thoughts.

It took another hour before two men from Helsinki arrived to escort Alex back, and it was clear from the deference in which the provincial police held them, and their attitude, that these were members of the security police, the ValPo. They held more authority than the local police in Loviisa and knew how to use it. Their instructions were to collect Alexander Carlsson and bring him back to Helsinki. There was nothing about bringing a girl with them, and despite Alex's objections, they refused to take Ines with them. The local inspector offered to allow Ines to stay with his family until things at the farm were sorted out, and Alex handed over the contents of his wallet to ensure that Ines could buy some feminine necessities. She clung onto him as the ValPo took him to their car, and they ignored the protestations of Alex and the local police as they physically separated her from Alex.

'Thank you for all you have done,' was the last thing she said to Alex as he was bundled into their car.

The atmosphere in the car on the way back to Helsinki that evening was tense. One of the officers tried to start a conversation by stating, 'You have led us a merry dance and tied up resources that could have been used to better effect than chasing after a Swedish newspaperman. It might be time for you to consider returning to Sweden.'

If they intended it as an ice-breaker, it was spectacularly unsuccessful. Alex sat in the back of the car and ignored both of the policemen. Even when they started asking more relevant questions and particularly making suggestions about his relationship with Ines, he just stared at them blankly. Unbeknown to them, he had been trained in deflecting interrogation, and eventually, they gave up.

The car swung into the courtyard of the impressive Secret Police headquarters in Punavuori and Alex recalled that the area previously used to be the area of prostitutes and brothels. He thought how little the district had changed in the past hundred years. As the vehicle slewed to a halt, the back door was opened by the policeman from the passenger's side, and he grabbed Alex to physically drag him out of the car. Another officer called from a doorway for him to stop, and he hurried over.

'Mr Carlsson,' the new officer said, 'it is so good to see that you are safe. Some people were getting quite worried about you, and from all accounts, you have been getting up to mischief again.

'The police in Loviisa have already filed a report, and it seems as though you rescued that young girl from a horrible fate and dealt with four ruthless and desperate Russian deserters. We might have a chat sometime about how you learned to use a puukko so effectively and how to shoot so accurately. It is not something ordinary people could cope with, and this is the second time you have displayed these deadly skills. Some might think it is becoming rather habit-forming.'

Although it was said in a light-hearted manner, it was clear that the sentiments behind the officer's words were that they regarded him with suspicion.

'Do not worry about Miss Lindgren. I have already ordered that her father be found and relieved so that he can go home to look after her. In the meantime, we shall ensure that she is looked after well. She has had a very traumatic experience and needs the support of her family.

'For the moment, you will be pleased to know that you are free to return to your hotel. If we need any further details from you, I am sure you will be happy to cooperate. I would ask, though, that if you are planning to leave Helsinki, please check with us first. I am sure it will not be a problem, but it is always wiser to check first.'

Was this a threat? Or a very sizeable hint that he was under surveillance?

Alex would have to be doubly careful in the future, especially when meeting contacts. The policeman ordered the driver of the car to take Alex back to the Hotel Torni and then return to headquarters.

XXIV

When Alex returned to the Hotel Torni in the back of a security police car, several eyebrows were raised by both the staff and the remaining journalists.

'I need a bottle of vodka and your assurance that I will not be disturbed,' Alex told the hotel receptionist as he collected his key from the desk.

'That's all right, Mr Carlsson. I am sure we can oblige,' the receptionist smiled.

'Thank you,' Alex said as he made his way to the lifts. He ignored the remaining journalists in the bar, who were keen to hear of Alex's exploits, but Alex knew he had a story to write.

Despite having asked not to be disturbed, after a short time, there was a knock on Alex's door. When he opened it, he saw a nervous-looking hotel bellboy with a sealed letter for him. 'This has just arrived, by messenger, sir.'

The letter was a short formal note inviting Alex to the Presidential Palace at 7.00pm, the day after next, *"where certain outstanding matters would be concluded"*. Alex was perplexed; he realised that his enforced extended visit to Loviisa had caused him to miss the reception to which he had been invited, but Alex did not think it overly significant, and yet he was again being summoned.

'Is the messenger waiting for a reply?' Alex asked. The bellboy nodded. 'Tell him "Thank you" and leave it at that, if you would.' The boy scurried away to relay Alex's response.

Alex ran a bath and poured himself a large vodka and settled into the hot water to soak away the degradation of the past couple of weeks. He threw the contents of his travelling case and the clothes that he had taken off into the bin. Alex dressed in freshly laundered clothes from his wardrobe and was intrigued to see that the suit he had ordered from Ekman's before leaving the capital had been delivered without him having had a fitting, and was hanging in the closet. When Alex tried it on, it fitted like a glove, and when the account was found protruding slightly from an inside pocket, he resolved to settle it promptly.

After his bath, Alex sat down and started to write his article on how people were surviving the post-war period in the provinces. He played down his involvement in the incident at the farmhouse and of Ines in particular, although he did comment on the danger from deserters who were still at large in the border country. Alex read his article through and edited it several times before he was happy with the result.

To say that Alex enjoyed a comfortable night's sleep would be stretching the truth, as he spent much of it tossing and turning and being plagued by nightmares of how his recent exploits might have concluded. He was worried about Ines, despite the assurances given to him by the police. Would she ever recover from her ordeal?

The next morning, as dawn's first light illuminated his room, Alex rose, and nursing a thick head from the quantity of vodka consumed the previous evening, he again bathed. It was almost as if he was unable to wash away the awareness of his actions in Loviisa. He dressed carefully and applied almost too much gentleman's eau de Cologne so that he felt civilised when he went down to breakfast.

The first person he met was Leona Guichard, who he suspected was lying in wait for him to make an early appearance. 'Hey, Carlsson,' she greeted him from her breakfast table, 'grab a coffee and join me. Tell me about your adventures. The scuttlebutt is rife with rumours, but I want it from the horse's mouth, as it were!'

Alex filled a coffee cup and joined her. 'What do you want to know?' he asked.

'Everything, darling, everything,' she replied. 'Did you honestly kill ten men with your bare hands to rescue a damsel in distress? That is the stuff of legends!'

Alex did not know whether she was deliberately exaggerating the rumours for dramatic effect, or to elicit a denial that she could whittle down to the truth.

'Good Lord, Leona,' he began, 'you seem to have cast me as a latter-day St. George, and that I am not. I did indeed meet up with some Soviet deserters, and, yes, they did indeed end up dead, but there were only four, and a pretty sorry bunch they were, too. It was a case of their or my survival, and I was damned sure my time was not yet up – besides, I had not yet written my weekly column!'

His light-hearted comments did not appease the curiosity of the Canadian. 'So what about the girl?'

'The ruffians had captured a woman, and she was freed after the deserters died, yes,' Alex replied, 'but honestly, it was nothing as romantic as you hope; it was a sickening incident that I truly want to forget. Tell me what has been happening here, while I was away.'

'You mean apart from being interrogated by the ValPo about you and your movements? Jesus, Alex, we thought you had been exposed as a Soviet spy or something. They kept asking who you were especially close to, and when they realised that Mick McMahon and Felix were both dead, you could see the cogs working overtime in their stupid brains wondering if you had any part in their deaths! You don't want to get on the wrong side of those guys – they seem to exercise their minds by letting them jump to conclusions!'

Alex's and Leona's breakfast arrived, and he was pleasantly surprised to see the quality of the food had improved since he had last eaten at the hotel.

'Food's getting better, I see,' he commented.

'Yeah, just as I'm about to leave. My paper has reassigned me to your old hunting ground; I'm leaving for London at the weekend.'

'You will enjoy that,' Alex assured her.

'Not with Herr Goring dropping bombs on it every night, I won't,' she replied. 'I'm sure *Le Nationaliste* wants to get me killed off!'

'I doubt the Germans have a bomb big enough to kill you, Leona,' Alex said with a smile.

'Nice of you to think so,' Leona replied without rancour.

'So, you are leaving at the weekend, then?' Alex asked.

'Yeah, my paper is trying to get me on one of the flights to Stockholm, but it ain't looking hopeful at the moment,' she said. 'God knows how I get to London from there, though. By ship, I suppose.'

Alex finished his breakfast and swilled the last of the coffee before smiling at Leona and saying that they should have a farewell drink before she left. By now, they were the sole surviving members of the original Torni Drinkers' Club left at the hotel and, in a way, Alex was surprisingly saddened by her imminent departure.

Having collected his report to send to *Svenska Posten*, when Alex left the hotel and headed to the main post office, he immediately spotted someone following him. The tail was so apparent that Alex wondered whether the follower intended that he should be detected. If so, why? Was it as a warning that he was being watched, or was it that another tail was following more closely to see what Alex did to shake the "dummy"? Alex pondered whether he should dive into Stockmann's department store to lose his follower, but decided against doing so, as that was a classic counter-surveillance move that would immediately be recognised by anyone else who was watching him. In the end, Alex strolled casually to the post office, waited while the clerk calculated how much it would be to wire the report before paying and stepping back outside. At first, Alex did not spot his follower and momentarily wondered if he was mistaken, but as he moved off, so the tail slipped back into position, and Alex's worries were confirmed. Who could have an interest in him; the Finnish security police, the Russians?

Returning to the hotel, Alex was only mildly surprised to find the kindly security officer waiting for him in reception.

'Mr Carlsson,' the policeman stepped forward, 'I thought you might be interested to hear about Miss Lindgren.'

'Thank you,' Alex replied. 'Would you like to come to my room, or will the bar be private enough?'

'The bar will be fine,' the policeman said and led the way as if he knew exactly where he was going.

When they had sat down, the policeman opened with, 'Miss Lindgren spent a relatively comfortable night with Inspector Laakso's family, and we have arranged for her to be seen at the hospital by a specialist in such things. She needs to be checked over for possible diseases that she may have contracted from her ordeal, and then there is the question of pregnancy, although it is too soon to know about that yet. But we are looking after her well, and the army has promised to send her father home as soon as possible.'

'Thank you,' said Alex, 'I am glad that somebody is looking after Ines. I am sure that the loss of her mother has not yet hit home.'

The policeman smiled, although that quickly changed as Alex continued. 'I noticed that I had someone following me when I went to the post office this morning. Was that your department?'

'Er, yes.' The policeman was embarrassed. 'We thought we should keep an eye on you, just in case you had the desire to go on any other excursions before your appointment tomorrow. You seem to have a nose for trouble, and it would be unfortunate if anything were to happen to prevent your attending the meeting.'

'Thank you for your concern,' Alex said with a smile. 'It is not my intention to cause any further difficulties, and it is so nice to know that someone is looking out for me.'

Alex stood, indicating that he considered the meeting over, and the officer followed suit and after shaking Alex's hand, he left, while Alex returned to his room.

Later that afternoon, he walked to Eerininkatu to settle his tailor's account at Ekman's and was welcomed by the tailor who had taken his measurements earlier. The tail that had followed him as soon as he stepped from the hotel took up position on the other side of the street and opened a newspaper. Alex smiled to himself at the sloppy conduct of his shadow.

Alex settled the account and complimented the tailor on the craftsmanship in his suit, at which the man blushed. 'We presumed it was an oversight when you did not come in for your fitting, and we also understood that you needed the suit for a significant engagement, so we were confident in the cut to be able to create the ensemble from your initial measurements. We are so pleased that you found it a good fit. However, should it need slight adjustment, please do not hesitate to bring it back to us.'

Alex could not resist it. As he stepped from the tailor's shop, he saw a taxi approaching, and so stuck out his hand to hail it, jumping aboard even before it had time to stop.

'Central railway station,' he instructed the driver, 'quick as you like.'

The driver let in the clutch, and by the time the follower had realised what had happened, Alex was driving quickly towards the station, leaving the tail standing in the middle of the road with his hands on his hips, looking dejected.

As the taxi crossed Heikinkatu, Alex changed his mind. 'On second thoughts,' he informed the driver, 'I'll go to the Hotel Torni.' The driver muttered something to himself and swung the taxi around. He was surprised by the generosity of Alex's tip when he deposited Alex at the hotel.

'Sorry to have bothered you, I just remembered something I had forgotten,' Alex explained. By the time that Alex's tail had resumed his position watching the hotel doorway, hoping to record when his mark returned to the hotel, the rain had started to fall again, and Alex was enjoying a relaxed drink in the hotel bar.

*

The weather throughout the day on Wednesday, 24th April 1940 was quite typical. The rain was falling and washing the pavements of Helsinki, but with it came a quite exhilarating freshness. Alex opened the windows of his hotel bedroom when he woke and drew in a lungful of fresh air, appreciating that spring had finally come to the capital. Not wanting to venture outside his room at all until the appointed time for him to go to the president's palace, Alex had ordered breakfast to be brought to his room and was quite surprised when the manager himself delivered it.

'Will you arrange a taxi to collect me at 5.30pm, please?' Alex asked as the man was about to leave.

'That will not be necessary, sir,' the manager replied. 'I understand that a car is being sent to collect you at six o'clock.' Alex was unsure whether to be pleased or annoyed. It seemed as though the security police were under orders that Alex should not miss this engagement.

The morning was spent writing another article for *Svenska Posten* that he planned to wire to Stockholm the next day, as a follow-up to the story about life in the provinces. It was not a story that Alex needed to write, but he had no desire to play catch and mouse with the security police who were evidently following him wherever he went, and the weather precluded sightseeing, so he stayed at the hotel all day. For lunch, Alex enjoyed a light salmon soup and a glass of wine and afterwards lay on the bed catnapping until mid-afternoon.

Alex felt distinctly self-conscious and awkward in the formality of the evening suit that he clambered into, and the impossibly starched wing-collared shirt that had been supplied by Ekman's was slightly too tight around the neck, making Alex feel as though he was enduring a blunt execution. The hotel's boot boy had performed wonders on his formal black shoes that had been waiting outside his room first thing that morning; they gleamed with perfection. However, Alex's preference for a wristwatch meant that he did not have a pocket watch and Albert chain to wear, which made him feel slightly underdressed for the reception, but he decided that it would have to do.

Arriving at the hotel lobby just before six o'clock, Alex was surprised to see Captain Toivonen, Field-Marshal Mannerheim's aide-de-camp, apparently waiting for him.

'Mr Carlsson, your car awaits,' the captain announced and, opening the hotel door, he guided Alex to the waiting staff car. Captain Toivonen opened the rear door and invited Alex to step inside before he took the seat next to the driver.

Turning slightly in his seat, Captain Toivonen addressed Alex. 'When you are taken into the palace, you will be escorted to an anteroom from where you will be collected. Please do not take it as a slight, sir, but unfortunately, President Kallio has been unavoidably detained this evening, and the reception is being hosted by Field-Marshal Mannerheim, who is deputising for the president. I know that the president was disappointed when you did not attend the previous appointment.'

Alex was vaguely apologetic as he muttered, 'Yes, well, as they say, necessity knows no manners.'

Captain Toivonen smiled. 'These events are usually held on Finnish Independence Day, the 6th December, but last year we were otherwise distracted, so the reception was postponed until April when necessity forced your absence.' Was there a hint in the captain's voice that Alex's flippancy had been taken as a slight?

'Regarding today,' Captain Toivonen continued without any apparent ill will, 'as the field-marshal is deputising for the president, the correct form of address at all times today is "Sir". Some find these events rather daunting, but my advice to you, sir, is to try and enjoy the occasion. Do you have any questions about protocol or anything you are unsure about?'

'I do not think so,' Alex replied, 'but this all seems rather formal for what I thought was merely an official reception.'

'Good heavens, sir,' Captain Toivonen smiled, 'there is always formality where the president is involved. Not so much as in some countries, I grant you, but we do like our little conventions on such occasions.'

The staff car drew up in front of the palace, and a sentry opened the car door as an official came forward to greet Alex and escort him to the meeting. As he climbed out of the car, Captain Toivonen said, 'Good luck, sir, and I shall see you later.'

Alex followed the official through the staterooms of the palace, and he was surprised at the quiet opulence of the building. The room into which he was shown was small but well furnished and lit by an enormous chandelier. The official asked if Alex required anything, to which Alex shook his head, and the door closed on Alex's solitude.

Less than five minutes passed before the door opened again as Alex heard the chiming of seven o'clock from a clock somewhere in the near vicinity, and the official invited Alex to follow.

'When you are admitted, please walk straight towards the single chair in front of those gathered within and take a seat. When Field-Marshal Mannerheim enters, please stand up and take one pace forward,' the official instructed. Alex was becoming perplexed by the whole situation, but as a door to a large reception room opened, he saw two banks of seats that were mainly unoccupied apart from a few military officers and a small number of civilians also wearing formal evening wear, none of whom turned around as Alex entered. Alex walked forward and took the single seat in the centre and front. Was this to be some sort of Grand Jury into his activities, he wondered?

After an appropriate delay, another door opened and Field-Marshal Mannerheim, accompanied by Captain Toivonen carrying a cushion, entered the room, and the field-marshal stood on the dais in front of Alex. He neither acknowledged Alex's presence nor spoke. A civilian stepped forward and addressed the assembly, reading in French from a script that he held in front of him:

'Par le présente je soussigné, Chancelier de l'Ordre de la Rose Blanche
de Finlande fais savoir que le Président de la République,
Grand-Maitre de l'Ordre a le 20 mars 1940
daigné attribuer a
Alexander Nikolas Carlsson
la croix du mérite de l'Ordre de la Rose Blanche de Finlande.'

By this I, the undersigned, Chancellor of the Order of the White Rose
of Finland inform that the President of the Republic,
Grand Master of the Order on the 20th day of March 1940,
deigned to award to
Alexander Nikolas Carlsson
the Cross of Merit
of the Order of the White Rose of Finland

Alex stood motionless in a state of abject stupefaction as Field-Marshal Mannerheim took a medal from the cushion that Captain Toivonen was holding and, stepping forward, he pinned it to Alex's left breast and said, 'For saving a Finnish officer's life in Suomussalmi.'

Field-Marshal Mannerheim shook Alex by the hand and pointedly looked at his lapel at a small decoration that was pinned in place and, drawing Alex slightly closer, he whispered, '*V temnote vse koshki sery*' – In the dark, all cats appear grey.

XXV

Alex was stunned. The last time he had heard those words uttered was at his wedding when Count Dmitry Sergeyevich Obolensky had brought dispatches from Grand Duke Kirill Vladimirovich Romanov, the titular head of the Romanov dynasty in exile and leader of the Russian Monarchist Union, *Soyuz Russkih Monarkhistov*. The phrase was given in recognition between members and accompanied by a discreet stick pin identical to the one that Field-Marshal Mannerheim was wearing.

The field-marshal stepped back and fixed Alex with a steely gaze that momentarily contained a twinkle in his eye, and he gave a very slight nod of recognition. Alex reciprocated and a bond formed between them, a connection that could never be publicly acknowledged.

The banquet that followed the ceremony was a discreet affair with only about half of those who had attended the ceremony staying to eat. Alex had been placed on the same table as Field-Marshal Mannerheim, who was on his left and Captain Toivonen, who was on his right. Alex was introduced to the others at the table, but he knew none of them, and they seemed content to talk amongst themselves.

Throughout the meal, Alex experienced a sense of expectation in the air, and whenever he spoke with Field-Marshal Mannerheim, he sensed that something was being held back. It was only during the dessert course that the field-marshal ventured, 'I recall when we met in Rovaniemi, I asked whether we had met previously, and you assured me that we had not.'

Alex was intrigued as the field-marshal continued, 'This continued to worry me, and when we met in Helsinki, I realised that I had been mistaken. I realised that I was confusing you with a young dragoon officer whom I once knew when I served the Tsar and to whom you bear a striking resemblance. His name was Aleksander Nikolaevich Karlov, but I knew that he had been killed in action. I made some discreet enquiries with friends that I have from that time in Paris and now realise the connection.

'Mr Carlsson, you may rest assured that your secret shall always remain such with me, but I should warn you that things are changing in our country and that it may soon be less safe for you to continue here. You might feel that you have served your newspaper well in the time that you have been here in Finland, but it is now time to leave. Your service to this country has been officially recognised, and you will always be a welcome guest here, but that may well be jeopardised should you remain. I have personally made provision for Miss Lindgren's future. She will be offered a position in the civil service in Helsinki so that she can leave Loviisa and the memories there—'

Alex interrupted the field-marshal. 'I thought her father was being released from military service so that he could join her?'

'Yes, sadly, it transpires that her father, Corporal Erik Lindgren, was captured by the Soviet in the last days of the war. His body has not been found, but he is presumed dead.'

'Poor Ines,' Alex said.

'Indeed, but after all that she has been through, it is perhaps better that she moves away and rebuilds her life.' Alex witnessed a rare moment of compassion that Mannerheim kept well disguised behind a stiff military countenance.

All of a sudden, the field-marshal rose and so did everybody else in the room, and he turned to Alex and shook his hand, saying, 'It has been most interesting to have met you, Mr Carlsson. Perhaps we shall meet again in the future. Thank you for all that you have done for our country.'

With that, Field-Marshal Mannerheim turned, and with Captain Toivonen in his wake, they briskly left the room.

*

Alex enjoyed the walk back to the hotel, and it gave him a chance to ponder over his discussion with the field-marshal. The sun had not long set, and there was a bright red glow illuminating the skyline over Heikinkatu as he walked up Esplanadi and past the Hotel Kämp. Had he not known the war to be over, he would have thought it the glow of burning buildings or a ship ablaze in the docks after a bombing raid. But this was the glow of a peacetime evening's sunset. He recalled hearing the English proverb about "Red skies at night, shepherd's delight; red skies in the morning, shepherd's warning!" If true, Alex thought, tomorrow would be a beautiful day.

Alex detoured down Bulevardi and came to the park where he had met Juha on his first night when he had arrived in Helsinki and sat on one of the new benches that the city authorities had thoughtfully replaced. The apartment house that Juha had indicated was where he had once lived, was being renovated very much in the style that had existed previously. It was almost as if the damage in the city was being replaced like-for-like so that nobody would remember the destruction caused by the war. Alex was unsure whether monuments to the future might not be a better testament to what had occurred, rather than trying to erase it from sight. He watched as a young boy crossed the road holding his mother's hand and went into one of the apartment blocks, and Alex unrealistically thought that maybe Juha's family had somehow survived and were living together normally again, but he knew it was a pipe dream.

Having sat for half an hour or so, Alex felt the chill of the evening creep into his bones, and as he rose, his fingers brushed over the leather box containing his award that was in his pocket. He walked pensively back to his hotel, and as he entered, he realised that he was not going to escape the staff and guests who had gathered to welcome him back. It was not every day that the president of the republic awarded one of their guests such high distinction and they wanted to congratulate him.

To an uncharacteristic round of applause, Alex entered, and the manager stepped forward to shake him warmly by the hand. He saw Leona Guichard over the manager's shoulder look heavenward in mock disdain, but she was clapping as enthusiastically as everybody else, and she flicked her head towards the bar, inviting Alex to join her after receiving his accolade.

The guests began to drift away, and Alex went into the bar. Leona had ordered a bottle of Krug Champagne, and as Alex approached, she said, 'The one thing my forefathers did well was making wine, and the one thing that Finns seem not to appreciate is fine wine. Otherwise, this bottle of 1929 Champagne would have been drunk already. It is one of the truly great vintages.'

'Thank you,' said Alex as he sat down and Leona discreetly removed the cage and cork. He savoured the creaminess of the bubbles, the almost toastiness in his mouth with a hint of almond, followed by an aftertaste of apples. 'My goodness,' he exclaimed, 'this is superb.'

'At long last,' Leona announced triumphantly, 'someone who appreciates fine wine. There's hope for you yet, Mr Carlsson,' she said almost mockingly.

By the time that they had finished the bottle, they were quite light-headed. 'So, what new adventures beckon you?' Leona asked.

'I really have no idea,' Alex replied and then remembering his conversation with Field-Marshal Mannerheim, 'but I think my work here is concluding. Who knows where my paper will send me next?'

'Perhaps back to London?' she enquired, and did Alex pick up a faint hope in her question?

'I doubt it,' Alex replied, even though he anticipated that would be precisely where he would end up. 'It is too soon after I left to go back. Knowing my luck, it will be Berlin or Moscow!'

They supported each other to the lift, and when it arrived at his floor, she leaned forward and placed a gentle kiss on his cheek. 'You look after yourself, Alex,' she said as he stepped backwards out of the door.

'You also,' he said, smiling.

In bed that night, Alex could not sleep. Although tired, he was kept awake by some sixth sense that things were about to change, and that this change would affect his whole life.

*

The pain that Teddy felt that night was excruciating. She felt as though her body was exploding, and her screams brought both Alex's mother and Klara running to her room. Teddy's bed was saturated, and she was writhing in agony.

'Go and telephone for Doctor Baxter,' the dowager countess instructed Klara, 'and tell him to come quickly.'

Klara ran downstairs and made the call, hurrying back to report that the doctor was leaving immediately but would still take a quarter of an hour to arrive. Alex's mother instructed Klara to go and boil some water, but such was her reluctance to leave her employer when she was in such pain, Klara ordered the housemaid to do so, who, along with other live-in servants, had come to see what was the commotion.

The doctor arrived along with a large and buxom midwife, who promptly took control of the situation and ordered the dowager countess and Klara to leave the room. Alex's mother swelled her chest and stood tall and proud, and Klara could sense that she was about to go into one of her 'Do you know who I am?' speeches, so she gently took the dowager countess arm and guided her out of the room.

After about ten minutes, the doctor emerged and said, 'Mrs Carlton is fine. The baby has decided to grace us with its presence a little earlier than we would have liked, but the indications are that there should be no difficulties. I anticipate that we have about two or three hours to wait, as the contractions are not regular yet, so perhaps somebody would be kind enough to fetch Mrs Armitage and I a nice cup of tea?'

Klara spoke to Alex's mother. 'Would you like to come and help me?'

'What?' exclaimed the dowager countess. 'Yes, of course,' and then added as an afterthought, 'thank God that Walter is staying in London. Men always get in the way at times like these.'

It was just after half-past four in the morning that a plaintive cry emanated from Teddy's bedroom and the doctor emerged from the room, drying his hands on a towel.

'It's a girl,' he said, 'five pounds and two ounces, so not a bad weight considering. She seems fine, and so does her mother.'

'May we go in?' Alex's mother asked.

'Let us leave them to rest for tonight,' the doctor replied. 'Mrs Armitage is staying with them tonight, and I shall call back out tomorrow morning. I am sure that they will benefit greatly from a sound sleep in what remains of the night and will be much more welcoming to visitors in the morning.'

The doctor collected his bag, and his jacket and Klara showed him out. As he was about to go to his car, he turned and said, 'It was not an easy birth, and tiring for them both,' he added, almost as if he did not trust Alex's mother to heed his suggestion. 'Make sure that they both rest tonight and are not disturbed. Tomorrow, Mrs Carlton will feel much stronger.'

The doctor had been entirely right, and the next morning, Teddy was starting to feel less fragile. She even welcomed a cup of weak tea that Klara brought her shortly after waking.

'That is not an experience I am keen to repeat quickly,' Teddy quipped, indicating that her sense of humour was returning. 'God only knows how some women have seven or eight children.'

'It probably gets easier,' said Klara, remembering that Rhodri had come from a large family and had similar intentions for his own. Mrs Armitage shooed Klara away, telling her that the doctor would be here shortly and that Mrs Carlton needed to rest, so Alex's mother and Klara went downstairs to try and start the day normally.

The doctor breezed in just before half-past eight in the morning and, after a short visit to see Teddy, he disappeared again equally as cheerfully, having told Alex's mother that all was as it should be, but 'Mrs Carlton still needs to rest.' The midwife rang down just after the doctor had departed and ordered that her breakfast be served in Mrs Carlton's bedroom, with the ominous warning that the doctor had asked her to stay on to ensure there were no further complications.

'Damned cheek of that woman,' the dowager countess grumbled as she helped Klara organise a tray of breakfast. 'It appears that she believes she is staying at the Ritz!'

Nevertheless, Mrs Armitage was a great help to Teddy in the first hours of motherhood. She explained how to encourage the baby to suckle and how to change the child's nappy, and she instructed Teddy that it was essential that the baby gets into a routine as soon as it is born; otherwise, it would benefit neither the child nor the mother.

'Mothering an infant is not a science,' the midwife explained. 'Women have been doing it for centuries with great success. Do not, however,' Mrs Armitage gave a stern warning, 'allow the child to control you. That is the start of a very rocky road to ill-discipline and one that many mothers take. You are not at the beck and call of the child, and neither does it harm the baby if you do not run to it whenever it makes a noise. The sooner your baby learns to sleep through the night, the quicker things will get back to normal for you.

'Now, the doctor is coming back after morning surgery, and he will bring a tonic to help you recover. Knowing Dr Baxter, it will probably taste foul, but it will make you stronger, so you must take it three times a day without fail. Is that clear?'

Teddy felt as though she was back at school and being admonished by a teacher, and before she realised it, she had responded, 'Yes, Miss.'

'You may call me "Sister", or "Mrs Armitage", but not "Miss". I am a married woman, and my husband is in the Royal Navy.' She was obviously annoyed. Then, with a radiant smile, she said, 'You will do very well, my dear. I am sure of it.'

Teddy drifted off to sleep and did not rouse again until Dr Baxter arrived shortly after midday. His examination did not reveal anything of concern, so he dismissed the midwife and went downstairs to inform Alex's mother and Klara that he was leaving.

'Mrs Carlton is still weak and should stay in bed for the next five days. Give her one spoonful of this, three times a day, and make sure she does not do too much. She should only spend half an hour at a time with the baby, or she will get too tired. If there are any problems, ring me immediately, and I will come out to see her. Meanwhile, good morning, ladies,' and with that, he turned on his heel and left.

'That man is always in a bustling hurry,' Alex's mother commented. 'He should slow down and not constantly seem in such unbecoming haste.'

Klara smiled. The dowager countess always took life at a gentle pace and was unnerved by anyone who tried to hurry her. 'It is his nature,' was her reply, and Alex's mother snorted in disdain.

XXVI

The morning of Thursday 25th April brought bright skies and a pleasant warmth to the long-suffering citizens of Finland's capital. Spring plants that many had wondered whether would bloom again provided a splendid blast of colour in the city's parks, and there was a distinct atmosphere of rebirth in the air. That morning also brought Alex a telegram that the hotel's bellboy brought to his room slightly after ten o'clock:

RECALL-TO-STOCKHOLM-IMMEDIATE-STOP-
REDEPLOYMENT-ON-NEW-ASSIGNMENT-STOP-
BOOKED-EVENING-FLIGHT-TWENTY-SEVEN-
APRIL-STOP-BON-VOYAGE-STOP-ASLUND-STOP

To say that his recall was a shock would be stretching the truth, but being given seventy-two hours to wrap up his affairs in Helsinki certainly was a surprise. When news travels, it travels fast, and by the time Alex had dressed and walked downstairs, the rumour of his imminent departure had already arrived at the hotel.

'Good morning, Mr Carlsson,' the hotel manager greeted him. 'I hear you are leaving us shortly.'

'It would seem so,' Alex replied. 'I shall be leaving on Saturday evening.

Will you please ensure that my account is brought up to date so that I can settle it before I leave.'

'That will not be necessary, sir,' the manager explained. 'We have been instructed to forward it directly to your employer in Stockholm.'

'And the private matter of the surcharge for the room?' Alex asked.

'That too, sir,' the manager said. 'The instruction was most specific.'

'I see,' Alex replied. 'Thank you.'

For the first time in months, Alex was at a loose end. He doubted that *Svenska Posten* would be expecting any further articles from him, so he wandered to the Stockmann store in Heikinkatu and looked for a small gift that he might give to Sigrid, but nothing took his eye. After a coffee at Café Fazer, Alex wandered aimlessly about the city until about six o'clock in the evening, when he found himself close to the bar where his rendezvous with Jarno had frequently occurred. Opening the door, he entered the welcoming fug that always seems to exist in bars anywhere in the world. Less than an hour passed before Jarno arrived and seeing Alex sitting at a table, ordered a drink and joined him.

'Alex,' Jarno began, 'it has been a while.'

'Yes,' replied Alex.

'I heard about Loviisa,' Jarno ventured.

'Yes,' Alex said.

'Good thing you did there,' Jarno stated.

'Thank you.' Alex was finding conversation difficult.

'I also heard about your award,' continued Jarno.

'It was a surprise,' Alex agreed.

'But well earned,' Jarno observed.

'Thank you,' Alex repeated, before continuing, 'I have been recalled to Stockholm.'

'I heard this also,' Jarno admitted. 'It will be nice to go home, surely?'

'Yes,' replied Alex, 'but I shall miss Finland.'

They both sat in melancholy silence, occasionally making an observation on which the other would briefly comment before silence returned. The four hours they spent together, gradually getting more drunk, seemed to drag, and when the barman told them that everybody else had already left and he wanted to go home to his family, Alex and Jarno got up and said their farewells on the street outside the bar.

'It has been a memorable experience knowing you, Mr Carlsson,' Jarno slurred as they were about to part, 'but you know that I was given scraps of information to feed to Mick McMahon when he first approached me. My superiors controlled the relationship between he and I.'

Alex was shocked by this revelation but tried not to let his surprise show. 'I had guessed as much,' he replied.

'But I had a more honest association with you.' Jarno was becoming more incoherent. 'I believed you had Finland's interests at heart and was not just interested in a good story. I gave you information that I should not have done, and that might be dangerous for me if my bosses ever found out.'

'They shall hear nothing from me,' Alex assured him, 'and thank you for telling me.'

'I shall miss our meetings,' Jarno said and gave Alex a bear hug. 'Take care of yourself, my friend, and if you ever come to Helsinki again, remember to look me up.'

'I shall,' Alex said, 'and give my best wishes to your wife, Katja.'

Jarno nodded in understanding, and they both turned and headed in opposite directions; Alex back to the hotel, and Jarno to his long-suffering wife.

*

The decision to recall Alex from Helsinki was not one that was taken lightly by his masters in MI2. Intelligence implied that Finland was smiling more favourably on the assistance being proffered by the Third Reich, despite all the efforts of the British and Swedish Governments to persuade Finland not to become allied with Germany. On the other hand, indications from their colleagues monitoring the situation in Russia were that Stalin was becoming increasingly less enamoured with the Molotov/Ribbentrop alliance with Germany, and tentative approaches were being made to Britain and her allies.

In one of the briefings with the First Lord of the Admiralty, Winston Churchill, Commander Jeffers raised the subject.

'God knows I am no lover of Bolshevism,' Churchill told Jeffers, 'but an alliance with Stalin does hold some merit. If Russia takes against Germany and forms a pact with Britain, France and their allies, then Hitler will become the meat in the sandwich that is Europe. He will be forced to defend Germany on two fronts. Even better should the southern states and those in the north over the Baltic join this alliance because then we should have Germany in a box from which it would struggle to become free.

'But despite our efforts, I suspect that it was always the case that Finland would align itself against whichever power the Soviets become allied with. Nevertheless, the might of Britain and her allies in the west and the Soviet in the east may simply be sufficient to quell the ambitions and warmongering of that Austrian corporal.

'Your man, Carlton, has done well in Finland and should be justifiably proud of all he has achieved, but I suspect that the time is nigh for his usefulness to draw to a conclusion. It might be time to consider bringing him home.'

'His reports are still providing useful intelligence, sir,' Jeffers ventured, 'and despite his more audacious adventures, we believe his position remains secure.'

'As you see fit, but my counsel is that he needs to come home.' The First Lord concluded the meeting.

Arriving back at Broadway, 2/O Daphne Devine told Jeffers that Colonel Llewelyn had been looking for him and did not seem "best pleased".

'Any indications as to the reason?' Jeffers asked.

'None of which I am aware,' she replied. If there was one thing that annoyed Jeffers, it was going into a meeting without knowing how and from where any ambush might come.

'Come in!' barked the colonel as Commander Jeffers knocked on the colonel's door. 'Ah, it's you, Roland.' Llewelyn appeared full of bonhomie as he welcomed the commander into his spacious office.

'You wanted a word?' Jeffers asked.

'Yes,' the colonel appeared distracted. 'Do you know what young Carlton has been up to recently?'

Jeffers smelled a trap. 'Nothing specific,' he replied, 'but he does file regular reports.'

'We knew that he was going off into the country to see how the peasants were surviving after the war, didn't we?' Llewelyn enquired.

'Yes, of course, we asked him to,' Jeffers responded, wondering where this line of questioning was heading.

'He did not happen to mention that he killed four Russian deserters and rescued some poor girl from their clutches, then?' Llewelyn asked innocently.

'No, sir, he did not,' Jeffers responded starchily; he was annoyed that he had not known of this snippet of information and that Llewelyn knew more than he did.

'Yes, it would appear that our man Carlton is quite the hero in some quarters.' Jeffers did not know whether Llewelyn was genuinely impressed or was being ironic. 'I thought we had discouraged him from being so noticeable and here he is again making the news and not reporting it.'

'If you say so, sir,' Jeffers responded, annoyed that his own intelligence network had let him down.

'I think it's time to bring our man in Helsinki back home,' Llewelyn ventured, 'and we shall have to see if we cannot find him something a little more discreet if such a role exists. Organise it, will you?' Llewelyn went back to his papers and Jeffers left the office.

Calling at 2/O Daphne Devine's cubbyhole of an office, Jeffers instructed, 'Make arrangements to bring Alex Carlton home, please, at the earliest opportunity.'

'Yes, sir,' she replied.

*

Alex and Leona Guichard travelled to the aerodrome at Malmi together on Saturday evening, as they were flying to Stockholm on the same flight. Alex was surprised at the transformation of Englund and Rosendahl's terminal building, which had been little more than a transit camp for the military when he was last there. Now it was bright and light and the epitome of efficient passenger marshalling. Having checked in at the Aktiebolaget Aerotransport (ABA) desk and left their luggage on the trolley to be taken to the aeroplane, Alex and Leona walked over to the café that overlooked the apron where incoming airliners were parked. Alex was pleased to see that the only ABA aeroplane was a Douglas DC-3 and not the usual Junkers that plied the route to Stockholm.

'At least the flight will be comfortable,' Alex said as they sat down to enjoy a cup of coffee while they waited for their flight to board.

'Has your paper told you where they are sending you next?' Leona asked.

'Not yet,' he replied. 'I hope it's somewhere quieter than Helsinki was, though,' he replied.

'If they send you back to London, perhaps we could meet up occasionally?' She persisted with the notion that he was going back to London – either her intelligence was better than it ought to be, or she lived in the hope of a future association.

Seeking to scotch the idea of meeting a fellow correspondent who he had met while undercover when his life returned to normal, he answered, 'I doubt it will be London. I've done two war zones now so I live in the hope that it will be a nice peaceful assignment. Who knows? Maybe Washington.'

'Who knows? But let me know. I'm staying at the Strand until I can get an apartment arranged,' she said.

The rudimentary tannoy system crackled into life, announcing that passengers for the ABA flight to Stockholm should proceed to the departure gate, and Alex and Leona swilled back the remains of their coffee and joined the group of passengers milling about near the exit. Having had their passports checked against the flight manifest, they walked over the apron to the aeroplane that was waiting to welcome them. As they boarded, the stewardess handed each a small packet of chewing gum, and when Alex looked at her querulously, she said, 'It stops your ears from popping when we land.'

Alex and Leona sat together on the starboard side of the aeroplane, as she was apparently superstitious about such things. Leona announced, 'My mother always said I was too posh not to heed that the word comes from "Port Out, Starboard Home" and I have always done it since, whether by boat or by plane.' Alex was less concerned, but he settled into the comfortable seats and waited for the pilot to start the engines.

As the airliner taxied out to the main runway, Alex heard Leona muttering to herself. 'Is everything all right?' he asked.

'Yes, it is a little thing that I do when I fly. I do not trust these things really, so I say the Lord's Prayer to myself as we are about to take off and land in the hope that if anything does go wrong, it will protect me from harm.'

Alex resisted the temptation to smile. He had not ever thought the hard-edged, seasoned correspondent would ever be frightened of anything, least of all flying and, furthermore, she had not once in the time that he had known her ever indicated that she had faith.

'I shall, of course, expect a gentleman to keep my little secret,' she said with a twinkle in her eye, but steel in her voice.

'Of course,' he assured her. 'I would not dream of telling anyone.'

The aeroplane turned into the wind at the end of the runway, and after a short delay that was only a few moments, it gathered speed and smoothly detached itself from Finnish soil.

Alex had left Helsinki.

XXVII

The flight to Stockholm's Bromma Airport was uneventful enough. There was a small amount of turbulence as the airliner crossed the coast, but the two-and-a-quarter-hour voyage was soon over, and the aeroplane began its descent to Stockholm Airport, and Alex reached for the pack of chewing gum. Leona had drifted off to sleep, and Alex shook her gently, offering her a stick of gum.

'Not long before we land,' he said and was rewarded with a smile and acceptance of his gum.

The pilot made a perfect landing, and the aeroplane taxied to the terminal building, and they collected their belongings before walking from the plane to where family and friends were waiting to greet arriving passengers. Leona spotted Sigrid before Alex and pointed her out to him, waving at him frantically.

'Your girlfriend is pleased to see you,' Leona said and pointed at Sigrid. 'At least somebody is here to greet you. All I have to look forward to is a day in Stockholm before flying on to London tomorrow.'

Alex almost felt sorry for the Canadian and was about to offer company for the evening, when he realised that it would appear strange if he had not wanted to spend his first night back with his "girlfriend". After clearing customs and immigration, which was perfunctory, to say the least, Alex and Leona shook hands and said farewell, promising to keep in touch, though Alex knew this would never happen. Alex and Sigrid hugged each other, and she took him to a waiting car.

'Your apartment has been let out, so the paper has booked you into a hotel for tonight, and tomorrow you are on the BOAC flight to Scotland. So, tonight you can take me to dinner to celebrate the ending of our brief affair.'

'You do know that Leona Guichard is booked on a flight to Britain tomorrow afternoon? It would be embarrassing to discover we are on the same flight again,' Alex commented.

'Do not worry. Miss Guichard is not flying tomorrow,' Sigrid explained. 'There was no room on the flight, and so there is a problem with her visa, which will delay her a day or two. The embassy will undoubtedly take their time to sort it out, so she will fly to London later in the week.'

Alex felt a little guilty that he was the cause of Leona missing her flight tomorrow, but he did not say so to Sigrid; he just smiled.

Sigrid had chosen the restaurant that they had visited the first evening that they had met. Restaurant Riche on Birger Jarlsgatan was still the same excellent value that Alex remembered, and he pushed the boat out considerably more than when he had last eaten there. After all, Alex still had his pay from the newspaper, and as he did not know how much he would be allowed to keep, he deliberately chose from the more expensive end of the menu. Even so, the bill still only came to less than Kr40, which equated to no more than two pounds, ten shillings.

After the meal, Sigrid walked Alex back to his hotel, before wishing him a good night.

'Alex,' she said, 'it has been wonderful knowing you, and I wish we could have made more of what we had, but you are going back to your other life, and I am going back to being a secretary at the newspaper. Maybe I will have some more excitement in my life, or maybe I will settle down and have a family, but whatever the future holds, I will always remember you.'

Alex held Sigrid to him and gently kissed her forehead. 'And I shall always remember you,' he said gently.

With that, Sigrid turned and walked out of his life forever, and Alex went into his hotel.

*

The next morning, Alex woke early, just as dawn was breaking over Stockholm, and as he lay in his bed, he wondered what the prospects were for him back in England. Would he still be attached to the intelligence services, or released for general duties? He was excited about seeing Teddy, and he had calculated that he should be home in adequate time to be a worried father pacing the corridor outside the ward when Teddy gave birth to the child. What would it be? Alex wondered. Secretly, in his heart, there was a desire for it to be a boy so that he could do all the things that Alex imagined fathers and their sons do together – there was even the prospect of learning how to fish so that he could teach his son. Or cricket, for which he had always had a penchant. Indeed, when the war was over and his son old enough, Alex would take him to Lord's to watch a test match, or to Wembley for a football game.

But what if it were a girl? How does one have fun with a girl? Alex pondered. Emphatically, he resolved that he would be a real father to his daughter, unlike the distant figure of authority that the brigadier had been to Teddy when she was growing up.

On balance, Alex decided that he would be content whatever the good Lord blessed them with, and he resolved to be the finest father that he could.

Alex bathed and dressed in a smart jacket and flannels and went to breakfast. The waiter brought the ubiquitous coffee pot to the table, and as he was about to pour, Alex rebelled against the life into which he had been thrust, and asked, 'May I have tea, please?'

The waiter was nonplussed, but he smiled indulgently and nodded before going to find some tea for Alex. As he savoured his first cup of tea with breakfast since he had left England last year, he sighed and welcomed the taste like an old friend. Even though it was not as strong as he would have liked, it was delicious, and Alex wondered at how the Continentals could ever prefer the bitterness of coffee against the delicate subtlety of a good tea.

Sigrid had instructed Alex to be seated at a table in the rotunda of Stockholm's public library on Sveavägen by 10.30am, and someone would contact him. Alex arrived at the library in good time and gathered a selection of newspapers, including *Svenska Posten*, to read while he waited for the contact. Some forty minutes later, when he had almost read all of the papers and was wondering how else to occupy his time, a familiar voice greeted him, and he turned to see Simon Potts settling into the seat next to his.

'Hello, Simon,' Alex said. 'How is life?'

'Well enough,' Simon responded. 'It's good to see you, old friend. You have caused us some sleepless nights, but I can see that you have thrived on the experience. Come on; I have a car waiting.'

Simon rose from his table, and they left the library together and climbed into the back of an almost new Volvo taxi that was waiting outside with its engine running.

'Back to the embassy,' Simon instructed the driver, 'and keep your wits about you.'

On the short journey between the aerodrome and the embassy, Alex asked Simon of news of Teddy, not forgetting to ask after Simon's wife, Cordelia, who had been Teddy's maid of honour at their marriage.

'There's not much to tell,' he reported. 'I understand that everything is progressing smoothly, with her and her expectancy; at least, I have not heard anything to the contrary. Your Uncle Walter is reputedly doing exceptionally well at the Ministry of Supply. It's all pretty much the same as the last report you received. But you will see for yourself shortly, so do not worry about it. No news, in these circumstances, is jolly good news.'

The new British Embassy in Stockholm was located in the diplomatic quarter and was an impressive redbrick building, much larger than its predecessor that had recently become the Ambassador's residence. The legation had only moved in the previous year, and there was still a sense of newness about the place. The driver parked the car near a discreet door, and Simon led the way, moving swiftly through the corridors until he reached his office that, despite the quiet opulence of the building, was furnished with civil service functional fixtures and fittings. It was definitely a place of work rather than somewhere you entertained other diplomats.

'Much to the annoyance of my boss,' Simon told Alex as they sat down, 'you are not being debriefed here, but in London. I shall be flying back with you on this afternoon's BOAC flight to Leuchars, and then it is straight to London where someone from the department will conduct your debriefing.

'If you can let me have all the documentation relating to Alex Carlsson, as we are issuing you with temporary diplomatic papers from the legation. Anything connected to Finland should be left here, clothes and whatever, but anything you acquired in Sweden is all right to take with you.'

'What shall I do with this?' Alex asked, taking his Cross of Merit of the White Rose of Finland, in its neat blue leather box, from his briefcase.

'What is it?' Simon asked and then opened the box. 'Good God, how did you get this?'

'Field-Marshal Mannerheim gave it to me on Wednesday last,' Alex said modestly.

Simon thought for a moment. 'It should really go in the bag,' he said, referring to the diplomatic bag, which is supposed to be the secure way of transporting sensitive materials, 'but providing you have somewhere you can secrete it, and as you will have diplomatic protection, it might be wiser for you to carry it.

'I had no idea that Finland had given you a gong.' Simon fished for more details.

'Yes.' Alex offered scant information. 'It was apparently for that Suomussalmi thing.' Simon nodded sagely, knowing Alex would expand further when he felt the time was right.

'Your weapon, however,' Simon continued, 'must go in the bag. The Swedes are very touchy about their neutrality and get a bit irritated if they suspect any intelligence activity by a foreign power. Zu Wied, the German Ambassador, despite all his connections, got the most frightful bollocking from the Swedes when one of his junior diplomats got caught with sensitive documents. It is challenging to keep smiling politely when all the time we are walking on eggshells!'

Alex recovered his FN pistol and ammunition from the secure compartment in his typewriter case and handed them to Simon. 'I hope I will get it back,' Alex appealed. 'It and I have grown rather fond of each other.'

'You can have it back as soon as we get to Scotland,' Simon assured him.

Alex handed over his Carlsson Swedish passport and other papers relating to his life as a newspaper correspondent but retained the photo of Teddy that had accompanied him throughout his adventures. In exchange, he received a diplomatic passport bearing his photograph in the name of Alexander Duggan, a diplomat listed as the passport control officer at the embassy.

'We have time for lunch, although it won't be much,' Simon offered. 'The food in the embassy is pretty basic, but we have to keep you here. Afterwards, you can have a bath and a shave before we shove off.'

'A shave?' Alex had become quite attached to his beard.

'Yes, we have to change your appearance a little, so the beard has to go, sorry; and you should part your hair differently. We also have a pair of glasses for you to try.' Simon produced a pair of horn-rimmed round glasses that were all the fashion at the time, which had clear glass lenses fitted. Alex was quite amused at how Simon had adopted the mantle of deceit so effortlessly.

The resident cook provided a light lunch on a tray in Simon's office. Despite the hustle and bustle of a busy diplomatic mission continuing outside the door, nobody knocked or entered Simon's domain, it was almost as if the staff had been told to keep out, as indeed they had. When an agent was returning, the fewer people that knew about it, the better. Even the Ambassador had not been given any details, in case he had to deny knowledge in the future – if he did not officially know, he would not have to lie.

Simon escorted Alex to a small bathroom on the next floor up from his office, and Alex found the suit that he had bought from NK, with a shirt and a tie that he did not recognise, neatly pressed and hanging on a coathanger behind the door. Simon left him to complete his ritual cleansing and shaving, and Alex was pleased to find a styptic pencil in the cabinet, as shaving his beard resulted in a couple of nicks that bled profusely.

Emerging nearly forty-five minutes later, he looked and felt like a different man. Gone was the adventurous newspaper correspondent and replacing him was a minor diplomatic functionary, who with the glasses was utterly unrecognisable as Alex Carlsson.

Simon was waiting for Alex outside the bathroom, and he smiled at the transformation. 'That's better,' he nodded approvingly before continuing, 'we've got about an hour before we need to go to the aerodrome, so we'll go back to my cubbyhole. Rumour has it that my boss may drop by, as he is quite keen to meet the infamous Alex Carlsson.'

As it was, his keenness was clearly not that imperative, as Alex remained on his own in Simon's office for much of the remaining time. Simon was off finalising arrangements before the appointed time when they were due to leave, and when he returned, Simon had gained an overcoat and hat and was carrying a raincoat and trilby for Alex.

'Come on, old friend,' he said, 'the car is waiting.'

Leaving by the same discreet door, Alex found the same Volvo taxi waiting, with the driver that had brought them earlier holding open the rear door for his passengers. The boot was gaping, and Alex saw both his and another suitcase had been placed inside, along with a heavy canvas bag with impressive wax seals.

The journey to the airport passed quickly, and soon Alex and Simon were checking in at the BOAC desk for the flight to Scotland. The officials only took scant regard of the diplomatic passports, and it was not long before Alex and Simon were walking across the apron to what appeared to be an impossibly small aeroplane.

The twin-tailed Lockheed 14 Super Electra that was to transport them the 800 miles to Scotland was the civilian configuration of the military Hudson and contained a mere seventeen seats, plus a fold-down for the steward. Simon and Alex took the last remaining seats either side of the gangway, and the door closed behind them. Passengers were asked to strap themselves into their seats as the aeroplane taxied out to the runway.

'It's a bit bloody cosy in here, isn't it?' Alex complained, to which Simon smiled.

'Since the fall of Norway, there has been a fair bit of hostile air activity, so we need something a little more nimble should we get bounced by the enemy. They have not shot down a civilian-registered aeroplane yet, but it is only a matter of time,' Simon explained.

The three-and-a-half-hour flight was a little bumpy to start with until they had cleared Swedish airspace and the pilot was able to climb above the turbulence, after which it was quite smooth, enabling Alex to catnap until the aircraft began its descent to the aerodrome at St Andrews.

XXVIII

It was early evening on the last Sunday in April when Alex stepped from the aeroplane onto British soil again. Dusk was falling, and it was raining heavily; one of the much-to-be-expected April showers. Most of the passengers scurried away quickly to the terminal building, but as Simon was fighting with an impossibly large umbrella, a naval staff car pulled up alongside the aircraft.

The Wren driver leapt from the driver's door and asked, 'Lieutenants Potts and Carlton?' Simon nodded, and she flung open the rear door for them, 'Welcome home to Scotland,' she said, smiling. After seeing her charges safely aboard, she closed the door and ran to the driver's seat.

'The weather has not changed since we've been away, I see,' Simon said.

'You are lucky, sir,' the driver replied. 'It was snowing last week! We have about 40 miles to go to Rosyth, which will take just over an hour. I can turn up the heating if you fancy a snooze, sir.'

'Thank you,' said Simon and both he and Alex took advantage of the warmth to drift into sleep.

Shortly after eight-fifteen, when the car pulled up at the gatehouse on Castle Road at HMS Cochrane, the naval base at Rosyth, the driver handed over her pass and orders to the rating standing guard. He checked the papers and went into the guardhouse, returning a couple of minutes later with the instruction that the driver was to deliver her charges to the wardroom, where Lieutenant Commander Campbell was waiting for them.

Campbell was a difficult person to try and age, his hair was steel grey, but his youthful looks suggested that it may have been premature. Nevertheless, he was a regular, and promotion to lieutenant commander in peacetime would have been painfully slow. Not a tall man by any stretch of the imagination and his jaunty walk gave Alex the impression that the man was a submariner.

'Lieutenant Potts?' Campbell shook Simon's hand and did likewise with Alex's, and continued in a soft Scots accent, 'Welcome to Rosyth. You are staying in the wardroom tonight and flying on to London tomorrow, so please accept our warm hospitality.

'First, however, we received a communiqué from Commander Jeffers this afternoon to notify Lieutenant Carlton that as of four days ago, he is the father of a bonny wee daughter. The message said that both mother and daughter are doing well. So, Mr Carlton, you will be joining us in the bar to wet the bairn's head, I hope?'

Alex was stunned. Teddy was not due to give birth for a few weeks yet, but at least she and the baby were all right. 'Erm, yes, of course, thank you,' he stammered.

'Excellent, laddie,' Campbell said. 'I'll get a steward to show you where you can sling your hammocks.'

Simon was beaming at the news as he clapped Alex on the back and congratulated him heartily. 'Admirable, jolly well done,' he said, almost as though Alex had somehow suffered the pangs of childbirth, instead of Teddy.

The rooms that Alex and Simon had been allocated were basic, but comfortable in their own way; government issue standard utilitarian furniture, but polished so much that it shone. When they reappeared, Simon had changed into his naval uniform, but Alex's was still God only knew where, so he had freshened up and combed his hair into a style that he preferred.

Campbell greeted them at the door to the mess. 'The admiral has a strict policy that uniforms must be worn in the wardroom, but in your case, Mr Carlton, we shall make an exception tonight. I shall sign you in as my guest, which means that you cannot buy a round, but on this auspicious occasion, you should not anyway.

'Cook seems to have made a fish stew for dinner, we get a lot of fish up here. I think he has a fiddle going with a local fisherman. I suggest we eat first, as the food has been hanging about for a while and is probably already past its best.'

The food was surprisingly good, Alex thought, and afterwards, those officers who were still in the bar when they had finished eating, joined Campbell and Simon in celebrating the birth of Alex's daughter. It was well past midnight when Alex and Simon unsteadily staggered from the wardroom and made their way to their billet, having consumed far too many Horse's Necks.

*

The next morning, neither could stomach the thought of breakfast, so both Alex and Simon contented themselves with just coffee, even though it tasted awful. The Wren driver arrived at ten o'clock prompt to drive them the short distance to RNAS Donibristle a few miles outside Rosyth, and by ten-thirty Alex and Simon were strapped into a de Havilland 95 transport plane that was taxiing to take off en route to RAF Northolt in north London. Joining them on the flight was a commodore who was going on to a meeting at the Admiralty, and two Wrens who had managed to persuade the dispatcher to allow them to hitch a lift so that they could go on leave in the capital. Flying was much quicker than the usual endless train journey, so quite what they had to sacrifice to convince the dispatcher was anybody's guess.

The four-hundred-and-fifty-mile journey usually took a couple of hours, but a strong headwind meant that they did not touch down at Northolt until 1.15pm and for the final hour they were forced to listen to the Commodore complaining that he would be late. He was even more annoyed when the staff car that had been sent to collect him was delayed, but the transport for Alex and Simon was waiting for them as the plane taxied to a stop. Their driver was quite firm in refusing the Commodore's insistence that he was commandeering the vehicle, and when Simon graciously offered a lift to the senior officer, he was most ungracious in his refusal, before storming off to the adjutant's office.

Due to the skill and efficiency of their driver, Alex and Simon arrived at Broadway less than an hour after touching down, and when they entered Commander Jeffers's office, he bounded from his desk and shook them both warmly by the hand.

'Welcome home, gentlemen, welcome home.' The commander pumped their hands with enthusiasm. 'Tell me, did you have a good flight from Sweden? No problems, eh?'

Simon assured Jeffers that all had been fine, and the commander took Alex by the hand again and congratulated him on becoming a father. 'We have arranged a bit of leave for you,' he said. 'You ought to telephone your wife and tell her you should be home by the end of the week, depending on how long it takes to wrap things up here. Sorry, it cannot be earlier, but we have to start your debriefing as soon as possible. Still, she will appreciate it is going to take a couple of days to get you back from Scotland. We have some correspondence that Daphne has been handling in your absence, so you need to read through what "you" have said in your letters before speaking to her.' The commander handed over a sheaf of letters from Teddy and a similar bundle of transcripts of the replies sent.

*

Alex had been allocated a room at St Ermin's Hotel in St James's, a short step from the office in Broadway and a regular haunt of members of the intelligence community. It was a place he remembered well with not much affection from the interrogation following the Horváth affair, and after checking in, he spent the hour before the scheduled time of the telephone connection reading through the letters received and sent.

The commander had arranged for the telephone call to be routed to Teddy in Gloucestershire through Scotland, and Alex picked up the telephone receiver in one of the enclosed booths in the reception area.

He was in little doubt that his conversation was being listened to by the service and that anything said that was controversial would result in an immediate dropped connection.

'Stow-on-the-Wold 7-5.' The crackling voice was indistinct, and Alex could not work out who had answered.

'Teddy?' he asked.

'No, it is Klara. Who is calling, please?'

'Klara, it is Alex Carlton. Is Teddy there, please?'

'She is resting at the moment, Mr Carlton, but I will go and wake her. I know she will want to talk to you.'

'Klara,' Alex interrupted, 'if we lose the connection, please tell Teddy I have some leave due and am hoping to be in Gloucestershire by Friday.'

'That is good news, sir,' Klara replied. 'I will certainly tell her, but please wait while I run upstairs to see if she is awake.'

As expected, the connection was lost before Teddy could come downstairs and Alex was left holding a silent telephone receiver, cursing that he had not been able to talk to his wife.

Alex joined Simon in the hotel's bar and the friends caught up on life, carefully avoiding discussion of anything to do with the job. Their attention was soon drawn to an increasingly rowdy group who appeared to be loudly getting more drunk at the bar. At the centre of the group was a gregarious and flamboyant fellow, whose upper-class drawl was clearly the loudest of the company he was keeping.

'What on earth is going on over there?' Alex enquired of Simon after the noise emanating from the group became unbearable.

'I think they are all from Six,' Simon said, using the abbreviation for MI6, one of the other shadowy departments responsible for liaison. 'I have met the loudmouth once at some diplomatic function. I believe his name is Burgess.'

'What is he? Army?' Alex asked.

'I don't think he's anything,' Simon replied. 'I seem to recall he is a scholar, some sort of specialist in Section D.'

'Well, if it is true that empty vessels make the most noise, that one must be devoid of any cargo whatsoever! In any event, I'm tired, so I might turn in. Will you be around over the next few days, perhaps come down to Ashton Court for the weekend? Bring your wife? I know Teddy would love to see you both.'

'Sadly not,' Simon responded. 'I'm spending the night with Cordelia, and then tomorrow, I'm travelling back to Stockholm. I have applied for a transfer back to the UK, but it is still going through the system. You know that nothing ever gets done quickly in the service, although I did ask Jeffers to see if he could try to push it along a bit. It's going to be jolly boring in Sweden now that Alex Carlsson has retired.'

Simon shook Alex's hand before leaving, and they gave each other a genuinely warm hug of affection before the loudmouth at the bar made an unsavoury comment about "pansies", and after delivering a foul glance in his direction, Simon left, and Alex went to bed.

*

Alex's debriefing over the next couple of days was to be held in the same room in which he had been interrogated over the Stefan Horváth affair the previous October, so he was already on edge. The debriefing could not have been more different; it was less a grilling and more a fact-finding mission to uncover anything that Alex had omitted from his reports. He was asked his opinion on various matters, and Alex genuinely believed that he was there to help colour in the overall picture of the war that he had just been through and to help inform the service as to Finland's future intentions.

Even so, the initial meeting took all day, and by the end of it, Alex felt drained, and after eating at the hotel, Alex collapsed into his bed and fell immediately to sleep.

The debriefing on Wednesday mainly comprised going over Alex's comments from the previous day and checking them against the reports that he had submitted, often asking for clarification or expansion on some point. Alex was asked to expand on the personality of several people whom he had mentioned, including Field-Marshal Mannerheim, former General Wallenius, Jarno and others. He tried to be objective in all of his responses. Afterwards, again, Alex felt exhausted. Being an agent in the field was so much easier than the subsequent post-mortem!

Alex's examination concluded on Thursday lunchtime, shortly after midday, and he was released with the caveat that his statements would be considered, and should intelligence need to speak with him again, somebody would arrange another meeting. Alex changed into his service uniform that had been delivered to the hotel along with the suitcase which he had last seen when he handed it to his surrogate on the train heading north to Scotland. Looking in the mirror, he thought the jacket hung a little loosely on his shoulders, and his trousers needed braces more than previously to stop them from falling down. Alex had lost weight, but he thought it befitted him more. After changing and checking out of the hotel, Alex walked the short distance to Broadway Buildings, where Daphne Devine met him and gave him a travel warrant and his post-operational leave chitty before expressing the hope that he enjoyed his time off. She added that the commander would telephone him in Gloucestershire, should anything arise that needed his urgent attention.

Leaving Broadway Buildings, Alex went first to his bank and cashed a cheque, as the one thing that the redoubtable and usually efficient 2/O Devine had omitted was some cash. The manager at the branch welcomed Alex and handed him a statement of account that showed considerably more than he had anticipated. Alex was less surprised when the manager suggested that Alex might like to invest some of his spare money into war bonds or other investments to help the war effort. Without wishing to be churlish, Alex agreed to think about his options, but privately he felt that he was already doing sufficient to contribute.

Carrying his suitcase, Alex hailed a taxi and asked to go to Paddington Station via Onslow Gardens, as he wanted to make sure that his house in London was undamaged. Alex asked the taxi driver to wait while he went inside. All the furniture had dust sheets covering it, and there was a distinct mustiness in the air. The house felt almost abandoned, but Alex was strangely gratified that Germany had not yet dropped a single bomb on the capital. The taxi driver told him that whenever the air-raid sirens sounded, most people now just ignored them and went on with their regular routines. Some might have a cursory look to the skies, but very few even bothered with that nowadays. *If they had seen what I have seen in Helsinki, people would not be so relaxed,* Alex thought to himself.

XXIX

The train from Paddington to Oxford was packed, and even with a warrant for a seat in first-class, Alex had to wait until Maidenhead before he found somewhere to sit in a compartment. He heaved his suitcase onto the luggage rack and flopped into the spare seat just as the train was pulling out of the station. The number of passengers gradually thinned at different stations, until there was just Alex and a middle-aged woman wearing stout tweeds and even stouter brogues.

'You on leave?' the woman asked.

'Er, yes,' Alex replied. In truth, he had been startled by the question.

'Navy, is it?' the woman asked; not a brilliant deduction as Alex was in uniform.

'That's right,' Alex replied.

'I run the Women's Voluntary Service in Abingdon,' she said proudly, although Alex wondered whether she should have divulged such sensitive information to a stranger.

'Oh, yes?' Alex tried to sound interested. 'They do some good work.'

'Just as valuable as the auxiliary services,' the woman went on, 'that's what the Home Secretary said.'

'So I believe.' Alex was starting to hope the train driver might just squeeze a little more speed from his engine.

His prayers were answered as the train slowed and came into a station. 'Didcot. Change for all stations to Swindon, Chip'n'am, Bath and Bristol,' called a porter. The woman gathered her belongings and bustled out of the compartment.

'Goodbye. Nice to talk with you,' the woman said to Alex, who nodded in return.

The journey to Oxford General was peaceful and undisturbed, and as he alighted the train, Alex smiled at how England was unhurriedly going about its business, even though they were at war.

Alex knew he had to change platforms to catch the local train to Adlestrop, but for his searching, he could not find a single sign to tell him which, so he asked a porter, who looked him up and down as if trying to decide whether Alex was a Fifth Columnist. He eventually decided that Alex was all right, as he pointed and said, 'Platform three, sir, due in ten minutes.'

'Thank you,' replied Alex and made his way through the subway to platform three.

The energy and vibrancy of the fast train that had brought him from London were conspicuous by their absence in the local train that wheezed into platform three. Only three coaches, one first-class, one second-class and a third-class carriage, neatly and methodically arranged in order from the engine. Only a handful of passengers waited to board the train and Alex was the only one in first-class.

The train had to call at four stations before it arrived at Adlestrop, at the second, Charlbury, the train was held for ten minutes while another whistled through without stopping. Alex was impatient for his train to get going again, but he had to wait until the signal changed, and the track was clear before the driver sounded the whistle, and the train gaspingly chuffed on its way eventually pulling into Alex's station at seven o'clock in the evening, twelve minutes behind schedule. Adlestrop was a small station that was lovingly cared for by a resident station master and his wife, and on that spring afternoon, with the flowers blooming in a spectacle of colour that would have won prizes at any Royal Horticultural Society event, Alex appreciated being back in England. He took in several lungfuls of fresh air and rejoiced.

'Afternoon,' the station master greeted Alex. 'Can I help you, sir?'

'I do not think so.' Alex smiled back at the official and offered the compliment, 'How wonderful your station looks.'

'Thank you, sir.' The station master almost puffed out his chest in pride. 'We do try. Are you going far?'

'Just to Lower Oddington,' Alex replied.

'Do you want a taxi?' the station-master asked. 'I could telephone my brother, I am sure he would oblige.'

'No,' Alex made up his mind. 'It is such a lovely evening, I think I might walk.'

'So be it,' the station-master answered. 'You take care now.'

Alex walked the short distance up the hill to Lower Oddington and was soon strolling up the driveway of Ashton Court. He knocked on the front door and was surprised when it was opened by a young girl whom he did not recognise.

'Is Mrs Carlton at home?' Alex enquired.

'Who shall I say is calling?' the girl asked politely.

'Mr Carlton,' Alex replied.

'I shall see, sir,' and she was just starting to close the door when the penny dropped, and she opened it again quickly. 'Oh, my goodness, I am sorry, sir,' the girl spluttered and held the door open. 'We were told you were arriving on the morrow!'

'That is fine,' Alex said as he smiled at her and he walked into Ashton Court for the first time in what seemed ages. 'Please see if my wife is available, or my mother.'

'Of course, sir,' the girl said and opened the door to the morning room, which was wholly inappropriate considering the time of day.

Alex placed his suitcase on the floor and looked around the house. The place had been transformed and was now the home he had spent the past months dreaming it would become.

There was a flurry of arrivals, beginning with Alex's mother, who held her son tightly to her as tears rolled down her cheek as she gave thanks for his safe return. '*Aleksander, Aleksander, moy syn, moy syn, Bog privel tebya domoy; Spasibo ogromnoye!*' – Alexander, Alexander, my son, my son, God has delivered you safely; thank you so much!

Teddy was next, still weak and needing the assistance of Klara, and she fairly launched herself at her husband, almost knocking him over. 'Thank God, thank God, thank God,' was all she said time after time as she showered him with kisses.

'Steady on, old girl,' Alex said when he was able to free himself a little. 'I run the risk of being more wounded by my family than if I had taken on the entire German army single-handed!' He smiled at his family.

'Come,' Teddy said, taking him by his hand, 'you must say hello to your daughter, but quietly, as she is asleep.' Teddy led him upstairs to the nursery and showed him the little bundle that was lying in a rocking crib. 'She was as impatient as her father to come into the world.'

Alex looked down at the sleeping bundle and said, 'She is beautiful, just like her mother.'

Teddy led Alex out of the room and downstairs, where she said, 'We must decide on a name. Mama and I,' Alex was a little surprised that Teddy had adopted the same familiar name that he used for his mother, 'thought about Viktoriya, after Uncle Walter's wife? We have not spoken to him about it yet.'

Alex thought for a moment. 'Yes,' he said, 'I think it would be a lovely name for our daughter. Have you thought of other names? Traditionally, in Russia, there is a patronymic name taken from the father's given name, so we could think about Alexandra, and what about a name from your side of the family?'

'I did think of that, and I wondered about my maternal grandmother's name, Catherine,' Teddy ventured.

'So, we have Viktoriya Alexandra Catherine or Viktoriya Catherine Alexandra,' Alex mused.

'I like the latter,' Teddy settled, 'it flows better off the tongue!'

'I agree,' said Alex, 'but let us not tell anyone until Uncle Walter is here.'

Alex helped Teddy downstairs, and they went into the drawing-room to join Alex's mother.

'You must tell us all about your adventures in Scotland,' his mother encouraged.

'Truthfully, there is not much to tell,' Alex said. 'it was all rather tedious, really. Just exhaustingly long hours spent deciphering coded messages. I'm looking forward to having a bit of a rest.'

If his mother looked disappointed, it lasted only until Klara opened the door and announced that dinner was served, and she smiled at Alex and said, 'Welcome back, Mr Carlton.'

'Whose idea was it that she should dress like a maid?' Alex said, noting that Klara was wearing black.

'It's not as a maid, but as a widow. Did you not read my letters?' Teddy admonished.

'Oh, heavens!' Alex tried to remember whether he had read anything in the pile of letters he had skimmed at the hotel earlier in the week. 'I do not think I could have received that one,' he muttered.

'Yes,' Teddy explained, 'with the BEF in France, or Belgium, or thereabouts. He's buried in France, anyway. Klara was upset for weeks, especially as his family treated her as an outcast. It has been a difficult time for the poor girl.'

'Well, she has us now,' Alex said as if that were a substitute for a husband.

*

Alex woke early the next day. It had been a restless night as he was not used to the quiet of the countryside or its strange noises, and he was lying in bed fully awake when the cock crowed to herald the dawn. Alex had heard Teddy get up twice during the night to feed their daughter, and it was not long before the child was mewling for another meal. Alex thought that it was no wonder that Teddy was tired if she had to get up so many times to feed their child, and he resolved to look for a nanny at the first opportunity.

He dressed in his silk paisley dressing gown and found his slippers in the place where he had shed them the previous night, and went downstairs where he found Klara already hard at work preparing breakfast.

'Good morning, Mr Carlton,' she greeted him cheerily. 'Did you sleep well? Would you like a pot of tea?'

'Good morning, Klara,' Alex replied. 'Yes, thank you to both questions.' After a decent pause, he continued, 'Teddy told me that your husband fell in France. Please accept my deepest condolences and let me know if there is anything we can do to help.'

'Thank you.' Klara continued making breakfast. 'It was a while ago now, and Mrs Carlton and your mother have been absolutely marvellous at helping me come to terms with Rhodri's death. It is getting easier now, but I still think about him every day.'

'I am sure that will continue all of your life,' Alex empathised. 'When someone close to you dies, their spirit lives on in your heart and memories, so although their body is no more, there is still their presence guiding their loved ones.'

'Thank you,' Klara said, pausing momentarily to comprehend what Alex had said. 'That is very true. I still believe that my Rhodri is with me, almost looking over my shoulder to make sure that I am safe.'

The moment of melancholia passed, and Klara brought Alex's tea to the morning room, where he was sitting and reading through yesterday's newspapers, with a more critical eye than he would have done had he not been recently engaged in the role of a correspondent.

'How was it in London when you were there?' Klara asked.

'Unnervingly quiet,' Alex replied. 'People were going about their business as if we were not at war. I even saw some children, which surprised me because I thought they had all been evacuated to safety,' Alex commented.

'I had heard that some parents brought their children home, as Hitler did not seem interested in bombing the city,' Klara said.

Alex's mind drifted back to Helsinki in a moment of déjà vu, and he thought of Juha. 'It is a mistake,' he pronounced quietly.

'I think so, also,' Klara agreed, before returning to the kitchen.

When he had finished reading the previous day's newspapers and drunk his tea, Alex took the tray into the kitchen and enquired, 'Has Mrs Carlton talked of getting some help with our daughter?'

'No, sir, she has not.' Klara paused thoughtfully. 'She will not let anybody help, even though both your mother and I have tried. I am a little worried that she is doing too much.'

'Yes,' Alex said reflectively. 'I am worried also.'

He went back upstairs and slipped back into bed with his wife, putting his arm protectively around her, before drifting back to sleep.

XXX

The mid-morning arrival of Walter Compton had a galvanising effect on the household. His appearance seemed to awaken everybody, and the atmosphere of quiet efficiency that had impressed Alex so much the previous day seemed to dissipate when Uncle Walter was in residence.

Alex's mother greeted Walter with a friendly kiss on the cheek as he bustled through the front door carrying his suitcase and several bags from a well-known London store. He instructed the maid who had opened the door to Alex yesterday, to take his case to his room and the other bags to Mrs Carlton. Clearly, Uncle Walter was feeling in a generous mood.

Uncle Walter greeted Alex by extending his hand, gripping Alex's and pulling him forward and encircling him with his other arm. 'Good to see you home safe and sound. How was Scotland?' Did Alex note a slight emphasis on the "Scotland"?

'Cold and wet mostly,' Alex tried to keep the meeting light-hearted, 'and jolly hard work. It is good to be home, though.'

'Have you met your daughter yet?' Walter asked.

'Naturally,' replied Alex, 'although she was asleep at the time.'

'Not to worry,' he smiled, 'you will soon know she is around. Your mother tells me that she has a fine pair of lungs on her, for someone so small!'

He ran up the stairs with the vigour of someone much younger, and shortly after, Teddy retraced his steps, carefully carrying her daughter. The family gathered in the morning room to await Uncle Walter's reappearance, and Alex took the opportunity of introducing himself properly to the child.

'Hello, young lady,' he began. 'I'm your papa.'

The child looked at him, and her bottom lip trembled before she let out an enormous wail. *Not an auspicious start*, thought Alex as he handed the baby back to Teddy.

Uncle Walter entered dressed as a country squire in a checked shirt, cravat, moleskin trousers and a tweed jacket; it rather suited him, Alex thought.

'Come, Uncle, sit with Mother,' Alex said. 'Teddy and I have something to discuss.'

He waited until they were seated comfortably before joining Teddy on the other settee. They looked at each other, and Alex began. 'We have been discussing names as it is only proper that the child should be named as soon as possible.

'Both Teddy and I have agreed that our daughter shall be called Viktoriya.' Uncle Walter looked up with a start and smiled.

For the first time that Alex could remember, tears welled in Uncle Walter's eyes as he remembered his own, dear wife, and he simply said, 'What a lovely choice, thank you.'

Teddy chipped in, 'It is unseemly for a child to only have but one name, so we thought it would be appropriate to add maybe Catherine and Alexandra. The first after my maternal grandmother and the second as a nod to the Russian tradition of a patronymic.'

'How very apt,' Alex's mother concluded, 'and Catherine appears in my family's lineage, also; several times. My own great-great-grandmother was a Catherine, so I think it most suitable.'

'Excellent,' said Alex, 'then it is agreed.'

Teddy took Viktoriya back upstairs to bathe and change her, and the dowager countess prepared herself to go out to a meeting of some committee or other in the village, which left Alex and Uncle Walter together.

'That was most kind of you and Teddy,' Uncle Walter began, 'and wholly unexpected.'

'I rather think that the decision had been made before I came home,' Alex stated, 'but it is one with which I wholeheartedly concur.'

'Tell me,' he asked, 'was your posting so terrible? Scotland, I mean?'

'No,' Alex replied, 'rather boring, really.'

Uncle Walter reached into his jacket pocket and took out a twist of sweets. 'Have you tried these? They are rather tasty and quite popular in England,' he said, offering the package to Alex. 'Of course, the English have a sweet tooth, so they prefer their liquorice oversweetened, some would say far too much so, but I am told that in certain parts of Scandinavia and the Nordic countries, they prefer it salty.'

Taking one of the confections and carefully placing it in his mouth, Alex said, 'Really?' noticing that Uncle Walter was observing him carefully. Was this his way of subtly telling Alex that he knew more than he ought? 'I imagine that it would be an acquired taste.'

'Yes, I imagine so.' Uncle Walter concluded the subject.

After the briefest of pauses, Uncle Walter brightened and asked, 'Tell me, how long have you got as leave?'

'I don't honestly know,' Alex replied truthfully. 'The project that I was working on is complete, and the department is trying to find something else for me to do. Commander Jeffers said that he would call when they have found something.'

'Let us hope that it not so far distant as Scotland next time,' Uncle Walter said enigmatically.

'I agree,' said Alex, 'what a shame they do not have a naval base at Stow-on-the-Wold!' Uncle Walter and Alex shared in a moment of humour.

*

Over the next few days, Alex tried to adapt to civilian life. He started to drive the Alvis again, and he spent time with Klara understanding how she envisaged the kitchen garden, which had been talked about since they moved in but had yet to be started. Alex spent time with Teddy and

Viktoriya, and the child no longer cried when she saw her father. He even learned how to change his daughter's nappy, but still, the contents of the one being removed occasionally made him nauseous. He admired Teddy's resilience, but it was clear that she was still not recovering quickly.

Deciding to take control, Alex arranged for Dr Baxter to call out to examine Teddy, even though she objected to wasting the doctor's time. The doctor's diagnosis was much as Alex had suspected – Teddy was doing too much.

'Darling,' Alex began after the doctor had left, having prescribed some other tonic to help speed Teddy's recovery, 'you remember when we interviewed for a helper back in London?' Teddy nodded. 'And we joked about how awful it would be having one of those harridans looking after our child?' Teddy smiled. 'You recall how grateful we were that we found Klara?' Teddy again nodded. 'And we thought she would be perfect for helping to look after our child?' Teddy could see where this was heading and stopped being so agreeable. 'Why is she not helping with Viktoriya?'

'She's far too busy,' Teddy answered. 'The house does not run itself, you know. She has not got the time.'

'Then let me get somebody who has,' Alex beseeched Teddy. 'You are working yourself too hard, you need some help.'

'I'm not having some interfering Sarah Gamp taking control of my child!' Teddy insisted.

'Of course not,' Alex was understanding, 'but you do need someone to help you. You can even choose who it will be.'

Teddy decided that the best form of defence was to attack. 'Are you saying I'm incapable of looking after my own child? Women have been doing it for centuries, you know!'

'Of course, I am not suggesting anything of the sort!' Alex retorted, perhaps a little more sharply than he intended. 'I would not want anybody but you to bring up Viktoriya. All I am saying is that you would benefit from having a little assistance so that you could rest more, and that would be better for both you and Viktoriya.'

Realising this was not going to be a battle easily won, Teddy acquiesced – after all, she could always reject all the applicants if she did not like them.

Thus it was that it was eventually agreed that Alice, the publican's daughter from the King's Arms in Stow-on-the-Wold, who had just left school, would bicycle over to Ashton Court three days of the week to help Teddy with Viktoriya. After the first two weeks, there was a noticeable difference in Teddy, whose strength was returning quickly, and she even let Klara help out when Alice was not due to come over.

*

Alex had been at home for just over two weeks, during which time the most notable event was when Winston Churchill replaced Neville Chamberlain as prime minister. Since the fall of Norway and Denmark, and only hours before Germany invaded the Netherlands and the low countries by circumventing the Maginot Line, the prime minister's position had become wholly untenable, and on 10th May 1940, Chamberlain had visited King George VI to submit his resignation. Unusually for a retiring prime minister, Chamberlain had nominated his successor, Winston Churchill, and the King had readily agreed.

The telephone call came in the morning on Wednesday 22nd May. Daphne Devine called and instructed Alex to report to Broadway Buildings at half-past eight the following morning. She apologised for the short notice and Alex was told that the dress code was civilian, but to 'make sure you have polished your shoes!' Alex knew this to be a euphemism that the commander liked to use when warning that the meeting would have a senior officer present, but although Alex tried to press her for more details, Daphne either did not know or was under instructions not to say.

Alex telephoned Uncle Walter and asked if he might stay at Bedford Square while he was in London, as he did not want to stay at St Ermine's and Onslow Gardens was mothballed.

'Of course, dear boy,' Uncle Walter agreed. 'For how long?'

'I really do not know,' Alex replied, 'but I doubt for long. It sounds like the department has found me something to do! I shall drive down tonight, if I may?'

'Yes, of course. What does Teddy say?' Uncle Walter asked.

'I have not told her yet, she was asleep, but I am just going upstairs to wake her now,' Alex replied.

'Give her my love,' Uncle Walter said, 'and to your mother, also.'

Alex replaced the receiver and went to the kitchen to request that Klara make up a breakfast tray for Teddy. 'Don't worry, I will take it up myself,' he said.

Teddy was just rousing when Alex brought her breakfast into the bedroom. 'Who was that on the telephone?' Teddy asked and then seeing the breakfast, a cloud passed over her face. 'Now I know it's trouble. Daddy always brought breakfast in bed when there was bad news.'

'Well, I have not brought bad news,' Alex said, 'but I do have to go to London today, and I shall have to take the car. I shall stay with Uncle Walter tonight, and Commander Jeffers wants to see me tomorrow morning – but I am sure it is not bad news, if it were, then I would have to wear my uniform. It is probably just some administrative matter that needs attention, so do not worry.'

'When will you be back?' Teddy asked.

'I don't know,' Alex responded, 'but I should not be long. Just a day or so, I would think. Can you manage without the car while I'm gone?'

'Yes, I should think so,' answered Teddy reflectively. 'Come back quickly, though. Your daughter will miss you if you are away too long – and so even might I.'

'All right, but you must promise to take care of yourself. If I am not back tomorrow, ask Alice to come over and help.'

Teddy smiled at Alex, and he started to collect some things in a suitcase. He chose one of his smarter suits that he had bought pre-war and selected a shirt that had not previously been worn and was still in the wrapping from the shirtmaker in Jermyn Street and completed the ensemble with his Old Lassitarians tie. It was just after midday that Alex drove the Alvis out of Ashton Court and headed south to Burford to join the A40 and to London.

*

Parking outside Uncle Walter's London home in Bedford Square was never a problem, and Alex knocked on the imposing door of the house that had enthralled him when he first arrived in England with his mother all those years previously. The door was opened by an ancient butler whom Alex had not before met.

'Hello, my name is Alexander Carlton, and Mr Compton is expecting me,' he introduced himself formally.

'Yes, sir,' the butler replied. 'Mr Compton telephoned to explain. Please come in, and I will take your cases to your old room, which Mr Compton thought you might like to use. My name is Williams, by the way.'

'Thank you, Williams,' Alex said as he entered the house.

'Mr Compton suggested that you might dine with him at his club tonight, at about seven-thirty, if that is acceptable, sir.'

'Thank you, Williams, will you arrange a taxi to get me there in good order?' Alex asked, mainly because he could not remember for the life of him to which clubs Uncle Walter currently belonged.

Alex followed the butler upstairs and lay on his old bed and promptly fell asleep, just as he used to when he was young.

The taxi dropped Alex at St James Club in Picadilly at 7.25pm, and Alex climbed the few steps and announced himself to the concierge.

'Indeed, sir,' the doorman said without any inflexion whatsoever. 'Mr Compton is expecting you.' He rang a bell, and an elderly retainer appeared and took a hastily scribbled note inside the building. After a few moments, Uncle Walter appeared and signed Alex in as his guest.

To say that Alex was impressed would be an overstatement. He found the club overbearingly stuffy and the food little better than he had endured at school. The wine, however, was excellent, as was the brandy after dinner.

'Have your people told you why you have been summoned back from leave?' Uncle Walter asked.

'No,' Alex replied, 'I was merely instructed to be at the office by 8.30am. I do not suppose you know anything?' Alex knew that Uncle

Walter's informal and official intelligence network extended far and wide, and if anything were amiss, then he would likely know about it.

'I have not heard anything,' he told Alex.

*

Alex was awake early the next morning and already at breakfast when Uncle Walter appeared in the dining room.

'Good morning,' Uncle Walter greeted Alex. 'I trust you slept well?'

'Thank you, yes,' Alex replied. 'It was a considerate thought to put me in my old room; it brought back memories of a carefree childhood.'

Alex was just finishing his final slice of toast and marmalade and draining the last remaining drops of tea from his cup when Williams announced that Mr Carlton's car had arrived. Alex bade Uncle Walter farewell and collected his coat, hat and briefcase before climbing into the black Humber car that was waiting outside. The journey to Broadway Buildings took hardly any time, and soon Alex was rattling to the fourth floor in the rickety old lift.

He knocked on Daphne Devine's door, and she smiled at Alex amiably as he entered her office.

'Good morning, Lieutenant Carlton. Sorry for bringing you back from Gloucestershire at such short notice. I trust you had a good journey?'

'Yes, thank you, it was nice to be driving again.' Alex was keen to find out why he had been summoned. 'What's happening?'

'The commander will explain,' she replied, 'but it is nothing to worry about. Just some final details relating to your recent assignment. It should not take too long.'

Commander Jeffers entered the room and saw Alex. 'Good, you have made it on time, Alex. Come on through.'

The commander led the way into his office before continuing as they both sat down in the two comfortable chairs. 'You know that Colonel Swann was promoted and we now have a Colonel Llewelyn running the show.' Alex nodded. 'Well, he wanted your take on some curious intelligence that is starting to filter through. It seems that Germany is increasingly reliant on Russia for grain and other supplies, which they have been obtaining for what is little more than a pittance under a hastily negotiated trade pact between the two countries. It would appear that Stalin is becoming progressively dissatisfied with Russia's compensation under the agreement and is wanting to renegotiate. The Germans are, needless to say, reluctant.

'The conundrum that we cannot seem to resolve is whether cracks are forming in the Russian-German alliance. The feeling is that it would be senseless for Hitler to try and invade Russia, as it would split his forces that are committed to the Western Front, although he might be enticed by Finland's defence against such overwhelming strength. Hitler might just believe that Russia's military is not as efficient as one might expect.

'On the other hand, we can see no significant advantage for Stalin wanting to take on the Third Reich. At present, Germany is paying for surplus Russian agriculture, although it is true that costs are rising in Russia, as a result of a few shortages. How do you see the situation?'

Alex thought for a while before responding. 'On the whole, I agree. There is no tactical advantage in Germany seeking war with Russia, just as it does not make sense for Russia to look for one with Germany. But I worry that we are not dealing with rational people. Hitler is a megalomaniac who believes in the ultimate superiority of the Third Reich, and Stalin is a paranoic who does not trust even his closest confidants.

'The policy of collectivism is central to Stalin's control, yet it patently does not work, and anyone who challenges his vision, disappears. He fears opposition, and most of the good men in Russia, both on the Central Committee and in the military, have been identified as a threat and killed.

'When you are dealing with such unstable personalities, you must expect the unexpected, so I doubt that the alliance between Germany and Russia will survive for long, as one or other of the leaders will think that they can win that gamble. When that does happen, and knowing that we are at war with Germany, would Britain want to ally itself with Russia, or sue for peace with Hitler and join forces against the Soviet? That is the real paradox that we shall face.'

'So the question is, which of the two evils would be the lesser?' Jeffers summarised.

'That's about the essence of it, yes. Speaking personally, I am glad that I am not responsible for making that decision, as I find little merit in either contender.'

'I rather fear that you could be right,' Commander Jeffers concluded. 'Anyway, we should be getting along to our meeting now.'

Both Alex and Commander Jeffers collected their coats and hats and made their way downstairs and out into the road, where the same black Humber was waiting by the kerb. The car took them down Tothill Street and around Parliament Square and into Parliament Street on the way to the War Office in Whitehall. As they passed the Foreign & Commonwealth Office, it slowed and turned left into Downing Street, before pulling up outside one of the most famous doors in the kingdom, the one with the number ten painted on the sombre black colour.

XXXI

Alex looked at Commander Jeffers in sheer disbelief, and Jeffers smiled as he said, 'The prime minister wanted to meet with you. Your assignment was, after all, authorised by him when he was at the Admiralty.'

The door to 10 Downing Street opened as soon as both the commander and Alex stepped from the car, and they entered the hallway tiled in a black and white chequered pattern. They divested themselves of coats and hats, which they handed to the doorman, who in turn passed them to another servant for safekeeping.

'If you step this way, gentlemen,' the doorman said, 'the prime minister will not keep you long.' The commander and Alex followed up the stairs, where the walls were adorned with the portraits of former prime ministers.

They were placed in an elegant anteroom where four high backed chairs stood, one against each wall. After a short delay, they were collected and shown into Churchill's office, where the prime minister was seated at a large desk strewn with papers and liberally covered with cigar ash.

'Ah, Jeffers,' the prime minister looked up. 'And this must be Lieutenant Carlton. Take a seat.'

The commander and Alex sat down opposite Winston Churchill, who opened the conversation, getting straight to the point. 'The commander tells me that you did a splendid job in Finland, young man.'

'Thank you, sir,' was all Alex could think of to say, as he was still wholly awestruck.

'Your reports were of the highest order,' the prime minister continued, 'and I speak as someone with not inconsiderable experience of being a war correspondent myself. Oh, yes, I wrote for the *Daily Telegraph* and the *Pioneer* from India, for the *Morning Post* with Kitchener in Sudan, and the *Daily Mail* from Ladysmith during the second Boer war, so I know the makings of a fine correspondent when I see one.'

'Thank you, sir,' Alex repeated.

'But your exploits in Finland were far more adventurous than any of mine,' Churchill continued, 'far more daring. That incident where you saved an officer's life, and another where you rescued the girl from those despicable deserters, is the stuff of derring-do. You did well, my boy.'

'Thank you, sir.' Alex was conscious of sounding like a broken gramophone, so he added, 'None of it was planned, sir. It was merely coincidental that I was there and able to help.'

'Let me tell you, my boy,' Churchill carried on, 'if you find yourself on the right side of happenstance, then give thanks; for surely the gods are smiling on you that day!'

Alex smiled.

'But the principal reason why I wanted to meet with you is that I received an unusual dispatch in the bag from our legation in Helsinki, enclosing a letter for you, which is most irregular.' Churchill slid open the drawer on his desk and handed Alex a heavily sealed envelope. 'Would you like to borrow my opener?'

The prime minister handed Alex a narrow blade, which he used to slit open the envelope. Inside was two sheets of paper, on which was handwritten a neat letter in Russian Cyrillic.

My dear Aleksander Nikolaevich,

Please accept my sincerest apologies for the abrupt manner of your departure from Finland, but I sensed that your continued presence might have proven an embarrassment for both your country and mine, had you remained.

You may recall our discussion at the reception held in your honour. Count Nikolay Alexandrovich Karlov, your father, was a good friend at the Court of His Imperial Majesty, Tsar Nicholas, and the family resemblance is remarkable. I am aware that your father gave his life in the noblest of causes and from your exploits while in Finland, I feel sure that you have inherited much more than just a remarkable physical similarity.

Your service to your adopted country in Finland was of the highest regard, but you also served, what I now learn to be the place of your birth, with high distinction and credit, for which our President bestowed a most worthy honour. However, protocol demanded that we followed convention in inaccurately recording your actions and I am pleased to have now corrected that inexactitude.

I am led to believe that there also exists some ambiguity over the record of your birth, which I should be happy to also correct at the appropriate time should you so desire, as this country would be both proud and honoured to welcome a man of such high principals as yourself, as a citizen.

With the eternal grateful thanks of our nation and esteemed compliments to my old friend, the Countess Tatiana Ivanovna, your mother,

I remain, dear Aleksander Nikolaevich,

Respectfully

C. G. Mannerheim

Churchill handed over a second document, which was the citation for the Cross of Merit of the Order of the White Rose of Finland, corrected to read *Count Aleksander Nikolayevich Karlov*.

'I do not understand.' Alex was confused.

'Because the previous citation was to Alexander Carlsson,' the commander explained, 'you could not officially wear the award, as Carlsson does not in reality exist. This, I believe, corrects that inaccuracy, and you may now correctly wear the honour.'

The prime minister rose from his desk and offered Alex one of his famous cigars as he said, 'Congratulations, my boy.'

'Thank you, sir,' was all Alex could think of to say.